PRAISE FOR SHELTER HALF

"Walt Whitman said, 'If you ever want me again, look under your boot soles.' Carol Bly might have said, 'If you want me again, read *Shelter Half.*' It is, and will be, Carol Bly's only long fiction, the summation of thirty years of short stories and essays—all the ideas, characters, ethical quandaries, sly humor, voice and wisdom—a capsule of her life's work between covers. In its pages, a world is created with great ingenuity that will surprise and delight the reader: a mysterious murder, shadowy characters, small town foolishness, and a heroine finding her path back from despair. This mirror held up to the world, is made with a wise hand that intends to reflect our own face. That is Carol Bly's genius—to bother our conscience, then to show us what a decent, honorable life might look like. Read *Shelter Half,* my friends, and be delighted and instructed together."

Bill Holm, author of *Windows of Brimnes: An American in Iceland*

"The question that drives this mesmerizing novel is not why someone committed a murder, but why ordinary people can sometimes rise to acts of great courage and compassion, at the risk of career, reputation, and even life itself. The answers are as various as the pageant of characters who fill these pages, from a German war veteran to a public relations executive, from a social worker to a strawberry farmer, from a bartender to a priest. In tracing the web of relationships in a northern Minnesota town, Carol Bly invites us to examine our own communitites and our own hearts. She draws on decades of observation and hard study—observation of her neighbors and our corporate culture, hard study of history and the human brain. Rarely does a work of fiction combine so much intelligence with so much gusto."

Scott Russell Sanders, author of *A Private View of Awe*

BOOKS BY CAROL BLY

Shelter Half, a novel (2008)

Beyond the Writers' Workshop: New Ways to Write Creative Nonfiction (2001)

My Lord Bag of Rice: New and Selected Stories (2000)

An Adolescent's Christmas, 1944 (2000)

Changing the Bully Who Rules the World: Reading and Thinking about Ethics (1996)

The Tomcat's Wife and Other Stories (1991)

The Passionate, Accurate Story: Making Your Heart's Truth into Literature (1990)

Bad Government and Silly Literature (1986)

Backbone (1984)

Letters from the Country (1981)

BOOKS WITH CYNTHIA LOVELAND (BLY & LOVELAND PRESS)

Against Workshopping Manuscripts—A Plea for Justice to Student Writers (2006)

A Shout to American Clergy (2005)

Stopping the Gallop to Empire (2004)

Three Readings for Republicans and Democrats (2003)

shelter half

A NOVEL

CAROL BLY

HOLY COW! PRESS | DULUTH, MINNESOTA | 2008

This is a work of fiction. No character in this story is intended to resemble a living person. There is
an Episcopal Bishop of Minnesota, but the Bishop in this book does not resemble him.

10 9 8 7 6 5 4 3 2 1

The publisher gratefully acknowledges the assistance of Mara Hart, Cynthia Loveland,
Bridget Bly, Micah Bly, and Lottchen Shivers in preparing this book for publication.

Several chapters of *Shelter Half* have been peviously published: Chapter 3, in
The Idaho Review, as "Crime"; Chapter 6, in *Prairie Schooner*, as "Love in a Time of Empire";
Chapter 7, in *The Idaho Review*, as "At the Bottom of the United States"; Chapter 8, in
Prairie Schooner, as "An Amateur's Story" and Chapter 14, in *Glimmer Train*, as "Therapist."

Library of Congress Cataloging-in-Publication Data

Bly, Carol.
Shelter half : a novel / by Carol Bly.
p. cm.
ISBN 978-0-9779458-6-3 (alk. paper)
1. Murder—Fiction. 2. City and town life—Minnesota—Fiction. 3. Minnesota—Fiction.
I. Title.
PS3552.L89S54 2008
813'.54—dc22   2008001860

This project is supported by grant awards from The Alan H. Zeppa Family Foundation,
The Lenfestey Family Foundation, The Elmer L. & Eleanor J. Andersen Foundation,
The Paula & Cy DeCosse Fund of The Minneapolis Foundation, The Margaret Wurtele Fund
of The Minneapolis Foundation, and by gifts from generous donors:
Carolyn & Robert Hedin, Joanne Von Blon, Miriam O. Hanson, Richard & Melissa B. Severance,
Warren Woessner, Nor Hall, Elizabeth C. Mason, Kenneth R. Skjegstad, and many others.

Holy Cow! Press books are distributed to the trade by Consortium Book Sales & Distribution, c/o
Perseus Distribution, 1094 Flex Drive, Jackson, Tennessee 38301.

For personal inquiries, write to: Holy Cow! Press, Post Office Box 3170,
Mount Royal Station, Duluth, Minnesota 55803.

Please visit our website: www.holycowpress.org

This book is for
John Washburn McLean
and
Malcolm McLean,
and in memory of
Charles Russell McLean, Jr.

For over three-quarters of a century, American infantrymen were each issued a "shelter half"—that is, half a pup tent with a button placket along one long side and grommets for staking down along the other. Other armies provided similar canvas protection for their ground troops.

When the day's fighting was done, you looked for your buddy. If your buddy had died that day, you looked for anyone left alive. A dead man's shelter would do, provided it wasn't full of shot or shrapnel tears. You buttoned your half to his half. You raised the tent.

Two people gave each other shelter. A question of trust, in civilian life as well as at war: if we say we are on the same side, are we really on the same side? When we are, how wonderful it is.

CHAPTER ONE

A young woman's body lay for over a week in mid-November, undisturbed by human beings. Then, one Friday morning, an old strawberry farmer named Dieter Stolz caught sight of it because he had crouched not four feet away in the highway ditch. He was helping a wounded hunter climb onto his back so he could carry the man up the embankment of Minnesota Highway 53. There lay the corpse with its face, edged in blown leaves and a little snow, its face half-turned to him. Some creature had eaten one of its eyes. If Dieter Stolz hadn't had the hunter getting onto his back, he would have shone his flashlight for a better look. As it was, he didn't even pause. He grasped his man's legs, and pushed his neck against the fellow's hands like a horse of good-will putting its shoulders against harness. He scrabbled his way up the embankment. It wasn't yet six o'clock so the smooth highway was dark. A few lights of St. Fursey shone a mile to the north. Above them the sky drew back its hood of stars.

Dieter Stolz had risen much earlier, in his usual way. He'd been married for years and years to a woman whose face had stayed motionless during whatever comment he was making on any subject. If she had been still alive on this cold morning, he could have told her about the mother bear and two cubs who robbed their Haralsons, and a hunter caught in a Conibear trap. However, he didn't wish her there to hear about his scared feelings. She'd been a wife who obeyed a law of manners that said, wait your man out when he is speaking. So she had never interrupted him. On the other hand, her motionless eyes were like the gun and cannon muzzles of a tank still pointed at you well after its captain or crew had died inside.

He did not rise some days at 4:30, others at 5:30. He rose every day about 5:00. Even this late in the fall, he carried a cup of his grainy coffee out onto his cabin's stoop. Like other poor men who acquired property in middle-age, he felt grateful for it every day. His stoop looked out over a small lake that still had no jet skiers thumping on it. Its fir trees were dying off at the south end and reseeding themselves at the north end, just as evergreens now did all over the top tier of the United States, but the change was slow. His heart wasn't constantly broken over reminders of global warming. As his father had in Germany, Dieter grew winter apples for the sake of their sharp bite.

The moon had lighted his path along the lake. Like others who were seventy-eight years old, he had to stand still for a moment after ten minutes' sitting with the coffee. But once the stiffness melted away inside his legs, he swung off the porch easily and went fast along his path. His hair was white now, not so thick as it had been, but thicker than most old men's hair. Most people in the town of St. Fursey called him "a character" as they tended to call anybody who had some foreign accent. Worse, Dieter Stolz could read musical score and was apparently educated, but somehow had a low income anyway. The man Dieter had bought his land from twelve years ago, Peter Tenebray, was never called "a character" or even "quite a character" by anyone because four generations of Tenebrays had had money—Mesabi Iron-Range money—what was more.

Women occasionally went after Dieter. The Episcopal Church shared an emergency organist with other churches in the area. One was Pearl. Pearl ran the St. Fursey Post of the Veterans of Foreign Wars and she gambled hard at the Black Bear Casino outside Duluth and at the Grand in Hinckley which she determined had looser slots than others. She was one of the worst organists outside of the Twin Cities. She noodled chords—that is, she rambled around the circle of fifths, resolving dominant sevenths into tonics while Lutheran pastors crossed from lectern to altar or from altar to side chair during a service. The Episcopal rector, a woman named Eliza MacInnes, told Pearl that she mustn't noodle-slop in her church, however, because the Episcopal Church had a canon against it. Noodle-slop. Pearl's face went stony. She herself knew she was a quick read as an organist. There were many, many fucking things to do in life before one wasted hours and hours a week in organ practice. Also, since when did some twenty-five-year-old woman getting herself up in cassock and all and intoning who knew what at the altar get the right to call an organist a noodle-slopper?

Pearl didn't tend bar at the VFW for nothing. She stood Eliza off. She said, might she ask what in the name of heaven was a canon?

The young rector explained. Then smiled. Pearl said, "Yeah? Maybe you don't need my services any more."

But Eliza had been rector at St. Fursey for nearly three years and wasn't shaken by the usual blackmail that organists use to face off clergy people. Eliza smiled. "No, Pearl, we all need you in town and you know it. I need you at my church. We all need you and we especially bless you for accompanying the ecumenical chorus rehearsals each fall."

Pearl had been the first of several women who hunted down Dieter Stolz after his wife died. Pearl was realistic. He obviously was some kind of a gentleman or something, even if he was a German immigrant. He went to the Tenebrays' fancy weekend dinner parties. He was a musical person, who held the whole tenor section of the ecumenical chorus together. Pearl was only a gambler and a bartender and a slipshod organ player, so she didn't want to marry Dieter. She simply knew in her heart of hearts that he would be a totally robust dream in bed. She wanted him just once, she thought. The way she had wanted a few other men, George Herzlich, for example. She always made it clear they didn't get to ruin her life and she didn't want to ruin theirs. The German strawberry farmer had said, "Don't explain that to me, Pearl," and took her into his cabin several nights. "Where did you leave your car?" was all he asked, since she hadn't driven right up his road. She had left it outside the abandoned Solid Waste Transfer Station. She explained that people would assume she was illegally dumping or shooting rats or shining deer, she told him. Half the town sneaked in there. Killing things, target practice, building tree houses. All the crap that people do. Tell you the truth, she had said to

Dieter, she liked animals herself. She liked people who owned them and she didn't like people who shot them for fun. She liked men who talked in bed. There were hundreds of things to talk about in the world so people should talk about them.

She never spilled drinks when she hiked trays of them around the good old VF on a crowded night. She was also careful-handed, oddly tentative-handed with Dieter. She unbuttoned his woolen shirt gently, as if she were his valet and he were a European dignitary, not just some character around a northern Minnesota town. The gentleness of that rough woman's hands poured into him, and stayed with him.

After Pearl came Imogen Tenebray, who was far too young for him. At that time, four years ago, she wasn't even thirty. They never talked about her failing marriage. If only he had been forty or even fifty, he would have asked her to marry him, but he had been 74.

On this particular morning, two of his still unpicked Haralsons had been smashed into. Whole branches had been smashed into and spoilt. A third tree showed signs of bear nesting. High up, the animal had crunched together enough small boughs to make a rough platform. She must have sat there quite comfortably, probably to feed.

He approached, but deliberately. It was one thing to observe last night's work by a mother bear, but another to find oneself right there under the trees with her. People at Denham's Bakery Cafe had been talking about a mother bear and two cubs. They had been around town these last two weeks, feeding up for winter.

Dieter bent to sniff a new dump. Rich and sweet, a powerful tincture of apples. Well, exactly. Of course. His Haralsons, likely a few dozen pounds of them. Under one edge of the scat, the small grass was still green. He went on double-guard, whistling Tallis's Canon to give the bear fair warning. He now made out at least one cub's trail as well. He crept along listening. Only the lake's moonlit wavelets patted and stroked the shoreline.

Then a branch broke close ahead of him, to his right, and above him. A huge bear sitting at her ease, a good fifteen feet up. Just below her, one cub clung frantically to the trunk. On the ground below stood another cub. An apple fell. Another. The cub on the ground dashed over to each of them, but then looked upward, at a loss.

Its gigantic mother descended, cracking and dropping small branches as she came. A number of apples fell. Her huge bottom knocked down the cub who had been hanging by claw-holds.

Dieter waited until all three animals had moved off southward, ahead of him. They kept to the shoreline, as he meant to. He recalled how Pearl, that usually rough-spoken organist, had said she liked animals. So did he, but he never started conversations with mother bears and cubs. He gave this one a good five minutes' lead time. Presently he heard splashing. She would have slogged out into the water, and the cubs would have followed. Dieter was close enough to hear her throttle-like call to them.

His intention was to turn west onto the rough track that led toward the highway, passing along the south edge of the old dump enclosure. From there he meant to walk the mile into town and get a hot chocolate *mit Schlag* from Denham's bakery. He supposed the bear family would keep to its southward course along the shore. Dieter turned into the woods now, unlighted by the moon. He didn't turn on his flashlight yet.

Then he heard from behind him sharp rifle fire. Next, a man screamed. Dieter trotted back toward the lake. He turned on his flashlight and waved it about. He set up a shout, "Coming! Help coming! Shout again so I will know where you are!"

The male voice cried out again.

Dieter kept shouting, both to cheer up the hurt man and to notify the mother bear that he was returning to the lakeshore and that although he liked her and her cute cubs very much he did not want to be clawed to death, so she should clear off.

He made out his man half-sitting, half-lying, right at the shoreline, at the place where a small stream ran into the lake. Dieter assumed the man had been drunk. He did not like coming upon drunken grown males in the woods. They usually had equipped themselves inwardly with rotgut and outwardly with firearms, with the safeties left off. If they had gotten into the woods by driving north from Duluth or St. Paul, they generally shot around happily for a while, then got lost, and felt cross, and with luck found their cars and tailed off southward on 53 and I-35.

This one was a local man. Dieter approached warily. He saw no rifle.

"All right," he said. "I will help you."

It was a fellow named Brad Stropp, the no-good husband of a cleaning woman in St. Fursey. Dieter knelt near him and went over the man's extended leg, turning the flashlight down the calf to where a small-animal trap had bitten onto the ankle.

The trap was a Conibear, a 330, Dieter thought, set for open water. The trapper had baited it with two fresh-cut young poplars so its chain pulled downward underwater just offshore. Dieter propped the flashlight to beam onto the ankle. He stood up, looking for a pry.

"What's the delay!" cried Stropp.

"Your rifle. I need something to lever it open with."

Stropp swore. "I don't have any rifle with me," he said.

"And no shotgun?"

"Why would I have a gun or a rifle around this time of year!" Stropp cried. "Jesus, will you get a move on?"

Dieter thought to himself, all right then. He knelt as far as he could rest on his heels, took hold of the bar, one breath in, back out, another in, held it, and brought the bar slowly back. Stropp didn't know how lucky he was. Dieter now slowly lifted the badly wounded ankle off the cut steel.

Dieter said, "All right now. You have to get up. Hang on to me."

But he had to lift him. Finally they got going, three-legging it together, arms around each other like soldier and wounded comrade.

Dieter kept talking so that Stropp would keep moving.

Dieter said conversationally, "Didn't have a rifle with you at all?"

"Jesus, I told you no," Strop said.

"Did you hear a couple of shots?"

"No. I didn't." Stropp was panting now, likely from the pain.

Both men were tired so even Dieter's desultory remarks petered out.

Their path had been down-leaves and light snow ruffled together. That would be Stropp's own trail from earlier. Dieter thought, good, we will find his car on the highway shoulder. If Stropp had come without a car, Dieter would let the man sit down on the shoulder and he himself would beg a ride. At least a few trucks would be coming past by now. It must be close to seven o'clock.

They came out of the pines and shoved through the opening forest edge of fireweed and other bramble. Then onto the highway clearance width of twelve feet, its scrub mown down twice a year by the district.

Dieter paused here. He had forgotten about the seven- or eight-foot rise to the highway surface level. He looked left and right, hunting for some spot with less gradient. No good. Yes, well, then, he would have to get Stropp up on his back. He noticed a place where someone had scrabbled up the slope, up or down it, the leaf and ragweed and scant lupine overturn not so fresh as Stropp's other track. More snow still floated on many of the leaves.

"All right, Stropp! Here we are! Your car up there? Good! I am going to carry you. Here's my back. Get aboard." Dieter got down on all fours, facing up the incline.

Then Dieter saw something else. A few feet from his right lay a human body, arms and legs flung out. Its smallish head was tipped and partly facing Dieter. The body must have frozen earlier, and now one eye cavity was half-watered with yesterday's partial thaw. About a week, Dieter supposed, but his knowledge of exposed corpses was now over a half-century old.

For one amazingly stupid second he went for his flashlight.

Instead he said heartily, "Hang on then! Here we go!"

He carried Stropp up the grade. Set him down, and asked for the car keys in a perfectly ordinary voice.

Dieter put Stropp into the passenger side, went around and got in. Straight stick. OK. Clutch, lights. Dieter drove slowly because half his brains seemed to scarcely work. Then he sped up some.

"That's more like it!" Stropp said in a jeer.

Dieter kept the car at fifty even into the St. Fursey city line and nearly to the Emergency entrance of the hospital. The ambulance door rose. A nurse with chilled arms across her chest, cardigan sweater drooping over her shoulders, came running crabwise to Stropp's car. A second nurse approached with a wheelchair.

Once those two women had him in hand, Stropp talked to them like a little boy. Dieter, listening as he followed them into the wide bay and down the hall, was reminded of how if you have lain wounded, sickening and cooling, and in danger of never being found at all, when people approach in the uniforms of help—whites or soldiers' Schürze with red cross—it is immediately all right to let go of adulthood. You change back to a child.

Brad Stropp chattered like a little boy to the nurses. Someone left a beaver trap on that path. The fool. You'd never catch him setting a line where people walk. Dieter half-attended. He waited for one of the nurses to finish calling the doctor from a wall phone. He took the phone, but waited until she was out of hearing range.

The dispatcher came on first. Then the St. Fursey chief of police said, "Stolz? Dieter? You wait for me right there. I'll be outside Emergency in two minutes."

Dieter went back outside, where day now filled the sky. It weakened the lights of the auto dealer's sign. His left hand was trembling. At seventy-eight, one trembly hand wasn't bad. He knew that trembling came on as soon as a person could unload some scary job onto someone else. Now the chief of police drew up, lights blinking, no siren.

There is an elegance about even a small-town officer's car when you've been waiting for it. There is an elegance about an officer himself, even if he is just a village chief of police, not a president of a country. The stripe down Bernie Stokowski's pant sides was the symbol of force—and help. Like anyone else, Dieter knew that the USA standards to qualify for local cop were supposed to have sunk like the standards for every other job, but still, still, the stripe had snap. All Dieter had left to do was tell Bernie about the dead body.

"Hop in, Dieter," Bernie said. The heater warmed the car. "South on 53, right? Dispatcher said that old track by the Solid Waste Transfer site?"

"Runs right along the south fence of it," Dieter said. "Down the embankment, just at the bottom."

Bernie told him, "So what we'll do is, you show me everything, I call in for help, you tell me everything you know about, and then Darrel here will give you a ride home."

For the first time, Dieter took in that a younger man in uniform sat in the back seat.

At the Solid Waste Transfer, Dieter pointed. Bernie said. "OK, we'll U-turn to right there." He gunned the car around and stopped. "Now," he said, "get out of the car, but don't walk around on the shoulder. Just stand right beside your door. Point her out to me." He said to the young man who had leaned forward to open the back door, "No, you stay put, Darrel."

They could see the girl's body perfectly clearly. It lay exactly as Dieter had remembered it, but now it was not night, but day, and it was only the dead body of someone he didn't know. He was not afraid anymore.

He told Bernie, "I pretended I hadn't seen anything, because I wasn't sure if Brad Stropp might be the one who killed her, and there he was with both his arms around my neck."

Dieter had never received any exhilaration from fear. His older brother had died in Egypt when he himself was 11, and his younger brother had been executed, by guillotine, in Linz. By the time Dieter himself was a soldier and was made sergeant, there was no winnable war to fight in. Waffen-SS fourteen-year-olds were assigned to hundreds of platoons to prevent noncommissioned officers like Dieter from surrendering to the Amis. That meant constant, low-level fear, which he disliked almost as much as high-level fear. He wasn't the least interested in bravery, not back then, and not now.

Bernie let himself down the embankment, bent over the corpse, but touched nothing. Then he scrambled back up to the cruise car. He told his deputy to get out of the back and into the driver's seat. He put Dieter in back, and himself got into the front on the passenger's side. He turned himself three-fourths around so they could talk to each other's faces.

"Tell me everything," he said. "Start at the beginning."

Dieter described finding the mother bear and her cubs in his apple trees. The policeman did not hurry him. From time to time he asked a question.

"What gave you the idea that Brad Stropp might have killed that girl?"

Dieter said, "He told me that while he was stuck in the trap, he didn't hear any rifle shots, yet I had heard two. If he was lying, there must be a reason. I guessed then that he himself fired one or both of those shots, then got caught in the trap, and began calling for help. Then when I answered him, he probably threw away the rifle so I wouldn't see it." He added, "Of course, he didn't kill that girl this morning, if he killed her at all."

"How so?" the policeman said quickly.

"Because her eye sockets were filled with snowmelt."

"OK," Bernie said. "Thank you, Dieter. Give this tired man a ride home," he said to his deputy.

The young cop kept eyeing up in the rear view mirror, his eyes, under the visor, like two muzzles pointed back at Dieter. He had the metallic voice of a completely confident person.

"Whoever they are," he was saying, "we'll get them. We always do. Like with 9/11. We'll get those people, too."

Take it all peacefully, Dieter told himself. Peaceful. Peaceful. This guy was just one more twenty-year-old like any other twenty-year-old, wanting to make an arrest, or even better, wanting to shoot someone attempting to escape—while Dieter himself was just an old man now. An old man growing strawberries outside a tiny American town, and no one was going to want to pick him up for anything.

CHAPTER TWO

The St. Fursey Police Department station had once been the Senior Citizens' Center. It inherited the seniors' flat-latex pink walls and white woodwork, and some womanly kitchen curtains. They hung in finger pleats all across the high windows, a yellow cotton with a pattern of ivy and baskets full of fruit of some kind that is always out of season in northern Minnesota. Bernie Stokowski disdained the look of the place even after everything his wife had tried to do to make it nice for him.

Gladys and he had shoved all the requisite locked file cases down to the far end of the room. A cross-stitched table prayer hung on one wall. Most police stations had patriotic messages, and a picture of the President of the United States. The senior citizens had left up a picture of President Clinton. There were a lot of Democrats in St. Fursey, so no one so far objected. No one was crazy about Clinton after the sex stuff, but then they hadn't liked anyone since, either. Bernie's deputy, the darkest bulb on any Christmas tree, envied the deputy at Cullough because of their office. The Cullough cops had two 36-inch wide commercial photos of patrol cars leaping forward, the front wheels nearly off the ground, with the manufacturers' names on them. Nice slogans. *A car you can count on, for the heroes we count on.* A cityscape of New York showing the World Trade Center towers with the legend in Old English semi-bold: *We will never forget.*

The St. Fursey station showed only blurry digitals of Gladys and Bernie himself and the children in metal certificate frames from the Ben

Franklin store before it closed its door.

This Friday forenoon the sun shined through the orange and yellow fruit and green leaves in the curtains. The deputy kept pacing around, clearly working up to beg for something.

Darrel had been training with Bernie for two months, so Bernie knew all his moves. He would start with some neutral remark. Then his own voice would give him courage. He would move into outright begging. This time, since it was a Friday, he probably wanted the rest of the day off. That wasn't going to happen. Bernie did not mind Darrel's whining and begging because he, himself, had been a bum policeman in his twenties. He had been a bum cop in a different way, but still, not much good. He had not tried out and flunked the state troopers' test the way Darrel had, but he had swaggered around the same way, longing, very secretly, for a chance to draw his revolver on someone while all the time maintaining, for old ladies and anyone else who asked, how much policemen really hated violence and all the time wished they didn't have to use force. In St. Fursey there was always some chance to sound off to old ladies. They called when they heard something scary in the Denham Apartments building, so you ran flashlights around and then stayed long enough to talk to them a little. It pained Bernie to hear old Mrs. Garris saying what a nice young officer Darrel was—it pained him all the more because it reminded him of how he had postured around in front of old ladies, too. But he didn't ever recall having given his chief the particular worries that this Darrel now gave him.

Darrel lied in a natural flow. The man's brain-dead waste ran out of his mouth like bad water from a culvert. It was the naturalness of Darrel's lying that irritated Bernie. It was no good speaking to him about it because Darrel would only be confused. To Darrel, words were something you used to relieve yourself of the moment's tension. Words did not symbolize a past action. Words did not constitute a promissory note for any future action. Darrel made promises because he knew he would feel better after he had spoken. It just barely mattered which words he chose to speak. Worse, he was a mama's boy.

Bernie wasn't going to make a fight out of Darrel's lying or out of his being so scared of facing old tough guys like Walt Steinzeiter who needed to obey the law the way everyone else was supposed to. He meant to bawl Darrel out for begging for hours off, and in the next breath inquiring about promotion. But Bernie wouldn't bawl him out for being a coward because that was what he was going to fire him for. He would simply wait and keep track, with each date, of the man's ducking his duties. Bernie didn't see how he could teach Darrel to have a conscience. His experience was that either you couldn't teach heartless people to feel remorse, or otherwise that he himself just wasn't a good teacher.

Now he said, "Darrel, why don't you go get fresh Danish and some bagels from Denham? And don't stop in there to talk to anyone."

"I was going to ask you, though, Bernie, I mean."

"Ask me what?"

"I mean, how come it's us hanging around the station and it's them guys from Homicide whoever they are who answered your call and are out there investigating that poor kid's murder? How come it isn't *us* investigating?" Darrel had got on his service jacket, but now sat down. Bernie found it painful to see the vivid St. Fursey Police patch on Darrel's shoulder. It showed a brilliant rose sunset over a northern Minnesota forest.

It reminded Bernie of a conversation he had had when he was a young policeman. He and his chief had been walking away from the yellow ribbon of a crime site between Cullough and St. Fursey. Along the highway shoulder lay the picked-over corpse of a rabbit. It had been yanked apart, and bitten into several pieces so that its parts now lay lightly as much as three or four feet apart. The men noticed that some crows stood poised at a thoughtful distance.

At that time in his career, Bernie had called corpses stiffs. "Boy, those guys—the crows—have already cleaned off this stiff all right," Bernie had said.

Now that he had seen a few hundred more stiffs, he called them corpses or just bodies.

His boss had said, "Those crows? They've hardly had a taste of this fellow yet. They're just waiting for us to quit jawing so they can feed. No, some very big wood folk, more than one, caught this rabbit and began tearing it open, rich, soft parts first, just about clean. Maybe a pack of something. Those crows are about fourth or fifth in line."

That cop had been the only man back then who used words like "wood folk." Nowadays the only person who talked like that was Peter Tenebray, well, and some of the summer people who loved nature and said so.

Darrel said, "If we ain't investigating, all those people in to Denham's Bakery are going to—"

Bernie said, "Darrel, how would you know there was a lot of people in Denham's? It wouldn't be that you already stopped by there on your way back from taking Dieter Stolz home?"

"No, heck no. I just looked in is all. Through that great big new window they got, you can see everything. The place was jumping. I didn't go in at all. I was only in there for a moment."

"You did go in?"

"No, heck no, I wasn't in there two minutes altogether."

Darrel went on. "Here's the thing, Bernie. When I go get the Danishes and bagels, they're all going to ask me, how is the investigation coming along, so what am I going to say? I mean, I got to say something."

"That's a good question, Darrel. And here's the answer. I think if you stand at the counter and don't go over to any of the tables, and order the buns and pay, and get out of there, you won't have to answer anything because no one will ask you anything. But say someone does shout at you from one of those tables they got. Say some loudmouth shouts over to you. 'Hi, Darrel, how's it going with investigating that young girl's death?' You can look at them and say, 'We're cooperating with the authorities, which is all I can tell you at this point.' You got that?"

Bernie looked at Darrel's face across the table. He thought to himself, I think I had better repeat that. "So you tell them, see, 'we're cooperating with the authorities which is all I can tell you at this point.'"

"Are you saying we ain't going to investigate this crime at all?" Darrel asked.

Bernie said, "That's right. We ain't going to investigate this crime. But we are going to cooperate. So if someone asks you, you can say 'I can't tell you much at the moment, but we are cooperating with the Homicide people.' You can say 'from Duluth.' You know, homicide specialists can be from just about anywhere, but since the road here comes up from Duluth you can say 'from Duluth' OK. Then if they say, 'Yeah but Darrel, how about that autopsy that Doc Anderson has on for tomorrow afternoon over to the Cullough hospital? That's for this dead girl, isn't it?' you can say, 'I can't tell you anything more.' Darrel, you make sure you're on your feet. If you stay standing up there, they will respect you for refusing to be unprofessional. But if you once sit down with them and *then* refuse to answer questions, you will just sound snotty. When you went in there already this morning, by the way, did you go over to any of the tables?"

"No. I was only in there a second. I went over to say hello to Vera, you know, from the school, where they were sitting. I didn't sit down with them. I bet I sat there all of thirty seconds, tops."

Bernie sighed. "You'd probably better go now so you're back and we can give those Duluth M.E.s and Homicide people a snack if they choose to stick their heads in here."

When the door closed, its ruffled curtain puffed out a second and fell straight again, Bernie let himself slope lower into place. He sat as deeply as he could in a chair like that old Meals on Wheels staff chair and thumped the table with the huge heels of his hands. He was not interested in this roadside murder and never would be because he knew in his heart of hearts that it was unsolvable.

He had to keep that insight to himself. Even if Darrel had been any kind of a promising cop, Bernie would not have shared his speculations with him. When a large organization, whoever they are, commits a crime for some reason of their own, Bernie's experience was: no one will solve it. To someone like those large organization leaders, everywhere outside their own offices and their own suburbs is just somewhere to dump a body, whenever you happen to have a body that needs dumping. St. Fursey, Minnesota; Paris, France; or Tokyo, Japan; Bagram, Afghanistan—all the same. This big, purposeful organization is going to have money and attorneys enough to head off any inquiry that any small-town cop in northern Minnesota might devise. Bernie thought, if he was them, he would even have people dressed up as cops. These people would very slowly and respectfully show you their I.D. so you could actually see the picture and read three or four lines of text. They would talk the talk just as convincingly as the two friendly, cordial guys this morning had, once Darrel had driven off. Nice guys, with their pale raincoats open and white shirts and tweed jacket fronts showing. Ties. Also that very courteous man-woman marks-and-photo crew.

Bernie did not think this murder was by a serial killer or rapist because the body was dumped off with no attempt to delay discovery. A rural-setting serial killer typically wanted at least a 24-hour cooling of the trail before you found the body. He would bury it somewhere, or at least drag it all the way into some woods or an unused meadow. Not these folks. It is true the body had not been spotted for several days, but it could have been. The murderer didn't care.

Bernie noticed he had begun to think of the young girl's killers as "these folks." It made him feel less scared and more indifferent. OK, these folks didn't trouble to hide the body. That suggested they got someone else, not themselves, to do the actual dumping, and this someone else *had* to do it, once asked. That suggested someone they had something on, but whom they would keep so completely in the dark that even if the dumper started to talk, he had no one very clear to point to. And as for the young woman, her death was probably a convenience death. She died because (a) the organization needed to punish someone, or (b) they needed to frighten someone.

It was this last likelihood that made Bernie uneasy. They might actually be trying to frighten someone. If they wanted a dead body found just right there, south of St. Fursey, they may have planned it for evidence designed to show up later, not now. The someone might be a local. So Bernie drummed his hands lightly. If these people were setting up a potential frame-up for a local, that local had either a *past* that no local authorities, meaning Bernie, would know about, or a *present* that no local authorities knew about.

The beautiful woods were full of knotholes. In the knotholes lived dozens and dozens of two-legged varmints and heroes and everything in between, eleven times as many in the summers as in the winters, but these days a few hundred stayed year round. The retired or pre-retired didn't make their living locally. In the last thirty years, even much younger people had built nice places back in the woods. They were dentists and doctors and investors, people who made their living somewhere else.

These people could have all sorts of enemies that Bernie would never know anything about.

Besides, except for the meth farmers and other trash, their faces didn't show up in his line of work. The more educated couples showed up at community events. If they were poor but not engaged in crime, they came to the annual ecumenical chorus rehearsals for the snacks that would be served during the breaks. When there was a veterans' evening lecture, like the one coming up soon, people appeared whom you never saw anywhere else—along with the regular crowd of the old and the poor. A lot of these people didn't do their regular shopping at Marty's Super Valu. Gladys had told Bernie that high-end people drove to Duluth for less sugar-based deli, more ethnic food supplies.

Neighbors no longer necessarily knew one another. That was not counting the meth tweakers or the think-tank people at a swish retreat-camp between St. Fursey and Cullough. Bernie saw those people because he occasionally dropped in to tell them to watch themselves—he would warn them that a bad type was out loose around, and he would keep in touch, et cetera. It was just a courtesy. That think-tank disguised as a duck-hunting camp had its own security as thick and implacable as the stars in the sky. Bernie's guess was that their weaponry was so electronic and modern he wouldn't recognize a lot of it.

Bernie wasn't surprised to hear there was a crowd at Denham's Bakery Cafe. There was probably a crowd at the other two cafes, too. There would be a crowd at the churches on Sunday. A roadside murder was like 9/11. A treat for ordinary people.

This particular roadside murder had its tiny blessings. The victim was not local so no one had to feel guilty about not mourning. You could just enjoy it. The crime was violent enough to be interesting—murder and very probably rape—so although St. Fursey people might intuitively decide that the perpetrator wasn't a local, they would speculate aloud to one another anyhow. The usual local suspects—who, this November, were St. Fursey's six year-round-trash types, one bad summer-people kid, and one old naturalized foreigner—would be raked out again. The old foreigner was the least intriguing since his only crime was to have been an infantryman on the wrong side during World War II. Still, the wits sipping coffee at Denham's usually shared a three-part philosophy: a) you never really knew, did you? And b) you can't tell, not for sure you can't, and c) frankly, they'd always been afraid something like this would happen. Their loose-limbed ideas left the field open for anybody.

Bernie would do the usual—let himself be seen driving here and there to interview those of the six year-round trash he could find. The bad summer-people kid from the last crime had grown up and gone away. The one foreigner, Dieter Stolz, was no longer a new kid on the block. Dieter had it in common with the Salem witches that he did hands-on nurture of fruit trees better than most farmers and his Midways and Sparkles were ten times sweeter than other farmers' strawberries. Often as not, the witches had nothing more against them than excellence at propagating plants and making wild-berry jelly.

A curious point about an external murder: it drew the town together a little. People would say "My treat! My treat!" and buy coffee for other people they seldom nodded to. With their heads thrown back like statues of lions or army officers of long ago, St. Fursey people would trade notes on who might have done it. Bernie knew all the conversations without hearing them.

For example, old Dieter Stolz was 78 and sure seemed to be more given to saving people out of illegal beaver traps than killing children, but you never knew. So what he spoke English so perfectly. He was a foreigner and everyone knew it. And in everyone's favorite war, he had served on the wrong side. That's got to stand for something, doesn't it? A lot of years of running a first-rate specialty strawberry operation—a lot of years of being a nice person, not to mention being a tenor who could actually read music in the Episcopal Church—plus being fairly recently widowed—all that might get him some natural sympathy, but suspicion would flare up anyway.

Darrel reached the bakery on foot because Bernie had told him not to park the squad car anywhere near or the place would turn into an outdoors movie set. Darrel got chilled walking. He hated getting a chill. He was already hung over and now he was going to get a chill. He and Bernie had already got cold out along Little Bass Lake, and the warm smell of the bakery was just killing him.

Bernie had guessed right. Darrel no sooner got in there, in his uniform jacket with the fur edging, than everyone paused in their talk. People looked hungrily at Darrel. When Darrel made it clear he would put in an order standing up at the counter, nobody dared ask him questions. But he could feel it. People were a little bored all the time. Most people didn't like their jobs much. They didn't mind them and usually were glad to have them, but the fact was their work bored them. They were probably bored a third of the time at home, too. They weren't ever going to be a policeman like himself. He felt sorry for them as he pulled his wallet out from his sheepskin.

When he got back with the paper bag, he told Bernie his idea even before he got his jacket hung up. Darrel was pleased to have got it right for once, about how people were bored. His boss liked deep thinking and sometimes seemed to be implying that Darrel didn't think deeply enough. Well, now he'd know. He could see Bernie was really listening. If he could get Bernie talking deep stuff, the man would be pleased and might give Darrel the afternoon off, even.

Bernie was doing his own worrying as he helped Darrel lay out the bakery stuff. The chief knew that people would start by pointing at Brad Stropp or Dieter Stolz since they had been near where the body was found. By tomorrow or the next day, they would give up on those two suspects for lack of evidence, but not yet this morning. Most St. Fursey people tended not to steal. They tended not to kill. Well and good, except that every year, Bernie, the other towns' chiefs, the county sheriff, and the state troopers plying that area came in contact with 16,000 cases of mental illness causing bad behavior.

When Bernie had been an aspiring young cop, all but two or three of the bad things that happened around St. Fursey happened because someone in a fifty-mile range did some logically motivated bad thing. Someone stole a good hunting dog because they wanted that particular dog or one like it. Bernie and the other city cops and the county sheriff would hook up and compare notes on the telephone. They would decide who *might* have stolen the dog and they'd drive out to amble around that person's place, one or two of them holding leashes. Usually the dog was there, so they would take it back. Nowadays, a dog got stolen, Bernie figured it might not have anything to do with the dog or its owner. Dog theft, like murder, could be just a red herring or something else. That social worker at the school, Imogen Tenebray, told him that sometimes people stole things while scarcely noticing what it was they'd lifted. So what did they want? He had asked. She said that they typically wanted the feeling of getting hold of something they hadn't ever had hold of before. Well, there wasn't anything much in police school that taught Bernie how to investigate that kind of crime.

Bernie told Darrel to look up the registration on Brad Stropp's rifle.

"That girl wasn't killed with a rifle though," Darrel said.

"That's right," Bernie said. "But look it up. Look up all Stropp's stuff. I think he has a varmint rifle of some kind, maybe a .22, but the one I think we're going to find will be a 30.30 Winchester. We'll go looking for it around down at the lake end of that path."

"Hey, I bet those Homicide people will show up soon," Darrel said.

"They might," Bernie said. They might show up to eat Danish and drink the coffee and share some conversation and philosophy and talk of clues left or not left. They wouldn't want Bernie to feel left out. The biggest possibility, however, was that they would just go back to Duluth and call, out of ordinary courtesy, from there. Or they would wait until they had that autopsy report from Doc Anderson, and then tell Bernie to just go ahead with the usual stuff.

"Come on, Darrel, let's us eat this stuff," Bernie said. The plate of buns had been smelling wonderful. Both men set to.

They waited another ten minutes.

Bernie stood up. "OK. Let's go out along that lake path and see what we can see. Don't forget your cap."

"I guess those guys aren't coming then?" Darrel said.

Bernie checked the car trunk to make sure they had the Sawzall. Then they drove south out of town.

They left the police car north of the old dump site.

The yellow police ribbon was gone. You could see that people had trampled the golden rod and burning weed, but that was all. A few late leaves cruised down. The forest was silent but for their feet on leaves already dried. They went past the bony aspen and birch, following a line parallel to and north of the path that Dieter had brought out Brad Stropp on. Bernie wanted to leave Dieter's route untouched until he could study it without the presence of his deputy. He meant to send Darrel out on an errand this afternoon, and then he would return alone.

About a hundred yards from the highway, he made a right turn, to cut over to Dieter's path. They came upon the Conibear trap and the smashed undergrowth and disturbed leaves where Dieter had freed Stropp. Bernie tied a length of pink tree tape seven feet up around a nearby trunk.

"OK," he said. "Let's walk around this going outward. Do one circle at about four feet, another at eight, another at twelve. I don't think he will have thrown that rifle very far because the odds would be it hit a tree before within 10 or 18 yards at the most. Besides, he was caught in a trap and he was in some pain."

"Here you be, Bernie," Darrel said in a casual tone, as if he were a man of such huge competence that of course he had spotted the flung weapon first. He shouldered his way back through some poplar saplings, holding up a rifle.

"Let's see what we got," Bernie said.

Fired within a few hours.

"OK. Hang onto it, would you, and I'll take the trap." He got down on his knees, held the chain taut, and Sawzalled through at the bolt. When he stood up, he paused, and stalled a moment looking around.

"Ain't that about it?" Darrel said. He rubbed his hands.

Bernie looked at him ironically. "You in a hurry to get somewhere, Darrel?"

"Heck no, but I mean."

"The man fired two shots. I thought we might see what he was firing at if we nosed around a little."

"All we got is that old strawberry farm guy's word for it, about the two shots," Darrel said.

"Yeah? I trust that guy more than I trust the 10 o'clock news," Bernie said.

He ambled ahead toward the lake. The path was arched with whitish trees. The whole forest was lightening now. It had the feel of woodland clarifying and shaking down for winter. Bernie heard his man following dutifully.

When they got to the shoreline, the water lay ice-colored and wide, still unfrozen.

"I guess if he shot something in the water it'd be gone by now, though," Darrel said.

"You still in a hurry, Darrel?"

"I was wondering about this afternoon is all."

"Don't wonder," Bernie said, now looking all around. "This afternoon you're going to see Steinzeiter and get him in compliance."

Nervousness transformed Darrel's mouth. It flopped open like a lasso.

"Steinzeiter is just about the toughest fourth-generation German-American in the county," Bernie went on, with satisfaction. His eyes kept moving along the shoreline. Here and there. Then along a line about a yard inland too. "He's tough. But tough doesn't mean armed. It just means ugly. So just tell him about having that flag draped out all over County 10. See if you can get it through his head that he can't interfere with a county road right-of-way. He will tell you how tough he is. Let 'im. When he's all through talking, you tell him to get in compliance." Bernie stooped over. "Here we are," he said. He picked up a baby black bear in his arms. It was stiffening curled up. It might have been about 40, 45 inches long, and except for the wild, red-rimmed eyes it looked like a toy bear. Bernie pressed the paw pads. Its already three-inch long claws spread outward dropping some lumps of leaf and mud. "See, he already had a lot of what he needed in life besides his mother and some luck. Good claws for climbing. Good for scratching anyone who gives him a bad time." Bernie kept looking through the little animal's fur. The bullet had struck him in the right hip, but passed on through.

"He ran out of luck all right," Darrel said in an indifferent tone.

"Yeah he did," Bernie said. "Look at this, Darrel. See how the leaves are all scratched up here? It wasn't a good shot. So the cub died slowly, and clawed around because it hurt. Here—you carry the Conibear and the rifle."

When they got back to the police car, Bernie put the cub in the back seat. It half-sat, half-curled over, like a baby who has fed and is now falling asleep. Its stunning dark head rested on its own baby shoulder. Bernie moved the rearview mirror to see it, and then shoved it back up into the right angle for rear-vision.

"I don't guess it will take too long to take care of Steinzeiter," Darrel said in a thin, conversational tone.

Bernie gave a laugh. "There's two ways it can go. You tell him what you want him to do in one minute and then he tells you what you can do with yourself for eight minutes, and you leave, telling him what he has to do for another one minute. That's a total of ten minutes. Or the other way it can go is you tell him what you want him to do for one minute, he tells you what you can do with yourself for eight minutes, you tell him what he has to do for another minute, you leave, and he joins you all the time you're walking back out to your car to tell you some more about what you can do with yourself. He'll probably work me into it, too. Yup. I wouldn't be surprised. He will tell you that you can tell me for him what I can do with myself, too."

"Heck," Darrel said. "I don't guess he'll actually hit me though."

"He hits you I put him in the slammer for 72 while I figure out something else I feel like doing."

They had drawn up alongside the station. Neither man got out.

Bernie said, "Cheer up. Either way it's over in fifteen minutes. And here we are on a Friday afternoon and you get done with Steinzeiter, you can go home."

"For the whole weekend?" Darrel said. He brightened.

"Sure," Bernie said. "Provided Steinzeiter doesn't draw on you, of course."

"Draw on me!" cried Darrel. Then he calmed himself and added companionably, "Oh God but he will be sorry if he draws on me." Then he added, "Just joking. I'd love to bring that guy in for assault with a deadly weapon, though."

Bernie said, "Speaking of assault with a deadly weapon, did you skip shoot practice again? Last week? The week before? When was the last time you practiced? I thought they sent you two warnings."

"Oh, those people," Darrel remarked. "They got nothing to do except send warnings."

OK. That went into Darrel's record, too.

"Well, yeah," Darrel said with a smile. "I mean. If I ever get through work."

"All you got left is talk to Steinzeiter," Bernie said. "Take some advice from me, all right? Don't be afraid of Steinzeiter. Just tell him if he doesn't get that dragline moved off from over the highway, we get him on a 160.27. You get to say anything else you want to say, too, just as long as you tell him the law. You can tell him you love the flag yourself. Tell him that flag of his hangs better than any of the other crap arrangements people have rigged up since 9/11. Flags on their bra-top bathing suits. Tell him his flag is so good because it is so big. It moves around, opening and turning the way it does in the wind nicer than the little flags that other people have. You can tell him I said that if you want to. Or you can tell him you said it. I don't care, either way. Tell him people can talk USA this and USA that, all right?—but the funny thing is, different people have told you whenever they've driven along on County 10 and seen his gigantic flag for the first time they feel like crying. Grown men."

Darrel said, "But Bernie, no one has told me anything like that. You want I should lie to him or what? And you always on me about lying, too."

Both policemen saw the school principal slanting his car into one of the 15-minutes-only places that Bernie and Darrel kept for people renewing licenses.

"Just tell him grown men cry when they see his flag. Just tell him. Then tell him he's got to move that dragline and get the flag out of the highway clearance."

Bernie added, "Hurry up now. Take the other car. I have to go in and see about whatever kid Donald's come in about."

Darrel glanced over into the principal's car. He said, "I used to hate that guy when I was in school. He'd knock kids' heads against the walls down in the basement where no one could hear."

"Quit stalling, Darrel. Go out and see Steinzeiter."

Chapter Three

The auto dealer found himself clinging to these last days' limbo before he was supposed to start chemotherapy in Duluth. Stan Garris was shrouded in a single obsession, a privacy, that reminded him of the privacy he had enjoyed with his Lab, Silver, before someone stole her. The two of them had gone about the slough paths alone with just one thought in their heads at any one moment. When Silver smelled partridge, then partridge was all she pointed out. She did it with eyes, tail, wriggle of her body, and Stan, once told, changed his shotgun grip a little and thought only of partridge.

Now that Silver was gone and he had cancer, he went around scattershot inside himself, glancing four or five times a day at his upcoming death—mini-versions of it swelling in his mind's eye, vanishing, then another one appearing like a new clip further on in the same movie.

Only two weeks ago he had gone to a GM dealers' enrichment session. Its centerpiece was sales knacks for auto-lot stock when a major design change was scheduled for the next quarter. Like every dealer-update conference Stan had been to in the last twenty years, this one had soft-fill inserted in the first after-lunch session. It suited everybody. You sleep through it and you haven't missed anything, yet the manufacturer comes on as attractive for having hired a woman trainer to do psychological stuff. Two weeks ago the focus was on how to get senior support-staff to do multi-tasking better and how to hire new staff who could distinguish between multi-tasking and just plain inattention. Stan and George, his salesman, had shaken their heads. In a small-town dealership like Garris Autos all you asked for was office and service-department help to do just any one thing without making a mess of it.

Yesterday made the eighth day Stan knew he had cancer. Doc Anderson had not said he was a dying man. He said the new chemo options were 100% better than even two years ago. But Stan had studied the physician's face and decided that what he read in it was: this patient is dying but needs to feel hope because hope helps medicine work.

One way he knew he was dying was that he usually saw Doc in one of the St. Fursey Clinic's patient examination rooms: this time the reception nurse guided him much farther down the short hall. They went past an open bathroom door with a mirror facing the hall. Stan saw what in his right mind he knew to be himself, passing, following a nurse. The fellow whose face he regarded morbidly was in his early fifties, with large eyes and a reasonable expression, but the skin was so colorless and the eyes so passive, as if looking backside-to, that Stan was shocked. The nurse and he also passed the technical room where two women in white bent over microscopes. Stan recognized the near one as the piece of work who recently had suggested that he fuck off just because he had offered to show her the wonderful Audi on his lot. Not an etching, just an Audi. That Audi being supposed to appeal to up-and-coming professional young women. He decided to cut her if she looked up when he went past. *Cut* her! He exclaimed to himself. No business-person in their right mind *cuts* anyone. You see an angel, who clearly gets around on wings, you *still* might sell him a car some day. Still, Stan told himself lightly, you're dying, you have to go on taking a little shit off people here and there because that's life and you are still in it, but you don't have to take it from everyone any more.

The reception nurse took him to an office he had never seen before. It had proper chairs like someone's living room. Chairs with colored upholstery, no exam table, and on one wall, real books. None of the usual feel-good posters of senior citizens taking vitamins, always senior citizens in couples, smiling aggressively. What about if the man of the couple was dying of cancer? They never showed you that. He noted Doc Anderson's medical books—at least, they looked very much like Stan and

Kenneth's parts books kept handy on shelves in his own office as well as in the Service Department.

Private items lay on Doc Anderson's desk. Clearly an unopened envelope from the Cullough High School. That figured. Doc had his older kid in high school. A grocery sales flyer from Marty Hanks's supermarket, which everyone around had gotten this past week. So old Marty Hanks was going to try to keep up with Denham's Bakery and offer Replacement Meals. Largest of all, a manila envelope with Stanford Garris printed by hand in the upper right-hand corner.

Doc Anderson said, "Take this with you to St. Mary's, in Duluth, next week. But I have also sent them everything from the computer. And Stan, ask them questions, but don't get upset if you forget the answers. Just ask again. One of the things cancer patients do is forget a lot of what they're told." Doc Anderson gave a friendly, sheepish kind of smile. "They just do it. In fact, some people take another person along, a relative, to take notes, even. They bring note pads. Clip boards."

Stan said, "Do men do that, or just women?"

"I don't know. I should think so."

Stan said, "In your practice though, Doc, do you know any men who take someone along to take notes?"

"I don't, as a matter of fact," the physician said.

Stan reached for the envelope now. He had been going to, a minute ago, but his fingers had kept moving around at the same time as they felt numb. The moment passed. He felt stable. He slapped the package of X-rays between his side and his elbow. He put together a grin and looked over. "I see you're practicing up for tomorrow!"

A piece of sheet music now showed that must have lain under Stan's X-rays. The doctor seemed to relax.

"I don't get this one part, Stan," he said. "The altos keep getting ahead of us tenors, and it shouldn't be like that. It should be that they start that bar first."

He moved the sheet over to where Stan could study it close-up.

"But by the end of the third bar we should be together."

Stan didn't read music worth two cents. Stan looked at the words, though, to see if he could figure it out. "From all transgressions, set us free, who would thy chartered freedmen be."

No one knew what any of that meant, of course. Stan had been brought up a Lutheran more or less, but even his mother had gotten bored with it and quit. He caught her letting herself into the library with her own key one Sunday forenoon, in order to go on the web. Stan himself went to services—what few he went to—to keep Ginny off his back and to be able to look old Pastor Niemut in the eye. Even really simple people like Menzies, the school principal, were bored with church. Menzies, that poor sap, had to show up there because the Board of Education members and a lot of other people knew that he slapped bad kids around some but if he showed up in church, it confused people's judgments. People would decide he wasn't all bad. Stan had to show up in church because everyone knows auto dealers will sooner or later just naturally shave you close as a snake but maybe they wouldn't, too, because at least—look—there was Stan Garris, along with the other usher, lined up at the back pew with the two collection plates, waiting for the organ to slam out, "All things come of thee, O Lord, and of thine own have we given thee." So Stan for years went smartly up the aisle with Donald Menzies.

As for this annual Thanksgiving ecumenical choir, he sang in it to be together with friends during the snack breaks but mostly because it gave him a community activity with Ginny without having to listen to any of her conversation. She was a soprano. The sopranos sat in front of the basses, so Stan, a tenor, got to be over on the opposite side, behind the altos.

"Doc, I can't tell," he said after a moment. He ought to stand up and go now, even though his mind felt rested, somehow, sitting there in that nice familiar doctor's presence.

He shook hands with Anderson. "Thanks for the directions sheet, too," he said.

Doctor Anderson stood up, as well. "I'm sorry you got cancer, Stan, but we're on it. And we have an excellent chance to win the fight."

But he used that elegant language—"excellent," instead of "real good." Stan wasn't so dumb: they were in the presence of death. That was what gave Doc the formality. Stan could hear that much.

His life did a complete U-turn when he left Dr. Anderson. His mind prodded him every three or four minutes. His mind said, "You're a dying man now, Garris."

He got back to the lot, geared to recall what everyone's work was for that day—his own, George Herzlich's, Kenneth's. His mind kept interrupting. "None of this matters, you," it said. "You are a dying man. Forget the day's schedule." No wonder he tied one on at the VF the way he did. Now, Saturday, he was not only a dying man, he was hung over.

Stan ambled casually from his glassed-in office out to where George was showing a car to someone Stan hadn't seen before. The car was one of this year's pieces of inventory trash—actually a perfectly good vehicle but both Stan and George got to hating any car that cost him $300 a month just because it's sitting there and the economy was down and people hardly bought Kleenex when they had a cold.

It wasn't anywhere near noon but Stan went over and slouched down onto the sofa in the new-car show room. The sofa was still covered with Silver's blanket. Her light hairs had felted into its worn upholstery. "Christ, Silver," Stan thought. "I wonder if you are dead or alive."

George Herzlich was showing a Suburban to a stranger from out of town.

Stan stayed put, playing the part of one of their regular deadbeat non-customers looking over new car mags. Deadbeat non-buyers were mostly wistful teenagers, who would grow up into car buyers, like Doc Anderson's nice kid, and old retired geezers who kept themselves looking nice in single-color woven shirts and Settesdal sweaters and khaki slacks because they had once had perfectly good jobs like anyone else and Stan wouldn't throw them out. Or they had been veterans in some war that seemed honorable. Old Ward Hines, for instance. Stan had to be careful which people he let hang around in the showing room.

Now he himself was too sick-looking to get into any part of a sale. Still, he listened carefully from the couch to the best salesman he'd ever had. Old George didn't miss much. He spent about two minutes explaining the FlexFuel option to the customer. Then because the man asked no questions about the E-85 stuff but was bent looking in windows, without a twitch, George went to talking about using the new Suburban for family. As in no one needs to be so crowded they're always sitting on some kid's abandoned Eskimo pie. The man kept looking in the car windows, so George switched fast again. Guns and dogs and a fast getaway he was on now. You got the weekend, but say that's all you got. You don't want to spend all Saturday morning of it wrestling with the car furnishings. Especially if you stayed late Friday making sure to wind up everything at the office. Stan shot a quick look up over a full-page ad for V-belts: George was a genius. George had clearly decided, as Stan did now, that this guy wasn't any executive around any office. He'd never stayed on a Friday night to sort out market decisions for any company or any staff problems. He sold insurance, maybe. He didn't hire or fire anyone. So George had brought out the line about clarifying all office issues with a firm hand before the weekend so you wouldn't have it all waiting for you on Monday.

The prospect said, "You said it!" Flattered.

George stayed firmly on the car's RV advantages.

"What I like about it," George said, "is kind of a personal thing with me, actually. It's how you can change all the arrangements inside so fast. Some cars, they say you can take a seat out here and put something else there, or you can turn it into a camper, all that kind of stuff, but when you get started actually doing any of that, you're suddenly tied up for an hour of monkey work. Not this one. I like it for hunting because it takes less than 20 minutes to set up for space in the rear, and you don't kill your back doing any of it either. That's just a personal reason, though. I suppose it's because I hunt."

"That George," Stan thought, "if he ever used a rifle except on a skunk this is the first I heard of it."

George's man wore cammos with the wet-woods deer pattern.

He now wore the classical half-glazed look. He pussy-footed slowly, slowly, around the whole car. George didn't follow him. George even backed away a foot or two. That meant George had decided the man was buying. The man trailed one hand with infinite delicacy along the hood design, the side, the back door, and now back to the opposite side where George waited with a very serious expression on his face. The man was making the car his own. A good two, three minutes ago, that car had stopped being some glossy E-85-equipped Suburban in a northern Minnesota GMC showroom. It was this out-of-town guy's car now.

Stan knew all George's moves from here on out. He fantasized the whole thing. George would take the fellow into his own office. They'd talk payment schedule. Then he would want to introduce him to someone else. This made a buyer feel he himself had gladdened a whole GMC dealership. The buyer up to then would have thought, wow, a big business for such a little town. But when Stan popped his head in wanting to be introduced, the buyer would get somber inside himself: what a good corporation this is, big and go-ahead where you want it, but mom-and-pop, too, so you realize there is nothing like the personal touch and this dealership has it.

George and his customer were emerging from George's cubicle.

"I'm going over to the police station to get your plates," George was saying.

Stan's mind cut in: George would be doing this after Stan was dead, too. His mind continued: everyone would do business in the usual way but he would be dead. His mind told him how George would call, "I'm on my way over to get your plates. Go get lunch. Go to Denham's, that's the bakery, south side along Fourth Street. They have deli sandwiches—thick on the meat, crusty bread, none of your thin flap of summer sausage and no Dijon." Stan's mind said, the man would do it and then George and his wife, Mercein, would drive the customer's old car up home for him, Mercein always knitting something, and the new car owner would feel strange with the paper flooring sheets still down.

And in the next instant, George began the scenario verbatim. Go to Denham's et cetera.

The customer fiddled his hands around the car papers, and said, "Deli sandwich sounds good. But it'd better not cost an arm and a leg! I just purchased a big car!"

Ah—the first twinge of buyer's remorse. The fellow's a good sport, though, willing to make a joke.

George was right on it. "There's people eating at Denham's who are never going to get a decent car in their whole lives. Not a chance."

The customer looked pleased. He left.

George came ambling over to Silver's couch and Stan stood up trying not to look sick.

High five. "Nice going!" Stan said. "The one great white hunter sells a Suburban to another great white hunter."

George said, "Time, too. Now we're down to only one of those bed-and-breakfast vehicles."

Stan said, "Can you hold the shop the rest of the morning and this afternoon?"

"I can leave Kenneth with everything this morning. I'll go get this guy's plates and Mercein and I were going to go to Duluth for yarn, but we can make a supper date out of it, and take the man's old car home for him. Not far, either. He's from Chisholm. Handy." He added, "No word of Silver, I don't suppose?"

They talked about the stolen Labrador for a moment, and Stan went into his own office.

Stan sat down, feeling rotten, and laid out his day. He would sleep. Then drive over to Tenebray Creek Drive and get to his two o'clock easily. After that, see Vera Hall, the school principal's secretary. If she was at home he would discuss her pickup with her.

Then he would see if he could find Peter Tenebray and pitch him the idea he had hatched up last night. A pretty good idea, considering he'd been so drunk he'd had to ask Vern Denham to drive him home from the VF.

He had fallen into bed to dream heavily. He had dreamed the idea to run past Peter Tenebray. Well, hell, actually—he never would have had the idea but for his mother. She was the one rooting around in internet chat rooms like a smart old sow and scooting all over the web all the time, hatching up ideas. Before he had become a dying man, he listened when she talked because she was a very likable person. Now that he was dying, though, he got more sense. He heard the goodness of this last notion of hers. She was a wonderful, ingenious person. She was likable all right. He loved her.

Now he was too tired to keep thinking. He lay down on Silver's blanket. Just before falling asleep, he planned what was left of his marriage. He intended to be a good-enough husband to Ginny until he died, but he absolutely was not going to sacrifice any more hours of his life to her than he could help—however he could decently manage it.

When he awoke, it was still only midday on Saturday. He went through his thoughts about Vera's pickup. Stan told her that he thought he could repair that pickup she'd brought in just for an oil change. He told her he could hear something in it and would she bring the old buggy in again and leave it with him until he and Kenneth—the mechanic—could figure it out?

"Can't do it," she had said. "School funding cuts. No raises this year."

He said, "Just give us a look. No charge. That sound could be anything from just a loose box for the exhaust to something about the timing or a flat place on one or more tires. You can't go by sound. I'll call you up and tell you what's wrong and I'll quote you a price. The price doesn't work for you, you tell me upfront, and we don't fix it until you have more money lying around." Then he laughed to show her this was a joke.

She laughed and said, "You got that much right—money lying around!"

He gave her shoulder a slap and said, "Think about it! The offer holds."

To himself Stan sighed, don't touch people's shoulders any more. He had picked up on a fast glimmer of horror Vera gave him. For a moment he had forgotten that he looked like hell and anyway, word was all over St. Fursey that he had lung cancer so he told himself, You are going to have to bite the bullet here. You tell someone some offer holds, but if you obviously are going to die soon they know the offer just might not hold up with whoever takes over your dealership when you're gone. Also, in places of business, women pretend to be mad if you presume to touch them. That was OK. All part of the game. But when you are sick with cancer, they do a fast cringe if you touch them. The way Vera had nearly ducked from his friendly pat.

She had brought the pickup in Thursday.

He took Kenneth off a juicy transmission job, and told him to do a worksheet for Vera's pickup. Kenneth listened to what Stan was telling him between the lines as well as what he actually said. Namely, he would understand that Stan wanted to know what all was wrong with Vera's wreck of a pickup, and he would want the diagnoses in two categories—expensive plus fixable and inexpensive plus fixable. He would all the while know that vehicle needed to be put out of its misery.

Kenneth had eaten and returned. He still had his jacket over his arm. It was a red and grey letter jacket, number fifty, from five years ago when he played at left tackle for Cullough High School. He came to stand over Stan.

"On that 1990 F-150," Kenneth said. "What about if both lists are so long that maybe we're talking going to the crusher?"

"Give me a look," Stan said. "Have a seat."

Kenneth started to lay his letter jacket onto the sofa arm, saw Silver's hair all over, and folded it up into his lap instead.

Stan took Kenneth's sheet. "I see what you mean," he said after a moment. "I was afraid it would be like that." He read aloud: "To start with the brakes, calipers and rotors bad in front and the pads gone, and in the rear the drums had shot brake linings gone. The catalytic converter worn out. Sulphur smell. The water pump was shot, so the truck overheated. The radiator needed to be flushed. The heater did not warm up, which might be the thermostat. This vehicle needs new plugs. The brake fluid was leaking at the wheel cylinders. The grinding noise around the rear axle might be, probably was, a wheel bearing—or it was a U-joint or bearing in the differential. The oil pump was not working. The radiator hoses were leaking oil onto the engine. There was a bad head gasket—very bad—sending black smoke out the exhaust. As for the body: chassis rusted through in five visible places. The back bumper is coming off. The tail gate can't be closed—well, the owner knew that: she had already tied clothesline around the bed and stabilized it with duct tape. The tires worn out, three with flat places. Wheels need alignment. Balancing."

Kenneth laughed. He said, "But you might keep it safe enough by fixing on the brakes, front and rear, and like get that oil drip stopped so it's not dropping right onto hot metal anywhere. A person could do that."

"I'll talk to her," Stan said. "Meantime, park it out on the back slab somewhere till I see what Vera says."

They both got up.

Stan climbed into a Savana on its last month of cheap inventory.

It was snowing heavily now. Bad on a Saturday. People didn't do inspiration buying of new cars on snowy Saturdays, although they would drive to a Wal-Mart all the way up to Cullough or even Chisholm.

He glided along Fourth Street, past the bakery, noting that it was full, as of course it would be because there was yesterday's murder victim to talk about. A nearby murder of a stranger was perfect for pulling everyone out of every knothole in the Superior National Forest: it gave you the shivers but you weren't obligated to feel anything at all about it if you didn't want to. Kind of a real-life substitute for reality TV.

Stan decided to cruise Tenebray Creek Drive. He had avoided it for a few days, since views of the meadows to the west reminded him of Silver. He and she used to follow Tenebray Creek south to the slough.

He decided to go up into the north corner where people lived who never bought a late model from him or any dealer and probably never would. At this upper end, Tenebray Creek Drive faded into a gravel road There were two ratty apartment buildings and a number of stands for mobile homes. Only three pickups stood near the stands. Down economy.

He passed the apartment building run by an out-of-town fellow who still drove a 1980 Honda. Stan had planned to wait until that Honda was a year older and then get into a conversation with the man about moving up in the world, say to a 1998 GMC something. Now that Stan was so sick, he shouldn't wait another year. Kenneth had fixed and shined up the 1999 Audi. It wasn't Stan's kind of car, but it had Audi mystique. He'd offer $1,000 plus or minus on the Honda and then let him have the Audi for $11,000 starting.

Stan slowed. His two o'clock appointment was in the other rundown building, but not for another hour. Why cruise around here now? He was embarrassed. He was actually yearning and yearning for that 2:00 appointment. Someone to talk to—someone professional who would keep her mouth shut.

All day he had been waiting and the hours scarcely moved. Now all of a sudden it was nearly 2:00. He U-turned in the snow and drove to his appointment. He began cussing aloud to himself in the car. He was not some pussy-whipped piece of sickness who would go to a therapist. He was doing a business-like thing. When he needed advice on extended cab pickups, he called up the technical man at Oshawa. When he had precise needs he got someone to address them. So it was the same thing: this woman was the expert and he was going to her to confirm what he already knew but needed to be sure of.

So what made him so sure Imogen Tenebray would be so smart? She had to be ten or eleven years younger than he. How could she answer any questions of his? He knew what it was. He was not going to her to find out how to die. He would do that by himself. Still, part of the reason he was going to her was that she knew something about death. He had heard the story that everybody in town knew. Years ago, when Imogen was just local big-shot Peter and Natalie Tenebray's daughter fresh out of college, she had married someone. They had had a child. That child had drowned in a flooded, open-pit mine that one of the mining companies was finished with. People fished in it, but it was hundreds of feet deep. You had to be careful. Town gossip was unreliable on this kind of subject. That is, since the young husband was not local, nothing stopped people from saying he had been negligent, taking a baby out in an open boat. Maybe he had been. Maybe it was not like that at all. The Tenebrays didn't share their private lives with folks having coffee at the bakery or even after church. They were said to give bash-up dinner parties on the weekends, where other Episcopalians who were college graduate types went— but news never sifted from those parties out to Stan's acquaintance, or the Friday night philosophers at the VFW.

Imogen Tenebray sat with the other altos in the weekly ecumenical rehearsals. Stan had been watching her. From the tenor section, he regarded the back of her neck. She didn't seem to whisper to people on either side. When it was break time, he edged around to where she stood talking to people, balancing the bendy little paper plates that tended to drop your crusts on the floor. He knew that she didn't jeer at people. His Ginny now—she always seemed to be in a little group with their heads lowered in close. They were always in the know about something that others were not invited to hear. This Imogen looked so different that he trusted she would be different. Now that he was about to step outside his life, he was so glad to get to talk to someone like her who was already, naturally, way outside his life.

As he parked the Savana among the wrecks of pickups outside Imogen's wreck of a building he wondered again: why didn't she live with her parents in their beautiful four-generation mansion? This place didn't even have an elevator. Its staircase was lighted by one low-wattage bulb.

By taking a break half-way up, making himself count to 100, Stan Garris made it up the second flight of stairs.

Its upper landing was very dark, but he found her bell. A scotch-taped sign said it was out of order so he knocked. He found himself delighted to be invited into her living room, like a new kid coming into a bright-lighted kindergarten. Two huge windows gave out to the west, where even so early, the sky was darkening behind the snowfall. The whole room was misty and gold.

He felt exorbitantly shy.

"Coffee over there if you want it," said the woman he'd come to see. "Take your time," she added. As for her, her eyes strayed leisurely away from his face. She appeared perfectly all right with looking out the huge windows over the rough grass toward Tenebray Creek. The new snow didn't yet cover the dull brome and quack of the meadow. All week there had been a mother bear and a cub out there, all around the town. Perhaps that's what she was doing, having a glance to see if she could spot them.

"Pretty," Stan said. He sat down.

Imogen now swung her face around to him.

"Tell me why you've come," she said.

Stan was startled, but the face across from him looked respectful and curious, not sardonic.

Being startled though, he blurted the truth at her. "I want to do three ideas that are a little different from anything I've done before—before—"

She waited. She didn't raise her eyebrows with a fakey expression of interest.

"The first one," Stan said, "is the easiest because it's in my line. I want to fix up a busted and worn-out pickup and do it all at low cost to the owner. Safety-wise, the darn thing ought to go to the crusher."

"But you're thinking of fixing it."

"Well, basically my mechanic will. Kenneth."

Imogen Tenebray smiled at him.

Stan checked her face carefully. He couldn't see any trickiness in the expression so he leaned back.

She was beautiful, of course, but then she would be. Her mother, who directed the ecumenical choir each Thanksgiving—Natalie—was sharp-looking even at fifty or fifty-five, whatever she was. Sharp-looking even when low-buzz drunk. Stan did not feel side-tracked by Imogen's looks, however. He was bracing up to his job here—his own agenda. He talked a little faster now because he felt he could make the important points clear to her. He felt he had better tell her exactly how Kenneth was a first-rate auto mechanic. And about George, too. You didn't have a good salesperson, you couldn't run a good dealership at all.

She was listening. Then Stan got confused because he realized he hadn't said who the owner was. It was terribly important to get it all clear for her. She needed the data. Vera Hall, he told Imogen.

Imogen spoke, "It's Vera who has the pickup needing a lot of work then," she said. Getting it right. Stan was glad she seemed to be someone who wanted to be sure she had the facts right.

She now said in a quiet voice, "Have I got this right? You are going to offer Vera Hall a repair job that she can afford even though a lot is wrong with her car?"

"Pickup. Yes—yes. That's it exactly!" he said.

Neither said anything for a second. Then Imogen said, "Did you want to say more about that or do you want to tell me the other two ideas you are working on?"

"Working on," he thought. That was a new one. Well, she was right. He was working on those ideas, in his head, just as much work as any other planning.

He said, "I'll probably just tell you the one and let the other go. Or maybe if there is time, I will tell you both. The other one doesn't matter so much, probably, so I'll tell you the one." His own voice, when he listened to it aloud, told him that the *other* idea was the important one and the one he proposed to tell this therapist was the less important. Live and learn, he thought.

"This project is about Dieter Stolz. He's in the ecumenical chorus."

Imogen exclaimed, "He's the one with the wonderful tenor voice. He has a terrific voice for a tenor, and he keeps the time right, too. I used to know him personally," she added. She seemed to be deciding whether or not to say something more. She said, "I know the gossip. Some people hold it against him that he was a World War II soldier on the other side."

"That's the whole point!" cried Stan. "That's what this project is about." He started doing that old elementary-school hands game in which your fingers act out the rhyme that runs:

Here's the church.

Here's the steeple.

Stan noticed his knuckles had gotten barked from connecting with Brad Stropp's chin last night. Oh well.

Open the doors. You spread your thumbs open as if they were great ancient oaken cathedral doors or something.

And out come the people. The eight fingers, dove-tailed, now turned upward.

Stan finished the game because it was addictive and then said, "You may not know because you probably don't have much to do with the police. Or maybe you do, since you are a social worker. Anyway, in this town, whenever there is a crime that isn't just USA vandalism but a major crime—well, like the one discovered yesterday—that dead girl found in the ditch alongside 53. The police go question the same old bunch of locals. It may seem like a dumb thing to do, but their budget is about a buck fifty. What can anyone do with that? So they get around to all their usual suspects, long shots or not. Here is my point. They always question old Dieter Stolz. Word is they are going to question him about this new murder, too. The girl out along Highway 53. Dieter has got to be seventy-eight, or eighty. He just isn't someone who would rape and kill and dump off a young girl. If he was up for that, he'd have been doing it ever since the late 1940s or whenever he got to the States. Not now, not out of the clear blue sky. But people get some one opinion and they can't drop it. Well—no, now that I think about it… it is fun for them."

Stan thought, I don't need to tell her that it's being married to Ginny that's shown me what people do when they're bored. They go after someone close by who is *different* from themselves. He thought of the trash around town, specifically Brad Stropp, talking at the VFW. Starting all his remarks with "Say what you will—"

Aloud he said, "Well, dumb or not, here is my idea. We do something about it. So here's as far as I've got. We plan our regular annual for old soldiers around the area. Veterans' night. This year we use it to head off all this finger-pointing at Dieter. We'll have a fancy lunch for after—stuff from both the Super Valu and Denham's so there's no bad feeling. We honor Dieter Stolz, who is as much an old soldier as anyone else around here."

Stan stopped talking and glanced down at his hands. They lay quietly enough on his knees but his face felt full of blood. He said, "My God almighty, but that sounds so dumb."

Imogen said, "How would you work it? Would it be a kind of surprise party for Dieter or what?"

He told her that his mother—she knew his mother? Bridget? The librarian? (She did.) His mother and he were running through a bunch of German and German-American websites, chat rooms—those chat rooms, now…to drop into a few dozen of those you'd think half the world were old Nazis still going strong. Or worse, fourteen-year-old American Nazi-wannabes. Some websites were genuine links to German archives, especially those in Bonn and so his mother and he had been chewing through a lot of them at night. Since—since…

"My mother is a computerholic anyhow. My mother lives in Denham Apartments, if you know them? Second floor, right above the bakery actually. Those old ladies have little supper parties, once a week anyway. At the last one, she said that two of the others had heard from an official that the cops always kept an eye on foreigners. So I asked, what official would that be? The official was the deputy who works with the Chief of Police. She was talking about Darrel, that kind of riffraff deputy cop. You probably don't know him."

But Imogen did. She said, "I know him. I know Darrel. We deal with one another now and again."

Stan's respect for her took a lift. He supposed anybody could be some kind of a psychologist or social worker or whatever she exactly was, but you'd need the money to get a college education. That was OK. That was what he was here for, because this Imogen Tenebray was a trained professional, but now that she had to deal with your very average cold-hearted trash same as he did, he felt more trust in her.

"My mother has always told me you can Google your way to anywhere except Heaven and she was going to—if I tell you what it is you don't tell anybody, right?" He looked over quickly.

"Nothing leaves this room, Stan, except what you tell people yourself."

"I knew that. I shouldn't have asked."

"Yes but you should ask. You have to be 100% sure. I'm OK with the fact that you asked," Imogen said.

"Well, yesterday, like everyone else, I dropped into Denham's to hear whatever the latest was on that dead girl. And last night. At the VFW. Every place crowded. And Brad Stropp was shouting around about *this* time, if this town and countryside was going to be safe for women and children, we were going to get that Stolz and make it stick. My mother thought she might do something in the library. If she's sitting at the computer all the time, it looks as if she's doing ordinary office work. She wondered if she might find his family. What if she found a sister or a brother, and we'd bring them over from Germany?"

Stan began to feel stupid, and then angry at himself. All this talk. He also felt a return of the morning's sickness. He hurried. He told her just the minimum. Some guy who works high up at a huge company in Roseville. His mother got onto him in a chat room so Mama asked him right away how he knew Dieter. It's the strangest thing. This fellow is a German-American who joined our army in 1943. This man had spoken German in his family, so they put him into army intelligence. He was serving in the Ardennes forest in the early spring of 1945. All the men he was with were killed. He himself was taken prisoner by a very young German sergeant. He remembered his name but that was all. He wanted to find him, to thank him, to see what he was doing. Of course Stan's mother, Bridget Garris, got all excited. Why wouldn't she? Imogen probably understood this even better than Stan did. What can your usual bunch of women in St. Fursey, Minnesota, talk about week after week? Those other old ladies up there in Denham Apartments—they weren't like Stan's mother. They couldn't any more double-click on a chatroom than they could shoot a bear. So of course Stan's mother got all excited. Here was American History connected right into her town.

He told Imogen they meant to pull this off the Wednesday before Thanksgiving. Every Wednesday was church night in St. Fursey—reserved for choir practice and all—well, since the all-churches' chorus would be singing Friday they could give up that particular Wednesday.

"Another thing," Imogen put in. "Some kids will be home from college for the weekend. They should hear this—grown males being serious. All so long ago, too. Now—Stan—did you want to say the third thing you had in mind? The reason I ask is you have time. You still have fifteen minutes, and I haven't got another appointment, either, so if you go over, that is OK. I will tell you, if you go over a lot, I will charge you for the next half-hour."

He said, "I have to tell you I was a little scared to tell you about this business for old soldiers. I know you work part-time for a peace organization in Duluth. You might not approve."

Imogen's face took on a hard look. Please don't be pissed, Stan told her silently. Begging. Please don't be pissed.

She said, mildly, "It has to be very scary, being a soldier. It has to be. You'd have to know that unless you were awfully lucky, you might never get to live out the whole grown-up adult life we think we have a right to."

She seemed to give herself a little shake. "Anyway, I'd be scared," she said.

"Wait a sec," Stan said. He put his head down between his shoulders and pretended to be fishing for his handkerchief. He didn't have one because it was Saturday and he hated carrying a handkerchief. He had to have one at work because a proprietor of a business like his can't pull a Kleenex out of his pocket, but he hated the idea. Still, having a handkerchief on you was being like those poor saps who leapt to their feet the moment the organist had finished playing the hymn once through, because they had a little kid's taste for obeying rules. He actually was crying for a second. He decided to tell her it was just for a second though. "Wait a sec," he said, "I am crying for a second. I'll be right there."

She waited without a motion or a sound. She didn't say any fucked thing like "It's good to cry. Go ahead and cry." She just sat there and stayed out of his face.

Soon he said, "Maybe my hour is up now."

"You have ten more minutes if you want them," she said in a very low voice.

"Maybe I will come back some day and tell you about the third thing. Maybe I will. Now that I know you don't think those two ideas are dumb ass." He said, "I don't know why I would use language like that with you. Such shit. I am a car dealer for God's sake. I know you can't use dirty language on the job. I know that! So why'd I do it?"

Imogen laughed immediately. "It's because I am a therapist. People feel free to use the worst language they know with a therapist. I think I know all the bad language now anyway."

Then he was out. It was awful to be out. He went carefully down the staircase of her building. He said to himself, "I am not in love with her. Not even thinking about it. So what is this all about? That's easy, stupid. I need a friend. She is going to be my friend. Hell no, she isn't going to be a friend. I will not go back to see her again. I may be stupid but I am not that stupid. Still, I will always know in some sense she is a friend."

Half-way down the now very dark staircase he stopped. "No, that isn't it," he said half-aloud. "She won't be a friend. Here's what it is. Now that I have talked to her, I have learned something. I've learned that there are intelligent people around. I now know that. The ones who are alive, like this Imogen, will be alive long after me. Millions of them are already dead, just the way millions of everybody are already dead. But millions of them are still alive. Intelligent people! Not just tricky operators. Not dumb asses. Intelligent people."

CHAPTER FOUR

At just before four o'clock on Friday afternoon, no one except Vern Denham himself was left in his building at Wrack Chemical. He was quitting. Quitting, quitting! For all the times that Vern had quit jobs, the happiness of leaving leapt up in him each time. Leaving, leaving.

He went along the silvery anti-personnel fence. The whole campus of Wrack Chemical was silent. He heard only the traffic on the interstate. When a company has 20% percent growth right along for a number of years like Wrack it needn't and doesn't hire riffraff for security: Wrack's armed people were never particularly visible yet they were always about, mostly near or inside 5 Lab. Oh, Vern thought, he was quitting, he was quitting.

He was passing it now, the earth-bermed Institute for Humane Research that Wrack staff called 5 Lab.

Vern had admired the outside of that building from the day he interviewed, two years ago, for the job at Wrack Chem. The building had one free, above-ground face entirely windowed in a steep-roofed assembly of glass. Its eaves were deep and low, precisely designed to let winter—but not summer—sunshine through all that glass. The architectural idea was a 1990s concept of rich people's workplaces designed to look like rich people's play places. 5 Lab looked like a Swiss ski hotel.

5 Lab was a first for Wrack, because Wrack had been just a conventional mid-sized chemical company organized in 1955. In a dozen

years or so, it had eaten its growth potential. Four years ago, the president bought a run-down adjoining site, put up the Institute for Humane Research, announced its project of looking for an absolute cure for red steel and other molds of interest to Minnesota and Wisconsin truck farmers.

Now, Vern marched along with heightened feeling. It was as if he literally could see farther. He felt the presence of small things—places where the silver was chipped away from the fence. He could already smell Wrack's weekend smell, piney from the spaced shrubberies. All weekend the campus would be free of chemical effluence.

He felt how sharp and clean Wrack's setup was at all times. Wrack was the first orderly workplace Vern had ever experienced. When nothing much was going on at lumber and construction firms, which, like Wrack, ran to a lot of woven anti-personnel fencing, the yards and dock drive-ins still looked as if violent work might start up any moment. Piles of lumber and half-unwrapped Tyvek or neat Lincoln-log piles of 4x6s lay around. You felt that at any minute a troop of men might appear, still wiping sandwich crumbs from their plaid shirts, replacing their helmets. Wrack, on the other hand, left nothing lying around. And why would it, Vern thought: chemical companies work with nearly invisible material. Chemistry is the ideas *inside* objects, not objects themselves. Construction companies sooner or later show everything they have here and there, right up front. When they have finished a building project, what you see and have been seeing is what you get. How different with Wrack! Vern had done promotions and image making for the company—it was over two years now—yet still he didn't grasp the crux of those chemists' work. Like any chem lecturer or teacher he knew some of the logic and a few formulas by heart. He taught them to high-school and vocational kids—but those letters and numbers and subscriptures had no real home in his brain.

Vern grabbed hold of the Administration door. Not exactly for the last time. He would want at least a week to get his present projects into other hands. Still, nearly the last time. He felt the heft of what he was doing. This might be the end of himself and Imogen Tenebray. It was her father who had gotten Vern this very high-end employment, the first he'd ever really had.

Good old dad Peter. Well, perhaps Vern would have to kiss goodbye to any more of the cheery, almost intellectual family dinners at the Tenebrays'—old Peter himself doing the cuisine, Natalie plenty juiced for the evening by that hour but still on her feet, and Imogen cutting them Stilton because the Tenebrays ate Stilton from Thanksgiving time through the Epiphany.

Vern imagined Imogen's oddly pretty face. You thought twice about such a woman. Vern had dropped in several times at her part-time workplace in Duluth. A shabby place it was. Women for Peace had the basement of some old failed church. In the Director's office, Imogen sometimes swooped down to pick up and stroke pets people brought in. Someone else's middle-sized dog often lay curled in her lap. Vern found Imogen once resting the elbow of her mouse hand on the haunch of a very mangy-looking creature.

When Vern first took to dropping in when he had to be in Duluth for anything, he had reached out a hand to pet the dog. It raised its nose exactly one inch above Imogen's thighs and gave a growl from deep as China. Imogen had grinned. "That's his best quality," she said. "Everyone else around this place is so non-violent you could choke but not that dog, at least."

Vern smiled now, recalling it. But when he recalled her long hair she would toss heavily back his heart shook.

He turned off the thought because now he was inside Wrack Administration, less than one minute away from quitting. Four more doors down the echoey hall.

He wore his most serious suit because Wrack's monitors were always on, making film whenever someone wasn't watching. Next week, next month, he didn't want Wrack's last view of him to show a nervous-looking man of 30 making a Major Life-Career Mistake. Quitting! His shirt was fine. Tie good. Haircut. He felt that if he quit the job wearing ironed cords and a sport jacket, casual Friday code, they would decide—and dictate into his employment record—that Vern Denham seemed to be going to seed anyway.

Vern wasn't a city man. Never mind that he had been east to college and he had had ten years of off-and-on employment, all of it in cities. He was a rural Northern person. He was the only person he knew who loved to go back to his parents' house—their second-floor apartment, the long comfortable sprawl of it, right over the bakery itself. Alongside other apartments they rented to old people. Vern didn't want to be reminded of boyhood but of young adulthood—of delicious earlier returns from college, from jobs he got fired from or jobs he had quit. He didn't pine for the Thanksgiving dinners of boyhood. His relationship with his dad and mother was merely so-so. Not sad. Not painful. Merely casual. Each time he came home, some job ended, his dad would say, "Now what happened this time?" Each time Vern liked telling him what happened anyway. His dad always looked doubtful. The two men didn't read each other very well.

It was his mother who didn't flinch from her serf-like loyalty. She would always say "I guess everyone can't be so lucky as to have the Tenebray family to work for." Then she would add, "Your dad never quit a job in his life."

Vern's parents lived in the dream world of serfs, then. They licked up a lot of crow from one Tenebray or another. When Vern's dad had been gardener and property supervisor for the old grandfather, Cornelius Tenebray, and after that for his son, James, and only recently for Peter— part-time—he wasn't galled at being called the Tenebray family's *man*. As if he were a serf. As a boy, Vern had been mesmerized by how his dad beamed when one or another Tenebray slapped his shoulder.

Vern never insulted his father. A previous girlfriend or two had thought him kind to the old man. That wasn't it. It was that he had known since he was 15 or 16 that he himself was dull. It didn't show on the outside. On the outside he was like any American who could imitate a smiley weather anchor. In fact, Peter Tenebray early on took Vern for a natural speaker. It was only inside himself that Vern knew he was dull. Not thick-headed like his high-school classmates. Not unthinking, like old Kenny who had become a mechanic for Garris Autos. He grieved at this dullness about himself, but could always gear up and be lively, even rowdy, when he had to be. He had to hide much. For example, who could he tell that he was glad he'd gotten laid off from such and such a job, and he was glad to be rid of it, rid of it, rid of it? Even the women he knew, with their sincere, or insincere, pose of being understanding, lost eye contact if you said you longed to be unemployed. A man who was unemployed…it was nothing you could put your finger on, but women felt an ancient dislike of such a man. Even Imogen, now, and she had to be an original if any woman was—even she would not admire him for *wanting* to quit. Even if the Wrack publicity job had come his way directly through her father— she might now regard Vern as one more colorless rural lightweight.

St. Fursey was full of them. Lightweights. People who did a little hunting. At least they made sure to get out for Opening. Some of them showed up to sing with the annual ecumenical Thanksgiving chorus but they could not concentrate. Natalie Tenebray shouted at them about making clean attacks—Please would they watch her! Please would they please, just this once, *watch* her—so they all came in at once? It did no good. They heard her shriek, they saw the high color in her face, but what was it all about? The old lady all worked up about something again?

He had already waited three or four minutes in the meeting room. A sharp-looking woman his age walked in—of course, he'd seen her. He placed her: she was the president's assistant, dressed expensively in khaki and black in the Twin Cities mode of the 1990s.

Now he had to concentrate sensibly. They, she, someone, would of course want some evaluative comment from him. They would of course feel some chagrin when he gave his two reasons for leaving Wrack. They would, wouldn't they? Somehow he had pictured being able to talk to Wrack's second-in-command, an older man with a kindly, too-soft face. He had imagined a sentient leave-taking. He had made a mental picture of the vice-president, silvery and gentle-mannered, who would twiddle a pencil and say, "Would it make any difference, Vern, if I told you that Wrack's senior people have been deeply concerned about the same issues as you are? That we have every intention of working on them? And…" and here he would pause, as if anxious not to be intrusive, "…I have to say your name has come up a number of times because we would like to ask you to help with working up the new three-year envisionment stuff?" Another pause here, Vern imagined, then: "You're good, you know, Vern. You are the best out-there speaker we have. Your conference breakfasts have made us some solid friends. Everywhere. Even in the Range towns. People in the schools say that kids actually love your lyceums. Do you think you could help us work this out? Vern, I guess I am asking you to stick. I guess I'm saying that what worries you at Wrack Chem is exactly what worries us, too."

Nothing like that was happening. The snappy young woman went around behind the huge table. She leaned across it to shake hands.

She would like to help him, she said, with whatever he had on his mind. Good, he thought. Her role here is just office staff stuck with the formalities. In a minute or two, she would call in someone who would accept his resignation.

"I am resigning," he said.

To her, he knew, he was a man acting on principle, leaving a job on principle, which meant he was a personnel problem pure and simple. She or someone would have discussed him already since he had asked for an appointment. They would have figured him. As an underling, a follower, a company person, she would have an ancient, inborn hatred of people who think for themselves. He felt the gelid disrespect veering at him from her eyes.

Apparently she wasn't going to call in anyone. She would either (he thought) accept his resignation outright or more likely (he thought) she would bid for time by making him an appointment with some HR person. Wrack now had on call not two, but four guided-imagery counselors. They were very thin young men and women, in Brooks at the least, Armani at the most, whose language was slack and friendly. When you explained anything at all to them, their eyes became doe eyes, as if you had just proposed marriage. The eyes also said that whatever you were saying, they had heard it all already and it was non-controversial and therefore didn't matter. Their invariable response to any insight was "OK, OK... OK." If you said, "My name is Albert, and I've got this idea about e=mc squared," they would smile and say "OK—*okay*." If you said, "My name is Gautana Buddha and I have this idea of an 8-fold path, right thinking and all," they would smile. That, too, would be "OK, *okay*."

One morning, when Vern had been with Wrack only a few weeks, he made to join a crowd in the largest staff meeting room for the morning session of two Spiritual Journey teams' half-day programming for employees.

The President of Wrack saw him in the hallway. He grinned, but firmly caught Vern's elbow and pulled him away. "No, no, Vern," the president said, smiling. He kept Vern's arm.

They went into the man's office with its huge shining desk top and the small iron safe draped with a yin-yang symbol embroidered on black velvet.

The Wrack president said, "You didn't want to go in there."

Vern said, "I didn't?"

"No, hell," the president said. "Sit down." He pressed a button. "Mervin, bring us a couple of coffees, will you, and open up the new box of the terrific stuff and bring us some and then go ahead and offer it around out there, will you?" Mervin left.

"No, hell," he repeated. "You would die in there. No, we get those folksies in here for two groups and two groups *only*—the people who need them."

Vern made interested noises.

Mervin was back in the room with coffee, an old-fashioned salver of cream and sugar and four dark chocolate truffles.

When Mervin left again, the president went on. "Group One is Chemists and Group Two is support staff," the president said. "Those're the groups. If there's any one group who can't seem to develop any loyalty to the firm the worst are the chemists. They don't even begin to get it about how we are a family and whatever other philosophy you have, you want to keep in mind what the whole family needs. Maybe only a business family, yes, but still, a family. Same with the support staff. Family— shit, Vern!—whatever language you want to use, the fact is, as a group, we have common goals, and you'd think they'd want to throw in with the company. But they never do. Not really. À propos, Vern, let me tell you a funny thing about industrial spying. You send out an industrial spy, right? They're supposed to find out the latest formulae from the competition, right? You know what they really find out? They find out that fifty-two percent of our own chemists are bad-mouthing Wrack everywhere. Not just in bars at New Year's, not just because they didn't get the Christmas bonus they wanted. Not just in bars but *everywhere*. And the support staff. They steal over seven percent of our Hewlett Packard laser-jet stock for their home computers. For their kids' computers. For all I know, they sell it to the Mafia for *their* computers!" The big man gave a fulsome, good-tempered laugh. He pulled the tinfoil off a truffle, and bit it in half. Then he plugged the rest of it into his mouth, too. "My God, but those things are good," he cried, when he'd bitten into a second one, "So it's the chemists and the office gals who get the Spiritual Journey, not you."

Vern asked, "Well, but what do they make of it?"

"They love it. They love it. The spiritual imagery people make the whole roomful of them fill out an evaluation at the end of the session. They all say they love it. At first I used to ask them, when I was working the crowd a little at the Christmas party or anything, you know, I'd ask them, in so many words, what did they get out of it. I never met anyone, chemist or office help either one, who could remember a single damn thing—*but* they felt so good. And it was a day of no work with full pay. You have to remember, those people are always slightly jeering about the company. They all sneer at Wrack's Weekly Dot Com Newsletter. At the same time, they have their noses to the screen looking for mention of themselves. Try forgetting that some couple had their first baby or some-one got a ribbon in a New Brighton art show! Tell you the truth, I think they like it that the Spiritual Journey people get $30,000 a go from us for doing virtually nothing. We leak the figures around. I think they like the idea that the top brass are being played for fools! It gives them a hoot."

Vern stopped stirring his coffee. "But..." he began.

To Vern's amazement, the Wrack president suddenly burst out laughing again. The laugh slung some chocolate juice onto the huge desk. The man mopped it up with his handkerchief. "You know, I love those new kind of Spiritual Journey types. Back in the eighties, we got a very different animal. Back then, it was mostly overweight middle-aged women who'd failed to build profitable, private practices out of counseling divorcees.

"They'd arrive in their layered silks. Real silk, too, but they still looked like they'd floated clear from an ashram in Jersey City, if there's an ashram in Jersey City. They would glide slowly around the room like huge, festooned barges. 'Now feel the sun is hot over your head,' they'd say. 'Yes, hot, but not unpleasantly hot. And you are relaxed. Really relaxed....'

"But that was then, not now. Our personnel people stopped getting those people in, for whatever reason. Maybe those huge creatures with their clipboards have died off. I wouldn't know. Or maybe those women generated some specialty gigs—nurturing sessions for people caught embezzling, or dynamic relaxation for prisoners caught molesting juveniles, whatever." (Another fulsome laugh) "Around 1995, we started getting these glamorous boy-and-girl teams. You could see our $30,000 three times a year right there in their clothes. Had 'em ever since!"

He laughed again. "You know something, Vern, I think they've got more panache than greyhounds let loose at a puppy farm! I love them!" His eyes squinted for a split-second. "You hire somebody to do some job, you look at what they do, but you also have to look at the crap they *don't* do. If you give 'em a grateful kiss, these kids in their this-year clothes don't call in the sex police from somewhere. They understand business is a trust thing and workplaces are friendly places."

"Well, are they psychologists, social-work background, or what?" Vern had asked, feeling around for some neutral ground.

"Who, those lounge lizards? No! No, if I got in a real psychologist or real social worker, now that's what I call asking for trouble. No, these folks are business people. Relaxation is billable hours, so they do it."

The man added, "Look. Example." He laid his head directly onto the desktop, left-ear down. A pulpy-looking eye rolled up at Vern. "I am relaxed, OK? Those people teach people to relax. Well, Vern, now—how much real thinking does anyone do who is relaxed? How much actual work does someone do who's relaxed?" The president dangled his tongue out. Vern was fascinated to see that a huge length of tongue lay out on the tabletop like a banana slug.

The president raised his head.

"No," he said. "Even if 66.66% of my company ever really relaxed that won't be you and me, Vern, thank God. You haven't been here long but I've learned that much about you. You can work. Wrack needs for you and me to do just what we are both already doing—working our tails off!"

Signal to go, Vern thought. Time to go. Stand up. Go.

One more full-throttled laugh from the boss. But before the man opened the door to the outer services office, he said, "Fair warning about the real world, though, Vern! Those Spiritual Journey people are geniuses! Geniuses! They didn't learn how to stroke my company—*my company!*—

for $90,000 a year from any state-paid counsel for small businesses, let me tell you. Geniuses! But," and at last he opened the door, his arm around Vern's shoulder so whoever was out there would see that this was his man of choice for today, "what can you do?" He put on a half-witty, half-rueful expression. "What can I say? Wrack is a genius-loving company!"

Heads had looked up when the president opened the door and Vern came out of the president's office to go through the general room full of cubicles. The people at work were those scheduled for the second sitting of the Spiritual Journeyers. The door to a side office was open—the executive assistant's office. A slender figure in black and khaki silk blouse turned at her desk to regard him. Yes, Vern thought, they will all slightly hate me now, and he noted how satisfactory that was, in a primitive way. Some were chewing gum. Some kept their feet behind the cubicles' modesty-guards but he caught sight of a loose shoe here, another there.

That day, he now recalled, like today, had been a Friday, too, so people slouched before their computers in Norwegian ski sweaters from Ely, Minnesota. Not all people obeyed the lower dress code for Fridays. Not the slender woman in that side office. Not the president. Nor did Vern.

And now Vern heard his voice explaining that he wanted to quit. The young woman waited. His voice went on. His voice went loping over the course of this last year's work—his traveling around giving lectures to college students, high school lyceums to Minnesota, some Iowa high-school teachers' retraining. He had shown up as consultant for kids' science camps in Wisconsin. He had prepared all-day workshops for area chambers of commerce and regional development task forces—those that hadn't already been disfunded down to their socks.

Oddly enough, he now explained in a low voice, he had never looked into Wrack's Institute for Humane Research until it was stuck in front of him. He had just glided past the earth-bermed 5 Lab the way your fingers slide over irrelevant listings in Yellow Pages. One day he had arranged to be taken through the Institute, however, to complete his grasp of Wrack's many entities.

The woman regarded him with no particular expression. He couldn't get any sense of whether or not any others had quit for the reasons he was quitting.

She said, "And what happened?"

Her tone said he was giving a muddled report and should speak more clearly. But her tone also said she was a professional and would therefore patiently wait out his story, however kinky it struck her. Only once did her eyes flicker upward at the clock.

Vern told her about two of the Institute's projects. One was a complex survey of diseases that ideally would have quick come-on, but whose bacilli had to be impervious to weathering of any kind for several hours. Wrack's interest in the project was the actual packaging of these microbes. They could be gelatinously or otherwise packed and kept with good integrity for extremely adverse conditions—extreme cold, desert heat, jungle humidity—and deliverable for use by non-technicians. They could be safely handled by briefly trained enlisted personnel.

"That's right," the woman said. "What was the second project that interested you?"

He told her about 5 Lab. At the same time as the disease research was started up, 5 Lab was reported, in Wrack's Weekly Word Dot Com, to be where staff were researching cures for red steel, a recurring curse to strawberry farmers.

Vern had gone to look over 5 Lab then. In one of the lower levels, lighting blazed down on four rows of white enameled containers, each with a half-sized clipboard hanging from a hook below a hinged cupboard door. Out of the top of these containers stuck small animals' heads. Those apparently in pain or general misery gave periodic screams, or simply twitched, their eyes now slatting shut, now opening, their small mouths, surrounded by white fur or white-and-black whiskers, oddly pink inside. The ceilings, Vern had seen, were low and made of negative acoustic material, but no one had yet invented the tile that drank up and off-directed screaming. Those animals able to sleep did so. They leaned left or right jowl against the clean enamel container hole, the fur lopping over the enamel. An assistant approached Vern, coming from the other end of this lab, carrying a wide, clean white dustpan. In it lay two still animals. As he went along, the assistant lifted a foot or a paw that hung off the pan and curled it up against the animal's fur, giving it the look of a puppy cozily asleep.

When Vern got to the far end, he had looked back. The assistant was now slipping the animals off his pan into a bin-style door in the wall. A framed directive near Vern ordered that no one was to carry "deads" in a disrespectful manner. No animal was to be transported by its neck or by any single limb. Subjects were to be placed on the subject pans just as a person would be laid onto a gurney. And important—this printed with a bellied exclamation mark like those on PCs—Are you sure you want to delete this document?—no subject was to be taken anywhere but between their hutches and the tall lab tables or to the terminal ramps on the north wall. Terminal ramps, Vern thought: those would be the bin doors, likely gravity tunnels to an incinerator area below.

"And?" the young woman said because he paused.

He went on talking.

"You see," he told her. "I was slow to catch on. There isn't any research into any garden bacteria or viruses or mold."

"Oh, yes, there is," the woman said. "We could show it to you. In fact," she added in a bright tone, "this might convince you. In that home town of yours, you've got a very savvy-planning strawberry farmer who stays in touch with us! No problem, Vern."

"I want to quit!" he cried. "I want to quit!"

She stood up and came around to his side of her desk. She sat on its edge and looked down at him. She said. "There's no problem, Vern. Is that all you came to me about?"

"Yes—yes, I suppose it is," he said. "Yes…" He shook himself. "What do you mean, no problem?"

She quite openly looked at her watch.

She said, "Just that." Her two hands, cupped like statesmen's hands, lay peacefully across her thigh. "Let's see. It is only 4:20 now, so you can gather your things and leave. I'll see that people get your paperwork to you Tuesday."

He told her he of course was prepared to spend another week finishing up the two departmental projects his sub-group were still tweaking. And the two road lectures that had been scheduled in stone for him three months ago. And some approvals for the website environment discussion project. "We aren't 100% out of the woods with that yet. A week should do it."

"Not at all, Vern," she said in a warm tone. "You go clean out your desk right now. Never mind the road show. Don't worry about the website thing. You can quit in peace. We think very highly of you, you know. But right now—you know how it is on Fridays!" And she gave him a smile that was oddly fleshy for such a thin face.

Vern started to his feet. Was it over then? He thought, was it all over so fast?

He tried to sound low-key. "I wasn't sure exactly whom I should go to for this—"

Again her smile. "You mean, you wondered—quite naturally, Vern, I mean, we're all human beings—am I senior enough to accept your resignation? Yes. I am so able to take your resignation. It's all A-OK. Everything is A-OK."

"A-OK," he said.

"Absolutely, Vern." The smile. It spread over the cool meat of her face. "You shouldn't worry whether or not you are making a career mistake. Absolutely no worry. Consider your resignation complete. Our people attending your lectures and taking part in two of the symposia you've put together have the greatest admiration for you. The greatest. You're just about as good as it gets. Actually, though, I would have had to let you go before Christmas in any case…so this is best, and you should feel you've made a wise move here."

He tottered back down the long empty hall, out the door, and started off like a robot along the mesh fence. Now the mid-November sun had dropped low enough to cast its mesh-cage shadow on his face.

Vern slammed himself into his car.

He drove along 694 safely only because he always drove carefully. Going east on I-694 and a quarter of an hour later north with the Friday afternoon traffic on 35E, he pounded his fist again and again on the rubber grip-covered wheel. He could hardly credit that that icy chic technocrat had contrived it so that the company he had meant to *reject* for gross cruelty had crippled his great moment into merely getting fired. His confidence lay shattered about him. She must have spotted some essential dullness inside him, and had decided, for the very fun of it, to turn his ethical stance into nothing but humiliation.

He tipped down the rear-view mirror. Its little coffin-shaped glass showed him his dull face. Well, it was a dull face. Reliable. Yes—reliable—but reliability is what a man wants from a dog. On the other hand, his eyes looked back at him like two jewels.

"All right," he said calmly aloud. "All right." He gave the mirror a few more glances. Perhaps women did not like such a face any better than he did at this moment. Was that true? No, that wasn't true. Women liked him. His guess was that even Imogen Tenebray liked him. And the Episcopal priest, Eliza, too. And Pearl, the foul-mouthed organist who did *locum tenens* for any church at twenty-five a time, she'd given him a friendly lewd look once that had made up for a bad day. And that woman who seemed to be the Program Assistant for Imogen at her mediocre Duluth Women for Peace organization—only last week she'd cornered him between the chuffing furnace and a broken file cabinet. She made him the classical speech of its kind—the point was, she explained, that unlike other women, she always tried to follow her most inmost intuitions because she felt they came from the deepest place inside her, if—and this said with eyes pinioning him—he got what she was trying to say. She was one of those people with the carefully straggled hair designed to look as if they'd either just got out of bed with a gorilla or were just about to get into it.

Still, outdoors people were outdoors people. If that made people laughable, then he was a fool but the fact was his heart was lightening. This was his favorite time of year. He settled down to the drive north. He felt happier every minute.

Outside the car, the forest began to change from deciduous to more conifers. The light was going down. At this time of twilight, the poorish farmhouses of northeastern Minnesota were lighted from within, so they looked as indomitable as pioneers' huts. Whatever life was going on in them, it was no more deprived than what went on elsewhere.

Vern began to feel peaceful, a little glassy. He would spend the weekend with his parents.

He was returning to the world of no particular ambition. So many people of his hometown simply ignored their own fates. It wasn't so much that they wasted their lives as that they never caught sight of them. They were like people with closets full of various nations' uniforms. Each morning they reach for one and put it on, without caring which. At least, Vern thought, from now on, he himself would no longer be just one more Ugly American making serious, ugly money.

It was absolutely dark by the time Vern pulled in alongside Stan Garris's convenience pump. Garris Auto Sales was basically a dealership and repair place, not a service station, but like other business people in any small town, its owners did extra favors. Stan kept a convenience pump. He'd once handed Vern two of the eight hundred dollars' worth of Vikings tickets that he gave away each season to car buyers and leasers and insurance guys.

Vern had done the last 60 miles up from Cloquet on a low tank so that he could fill his tank at Stan's. He waited in the shadowy interior of his car. Vern expected Stan's mechanic, or maybe Stan's elder statesman of a salesman, George Herzlich, would come out and pump for him. It was Stan himself who approached, looking shaky. Vern had never heard any talk about Stan drinking on the job.

Stan set the nozzle and worked around wiping headlights, the windshield, finally the outside mirror on Vern's side. The man looked terrible. Not drunk, Vern thought. He might be sick.

Vern leaned out his window a little. On impulse, he said, "Let me tell you, Stan, I just got up here from the goddamned Twin Cities. Let me tell you, Stan. It's a been a bad week down there."

Stan stopped wiping. He looked touched by the friendly, tasteless speech. He looked in at Vern with his old-man's wrinkled eyes.

"Today was a terrible week anywhere," he said.

Vern considered, then asked, "What happened?"

Stan's eyes filled with tears. "Silver," he said. "It's Silver."

"Ah," Vern said, "It's horrible when a nice dog like Silver goes. I'm sorry, Stan. She didn't look that old, either."

"She didn't die," Stan said. "Someone stole her. A couple of days ago. She'd never run. Someone either got in and stole her from where she takes her naps on that couch in the car show room, or they could have got her while she was out back. "

"That's horrible," Vern said.

Stan brought over the signing board.

Vern took the ball point. "Listen, Stan, how about you get in with me and we go over to the old VF and I buy you a drink?"

By that time of year, the VFW's fake bare-branched trees already stood in their Christmas pots along the front sidewalk. The tiny twinkling lights already twinkled. The two men felt mollified and went in.

All booths up and down both sides were filled, but Pearl pointed them to a table jammed in the middle of other tables full of people.

"Go ahead, Stan. Go ahead, Vern," she yelled from the liquor shelves behind the bar. "Take that table. I haven't had a chance to wipe it off yet but no Packers fan threw up on it far as I know. I'll get you guys in one second flat."

Stan and Vern slunk into their chairs and praised her a little. Pearl might be a generally terrible organist and an unusually terrible accompanist for the ecumenical chorus each fall but she was a wonderful bartender. Her passion in life, however, was neither playing the piano badly nor minding the VFW post well: she was a casino addict. Stan had a new Pearl/casino story to tell Vern. Fresh from Bernie Stokowski who had got it from his deputy who wasn't good for much except telling anecdotes. Pearl had been waiting for a certain hot machine that she liked in Hinckley one night but a guy had been holding it down for hours. Finally the guy asked for the girl to come around with the ice cream carton for cashed-out coins. He took the bucket of coins and peed into it so he wouldn't have to leave the machine. Pearl raised a howl because she'd wanted that machine for so long. The guy made a mistake. He laughed at her. She got her fist under the bucket, as for serving at volleyball, and splashed the whole bucketful of quarters and pee into the man's chest and neck. Security threw them both out. Vern appreciated everything about that story. The combo of his first beer and the mental image of urine and coins flying restored him.

At a table right behind Stan, St. Fursey's all-purpose slob, Brad Stropp was carrying on, nothing new about that, but Vern was surprised that people were listening to him. Asking him questions, even. Who would wreck part of their Friday night listening to Brad Stropp?

Vern said to Stan, "What's that all about?"

Stan said, "That's right. You just got back from the Cities, didn't you?" He told Vern what had happened in St. Fursey that day. A young girl's body had been found rolled down into the ditch on the east side of 53, just south of town. No one anyone knew. And Brad had got caught in a beaver trap right near by. Vern and Stan let themselves listen to Brad ranting at the table behind Stan.

What Brad was telling everybody was that, "...by some coincidence, that old kraut, Dieter Stolz, had come along when I had my ankle stuck in a beaver trap, just a coincidence, hey that's all he was saying, but hey, it kind of was a coincidence, wasn't it?" Brad explained that Stolz could have been actually murdering that girl while Brad was still stuck in the trap and then he comes along and acts like a boy scout and gets Brad out of the trap, and helps him out to the highway, but wouldn't you think it was kind of funny they must have went right by that girl's body, but did Stolz mention it to Brad, no, sir, he didn't, so hey, Brad was not pointing fingers, but it made you think.

Pearl had come up with her tray.

"Yeah, well, it doesn't make *me* think," said Pearl. She gave Vern and Stan a new pitcher.

The early, serious drinkers were already there, but they hadn't wound themselves up to any ugliness. Among them were people whose driving, over the years, had given Stan Garris's auto lot its most reliable repair and replacement business. These people wrapped their cars around trees at 1:30 or 2:00 in the morning. To use Bernie Stokowski's official language, these people "lost control of their vehicles." If they had totaled whatever they had been driving, Stan got to hear about it. He would wander by their place of work, if they had a place of work, and mention that he had just got in a '94 Honda hatchback, no rust. Some Californian had traded it to him. Stan would add, he wasn't much of a Honda man himself, but this one looked good. And he had had it out himself, and taken it here and there. It went down the road good.

Vern had once bought a car from Stan. It happened during one of his between-jobs times. He remembered how warm and full and friendly Stan's voice said, "Hell, Vern, try her out." They were standing out back of Garris Autos where the very, very used cars were. "It runs very quietly,"

Stan remarked. "But it was manufactured by human beings. It's been *driven* by human beings. So it isn't perfect. I don't know about you, Vern, but pretty much what I want out of a car is it goes down the road good, and I like to know the guy who's selling it to me." Even though Vern would be buying a piece of transportation from Stan's back concrete slab, not anything from his nice show room, Vern felt sure that Stan respected him and the car both.

Now Vern knew he was getting drunk fast, but there you are. Feelings are feelings. He threw back the rest of his beer and made Pearl come back with another pitcher.

He got Stan to tell him about Silver. Stan said he had checked everywhere, even at the Range Shelter for Dogs. He told Stan how everyone in town loved that dog. And everyone in town knew her one trick.

"J'ou know about her one trick?" Stan asked.

Vern said he was fuzzy about it. "How did that go anyway, that trick?"

Stan told him, "Oh, it wasn't that much."

"How'd it go, though?" Vern asked.

Stan would tell Silver, "Listen, Silver, you know life is cruel? A man doesn't have a sporting chance if a bunch of rich guys organize against him? You know that, don't you, Silver?" [Silver would whine, right there.] Then Stan would say, "Yup, Silver, a bunch of people, they organize, they decide to screw you, and you know what, Silver? You get screwed, that's what. But I don't know..." Here Stan would pause, and put both hands on Silver's cheeks below her ears. "Gee, Silver, I should give you a chance to say what you think. People are always telling dogs what to think. They never ask dogs for their opinion. What do you think, Silver?" At that cue, the intelligent Lab would lift her head from his hands and give from her powerful throat an incredible, wonderful howl, and she'd keep it up and keep it up.

But Stan didn't go all the way with the story this time. He didn't imitate her howl the way he sometimes did. He just went on talking to Vern. He told Vern he would take Silver out walking around in that slough near the old Tenebray family bridle path, south and east of town. He and Silver knew everybody who walked around in the woods. They were a different breed from other townspeople who never went outside, no names mentioned. Vern egged him on, and he also discreetly caught Pearl's eye. She came over with a fresh pitcher and she refilled their bowl of chips. She handed Vern a bowl of salsa, too. "Try this Twin Shitties-type stuff," she said. "I think it tastes like rat blood. Looks like it, too."

Stan was now saying he and Silver didn't use the slough just for serious hunting. They went out there all times of year. Silver knew when it was season and her job was to raise a bird at the right time and at the right distance for whatever Stan was carrying. Stan swore she would check which gun he'd brought along that day. She would figure the yardage to get up birds for him. She also knew when it was off-season and therefore OK for her to go after other stuff that didn't mean anything to Stan. She went after stuff that was passionately desireful for her to kill—creatures low to the ground and pungent and disgusting, creatures that needed to be killed and it took her, Silver, to do it—muskrats and ordinary water rats and other varmints—animals she despised. She was careful to get her teeth into their necks just so and then flip them up into the air so that at the top of their helix the neck snapped. She would listen for that snap.

Now Stan and Vern felt happy, both of them, even Stan, just thinking about how good that sound felt to Silver. "Right at the top of arc," Stan repeated. "You'd hear that little beast's neck bust clean."

A fellow who had been seated with his back to Stan now turned around and gave Stan and Vern a primitive jeer. Vern knew he had already looked at that ugly face this evening but now the beer inside Vern blurred the man's face.

The man said, "If you two guys don't sound like a couple of environmentalists!"

Oh yes, Vern thought, that's who that was. Brad Stropp.

Not good, Vern thought. The word "environmentalists." Not a good word at the VFW. In St. Fursey a lot of people had the idea that environmentalists were out to wreck your job or your pastime or both. If you were prospecting for gold twelve miles farther north out of town, environmentalists would be the ones organizing an attack on you with their desk-top-published brochures about how washing gold flushed cyanide into the land. If you were anything to do with the Rocky Mountain Prospectors, environmentalists would try to get the state to plug your trial holes with concrete because uranium was supposed to be something bad. If you were not doing any of those projects but were just eking out a little weekend cash flow when the taconite hiring was thin, then environmentalists got you fined for just laying a line or two for beaver.

Vern felt sorry that Brad Stropp was coming on like someone who might in the next moment relieve his concerns by deciding to slap someone around. Now that could be a bad end to an already very bad day, especially when Vern had begun to feel human again, with some self-respect.

Well, he'd been a public speaker for a few years, so he gathered himself to speak in a sharing, nurturing, crowd-soothing way. He said, "Actually we are talking about how someone stole Stan's dog, is what we're talking about. Actually one of those really great dogs, too."

Brad said, "You want my opinion? Dogs are dogs. People keep talking, they have this great hunting dog. They have this great show dog. They have this great something-else kind of dog. Well, since you asked, a dog's a dog. Dogs bite. Dogs bark. Dogs fuck. That's pretty much *it*, for dogs."

Stan hadn't moved. Now he did. He slowly rose to his feet in his crabbed, unhealthy-looking way that was so saddening now Vern was there to see it. Stan turned around so he could place the heel of his right hand onto Stropp's nose and left cheek. Then he arranged his thumb into Stropp's right eye. When he was all set, he shoved.

Stropp gave a howl that converted into a little scream.

In the blurry background, far away, Vern saw Pearl rise from her stool behind the bar. Vern himself came around the table to get between Stan and Brad. He braced himself and got off what started as a nice, ordinary, practical haymaker except someone slapped his arm down. His fist went into the man's chest. Oh God, but that hurt. How come they never told you anywhere the real reason not to be violent—that it hurts to hit someone with your fist.

Brad Stropp's face still flapped like a piece of laundry right in front of him.

Pearl had made her way gently between the tables. She didn't elbow into people on her way. She came gently. Now she was here. She sighed. She looked down. She saw Brad's bandaged ankle. Pearl reached out with her right foot and hooked it and gave his ankle a swift half turn. He went down. His shoulders tipped over and wasted the whole hardly touched pitcher of beer.

Then Pearl returned to the bar and removed the wall phone earpiece from its hook. She gave a fine shout that everybody could hear.

"All right, everyone! All right! All right!"

Stan Garris must have heard her just as well as anyone else, but Vern saw that Stan couldn't resist one last quick moment's work. Stan reached for Brad Stropp's knees. He lifted them high above the table level and then gave a push, as if the head, shoulders, stomach, the rest of the man, were a wheelbarrow. Brad Stropp's whole body flowed smoothly across the beer-wet table like a new ship going down its ways. That got some clapping. High fives. More clapping. The whole room.

"All *right*, damn it," Pearl shouted over the laughing. "OK! I've dialed. All right? Would you listen up now?"

She was holding the receiver way up in the air.

The room stilled.

"OK, guys," she said with perfect enunciation. "I've got the chief of police on the end of the line. We do Plan A or we do Plan B. Plan A is you keep on fighting and spilling drinks and tearing up my Post. Then a lot of you spend the rest of your Friday night in the slammer at Cullough. Plan B is you quiet down as of right now and Bernie and Gladys get to have the rest of their supper in peace. So what's it going to be?"

Everyone sat down except Vern and Stan. Brad Stropp rose from the floor, but only as far as to sway on all fours, hands and knees, not hurting anyone.

Pearl said, unnaturally loudly, "OK." She turned to the wall speaker of the phone. "OK," she shouted into it, "Bernie, they decided to get their butts in gear." She replaced the earpiece into its cradle.

Vern offered his arm very formally to Stan, the way he had once seen some Buddhist kid hanging around that Duluth Women for Peace help an old, visiting rinpoche.

"Here we go, everybody," Vern said loudly to the whole room. "Yup…here we go! Right!" They processed towards the front like church ushers.

People clapped for him and Stan. They owed those fellows. Sometimes you sat for hours at the VFW and nothing worth mentioning happened. Well, not this Friday night.

Vern had to put his arm around the tired Garris to steer him through the crowded tables. "Here we go! On our way, Pearl!"

When they had got to right alongside the bar, Vern managed to pull a twenty out with his free hand. With a great arcing reach he got it over to Pearl, like someone semaphoring from the bridge of a major ship.

Pearl gave Vern a brilliant, compassionate, utterly feminine smile. She pocketed the Jackson and said in full musical voice, "Well, Denham! What'd'y know?" She added, "You just never know who's going to do what, do you?"

He thought, full of love, how that old Pearl knew a man when she saw one. Then he had to figure out where the door lever was. That door had to be like other doors. It had to have a lever or a knob, so he concentrated to find it.

Vern sobered a little as he drove Stan to the lot. Stan's own car stood there, looking very lonely under the overhead yard light. Vern got out his side of the car and went around to open the passenger door. Stan didn't get out, somehow. Maybe he had hurt his back hefting most of Brad Stropp all the way to shoulder height like that.

The two men just paused. A loon gave its nervous trill, once, then again, from the direction of the lake.

"I've always been partial to loons," Stan said leisurely. He added, "You'd better give me a ride home, Vern. I'll leave the car here."

When they were on their way again Stan said, "Know what, Vern, I am actually a sick man." Stan's hands kept climbing over one another in his lap.

Stan said, "It's true. Apparently I am awfully sick. Now they want to do chemo on me and all. But here's the thing, Vern. If I could just get Silver back. If I could just get her back. I would make sure she was taken care of OK."

Vern tried to pay attention to Stan but it was very difficult because he himself was so drunk. No, he thought, that's a lie. That wasn't why. It was very difficult because his own heart was flaring and flaring with happiness. He was designing the proposal he would make tomorrow. He was working on the phrases. He would tell Imogen Tenebray, "Listen, you have to marry me. You have to let go of your softhead father with his cheery Republican buddies and his crooked contacts with sadistic chemical companies and all the other crap-filled spooky money bags he wheels and deals with. You have to just leave him behind because you and I are going to get married so we will be happy. We will be happy Americans. What a concept, Imogen! You think Americans are too full of shit to know how to be happy? Forget it! You and I are going to be happy."

Vern felt there might be things wrong with that speech, but tomorrow was another day. He would have time to get the bugs out of it.

CHAPTER FIVE

Pearl got old Bridget Garris safely through the shining revolving door. She got into the same door quarter as Bridget was in, just to be on the safe side. Some basic jerk, however, entered the next door quadrant and sure enough started pushing to make the door revolve faster. Pearl often thought she knew of all the ways that bullies wreck things for other people, but here it was again—a new wrinkle—a big guy trying to frighten an old lady and maybe make her lose her step, when all Bridget was doing was minding her own business, trying to get into that rich munitions building like anyone else. There wasn't much space to operate in, but Pearl craned around and gave him the finger so he could see it plainly through the glass, right up close to his face. He quit shoving. She was very glad he did quit, because this wasn't a casino where she was on her own time, and could possibly educate him a little, once they all got out of that door. Today she was on duty for Bridget Garris. What's more, she was in VFW Auxiliary uniform.

Pearl kept right with her charge. Without trembling, the old lady went straight to the center of the room. It was a gigantic reception area, two opposite sides of which were fitted up with eight-foot high glass cabinets. Inside them, life-sized figures carried machine guns and rifles. Placards stood at the toes of the statues' boots. This was a weapons manufacturer so they were likely just models of infantry weapons. Fake forest was painted onto the walls behind the figures. Some of the soldiers wore

American uniforms, some German. A few others wore uniforms that Pearl never kept straight since she recognized only present or past allies of the United States or present or past enemies whom the United States had defeated. Pearl was sergeant-at-arms of the VFW Auxiliary of the St. Fursey Post. She made up the values of the job description herself. That is, she saluted and carried colors the way the manual said to, but she felt that how a VFW Auxiliary sergeant-at-arms was *respected* was up to her. She saw no need to memorize the military uniforms of the countless weaselly nations around the world.

At this moment she didn't like the way two seated receptionists in the huge oval-shaped space behind a wide counter did not rise and ask how they could help Bridget Garris. Two men outside the counter were dressed as security, but Pearl assessed each of them as straight wind tunnel ear to ear. One good looking, one not. She figured no one trusted either one of them for much.

One or both of the women suited up as receptionists were probably the real security. The front one waved a hand that was fragrant with freshly painted lacquer. She was probably using dumb-receptionist as a cover.

Pearl hated being made a fool of, even in the reception area of a huge weapons manufacturer. So she narrowed her eyes, not to see better; she had good vision for a forty-three-year-old. She wanted to show these people that the whole charade wasn't going to work with her.

She took Bridget's elbow gently.

Pearl said, "This is Ms. Bridget Garris to see Brigadier General Goretter."

Drying-nail-polish said, "Actually, General Goretter comes to his office here only once a week."

Pearl said, "That is 100% right. And today is the day. And Ms. Garris has an appointment with him at eleven."

Nail-polish turned around to the woman seated behind her.

"Eleven o'clock is correct," the second one said.

One of the men now came forward.

"Will you take these ladies up, please?" Nail-polish then spoke slowly and very distinctly to Bridget. Not so dumb. She'd apparently noticed both Bridget's hearing aid and her puzzled expression. "Will you please sign—just at this place?" She had reached for the clip board and placed a fresh sheet on top of the others so you couldn't read who all had been there already today.

The better-looking of the two uniformed young men now indicated their way to a double stand of elevators. Pearl could relax. All OK so far. The elevator had only the faintest sound. It was not made by Otis either. Probably some German company. Their guide pressed the button for them but stood against the opposite side of the elevator. Yeah, Pearl thought, not exposing his back to us. Of all the tools she'd taken up with in her life, none of them had been this good-looking. On the other hand, she wasn't sure he could make two plus two come out the same each time. It was too bad. Wastage of that sort was very natural in this world, however. Pearl did not sink into a bitter mood about it. Today she felt very interested in everything. It wasn't every day that a big-shot like Stan Garris hired her to come in uniform and take his mother to Roseville to a huge munitions company and back, with fifty dollars extra thrown in for food. He gave them a waxed new Tahoe for the trip, too.

The elevator kept going up.

Clearly Stan Garris's mom was into major stuff. Pearl smiled at the old woman.

"You look nice," Pearl said to her. "Christ, that's a nice dress."

Bridget had clear skin and open eyes for someone however old she was. And now color came up in her cheeks, too.

"You look very pretty," Pearl told her. "This general'd better be worth it."

"Shame, Pearl," Bridget said. "This is strictly business."

Clicking. The door slid soundlessly open.

Down a long beige carpet without one single spot of spilled anything on it.

Door. Knock. Come in! shouted from inside.

Their soldierly guide said, "General, sir, this is Ms. Garris, and her driver, Pearl."

An old man rose up straight as an aging G.I. Joe. He wasn't in uniform but he gave off soldiery. Pearl wasn't sergeant-at-arms at the VFW Auxiliary for nothing. OK, she said to herself. Whatever Bridget was doing, every minute it felt more awesome and good. A person could very easily spend their whole life among slobs, nobody knew better than Pearl, without ever getting to do any business with a true, old, high-ranking soldier like this.

Pearl commanded herself, At ease, left hand grasping right thumb behind her back.

When Bridget had shaken hands and spoken to the general, Pearl made sure the old lady backed up into her seat squarely.

She told Bridget she would be very happy to tool around outside and pick her up in 25 minutes. Very happy to. No problem.

Bridget Garris said, "No, Pearl. You might be interested in this, and I trust you not to mention any of it around town until next week when we bring it off."

They were talking about Veterans' Evening in St. Fursey. The old lady had somehow gotten this general to offer to speak. As they smiled and talked to each other, you could see they were each gratified by the other one. Pearl couldn't hear anything to suggest money. What surprised her most, somehow, was that apparently Bridget Garris, who was on the internet a lot since she was the St. Fursey librarian, had met this big shot with this big-shot office in this big-shot armament corporation—get this, Pearl told herself, in a damned chatroom! When Pearl thought about the people she met in a chatroom! Of course she herself never went to a chatroom except to get the word on which casinos had loose slots these days. Which exactly were the decent quarter slots, looking at it as you entered. Where the dud machines stood, left or right, as you came in from the main parking lot. None of those people seemed likely to be retired brigadier generals.

These two seemed to have met in a chatroom called 101st Airborne. Pearl noticed, however, that they both knew other places. Something called Boondess Arkeev and somewhere called Rink. Some guy named Montgomery. Some guy or place named Stolz. There was a Stolz in St. Fursey, but she guessed they weren't talking about him. They were speaking English but with so many non-English words that Pearl couldn't follow. One thing she learned for sure: this Bridget Garris, whom she had tolerated the way you tolerated all the old folks in St. Fursey, was someone significant. This old lady apparently was arranging this general to come for Veterans' Night. That kind of top-drawer doings you expected from the Tenebrays or the town clergy, not from the auto lot guy's mom up there with the rest of them in Denham Apartments. It went to show— exactly what it went to show wasn't just clear to Pearl, but whatever it was, she snapped to when Bridget and the old retired army officer at last stood up. They were shaking hands across the table. Pearl believed she knew a class act when she saw one. She stood up very straight, just behind Bridget, and turned back to get the door like an official driver.

Pearl knew her weaknesses and strengths. She had been meaning to ask Bridget if they could make a bathroom stop at Hinckley where Pearl would be real glad to treat lunch—and maybe just do a couple dollars' worth of quarters at the casino. She sure wasn't going to ask that kind of favor now, not now that Bridget had risen in her estimation. Pearl had used to kid sometimes, at the VF or during the breaks at ecumenical chorus rehearsals. She would kid about the old folks, Ward Hines and Bridget Garris and the others, who lined up in the back and scarfed up the food, whatever they had. From now on, if Pearl ever heard that deputy policeman whatshisface Darrel making smart-ass remarks about the old residents in Denham Apartments she would go for him. She didn't worry herself about how she would go for him. Something would come to mind. He was no one to be afraid of anyhow. At the VFW Post planning meeting, old Walt Steinzeiter had told Pearl that the deputy had dropped in at his gravel office just this past week to tell him to take down the big flag he had hung from his excavator. Walt explained he had run him off. That was the only thing to do.

Let's face it, Pearl said to herself, when you live in a town, probably most of the United States, where most people are too chicken to look out for one another, and you have the good luck to meet some old lady like Bridget Garris with a whole lot of backbone, and who is equals with a retired brigadier general, the least you can do is make sure nobody motormouths on her.

They headed back north. Pearl didn't venture any conversations. When they were picking up billboard notices of the Hinckley casino, Bridget said, "Oh yes—that's the place with the casino. You know, Pearl, would you want to stop there or anything? I bet you could show me how to work one of those gambling machines. You'd have to explain slowly. I heard from my son Stan that the buffet is good. It'd be my treat!"

Pearl's heart danced. The very thing she wanted! How lucky can you get? Besides, what if she showed that nice old lady how to work one of the quarters, maybe not one of the blackjack tables, though. But say Pearl moseyed around and found Bridget a hot machine, and old Bridget won a bundle, wouldn't that be a nice thing to do for her? How about she took that fifty that Stan had given her for food and she helped Bridget win a couple hundred? That would go down pretty well, she bet.

She turned her eyes briefly from the road. Bridget's face looked like a pale flannel cloth. The mouth was still smiling, but all the rest just cried "exhaustion."

Pearl gathered herself. She said, "No, you don't want to go in that dump. Even the buffet has slipped, too. It doesn't hold a candle to the new Meal Replacement options at Denham's Bakery. It's only another hour and a half to St. Fursey, Bridget. Let's make it home, and get us some sandwiches and then you're right there, home. You can eat in your own living room."

The old lady smiled. Her eyes closed and she slept the rest of the way.

CHAPTER SIX

erious snow fell on Sunday afternoon, when St. Fursey's ecumenical choir were rehearsing. Another several inches fell in the night. The snow was great as always, but especially for people who lived in ratty neighborhoods like Imogen Tenebray's. It gentled the yard butt and the derelict cars of the poor.

"Chill, chill," the snow said. "Of course, this dump and most of our planet are a shambles but it looks as good as ever, doesn't it?" The new snow said, "This is really just the nineteenth century, not the twenty-first, when the males of every household hitched horse to sleigh and everybody glided over to Grandmother's house. The males are not incompetent or sadistic. The males are very caretaking fathers. The world is not overpopulated. The streets of neither St. Fursey nor Duluth, Minnesota, are salted, and America, a republic, protects its poor from the hobby wars of the rich."

Imogen drove happily in the dark, past the lighted reindeer of her neighbors' yards. They were not the reindeer of last Christmas or even of recent years, but from Christmas of 1998 or 1999 even. No one took them down. The reindeer were always lighted, except when the owners had defaulted on St. Fursey Area Power & Light.

On Mondays and Fridays, Imogen drove into Duluth to be executive director of Women for Peace. On Tuesdays, Wednesdays, and Thursdays, she was the school social worker at St. Fursey Elementary and Middle.

Over the weekend she had seen one private client and gone to her dad's usual Friday night gathering of local Episcopalians. Episcopalians and any intellectuals he had rounded up during his convivial weekdays. The party had the usual pleasant people, even Tip, the Bishop, had turned up. And her dad's big buddy, John Rubrick, whom nobody liked *except* her dad. Imogen had practiced social work long enough not to trust character judgments made from people's looks. She felt confident, however, about John Rubrick. Some handsome, ageing preppy who went to her dad's school or something like it. An empty man. Nothing major wrong with him, she said to herself. Just not much there. Gorgeous clothes, though. Aberystwith tweed. Gorgeous manners, too. He leased Volvos to get where he needed to be. Although whatever his work was took him on airplanes midweek, he genially kept track of the trivial news of St. Fursey. He asked about the mother bear and her cubs who were prowling around the edges of St. Fursey.

John Rubrick moved about slowly, here and there, smiling at people. He helped Imogen's father serve drinks and load the buffet. He twice made swift but non-intrusive moves that kept Imogen's mother from falling on the floor. He made it around to everyone at a party without seeming to work the crowd. Imogen joined him at one point in a short mutual-admiration conversation with a couple of the community singers. They were grateful for her leadership in the alto section. The altos were always weak since you had to read music and few of them did. Imogen caught sight of Eliza, the Episcopal priest, and dutifully went over to greet her.

Eventually Peter and Natalie, who wobbled but not badly, swept people up to the table to fill their plates. A pleasant crowd. Imogen looked around for Tip, with the idea of sitting near him. He was talking to John Rubrick in the small ante-room which had been a small library when she was growing up in that house. Peter and Natalie still winced when people called it a den.

Imogen had sat down and listened with the others while Tip told them how in high school he had slugged someone in the face and that he never went to a non-violence protest vigil now without recalling the painful but delicious crunch of it. The other boy's sudden cry. He'd do it again, he told the delighted group—well, but with the caveat that that boy hadn't grown up into prize fighter over the years, while all he did was become a Bishop.

That was Friday. Imogen had two clients on Saturday.

On Sunday morning, Imogen had made herself read and print off much of the online news services she subscribed to. She decided to go to Eliza's early service, then let herself putter around her apartment and be domestic until choir practice. At dusk she trampled out across the rough meadow behind her building. It was stuck over with the afternoon's snow. The woods hung cavernous with snow roofing the oaks' clusters. Imogen returned in the dark full of fresh feeling, though she hadn't caught sight of the mother bear and her remaining cub.

Now, Monday, she didn't have to plan the day because it was Volunteers' Monday. She and Kay Bettis, her program person, had already laid out the short housekeeping agenda to start everything. One item of their agenda they did in order to buoy up the young women in the group. They would update the group about new protests for peace around the United States. The idea was to buoy up their spirits, whereas the fact was, the older, professional women in the group hated any off-beat testimonials and radical posturing.

This morning she and Kay were to show the volunteers new pamphlets available from COPRED and the new lot from the National Peace Studies people. Kay would pass out sheets listing good websites. Kay would read aloud letters from sensible websites like MoveOn.org and Orion.

The Duluth volunteers were three-fourths young-middle-aged or middle-middle-aged people either in professions or married to people in business or professions. These people's husbands on average made two or three times as much as the wives. At Women for Peace open houses, they spoke courteously of their wives' jobs. Still, one felt the weight—not bad weight nor good weight, just weight—of those men's actual incomes, their bonuses, their stock options.

After housekeeping, the volunteers got to do projects they liked. They sat at the long, scabbed tables, still left from when this basement had been a church basement. The women stapled together the WFP pamphlets. They painted quite beautiful signs to be jounced up and down by the considerably younger college people and the considerably older, retired peace-vigil keepers, on street corners.

This morning Imogen found no homeless people on the familiar shambles of the WFP staircase. Six or seven of them, now that the cold weather was coming in, tended to spend the night on the staircase, trying to look as if they were clients of the social work teams who leased the rest of the basement space. They usually smiled at Imogen, and did their best to crowd to either side so she could pass. They drew their dogs' leashes in closer. This morning, though, she saw neither dog owners nor dogs.

Imogen's program assistant, Kay, and Muffy Lazer, their steadiest volunteer, hovered in the hall outside her office door. Behind them straggled four or five volunteers, who stopped talking to one another the moment they saw Imogen. Trouble. Clearly, trouble.

Imogen thought, well, it likely always had been only a matter of time. Members had been warning her ever since they leased that old church basement that if she went on letting homeless people sit on the basement staircase during the days, sooner or later either of two things would happen: people would pee where they shouldn't, to save going out in the cold, or someone would molest some Women for Peace staff member or a volunteer. Since the old staircase did not smell of pee this morning, that left attempted rape. In any case, here stood her program assistant, Kay, and her lead volunteer, Muffy, both with the grave, weak-minded smiles that some people give when they are about to attack. Behind them, the other middle-aged women—heads up, here's Imogen!—swept back like jetsam away into the Volunteers' Room.

The furnace kicked in. Imogen, like any administrator in a shambles of a facility, noticed such things even in times of crises. The furnace snuffled and rattled its two filters and its yards and yards of fat tinwork that still held up from Imogen's and Kay's last duct tape job on it.

Muffy gave her a handy smile. "Can we go somewhere and talk?" Muffy's middle-aged face looked crafty above the peasant Fair Isle sweater design.

"We're right here," Imogen remarked, key in hand. "Come in, come in."

Kay Bettis took her usual chair just as if everything were OK. Muffy took the guest seat, but first gave it a fast rub with her hand, since Imogen quite often had one or another of the staircase dogs drowsing in it.

Imogen now waited, social worker style. Muffy and Kay gave off an aura of determination, irritability, and shame. Bad, Imogen thought. The empty staircase this morning… maybe someone had at last tried to rape someone else, so Muffy and Kay had already run all the trash, as Muffy called them, out of the building. Imogen felt the woman gearing up to do the talking. She felt Kay standing by, like a tender near a major ship.

Muffy said, "We want to voice some concerns everyone's been having."

A pause.

"Actually, Imogen, my husband has been concerned about this longer than I have."

One by one, Muffy laid out the husband's concerns. Every so often Muffy interrupted herself—she was holding a 3x5 index card with notes on it—to say, "But these aren't just my husband's concerns, Imogen. They're mine, too. In fact, the others', too. The whole group, really…"

In a word: they wanted to put a halt to all present vigils for peace in Duluth, all sponsoring of fence-climbing at Wisconsin military installations, all placard marches on Superior Street, London Road, and especially Canal Park Drive. Muffy said, "We want to turn a fresh page. We have been putting together some ideas for innovative approaches to peace work."

Imogen recalled some ancient page of an ancient MSW course text. "It is always good to look at new ideas. What have you got?"

"We want to organize travel tours with a peace theme," said Muffy.

Imogen sat up straighter.

Their idea, Muffy told her, was to quit all protesting as such and get started with two travel tours going this coming winter, for which either Icelandair or Northwest Airlines promised, if the tour filled, free fare to both the Women for Peace leader and one assistant.

Imogen said, "Women for Peace would become a travel agency based in Duluth—a kind of travelling theme park?"

Muffy said, "Perhaps you are feeling hurt, Imogen, but that was *such* a cheap shot. I'm surprised it came from you." She paused, glanced at the 3x5s in her hand, and picked up briskly: "We'd have lectures planned as part of it. Real lectures, like Elderhostel, but not wasting so much of people's valuable time the way Elderhostel does. For example, on the Irish tour, we would have someone telling us the history of the conflict between Ireland and England. That would fulfill the category of peace versus conflict. On the Rome trip, we would have a discussant sharing with us about how the republican government of Rome gave way to empire."

There were other points. The husbands had never liked their wives' scrambling up the anti-personnel fence at Minneapolis-St. Paul International Airport and especially had not liked— "before your time, Imogen," Muffy said—that respectable professional women were hosed off that fence by order by some colonel at seventeen below zero.

"Not Women for Peace," said Imogen.

"Nor having civilized women arrested outside the School of the Americas at Fort Benning."

"Those protests were not sponsored by Women for Peace," Imogen said.

Muffy cried out. "It's all the same rinky dinky kind of behavior!"

She seemed to recover control of herself, and continued, "The husbands also made it clear that if there were peace-themed tours to places that any sane person would want to have a look at, they might even go on some themselves. And they would contribute. They would *contribute*. All this makes some fund-raising sense."

"Fund raising for what cause would this be, then?"

Muffy cried, "For peace, of course, what else? But indirectly. Reg said they would contribute to getting the tour business on its feet and then the business would be the rainmaker for peace organizations and most everything would be tax deductible."

Imogen said, "Sounds like a plan. And clearly you have given it a lot of thought. And I can make you a terrific, first-rate recommendation for a new executive director."

Imogen sent a very glistening smile across to Kay. "Kay's as good as they get," she said, in a slangy drawl to show how relaxed she was and not thrown off-base just because a 100% creepy, serious asshole like Muffy Lazer and likely her equally asshole husband had corrupted a fragile peace organization. "As good as they get," she repeated. The other two women looked away.

"Actually, we couldn't agree more," Muffy said. "Actually, Kay, here has been good enough to agree to be our next director."

Imogen said, "I tell you what. You give me today and then my next regular day, Friday, to clear up my end of things and I'll be out."

Muffy said, "Actually we thought—actually it would be just as easy, we thought, to make a clean break. Kay has been working so closely with you, she can easily transition everything into her own hands."

It was the modern way to let people go, if you were downgrading. All at once, so the HR person need see those fired-looking expressions for only one half-hour. Besides, who cared about their unfinished current projects? If those projects were attractive, the organization wouldn't be firing. It was the psychology of a planned downgrade. When you were planning an *up*grade, you read the dropped employee as good riddance. If they looked licked they had it coming. Like Hitler getting rid of Roehm's S.A. Imogen had mistakenly majored in music at Oberlin because at seventeen, she had respected her mother's values. But she had taken modern European history on the side. The Third Reich was like something out of Ecclesiastes. The United States was like something out of Ecclesiastes. Everywhere was like something out of Ecclesiastes, now she thought of it.

Kay said, "I've really enjoyed working with you, Imogen."

"Oh good," Imogen said.

The other two still hung there, so Imogen thought, Oh yes, they need me to help them get out of what used to be my office. Anyone can see that they would give a hundred each not to be in this office one more minute. Besides, they will want to go into the Volunteers' Room and give the high sign to the women waiting in there that all has gone as planned.

Imogen got to her feet. She smiled. "I am going to throw you guys out because I want to sort out my computer. And what about the dry dog food, you two?"

"Take it! Take it! Take that with you!" exclaimed Muffy. "We won't be needing it. And all those cans, too."

"No more feeding dogs on the staircase then?" said Imogen.

Now that Muffy saw Imogen's grin, she reseated herself but only on the edge of her chair. She said, "Frankly, this whole thing about the dog food and the people on the staircase, Imogen. I wasn't going to mention that—but since you brought it up. That's a thing that has concerned me, and Reg, too."

Reg. The husband.

Muffy said, "Imogen, we are all sick of those people squatting on our staircase. Sick of their dogs, and sick of having cans of dog food stacked up in the stock closet so when we go for the high-brightness paper we have to shove aside tin cans. Sick of it! I want to be upfront about that! Another thing, Imogen, this place is just too much of a dump. I think you ask an awful lot of your volunteers, you know. I wonder if you realize how much! These people volunteer in a lot of other places. Who do you think races all over the whole damned Arrowhead Region in the middle of winter at twenty below not to mention on summer weekends instead of going to the lake, raising money for the orchestra and the playhouse and the library? These are hard workers—but no one except you expects them to work in such a, such a—well, for goodness' sake, Imogen, this place is just a, just a *dump*—you know that as well as I do..."

She dwindled off. She had got to the door.

Imogen was left to surmise just how Muffy and the other volunteers—or maybe all it took was Muffy and Reg—had co-opted Kay. She thought how she and Kay went back a ways. On the other hand, everybody goes back a ways. She and her ex-husband went back a ways. Hitler and Churchill went back a ways.

She wondered what kind of money they meant to pay Kay to be executive director. They were business-minded. Jobs were scarce. They might well have decided they didn't have to offer Kay Bettis much at all, perhaps less than what they had paid Imogen Tenebray. Imogen carefully role-played Reg and Muffy. If she were Reg and Muffy, she would invite Kay for a martini and point out that early on in any organization you had to have muscle-bound, no-scruples, bad-manners people. True, Imogen had more or less stiffed a tough real-estate team to get the lease for that Duluth church basement at half what the owners had wanted to charge. Good enough at the time, Reg and Muffy would say, in a generous tone, giving credit.

Imogen thought some more. She thought, "If I were Reg and Muffy, I would tell Kay, 'We see you very big in our concept. Frankly, Kay, we don't want to see anyone with your potential slippy sliding down with the

Imogen Tenebrays of this world.'"

Imogen copied her own letters and memos as well as she could onto her pre-Flood floppies, the WFP budget never having sprung for decent electronics. At last she deleted from the computer itself everything she had copied. She left saved the volunteers' records and their primitive finance program. She opened and read over the document called "Good Quotes—Use Somewhere." She had made a beautiful default—an Old English font that made everything look like an Episcopal Church newsletter. She scrolled through a few quotes. There were a lot of wonderful people in the world, actually. She wasn't just being a wishful-thinking ass. It was true. Susan Sontag and Michael Moore and Michael True and Senator Robert Byrd and Edward R. Morrow. In that seriffy print face, Molly Ivins looked permanent, like Thomas Paine, someone to last.

Someone knocked. "Come in, come in!" cried Imogen as much like a ray of sunlight as she could. It might be one of the homeless. They sometimes came in to explain their kid got a new puppy and did Imogen have any extra of the dog food, canned, hey, better than dry. She was going to fill one of the black Hefties with all the remaining dogfood and tell them to take it away.

"Hi, Imogen!" said Kay.

"Hi, Kay," said Imogen, cordially enough because she still had a quote from Thomas Paine in her ears and it still held her up. She did not say, "How is every little fucking thing with you since two minutes ago? Good, I hope?"

Instead she said, "Come in, sit down."

Kay said, "I want to be very upfront with you about something, Imogen."

Imogen waited.

"You know, the receptions we've had after some of the vigils and all. I wanted to tell you straight upfront that a couple of weeks ago, I met a guy from your town, St. Fursey. I like him a lot, Imogen. So I just wanted to tell you that. I think we may be seeing each other."

Imogen said, "Who's that?"

"His name is Vern Denham, actually. I know you and he kind of know each other. In fact, he mentioned you, I mean."

Imogen said aloud. "I do know Vern. Nice guy, too."

Kay stood up now, smiling, looking relieved. "Well, I thought it only right to let you know."

"You bet," Imogen said.

The Mac's old hard-working After Dark was now bannering across with *Please wake up, please wake up, please wake up.*

In her car, Imogen was listening to the history of everywhere, thanks to The Teaching Company and the Duluth Public Library. She listened to one audio book after another, going backward and forward in time. She had listened to the history of creatures on earth before homo pre-sapiens ever got erectus enough to be the cause of the fifth huge extinction.

Imogen left Duluth listening to Ice Age times on the car audio. Soon the ponds and thousand-mile sloughs of one or another inter-glacial period were so vivid to her that her own species felt like happenstance. Clearly, easily, this globe would have got along without us. And maybe— she remarked to herself this noon, pushing in a CD about the huge Romford elephant found in the north of England now being repaired in St. Louis—maybe our species will get wiped out, too. She listened.

She let the truthful science quiet her feelings.

Gradually her outrage settled out. It became the new river floor of her mind.

Mid-morning sun shone on what was left of last night's clean snow. It warmed the still-green meadow grass that poked through it, so that in the fields that Imogen passed, whiskers of green rose everywhere through the white. How valuable it all was.

Then a strange thing happened. For the first time in the four years since her then-husband had sat, without moving, in a fishing boat and somehow allowed his infant son to drown overside, Imogen felt suffused with desire. Back then, her father had cried, "Oh but you must forgive him, Immy! You must! you must! You must! Oh, Imogen! Forgive him!"

"I do," she had said. They were being returned home in a Cullough funeral director's limousine. Oh, she did, she did, she did forgive him, she told both parents. She sat motionless as cut flowers.

Her father, even her mother, who was more or less sober at the time, had urged further: this could happen to anyone—the soul suddenly freezes and then you are unable to save a life.

"Yes, yes, of course," Imogen had said. Oh, of course she forgave him. "Dad, Mom, believe me. I forgive him."

The only trouble was she could not touch him again, ever again, not for any reason. Then, worse, after a year had passed and he and she were formally separated, she discovered that she couldn't touch anyone.

That is how it had been, for four whole years. But now this—here in the car, a burst of pointless lust! It was the sight of the green grass that did it, coming up through the snow. Good God, she thought. She fought it off. She did not want a gratuitous aberration of the mind.

Too late. Her mind had begun to sing with lust. It was flying, and slipping its song down upon her. It thought up possibilities. She tried to shut up her mind, but push had come to shove and her mind went turn-coat—betraying her will, it went over to her body's side, and deeply every minute her body kept hollowing and hollowing.

Her mind said lyrically, look, why didn't she stop the car, take most of the air out of one tire, open the trunk. and pull clear the jack, the spare, the four-end wrench, and the pad for kneeling. Shut up, she told her mind. Her mind explained that she could stand there outside the front door without doing anything and carefully look into the faces of truck drivers coming northbound on 53. When one stopped, and her mind pointed out that someone might stop, because she still wore her fairly OK WFP work clothes—OK stockings, requisite USA-black suit and khaki silk blouse, her only pair of boots with the classy clumpy heels. Her mind said that what would happen is, a guy would drop lightly down from the baby staircase of his semi cab and amble back to her. Did she need help?

She could explain that she did not want to tie him or anyone else into a commitment of any kind, not even a one-night stand, that what we are talking here is a quarter-hour, or less, to whatever he was up for—she meant only, if he—if they—she meant...

Such a pickup would be the first for her, but Imogen was a social worker so she expected to be patient as he moved through the communication stages—surprise, amusement—not disdain, she hoped, though that was always possible. If he wore one of those outsized crosses that Born Agains who were Republicans wore, then the whole plan was off, of course, but if it *wasn't* off, then he would next, she expected, feel vanity and then delight maybe. Then there would have to be a moment of practicality—it would be his semi, not her Civic, more room, then back to delight, she hoped, without jeering, she hoped, just pure delight, and afterwards she would tell him an admiring thing or two, about how he was an absolute doll and he would believe it. And drive off thinking about it, and so would she.

That is such a dumb idea, she told her mind, not only dumb but gross, although she noticed that she had let the car slow all the way down to 40 as if to go off onto the shoulder and stop.

Her mind wasn't through. It imagined another instance for her. An elongated limo with black-glass windows would pass her. It would slow, and stop, and back up—one of those big cars that are so expensive they are as quiet in reverse as they are in drive. It looked like a serious car full of criminals. She imagined they were stopping to murder her as she stood there, so she lifted the wrench and kept hold of it. She wasn't going down without a fight. The driver got out. He did not wear the down-scale tux of limo drivers and musicians who must have black tie before they can afford it. No Mafia camel's hair overcoat.

He was beautifully dressed. He approached her briskly. His face was poker-grave. "I will escort you to the limousine," he said. "The President has asked me to tell you he is at your service."

Oh give me a break, Imogen said to her mind. "Would you please give me a break?—besides, since you brought it up, not *this* President."

Her mind didn't care. It was getting off on its own little chemo-electric fires and flaring all across the cortex.

At last Imogen drove along with only a philosophical problem: If desire was now coming back to her, after these four years, did that mean she would come out of her cocoon of hard work and away from her hundreds of nightmares about that little boy whose name she still could not say aloud? And had she enough poise left in her heart to enter the world of men again?

She thought of Vern Denham. In fact, he had come to her parents' house for dinner just a week ago, as now she recalled. Her mind reminded her of how he had stood without leaning on anything in the little anteroom with its entire wall full of bookshelves.

Men, with all that musculature and their readiness to move quick-ly—they had that, the good ones had muscle and they moved fast—men were most interesting looking when you saw them in places of culture. That is, there is nothing much engaging in the muscle of someone dig-ging a ditch or strangling somebody. But when males stood with a baton or in front of a whole wall of books—then you felt two things at once: the man's muscle, of course, but also the private power hidden in any human cranium. Inside yourself lurches the pull between those two—mindless body and the brain with its genius for constraint—if either wins, the man is ruined, and you with him. But if both are there, he might be OK. She might be OK.

Imogen went over it to herself, but after a few minutes she was re-ally paying no attention. Really what she was doing was visiting old sites in her mind—the way you stop here and there when you revisit an old hometown. You don't start some intelligent quarrel with those who greet you at their doors. You simply ask them: how is everybody?—after all this time—how are you? And you? Actually, how are you all?

CHAPTER SEVEN

Whoever said the meek shall inherit the earth didn't know anything about being on the bottom of the system in your own hometown. And another thing, Brad Stropp was sure of: those ancient people like Jesus got to live outdoors all the time, keeping sheep from falling into hot sandy ravines, and kicking back with strangers at wells and saying wise things which people actually stayed to hear—nothing was like that now, and people weren't like that now. Brad Stropp may not have gotten much out of church when he was a kid but he remembered about the sheep which they let you color in Sunday School and the hot sand and grass. And those shepherds weren't just out to shove other people around.

Judea was not like St. Fursey with its thousand-plus people whose shitlist never changed. No matter how true some insight you told someone, if it was something they'd never heard before, they jeered at you. You tell your boss something they really don't want to hear, they fire you.

A few days ago he was fired from Marty Hanks's Super Valu. Today Brad had something a lot better going. He told Arlene, at five in the morning, when she was already spreading out her sweepstakes paperwork, "I need the car today, you'll have to walk today. Who do you clean for today anyway?"

She already had her nose moving along close over the spread-out sweepstakes sheets. Arlene looked more like a bear following scent than a grown person reading.

"Anyway, you'll have to walk," he said.

"How come?" she said.

"I am going to apply to Garris Autos for a job and I can't arrive there on foot like some hitchhiker."

Now she looked up all right. "Hey," she said, but not in a mean way, "What happened to the job at the Super Valu?"

Brad said, "We parted ways, Hanks and I did. You'd have to say we parted ways." Her jaw hung open: she regarded him in that slack way she had. He said, "There's a time for people to work together and there's a time to part ways. I decided not to stall around, just cut it off clean."

Truth was, all the time he had been working at Marty's Super Valu, he had already been making roundabout inquiries about Garris Autos. Marty's after-school help, the doctor's kid, knew a lot about the car lot. Marty himself worked with the experienced guys in Meat and Frozen. Brad got to know Simon Anderson because he was the latest hire. He and Simon were often relegated to the huge, lonely warehouse together. They talked steadily as they sliced cartons with their box cutters. Then all the dry line, canned and boxed, for the center aisles would go to the other end. In staff meetings, people feel fairly equal, but when you are box cutting with a sixteen-year-old, you know you are at the bottom.

What Brad and Simon saw in their imaginations was not the dreary warehouse but new cars and the people who sold new cars or serviced recent models. Simon knew about cars and dealerships the way some boys know about F-16s.

Simon told Brad that no one could ever get that job of go-fer at Garris Motors in town because Garris's go-fer was old George Herzlich who was top salesman and go-fer both, all sewed up. Mr. Herzlich did all the driving when dealers traded models. If someone in St. Fursey wanted a new car from Garris's inventory but the one in his show room was the wrong color, Garris would call up the GM guy in Hibbing or Chisholm or Cook, or even all way down to Duluth. If the other dealer had it on inventory they traded. George Herzlich looked more like a diplomat than a half-retired car salesman now doing odd-jobs around the lot. He would go pick up the car. For actual deliveries, Simon told Brad, George Herzlich's old lady would go along. People would see them out on the road in the shiny new car, him wearing shirt and tie and Garris uniform sport jacket. Her knitting.

More and more, Brad realized that his own real skills would be recognized not here at the dumb Super Valu, but at Garris's dealership. Brad dropped a jar of Miracle Whip onto the concrete floor, where it made a serious crunch. Its white, custardy glob full of shards spread itself out a little but Brad managed to edge it more or less together with the side of his tennis shoe and then shove it under the warehouse racking. Then the owner, Marty Hanks, came up silently from behind him. Marty might have been there for the last five minutes for all Brad knew. There's a type of people who sneak up on you. They just are that way. Marty bent over, scraped the half-smashed jar and glop back out and onto a dustpan and took it over to the nearest waste bin. He gave Brad a nod and passed on. He could have smiled but he didn't because he owned the place and he liked to make you feel bad.

The kid kept talking about new GM cars. He gave a laugh. "Well, I can't afford anything except a junker, myself, but I sure would like one."

Brad thought, how come he didn't have some OK car? He's the doctor's kid? Yet, maybe that doctor wasn't much of a doctor, either, since he practiced in their dumb town, St. Fursey, and drove only a Garris Autos Chevrolet, too.

Brad and the kid finished cutting all the freight and started stacking it by aisles, ready to move to the floor. Brad imagined himself working for Garris, gradually rising to the sales department and then something might happen to Garris. That was not a dumb idea, because things happen to people, and Garris's wife would come up to Brad, and tell him that he was the only person around the lot who seemed to know the business and would he take it over?

Brad's wife, now, she wasn't anyone who helped a man get ahead. It wasn't that Arlene had got fat or was an alcoholic or pretended to be sleepy. It was that she somehow was like a pile of human parts instead of a real person.

Last week a lot of bad stuff happened more or less all at once. Brad was out down toward Small Bass Lake and got his foot half busted off in a Conibear trap. Then he got fined for shooting a bear cub, and then the chief of police took one of his guns away. Then there was that dead girl. Then Marty Hanks fired him from the grocery store. About the only thing he wasn't worried about was that Stan Garris had decked him at the VFW on Friday night. Brad knew Stan was very drunk and wouldn't remember.

On the day he got fired, Marty had said, "Simon, when you and Brad get through out here, pile up all the Charmin toilet-tissue cartons and put the cloth over it for the staff meeting. And pull the chairs around."

"OK," Simon said.

Brad tapped his cutter back into its sleeve. He liked that Marty told that kid, not him, to set up for the staff meetings. Even if Simon had been there longer, the fact was Brad was 48, not 16. What you got with Brad was an older person's judgment for one thing, and that's got to be worth something, even in the dumb-ass grocery business.

But he hated staff meetings. They were always at 11 am and 4 pm, so half the employees went to each meeting, and the other half covered the store. Marty would send the meeting half out into the deli to choose what they wanted to eat and one pop of their choice.

Marty ran the meeting from notes in front of him. He said in a loud voice, he wanted to thank the checkouts and the baggers for not having jokes among themselves when customers were going through. "It makes us a friendly store," he repeated for the thousandth time. "Look, next time you go to Duluth," he told them, "go get some groceries—don't get too many, hey, remember you're supposed to shop here (everyone dutifully grinned)—but go in and see how the checkout and the carryout treat the customer."

Then Marty brought up some other items, and finally said that was it.

Brad got up.

"Stick around, Brad."

When the others had picked up their aprons and gone out front, Marty said. "Have a seat a second."

Marty paused. "I'm not going to beat about the bush. I have to let you go, Brad. The town's not growing, let's face it. What mining they're still doing at the other end of the Mahoning, that taconite and all, if they're making money at all, it doesn't rub off on us. Business is smaller. Not down, but smaller. I can't use as many people."

Brad knew shit when he heard it.

"You just took on somebody last week!" Brad said, "and anyway, I sure as hell have seniority over that Anderson kid."

Marty didn't look upset. "That's right, Brad. But I have to look at everything. He's a good worker. I'm a businessman. I look at that."

Brad felt shrunk but he knew enough not to show it. "He's a dumb kid, if you want to know."

Marty now looked even more relaxed. He leaned back against the Charmin tissue stack. His voice was almost cordial. He said, "OK, Brad. I'll show you what I mean. What was last week's special in the deli promotion?"

"That's not my job to know that stuff," Brad said promptly.

"That's everybody's job," Marty said. "That's why we have it at staff meetings. What's Minnesota Lottery's new scratch-off this week?"

Brad said, "Who'd ask me? I don't have anything to do with the customers. I do the heavy moving. I do the real work around this place. You hire someone to chew the fat with customers or you hire someone to get the work done."

Marty then said, "One thing more. You were supposed to take Bridget Garris's groceries and Meal Replacements up to her last Friday. She asked you if she could get things brought up from the deli for Saturday because she was having friends over."

Brad grinned. "Her and all those other old biddies in that building."

Marty said, "You told her you didn't know if she could order deli delivered. You didn't bother to find out. You didn't come back and tell me to call her up and see what she needed. She and her friends have supper parties nearly every weekend, one night or another, usually Fridays. This one happened to be Saturday. That's fifty-two plus or minus deli orders sent up there in a year. That's five- or six-hundred dollars' business in a year. And—*and*—when they come into this store—"

Brad said, "Them go any place? Hobbling around with them walker cages?"

Marty said, "When they come in here, hobbling or not, they come hobbling into *this* store instead of getting their relatives to drive them to a Wal-Mart. And so do their relatives. And anyway, Bridget Garris doesn't hobble."

Brad stood up. He took his apron in his right hand and swatted his left palm with it—but Marty had risen, too. His face, so soft and wide, was blank as plywood and Brad knew that man was one more guy who wouldn't listen to anything. The guy was dug in against him. All the different things that Brad could have told him to help him run a better store, forget it.

As he left the warehouse, Brad already heard himself explaining it to Arlene. He saw her face, looking at him full of kindness. Even if it was hard to look into her face because the bruises had faded to the yellowy stage that made any woman look like shit, she was his wife and she was loyal. When he explained what a shithead Marty Hanks was she would get it.

He drove straight home, glad to be outside. He was especially glad to be outside now it was late fall. The leaves had long since fallen and browned. They lay torn on the ground. This wasn't tourist time: this was hunters' time, and the old trapping urge glowed in Brad. The chief of police was going to have to give him his gun back from the last time. OK so he had lied about firing his gun in the woods, there was still no way could they figure he shot that kid they found in the ditch. They couldn't really prove that he had shot that bear cub, either.

And so what if he and Arlene weren't very well off? Still, they got to live at the edge of their own town. He hadn't given up, like those trailer house people. He hadn't dragged his wife down to live in some bad part of Minneapolis. Their back porch looked out over nearly an acre of uncut sedge and cattails in the low places and brome grass and quack on the higher ground. St. Fursey Creek ran its pebbly course from north to south. On its far bank stood the serious forest. Look, Brad said—going along snappily because he had now got his thoughts together—he could almost physically feel his confidence returning. He could feel how his confidence went jolting along and growing from his mind to his whole body—so, look even if maybe he was still in shock a little, and his brain felt jerky, but he was coming back together as a man. Soon as he got his

weapon back he was going to get something, that other bear cub or whatever. And he would get a good job, too.

Look, he said to himself, I will make it. And why will I make it? I
will make it because I have enough sense to plan ahead. I will apply to
Stan Garris for a job at his dealership. He took a couple of days, though,
to get up his nerve.

This was the day, finally. In the dining room Arlene had left sweepstakes papers and Publishers Clearing House sheets all over the table. He
sat down and idly picked up one of Arlene's papers. "If Minnesota resi-
dent Ms. Arlene Stropp is positively identified as a winner by having and
returning the winning number by April 3rd, we will be required by law
to file Ms. Arlene Stropp as the winner of One Million Dollars." He read
along. The main prize was more like fourteen or fifteen million: Arlene
was careful to keep up with the side stuff, too, the scatterings of one million here and there. He raised his head and looked out at the field, already
darkening over the cold, rotted grass. A million dollars.

It was still only six a.m. when Brad made his first pass by Stan Garris's auto lot. The early morning was luminous full of stars. He looked
out the windshield for a second before putting the headlights on. Part
of him dreaded asking Garris for a job. Garris looked like a nice enough
guy—so tall and thin-faced. It was right and just that this man was so
successful in business. Still, Brad dreaded asking him for a job. Quit crying, he told himself, you've had jobs ever since senior year in high school,
which means you've applied for well over 20 of them, so what is there to
be scared of? You have to get your guts together to apply for work. He
sure knew how to do that.

The stars paled out like scattered coal. Brad wished he never had
to work indoors anywhere, not even in the wonderful Garris Autos. He
wished he could live his dad's old life, hunting and trapping and standing
around the icy lakes' edges with his friends. His dad and those guys were
always speculating, would it be a hard winter or an easy winter, would
it be an open winter or a snowy winter—as if life itself shambled along
in such beautiful places that you could move peacefully, very slowly,
through your thoughts. Yup, they'd say, bet it will be open. Yup, supposed
to have heavy snowfall this year. No one carped at anyone else. Almost

every idea Brad as a boy had heard those men say was just speculation. All those men—their minds were just bungee cords of guesswork. They didn't know anything. They accepted one another's guesswork without carping. They didn't put other fellows down. It seemed like a gentle life. Brad hoped Stan Garris wouldn't just put him down.

He opened the car window as he drove along Fourth Street. He drove through some fragrance of deep-fat frying from the bakery. That's right, Brad thought, those guys, father and son, they were always up and hard at it before anyone except the state troopers. Not a dumb move to vent the hot grease smell outside the way they did. Made you very hungry. That must be a very nice life, too, Brad thought. Running a bakery. No one to smart off at you like Marty Hanks. And everybody loves someone who makes bread and Danish and all. One of the pleasures of Brad's life as a kid had been cutting school at noon. The teachers and administrators couldn't keep much track of where kids were, since they had every-18-minute seating in the cafeteria. Brad and his buddies would trot along Fourth Street, same as kids did now, and go into the bakery and get a Danish so they wouldn't have to eat the crap hotdish the school wanted to throttle you with.

Garris Autos was a modern building with concrete slabs in front for customer parking. The whole business site was a square of concrete laid over what had been forest on the east side of the highway. On the south slab, Garris's men would pump people some gas if they were low. Around on the rear side, they parked the used cars. Brad tried to keep some of the Garris operation in his mind so he would do a good interview.

Brad made another round of the town but stayed clear of Park Road where Tenebrays still lived in the same old family mansion. St. Fursey cops didn't formally *patrol* any streets, but they kind of noticed if they saw ordinary people cruising too slowly where the big shots lived. Of course they often saw the Stropp car over at Tenebrays', because of Arlene cleaning house there, but Brad remembered that a while back, once when it was Brad in the car, not Arlene, the cruise car had followed him for a few blocks.

So now he kept to the center and north parts of town. He had to pay attention because his brace/bandaged ankle was clumsy. He felt full of intensity. He knew all about that feeling, half-philosophical, half-adventurous. In a mood like that you realized that, if you put your mind to it you could make a good job of applying for work, especially if you had a plan and followed it. The exhilaration that he felt now was about 90% panic—he knew that much—so he calmed himself. He had been imagining this moment—for now it was getting up to 7:00 a.m.—when he would ease the car onto Garris's front slab. Out of consideration for any early customers he would park at the far edge.

It was just as he had visualized it. The large car show room lay in shadow so Garris's brightly lighted, inner office, with its mostly-glass-pane walls, showed the great man himself at his desk. He was eating something. He looked pretty human, Brad said to himself. Eating, just like any human being. If he were rich, that was what he would do. Each day he would get away from Arlene early, tell her he had office work, take a sandwich, and then enjoy himself, hiding in his own glassy office, away from all the unpleasantness of life.

Brad was now walking up, feeling respectful of the dark new car show room in front of him. Light fell upon a fender here, a corner of the sofa there, a huge triangular ad placard on top of a huge Buick.

He had figured just right. Stan Garris's men weren't there yet.

Brad considered his script. Things in common. That was going to be one thing to emphasize. He and Garris had things in common. He wanted Garris to think of him as someone not just to hire for the bottom of the totem pole, but as someone who in a year or two would help him with the major sweat of doing business.

Now Brad saw that the man was eating a thick sandwich. It wasn't like those one-luncheon-meat-slice deadbeat sandwiches that Arlene made for him: it was a manful sandwich, with at least two inches of chicken in it. Brad slowed.

"Hi, Stropp," said Garris in a wonderfully friendly tone.

Ah. Every omen was good. The man was obviously in a happy mood, even though he looked awful. Stan Garris was a huge fellow, but under his eyes hung soft pads of dark skin. Brad had applied for jobs from people who had hangovers. It was uphill work. This morning would be all right. Stan Garris was just naturally unhealthy looking or he was sick or something. It didn't matter. The point was, he seemed to be in a good mood. Garris said, "What brings you here at this godforsaken hour of the morning?"

Things in common, Brad reminded himself. "I'm a morning person," Brad said. "It's just a great time of day, is all. People who sleep through it are missing half of life, is the way I look at it."

"You want some coffee? Half a sandwich?" Garris gestured with a thermos, and now Brad saw he had the sandwich half he was eating but there was another untouched one lying on a piece of wax paper. A nice guy. It was very damn smart of Brad to apply to work for this guy. Brad shook his head to the coffee and sandwich, but decided he could sit down on the wood chair near him. He'd been a fool to fool around working for a dip like Hanks. Garris was a real man.

Brad explained he hadn't actually intended to come in until eight when the dealership opened but then he had seen Garris there.

Garris told him that was OK. What could he do for him?

All the time Brad was asking him for a job, Garris didn't take a bite of his sandwich half. He set it down.

At last Garris said, "This isn't a promise. But if you want to start, you could start right now, and then we'll talk later. All the work stations need cleaning up. I lost some help last week. The showroom needs the usual vac. I'll show you the job. Then we'll have some cars and trucks to wash. You up for this?"

Garris lifted himself delicately out of his chair, using both arms.

He took Brad down a night-lighted hallway towards the back. Garris put the regular lights on as they went along. Dark green uniform jackets and trousers hung on hooks, with names on the wall above each. Garris told him to lug the cleaning cart on its casters over to the long garage where his mechanic had his own station. Garris walked beside Brad.

"You can catch Kenneth's station before he gets in so you'll be out of his way by the time he wants to start work." Garris looked out a smeary back window. "Yeah and wash that window," he said. "You can't tell night from day."

Day was coming. Brad could make out a beat-up pickup parked just outside in front of the row of used cars. "Kenny has a '96 Ford to work on this morning, but he might get to that pickup out there, too."

"A Ford!" exclaimed Brad.

Garris said, "We don't turn up our noses at anything around here. Whatever they drive in here, we fix it."

He spent a quarter of an hour showing Brad how to do the heaviest dirt first, then move to the light dirt, which meant oil and grease spills first, then ordinary floor dirt with the other compound on the shelf, then after that, go to the piled, folded rags and do the window sills and every horizontal surface. Then he could use that ammonia mix for the glass panes.

Brad said, "What about the show room?"

Garris said, "I have to take a truck to Chisholm in another hour or so. Let's see how far you get. If you do get through with everything, you can vac and wash the wrecker truck." He turned to go, but swung back around to Brad.

"And oh yeah, when you're doing the shelves over the work station, be sure to leave Kenny's thermos and stuff just the way he's got it!"

"You bet!" Brad said with a smile but he felt a twinge. Garris spoke of his mechanic with such respect. Brad got the rest of the cleaning equipment out of the utility room. Someday he bet he would overhear Garris saying to someone, "Get Brad's station first, would you? He's got a busy day. You can get around to the other stuff later."

Brad thought about what Garris had said about heavy dirt first, light dirt later. He thought, yeah, that was logical enough, except that the heavy dirt was underfoot and the light dirt would fall on it. He decided to start with dusting instead, and then move downward, catching and cleaning any dirt that fell. Well, but Garris was right about the windows looking like shit. Brad got up on the stepladder and started in on the window that overlooked the back slab.

Daylight now bathed the ratty pickup out there.

Brad did good work. He had wiped off everything, even the compressor hoses and the hydraulics casings. Garris had told him to grab a pair of gloves from out back, but Brad worked barehanded because he wasn't chicken. After all, here he was dragging his shit-bandaged ankle which weighed an even ton, up and down the stepladder. After another half-hour, he could feel a tingle all over his fingers. It reminded him of the first year of his marriage when Arlene had got him to help her strip some furniture. "You'd better put on gloves for that, honey," she said. Christ, he had explained to her, if a man was afraid of a few chemicals, what was he good for? Arlene had given him a fast glance. He was sure a woman got sick of all the safety rules her mom and dad put on her. So then she meets someone and marries him—and she sees him *break* a few of those wimpy rules. It wakes her up somehow. She feels that man is free, not all tied up in knots like other people, and she gets free with him, because of him.

He was running the vacuum around some coiled hose on the floor when he noticed Garris's new-car salesman had come in. He looked like any old man around town in his jeans and jeans-jacket. Any old man except very good looking, Brad thought. George was old now, but Brad expected the man had had a lot of women in his day. He imagined George making out with a woman, maybe starting at the VFW and then moving over to her place. But whoever those women were they'd be old now, too. Dead, more like.

George came over and said hello. Brad was glad he didn't ask, hey, you working here? Because he would have had to admit that he didn't know yet.

George wandered off, and next time Brad got a glimpse of him he was wearing sharp-pressed navy green pants, a white shirt, a light green tie, and the dark green jacket that said, in very small gold-thread embroidery, Garris Autos over the breast pocket.

After a while, Garris himself came to Brad and said, "You can quit here because Kenny is coming. Go vacuum the new car show room. You're in luck, Brad. I had to let that girl go who does that. Go anywhere you can get without even so much as *touching* those fenders or anything. Don't even touch the wheels. Get down on your knees and look under, though. Sometimes people roll a Pepsi can under there, or they drop gum wrappers and shove them under with their shoes. Then, when you got that done, take this neat little gizmo and very gently dust off the roofs and hoods. Got any questions, I'll be out in Service. Come find me when you're through." He handed Brad a long-handled pink fuzzy duster stick.

An hour went by. Garris came up. "Here," he said, "Can you run the washing equipment?" He took Brad over. "And be careful, Brad," he said. "This place is dangerous. We got static electricity up the wazoo. We got chemicals that could bend a wrench. You have to remember, where there's cars, there's accidents, no matter how shiny the cars are. Talk about 'moving violations'! What scare me is the ones someone left in park."

Brad figured that was a joke so he laughed.

"You ever use a posthole digger at all?" Garris said.

"No."

"Too bad. I am thinking of fencing for all those deer that have been yarding up around my used cars. OK. I have to get to Chisholm. Work hard and we'll talk when I get back."

Brad watched Garris and Herzlich open the doors of a new mid-size pickup parked at the side.

A half-hour later, the mechanic came up behind Brad without his noticing because of the noise of the washing. He pointed at the handle. Oh. Quit working so he could tell him something. OK. He turned it off and hung it up.

"Stan had to pick up a car in Chisholm. It's my coffee break. Would you mind the shop for us?"

Kenneth wore the other Garris uniform—not the salesman's jacket but dark green pants and lighter green shirts. A mechanic's uniform.

Brad knew enough not to just nod and go back to work. He said "Sure" in a very willing tone.

Brad reached for his hose. Next thing he knew, the fender of the truck he was washing popped. Jesus. Steam and spray flew up. The hell with it if a truck couldn't take a hot-water wash. Brad went to re-hang the nozzle. He then saw that he had picked up the steam-cleaning hose instead of the hot-water hose. It didn't look to him as though he could force that fender back right either.

He hesitated about what to do next. A voice from behind him said, "Sir?"

He turned around.

The teenager looked surprised. "Oh," he said, "Brad Stropp! Gee, I took it for granted you were George or Kenneth."

It was Simon, the doctor's kid, who had worked part-time alongside Brad at the Super Valu.

Brad drew himself up. "How you doing, Simon?" he said. "And what can I do for you?" The boy looked abashed.

He explained he wanted to see how much a used pickup might set him back.

Brad strolled to the back doorway, with Simon following. After all, Brad was minding the shop. He should take care of whatever came up. "Well," he said in a leisurely tone, "I could let you try one. That one over there. It's not for sale but I think we have something like it that we can show you later."

Simon's face lighted up. "Really? Really try it?"

Brad said, "Listen, Simon, you're a reliable kid. I let you try it, you have it back here in ten minutes flat. You don't drive all over town. You go west on Fourth and south on whatever street you want, back east on Park Road then back up on 53 to here. You don't take this car out of town. Not back to show off at school where I bet you're supposed to be."

"No, sir," Simon said.

Inside himself, Brad heard the holy chime *sir*. Brad thought. "Sir."

Brad went over to the Service cubbyhole and brought out the keys from under the worksheet laid out for Kenny.

"OK, then. Nice truck. Not beautiful. Just nice. See what you think. Mr. Garris gets back, you can look at some others."

"Gee, thanks, Brad!"

In a half-hour, Kenneth returned. He went to some papers stuck up on his pegboard and started looking for a parts package. Then he went to the Service window and around behind to the keyboard where people clipped worksheets. Garris showed up a minute later.

The mechanic said, "I thought you had that pickup of Vera Hall's that needed drums and lots else."

"Yeah," Garris said, taking off his jacket.

"Where's the pickup, though?" the mechanic said.

"Out back where it was," Garris said.

Both men looked out the wide door. The mechanic turned back.

"You see anyone?" the mechanic said to Brad.

"No," he said fast. Oh no, he said to himself, why didn't I tell him that this shit kid had gone off with that pickup and promised to be back in ten minutes? The doctor's shit kid never got back.

The other two men walked farther out on the concrete outside. Then they returned and went through the building and out the front door. They left it open in the unnaturally warm autumn day. All three men heard the ambulance from across town, and next, the two-note throbbing wail of the police car.

Garris turned to Brad. "You say you didn't see or hear anybody?"

"No," Brad said, and to his own humiliation, he added, "Sir."

Garris said, "Some guy comes in here, lifts a set of keys off the Service board and drives one of our fixers off and you didn't *hear* him?"

Brad said, "You have the sprays on, you don't hear much."

"That's true enough," Garris said.

The boss went into his office. They saw him pick up the telephone. Whoever Garris was talking to kept him on the phone. Brad saw Garris raise his head and look directly over to him. He kept talking on the phone but he kept looking at Brad.

Meanwhile, Kenneth had brought a car into the wash, so Brad started doing spot cleaning. He rubbed at a rust spot. Trouble, ancient, familiar-type trouble, was cantering around quietly toward him. He told himself, "All I have ever done is tried to support my wife and family. My wife and my kid." He kept repeating it to himself, as if he were rehearsing some dread part in a play. "My kid," he repeated to himself. He tried to make a mental picture of himself playing with little Dianne, before she got to be a sassy high school kid who smarted off to her parents and later ran away and never came back. He tried to keep a good picture in his mind, but the dread smoked around everywhere deeply inside him.

A huge voice, calm and confident, spoke from behind and above him.

"Once you start rubbing down on a spot like that, you got to make sure you put a stop agent on it or you're going to give that owner a lot worse headache than that little place. Rust travels under paint at the speed of sound, Brad."

"I was going to, soon as I got it clean," Brad said fast.

Garris's voice said, "So where do we keep the body putty?"

"I don't know yet. I haven't figured out where everything is yet."

Kenneth had now come to stand next to Garris. Both men looked down at Brad. The mechanic said, "So if you didn't know where it is, how did you figure you were going to put it on this car?"

But Garris said, "Never mind, Kenny. Come on into the office, Brad."

"Sure, Stan," Brad said gratefully. "Wait till I wash my hands."

"Come as you are," Garris said.

In the glassed-in office he said, "Shut the door, Brad."

Then he said, "No, don't even sit down. That was the police on the telephone. I probably don't have to tell you much about what they said since you seem to know a lot more about it than I do. I sure would have appreciated it if you had shared with me the really swell information that you sent a minor out of my lot in a vehicle with no brakes."

"It won't happen again, Stan."

"That's right. It won't," Garris said. "I figure you worked here four hours this morning. Brad, would you figure you worked here four hours?"

Brad knew he hadn't done any four hours' work, no matter how you figured it. He opened his mouth. He meant to say, "More like two, really," but he couldn't say it. He couldn't make himself. He watched while Garris wrote him a check for four hours' work, and then handed it up to him.

"Just one other thing," Garris said. "You never asked why the police called. Don't you want to know why?"

Brad's face heated.

"I'll relieve your mind," Garris said. "A line of kids were walking out of the bakery, side by side, right down the middle of the street. So Simon's coming along in that pickup. He jams on the brakes. But no brakes. So he turns Vera's pickup 90 degrees left at 20 miles an hour and drives it right through that new huge window that Denham's just put in the bakery. Right on through. Totaled the day-old cart, but that's all. Didn't kill any kids in the street and no old folks in the bakery."

Brad kept his face down. He took in that the check wasn't even a big business check. It was just a personal check of Stan Garris's. He'd never even made it onto the payroll.

Stan looked at him. "Aren't you even going to ask if Simon's alive or not?"

Brad said that of course he wanted to know. Christ, think how he felt. Simon was bruised but he was OK, Stan told him.

"Well, thank you for paying me for the morning's work," Brad said.

"That's right," Garris told him, standing up now. "That's what I'm going to pay for all right. A morning's work. Seventy-two bucks for you and twenty-five hundred for Denham's brand new whole-wall-width window and a comparable or better used truck for Vera. You know something, Brad, you come with one big price tag on you."

Brad suddenly remembered the fender of that truck that popped off when he hit it with the steam hose. He mumbled goodbye and left.

Brad felt reamed out at first. But then he realized he had the afternoon off, and he had the car. He could drive along 53 and park, and check out that path that ran in toward Small Bass Lake where he'd seen that mother bear. She and the cub she had left had to still be around somewhere, dangerous as all get-out. You couldn't trust a bear this time of year, especially a mother with a cub. Anyone who'd seen how she had gone and tore up those old apple trees of Stolz's could get some idea what a bear can do.

A town was like a country in one way, Brad thought aloud in the car. You have to look out for it. Somebody has to. Once a bear like that gets hold of you, Brad didn't care if it was a polar bear or a grizzly or just a Minnesota black bear, you can say goodbye to your eyes and your face and your brains. One swipe of those claws could rout a clean channel down you, top to bottom, and open out a man's heart like a butterflied fish.

Chapter Eight

People supposed Dr. Anderson was excellent in his profession, family medicine. They had to believe that, since no one wanted to make the eleven-mile drive to Cullough to see the doctors there. St. Fursey people told one another what a good man Anderson was the way parents tell children that Santa Claus is always full of good will. Nobody told their children that Santa Claus got tired and short-tempered from year-round holiday preparations.

Still, something held them off a little about their doctor. It was his politics. It was not that he was Republican or Democrat or something else; it was that he was political at all. Dr. Anderson sometimes brought up miserable subjects that people needed like they needed a poke in the eye with a sharp stick. They wanted him to live the life *they* lived—interested in his work, interested in his family. They felt sorry that his wife had died and he was raising two children alone. But... but... if only he would stay on task...

One person in all of St. Fursey approved of him completely. That was the chief of police. Stokowski's and Anderson's conversations with each other were usually horrible. Bad luck or bad human behavior were what brought them together in their work. What made them like and trust each other, however, was that neither of them tried to find any silver linings in any clouds. Neither of them tried to put a good face on any happening. They talked about the most grievous subjects, of course, since they were a cop and a physician—with this major difference from casual pessimists: their professions gave them a respect for accuracy. They had the habit of checking out whatever guesswork they had to do. They were exact, rather than romantic. They shared an abiding hatred of such horrible human behavior as they came across in their work.

What Stokowski knew was an eye opener to the physician. What Anderson knew was an eye opener to the policeman. They commonly met alongside yellow tape, in hospital hallways, in the holding tank at Cullough, in the St. Fursey Clinic's Physicians Only parking lot. Neither of them ever had a deli sandwich at Denham's Bakery or a drink at the VFW Post. They ate and drank in private.

It was an early weekday afternoon. The inside back hallway of the St. Fursey Clinic was crowded nearly shoulder-to-shoulder with ordinary people, even the chief of police. People peered in from alongside the registration counter. Dr. Anderson was prancing like a teenager up and down the hallway, hugging his sixteen-year-old son, kissing him, never minding the boy's red face. Simon could have been killed a half-hour earlier, but the boy had used his head and had a lot of luck, so his father was laughing and crying in the hallway of the St. Fursey Clinic. The med techs, especially the touchy, low-spirited one whom no one particularly liked, carefully backed away with their plastic cups of urine, and the two office nurses held their index boards close so that their nutty boss and his son wouldn't barge into them as they reeled and zig-zagged past.

Of course it was wonderful that Simon Anderson had survived crashing a pickup with no brakes right through the huge north window of Denham's Bakery. Everybody had learned the details within a half hour. Of course everyone smiled. Of course people said that it was a near thing. But in that less voluble neighborhood of their upper cortices, the six inter-conversant layers of the neocortex, what people in their right minds call their heart of hearts, they did not completely admire their doctor for cavorting like that down the clinic hall. OK, so Simon Anderson had not been killed. Simon Anderson in his wisdom had cut school that day, apparently in order to go into the auto lot right on Highway 53 and "try out" a second-hand Chevy pickup which had come into Garris Autos expressly for brake repair. The onlookers, grinning and clapping, remembered being sixteen years old. On the other hand, they did not all remember their own dads ever expressing this much love for them. These grown men's faces, despite their smiles, looked a little strained with envy.

The previous few days had given Dr. Anderson exercise in most aspects of his practice. He endured each of the two smells he never could really accustom himself to—the fetor from his first tipping the blade into the chest to examine a rotted human body. And then, today, on Monday, the classical, pallid stench of semen on a battered patient.

On Friday Dr. Anderson pronounced on the body that had lain beside Minnesota 53 for ten to twelve days, twice lightly shawled by snow. Animals or birds had eaten its eyes. On Saturday forenoon Dr. Anderson had done the examination as a favor to the county M.E. who didn't sing in St. Fursey's ecumenical choir, and therefore had had the weekend away.

The official cause of death was two blows to the head in the upper left parietal area. They could not have been self-inflicted. The body had been in sexual intercourse before the head was struck. For the present, it would be held chilled until someone claimed it. For now it was essentially a legal possession of the State of Minnesota. The doctor and the St. Fursey chief of police talked about it.

Bernie Stokowski said that this particular murder looked like work by a very large organization whose resources, or you could say, whose skills, included getting rid of any bodies it wanted to get rid of.

"How do you know?" Dr. Anderson said.

The pattern was classical. Neither the body when *in vivendi* nor anyone else had handled any of deceased's clothes or shoes, the chief said. There were no partial prints on anything. Human beings use their hands to get dressed. If they are dressing someone else, either a live or a dead someone else, they use their hands. Everything on the dead female had been wiped clean. Sunday School teachers do not wipe prints off young women.

Earlier that same Saturday morning, between 3:00 and 3:45, Dr. Anderson had attended the delivery of a moribund baby. Its parents had refused any medical intervention throughout an unpromising and potentially dangerous pregnancy because they were practicing, they told him, the full power of prayer. Each of the four times the doctor had pointed out to them that the pregnancy was not good, they had smiled at him. Their smiles were the smiles of a fourth-grade arithmetic teacher. If you don't understand long division today, such smiles say, you will tomorrow.

They were inspirited Christians tolerating a dim physician. The father had explained that both he and his wife were in personal relationship with Jesus Christ. The doctor took their smiles and their remarks like blows to the face, but he had heard worse. The baby lived for three minutes before it died.

The next day was Sunday. Dr. Anderson had only rounds at the hospital. Rounds included checking on the mother who had lost her baby. He started off down the maternity wing, but turned back to pick up one of the nurses to go with him.

In her room the mother told him that she didn't like to be negative but she had concerns. If her attending physician had been willing to pray with her and her husband the way they had four times requested, instead of allowing the devil to fill him with pride in his technical professionalism, they would not have lost their baby.

Dr. Anderson raised his eyes from the clipboard of her vitals. He told her again how sorry he was that her baby had died.

He returned to the nurses' station to fill out his report. The senior nurse handed him a cup of coffee without his asking for it. She said, "I thought you handled that just perfectly, Doctor." Her eyes filled and her voice thickened. "I've always noticed—we've all noticed—how gentle you are, too, when you have to blanket and hand over a dead baby to its mother. Like yesterday. I know it's your job and all, but not everyone's that gentle. Not everyone's that caring. We noticed."

The other nurse who was on duty that morning returned to the station from a patient call.

The doctor stopped scribbling his codes and signatures and remarked, "You know an experience I've never had?"

The first nurse now decided it was time to cut the sadness. She said, with a brightening face, in a witty tone, "Of course I do. You have never delivered a baby yourself, Dr. Anderson."

He said, "I have never attended the delivery of a healthy baby, handed it to its mother, and then heard airplanes fly over and then had bombs drop on the hospital and kill the new mother and the baby. I've never had that experience."

Both nurses stared.

The younger one began to cry.

He paid no attention.

"No," he went on, in his odd-ball, nearly languid tone, "Turns out I've never had that experience. I wonder if the President has ever had that experience."

Now the one nurse wept in a florid, nearly vomitous way. The two nurses handed a Kleenex box back and forth, very gently.

Soon Dr. Anderson was done, so he lifted up the little Dutch door and left them. From the coat hooks, however, he overheard the senior nurse say, "I like Dr. Anderson a lot, but I really wish he wouldn't do that so much of the time. Dragging in stuff. We had enough sadness around here this weekend, what with someone left dead out on 53 and then that dead baby, without him dragging in other stuff that hasn't got anything to do with anything."

That was early Sunday morning. The Anderson kids had fried pancakes at home. Simon was an awfully good tenor for someone sixteen and Katie was a focused nature-lover who would sit for quarter-hours on end to observe deer or bears. They were both such terrible cooks that their dad had to master his aversion to the burnt edges and running mucus of the pancakes. "Have seconds, Dad," they told him. "Here, we made plenty."

"Gee, kids. OK. Seconds."

The doctor got a beeper call at 10:00 but only to arrange a 72-hour hold for his repeat bi-polar. One of his repeat husband-battered patients called but called back two minutes later to say she sure didn't know what was wrong with her. She giggled. She guessed her head would come off if it wasn't screwed on—how could she have said anyone pushed her down the basement staircase when what had happened was the usual? She'd just lost her balance with a basket of laundry, and she bet even the doctor did dumb stuff like that *once* in a while, and she gave the good-sport laugh which he knew from the years of his practice meant she had decided on this version of the script.

No one delivered a baby. No one called from the hospital to say anyone was claiming the murdered woman's body. He was free to finish breakfast and eat lunch with Simon and Katie, and even get in a full one-hour nap, and still make it on time to the 3 p.m. chorus rehearsal.

Now he was doing a Virginia reel up and down the hallway and didn't mind that Simon was embarrassed. He didn't mind that he thought he had a 1:00 appointment with someone but absolutely couldn't recall whom. He couldn't feel any weight in his right white-coat pocket which meant he had again misplaced both his cell phone and the new stethoscope. Never mind.

His appointments nurse elbowed through the crowd. "Dr. Anderson! Do you want to pick up?" She held out a wireless.

He laughed and practically sang, "No, but I'll take it!"

He let Simon go but said, "Don't leave."

The show seemed to be over, so the crowd politely drew back a little, to allow their doctor some privacy on the telephone. In the next moment, however, they heard him give a shout, a shout that was one part shout and nine parts snarl. Nobody could resist eavesdropping.

"You're saying *what*?" the doctor shouted into the phone. "Yaaas, I know who you are! You are saying that Simon skipped school and missed four classes? I believe you! I am sending him home for the rest of the afternoon, too, Principal! So he will miss whatever he's got for the afternoon, too! I am ordering up bed rest. You'd like to know why? I will be happy to explain it!—you *what*! You resent my tone! Listen! Do you realize that my son could have avoided risking his own life by driving through a bunch of younger kids in the street! He could have done that! That's what people do, Principal! Whatever they're doing, they just keep on doing it, never mind that they can foresee what will happen! But Simon didn't!"

The clinic crowd were utterly delighted. Even one of the techs, not the dour one, grinned. No one much liked the Cullough high school principal, but up to this minute they had felt vague about it. Now they knew they'd always been right. The fellow so totally sucked.

"Jeez, Dad," Simon said.

The doctor held the phone away from his mouth long enough to say, "Pipe down, Simon. I want to look at your signs again."

Back into the phone he said, "He could have done that, you know.

Half the world just keeps doing whatever they're doing even if they could save lives by doing something else. Not Simon. He made a 90° turn and drove through a building so you know what? You know what's going to happen to that string of kids? They are going to grow up and go to your high school some day! Now, I have to get off the phone and let you get back to your work."

The doctor said to Simon, "I want you home, on the couch or in bed. Lying down. I will come check you after a while—wait a minute! I don't want you there alone! Oh good—" he cried, and pointed at Arlene Stropp, a woman he knew, who was standing among the crowd.

"Arlene!" he shouted. "Is today the day you clean my house? Could you take Simon home with you and stay with him?"

His appointments nurse said severely, "Dr. Anderson, Mrs. Stropp is your one o'clock and she's already been waiting a half hour."

"Go home," he said to Simon one last time, "If you feel even the least thing, dizziness, nausea, anything, call me!"

The chief of police came forward. He said, "I'll drive him home, Doc."

Dr. Anderson hugged *him*, too.

His happiness lay all about him, as though he himself, some vessel of himself, had poured out.

He rushed toward his nice cleaning woman. "I'm so sorry, Arlene! I wasn't thinking! Here—" and he took her folder from the nurse, "Come on in here."

He pushed up the orange patient-in lever. "Don't be cross with me!" he said, following her in. "My son is alive, you see."

His patient was far from cross with him. She looked at him with a face full of love. Her face also showed a fresh five-centimeter bruising on both left and right side, with several-days-old dark black and blue in the periorbital area around each eye. Dr. Anderson began lightly touching her face. He figured the original bruise site was on the left cheek, but she had turned when struck there, to the right, likely to stave off further blows to the left-side damage done to the jaw three months ago. Macroflages had eaten the old blood, and scavenger cells in both cheeks were well into several days' worth of remaking blood. Destroyed hemoglobin gave one cheek surface a brownish green.

He wheeled a little closer to Arlene and lifted her hands. The undersides of both arms were yellow, where they would have caught some of her husband's blows when she raised them to protect her face. Dr. Anderson set one assault on Arlene Stropp at about five or six days prior, and new trauma today.

He asked her a few desultory questions while he wrote on her sheet. She never paid any attention to his advice, but he always kept her in the clinic as long as he could. He kept half an ear cocked for an opening when he might talk her into making a charge and leaving the brute of a husband. There was no single reason that Arlene should stay to get beaten up every—he peeped into three previous pages—every four months or so.

Arlene Stropp, so far, had followed a conventional pattern. She always gave Dr. Anderson a specific, partial subject to advise her on. "Just look at the left side of my jaw, would you, Doctor, please?" she would say. Keep away, her tone always said. Keep from any holistic remarks about my life. Over the past few years, he had several times given Arlene Stropp his shaky speech on the subject. There is a law now, Arlene, he would say, as though it were nothing to do with him and he was helpless in the case. He would tell her, I have to report such bruising as you have. He always offered it all in a very low-key tone, matching her typical lifelessness of voice. You know what that means, Arlene? It means you have *more people on your side than you know about.* Not just me and my staff but people with authority in Duluth.

She never paid any attention.

He didn't think it was money. His other battered wives needed to stay married for the husband's income. They had to feed their children. Not Arlene. She brought in the only regular income they had. He knew she cleaned the elementary school and the St. Fursey Episcopal Church, and a number of individual homes such as his. He himself knew of four people who had her come for half-days. In the way that word got around, Dr. Anderson knew that Peter and Nat Tenebray and he paid her $25 an hour but another three of her employers whom he knew of stayed at $12 an hour, probably the rate they had hired her at years ago. Practical enough. They knew as well as Arlene knew it that they didn't have to pay more. She wasn't going anywhere. Everyone knew her husband couldn't keep a job. That lady was good and stuck. Twelve dollars an hour was fine.

Arlene would actually *save* money by throwing Brad out, the doctor figured. What kept her in the abusive marriage wasn't hard to understand. First, if she tried to get out of it, Brad Stropp would beat her up. The chief of police was a nice and very savvy cop but she would get beaten up before Bernie ever got there. Second, even if the chief fixed up a restraining order on Brad, Brad would beat up Arlene, get put in prison for a while, then get out and beat her up again. The clincher reason though, Dr. Anderson thought, was that Arlene was caged in her own ideals. She was *married*. She was a married woman. Whatever impenetrable fog of disrespect the rich and the near-rich of St Fursey, and especially the women's church groups, let fall upon Arlene Stropp, they couldn't take it away from her that she was a married and gainfully employed woman. She crouched in her marriage the way a live-caught mouse crouches in a humane trap. Arlene did not see it as a cage for holding prey ready for a predator.

Today Dr. Anderson's heart was so full of joy about Simon he had to order himself to stay on task with Arlene. He let her talk. Even on this November day at 47 degrees of North Latitude, she wore a print cotton dress. She kept one knee crossed firmly over the other with the lower legs and ankles held together, then tipped to one side, like a college girl on television. He was not sure whether her dress, the more pathetic for looking ironed, would be her clothes for cleaning houses or if she did her cleaning in pants but had put on this dress for her appointment with him. He knew she loved him. How could she not? He didn't take it personally. In a culture so full of cruelty as the United States was, people loved anyone in the helping professions who was civil or just minimally kind. Of course she loved him.

It was as they sat there, he trying, as usual, to conjure up some way to convince her to leave Brad, that he caught the floating fetor of semen.

That smell changed everything. She always came to his office fresh-bathed. Only force, force at the noon hour, so she could scarcely keep her appointment, could have made her come to him with her husband's seed spilled on her.

The repellent odor gave him a new idea.

"Open your mouth, Arlene," he said peremptorily. "No—wait a

second. Is your jaw OK enough now so you can open your mouth wide without any discomfort?"

She opened her mouth.

He said, "Yes—like that, but wider. Now," he said almost harshly. "Say 'Ahhhh.'"

"Ahhhhh."

"Good. Now listen carefully, Arlene. Say 'ahhhhh' this time just the same way, on the same note, as I say it." He sang "Ahhhh" very loudly.

She imitated.

"Good!" he exclaimed.

She looked at him as though he'd lost his mind.

She tried to shrink from his handhold: he had taken hold of both of her hands several minutes ago and was still holding them. He let go.

"Now," he told her. "You say 'Ahhhh' on that same note. I am going to start out with you. Then I will change my note, but *you keep yours*. As I raise my voice, don't slide up with me."

He took his note and she picked it up. For a quarter-second, they held it together, he at his octave lower. Then he slowly went up a fifth.

She kept her note.

He cried, "Arlene, you are a natural!"

He then said, "I'm just going to suggest one more thing." Dr. Anderson noticed he was using the silky language of a family physician doing an internal exam—it was the language that said, "I know what I am doing is intrusive but it has a purpose and I promise this will be over in just a moment."

"Just one more thing," he said. "Please take a good deep breath and let it out, then take another, and let it out, then take another. Then, sing the same note I sing, the way you did before, and hang onto it until I stop singing completely."

He smiled briefly at her face. "No, I have not gone crazy," he said.

They each breathed in and out together, twice, and then took their note, which was the bottom of the same fifth they had sung before. They were both using "Aaaaaah" as before. Then he jumped clean up a major third. Arlene held strong, so he rushed singing through the first bars of the "Ode to Joy." He knew that whatever music she didn't know she would know that melody. It was jammed into the culture as firmly as the national anthem. Even Arlene's repulsive husband probably knew it and loved it.

He sang loudly. The cramped little consulting room with its glass of cotton swabs and its folded paper gowns and its skeletal heel rests and its posters about the difference between a bacterium and a virus and its Norman Rockwell print of a white-haired physician with his stethoscope pressed on a doll's chest while a little girl watched—Dr. Anderson's consulting room blared with his sound. Then he, and no doubt she, too, ran out of breath. Silence.

"Oh!" his patient exclaimed.

He waited. Please, he begged her silently: Please actually say *something*. Please commit yourself to some opinion or other. Silently he begged her: Oh *what*?

Arlene said, "That was so pretty!"

But she added in her usual gravelly tone: "Dr. Anderson, why did you want to see my tonsils when I haven't got a sore throat? And anyway, you told me ages ago my tonsils were shrunk up by now..."

He said, "I want you to sing in the ecumenical choir," he said.

"I can't sing with those kind of people," she remarked without any particular expression.

He told her she had ear. She could hold a note even though other people very nearby were singing on a different note. He told her without lying that she had musical taste. There was nothing wrong with old Beethoven, he thought a little wildly to himself, and there was nothing wrong with Arlene for liking him. He told her the next rehearsal was Sunday afternoon at 3:00. He was going to get that music to her ahead of time.

"Wait a minute, Arlene," he interrupted himself. "Do you read music?"

"The words part, not those lines things," she said.

She added, "Dr. Anderson, I can't sing with those people."

He stood up. "You're right. Not today you can't, but by Sunday you can. It's only Monday. I will get the music to you tonight."

Her head came up fast. "Not to my house!" she exclaimed.

"No," he said. "Are you cleaning at my house this afternoon?"

"At the school," she said.

Then he would get the music to her at school. He was going to set up times to sing with her so she could memorize everything before Sunday. To himself, he said, that little devil Simon who'd skipped school and put a pickup through the whole front of a grocery store, that boy was going to do a little work for the old man—he could do five half-hour singing practices at home with Arlene. He himself would sing on the melody to teach her, and Simon, who was in the tenor section anyhow, could do the tenor line, and Nat could take the alto and sit off to one side of Arlene so she would get used to hearing the opposing women's part on the left. Nat wouldn't give him grief about this, because they'd do it during the main one of her five or six happy hours of each day and she liked music at any level anyway. Drunk or sober, at least so far in her alcoholic pattern, she always came through for the ecumenical chorales.

Dr. Anderson noticed he was fast crumbling back down to practicality after the passion of gratitude for his son's life. He explained that he would pick Arlene up on his way home from the clinic at 5:30 tomorrow and Wednesday, Thursday, and Friday. He thought to himself, he wouldn't offer the Saturday, though. He'd done last weekend for the coroner. He wanted a weekend off.

He had the door open and held it for her.

"I will have to ask my husband," Arlene told him.

He said, "I come pick you up at your house and either Simon or I drop you back home a half-hour later. You don't have to ask your husband anything. If Brad has any concerns, he can ask me. Will you tell Brad that? Tell him that I will be really glad to come around to your house and help him with any concerns he has about your singing."

"Those people though," she murmured, now that he and she were out in the hall where they might be heard. She added, "Big shots."

A tech and the appointments nurse hovered near.

Dr. Anderson said very loudly, "We're using the Episcopal Church red robes this year, Arlene. I'll see you get one." He went on in such a loud voice she had to realize he actually wanted others to be listening... that nurse or two, a passing patient, a tech.

"Since we talked all the time about the ecumenical choir rehearsal, this was not a medical consultation."

He followed her all the way down the hall toward Reception, still talking loudly. He said to the receptionist, while helping Arlene Stropp on with her jacket, "We never saw Mrs. Stropp here this afternoon. She was here about the ecumenical chorus. No meds."

At last she was gone.

He thought: I will call Simon and see how he is. Where'd I leave my cell phone, though?

He returned to pause at the door to the blood room.

His least favorite of all the techs the clinic had ever hired was pulling a slide out of her microscope. Without even lifting her head, she said, "On the baby scale, Doctor."

He took up the cell phone from the soft flannel.

"And your stethoscope's in the clinic jacket you left in the doctors' lounge. Right pocket."

She clearly made her voice express as much disdain as it could.

That medical technician had come to St. Fursey Clinic at age 20. She was the doctor's own fault He didn't know anything about hiring and he'd hired her. She must be only 22 or 23 now. He supposed she might still grow up to be a friendly or affectionate human being. He bet she might. Then he thought, that's not true. He bet she wouldn't. He bet she would stay the same. He wasn't a psychologist. He was a physician who had a family practice but he wasn't completely stupid. Chances were, she would go on doing what she was doing, and being the kind of human being she was being. She would slouch through the other three-fifths of her lifetime just like that, with her taste for low-key bullying when a chance offered. People might hint to her about putting people down so much, but no one would tell her in a straightforward way to be more, say, kindly disposed, because she lived in the same work world Dr. Anderson lived in, where people took care not ever to come off as judgmental.

CHAPTER NINE

John Rubrick's job was to mix business with pleasure.

He had known how to do business in living rooms since he was a little boy. He had never been one of those tall, idle fellows so good looking that older people smiled and said, "He hasn't found his feet yet." You always got the feeling when you talked to him, that he had already thought through your subject, but was too tactful to say so. He was always on his feet. He first worked in Washington for four years, and then joined his present organization and stayed there—32 years it was now. He was still tall, and fine featured, and good looking. Most people smiled when his name came up. If charm is a matter of having a humorous face that gets solemn the moment you mention any sadness of yours, then John Rubrick had charm. It was a grown human being's charm. He was fifty-seven.

John never talked about people as "contacts," yet he entered and annotated all his business acquaintances in four address books. Two of them were electronic, and duplicated many names that appeared on the third, which was a personal, scribbled mess of a notebook. His annotations looked like the jottings common to people who bump into old friends now and then and wish to stay in touch. It was awfully nice to see so-and-so again, surprisingly so, and wisely not trusting one's own memory over the age of 21, one scribbled a few things about so-and-so. Marriages made, job changes, children born or succeeding at such-and-such. Moved to somewhere.

John's fourth address book had the peculiarity of being in Norwe-gian. It looked like a novel, not an alphabetical listing. It had indented paragraphs of narration. It seemed to have dialogue, a lot of it, each speech introduced by a long dash, European style. Unlike most fiction, this text had the peculiarity that any of its characters who were described, and who got to say things to one another, never appeared more than once. To read through such a narrative would be like reading *Gone With the Wind* and finding Rhett Butler early on saying, "Frankly, my dear, I don't give a damn," and Scarlett O'Hara appearing considerably later saying, "I'll think about it tomorrow," after which we never hear from either of them again. If you paged through this double-spaced manuscript you might notice that characters in the early chapters had names beginning with early letters in the alphabet and characters appearing later had names like Erik Peter T. Ødsel or Anne Michelle Langley Yttervind or so-and-so Aetterbok, O and Y and AE being the last letters in the Norwegian alphabet.

No one paged through the manuscript, however. Rubrick never showed the book to anyone. No need. John's north-midwestern acquaintance who claimed to speak Norwegian didn't speak it past knowing enough to grin when someone mentioned lutefisk or to say "Takk skal De ha" when offered more of whatever people were drinking. They didn't even know that the respectful "De" scarcely existed any more. Besides, the book was impenetrably uninviting, with handwritten insertions all through it. John sometimes told people that he was plugging away translating a nineteenth century novel by someone whose career had been wrongly overshadowed by Bjørnstjerne Bjørnsen. "Oh, yes, of course," people said, "You were our American cultural officer in Norway for a while, weren't you?" John hadn't been but he would beam a grateful expression.

His real address books sometimes revealed anomalies. So-and-so told John about a degree in history taken at such-and-such a college but that college had no record of that person's having graduated in history or with any other major. More of these irregularities, actually about twice as many, were showing up in recent years than earlier; lying in corporate life was trickling into academia. Resumés were full of lies. John's particular work had little to do with lying done by young adults. When he came across their falsification of personal records, he simply passed along the information to the appropriate colleagues in his organization.

He regarded himself as a lucky man in that respect. He worked with people he often came to like. He liked Peter Tenebray, for example, the present head of a four-generation family of some substance in a small northern Minnesota town called St. Fursey.

He knew exactly how Peter regarded him, John Rubrick, because it was precisely how John designed for Peter to see him. Peter took him for someone more estimable than the shallow-hearted pool of executive-level technocrats whom Peter shuffled among. Peter admired John. Peter took him for someone who had graduated from either St. Cloud State or Bemidji State. Peter apologized gracefully each time for not remembering which it was. After four or five times, a few years ago, John only smiled back at him and forbore to repeat that his alma mater was the University of Minnesota Duluth. Peter had never asked so he didn't know that John had a minor in Art History.

Whenever John quoted Mencken or Edward Murrow or Molly Ivins about America, Peter gave him a curly smile and a small shake of the head. "It's amazing! Amazing, John!" he would say—a comment that said *sotto voce* you just made the perfect allusions of a liberal-arts background.

Even Peter's banal snobbery didn't wreck John's enjoyment of any dinner he could take off the Tenebrays. Today, when John got through with the lunch meeting in Ely with his supervisor, he would take dinner with Peter and Nat Tenebray. Sometimes he ate with the Tenebrays because his supervisor suggested it. Sometimes only because John was passing on 53 or 169. This time it was at his supervisor's suggestion, and John was glad to have pencilled it in.

Peter Tenebray wasn't just an affectionate fellow with a knack at both Thai and French cooking. He was a loving man. Some people lighten your heart merely because you have wandered into a room where they happen to be holding forth. You could have spent the preceding hour deploring that person's naïveté, as John did Peter's, but when you knocked on their door, and they opened, they smiled at you, and their genuine molten bonhomie flowed over you. That was Peter.

Good thing, since John's profession required him to make himself welcome in the homes of his charges. He gave out to everybody that he was unhappily married. This cut down on the personal questions. Only at first did people give tentative invitations: would his wife come, too? John's being a frequent dinner guest meant arriving with more and better gin or single-malt than people expected. He listened to marital miseries. He was occasionally asked for advice in such things. He gave the most generic advice possible.

John's colleagues were of two kinds. There were the toughs, people who looked more vicious, not less, in dinner coats. John saw little of them. His usual associates were upper-level public service and corporate managers. He was seldom surprised, but when he was, it was almost always unpleasant.

John had only recently received an unpleasant shock. An on-site special-program man in his organization had proposed that they dispose of a young kid whom they had hired for sensitive one-time-only work. The eighteen-year-old kid had done the job exactly as instructed. It wasn't a difficult task. All he had to do was roll a body off a truck bed and down a highway embankment into the ditch. All he had to remember was to get her rolled out of the tarp and to replace the tarp in the truck bed, weighted with a spare wheel. The boy had done it exactly as ordered. What's more, the kid's own repulsive sex-offense background ensured he'd keep his mouth shut. John had gone out on a limb urging that they not dispose of him. John's supervisor had listened and, John thought, agreed.

For a week John believed he had saved the kid. Only yesterday, however, he read in *Twin Cities Online* that the boy had died in a tragic highway accident. He felt shaken.

Sometimes when John stood around at a reception somewhere, he heard—especially from young women in one business or another—that some job was a great job "because the *people* were so great." He always commented, that "You got that right: the people make all the difference." In his own work, however, great or not-great people made no difference. He was mildly gratified that Peter Tenebray liked him. Even though Peter patently liked more or less everybody, he clearly preferred John to most. John chose not to feel cynical about it because it was Peter's liking everybody that made him absolutely superb at the work that John and his supervisor gave him. No one did Peter's work better than Peter. Not on either of the Coasts.

Peter was a whitener. He was brilliant at it.

And Peter also was economical for them. They paid him $230,000 a year to do what their consultants in San Diego or Atlanta or upstate New York wanted $600,000 for. Not to mention that the others wanted and gouged them for bonuses and stock options as well. Peter didn't even ask. All Peter wanted was the honoraria they made sure he received, and one oddball thing: he wanted speaking gigs. He wanted to give talks in churches. He wanted to keynote meetings of alumni groups. The man was not a pig, either. He didn't hint for many such speeches. Four or five a year kept him happy.

John was on 169 going to Ely for his lunch meeting. In the car, he languidly asked himself for the *nth* time, how could someone like everyone?

He looked at the snow starting lightly outside, making John think, as snow always did, of his childhood. The thought of childhood made him comment to himself, he hadn't particularly liked the adults of his childhood. He hadn't even had a favorite teacher. Maybe Peter had been brought up in such a loving home that he didn't really know anything *except* (a) love and (b) parlor talk. Whatever the reason, Peter was a first-rate whitener.

John didn't have to worry that Peter might take Natalie off to live in Boston or New York to work for serious dollars. Peter loved his family background in that rundown little hole of St. Fursey. John had known for decades that either love of your hometown, or love of your family, could have you by the balls—even if the town was doomed and both parents dead. Peter had recently shown John a nearly invisible patch job on his grandfather's old Rockefeller desk. The desk itself had to be worth tens of thousands. Just the patch job, those two satin-smooth joins, had to have cost thousands. Peter had laughed, "—Of course!....if it hadn't been his grandfather's desk....he might not have..." The man hung fire, to see if John would jeer. Jeering would not have been a mistake John would make: "I like your values," John told him solemnly, his fingers still caressing the patch. "Other men wouldn't see the point," John had added. Peter looked so pathetically grateful that John told himself, I am not so nice a person as Peter. Perhaps that was an advantage of not being born with a silver portfolio stuffed in your mouth.

When he had first started getting jobs for Peter to do, he didn't bother to interpret why he enjoyed the man, and even Nat. He even got a kick out of that sharp-tongued daughter of theirs, with all her evident disappointments in life. It was a great thing to go to the Tenebrays' for dinner, period. Peter might be a flyover provincial prince but he was princely, and the whole family were kind of a hoot as families go—the princely, naïve, motor-mouth dad, the drunken wife, and the sharp fox of a daughter. They all just naturally and frequently did *noblesse oblige* with one brain tied behind their backs.

Natalie Tenebray clearly couldn't stand him. John was proud of that. She was smart. John felt that she realized *he* was smart in some way that Peter was dumb. So she disliked him. He hoped she wasn't so smart that she got to realizing that John did sophisticated, grown men's work, part of which was that he *ran* Peter. It wouldn't matter if she came to such a conclusion, but it was preferable that she stay blinking, hostile, low-buzz drunk.

Over a decade ago, his supervisor had said, "Is that something we should be taking into consideration—the wife? Drinks and all, anything else?"

John had let himself appear to be thinking it over. Then he said, "No, she will be all right."

Natalie was one of those people who got called attractive when actually they were quite beautiful. In American or Japanese business, however, it was not vital that an executive have a *beautiful* wife, whereas it was absolutely vital she be in the category called *attractive*. John thought, when Natalie stayed on her feet or in her seat, and didn't slide under the table during dessert, she was more than just witty and mean as a witch with ten moves for every one of her husband's. John loved to look at her. The fair, thickly waved and shining hair was as good as a girl's. The dark, blue-green eyes under carefully arched eyebrows looked at you with a startling directness. No spillage of sentiment there. Maybe she was no

more than a civilly spoken Midwestern wife and mother who could get
a mixed bag of a community chorus to outdo itself once a year—maybe
that's all old Nat was good for—but he doubted it. He read her as the
kind of alcoholic who develops a pattern you just needed to keep an eye
on. It would worsen, of course, but only slowly. He knew, from happenstance comments of Peter's, that although she routinely drank herself into
a heavy nap on one or another of their guest room beds, she always rose
to the occasion when needed.

Even John's supervisor regarded Tenebray as a genius at whitening.
"How'd you find that fellow?" he said. "Worth his weight in gold. No, don't
tell me. I don't want to know where you got him. Wherever you got him
from, he could be lecturing at twenty-five thousand a shot at Wharton
or Darden or the Harvard B School or somewhere. Can he do anything
besides whitening? No—don't tell me, I know he can't."

"Oh yes he can though!" John had laughed. "He can cook salmon,
Thai or Norwegian, and his crème brûlée doesn't break apart."

When John listened to Peter's speeches or read his essays, he felt as
if all the world was basically good-hearted. If whatever corporation Peter
was hired to whitewash had got into a jam, it disguised it as a forgivable
error, and very much the lesser of two evils. Peter could actually make
fraudulent advertising and criminal refusal to remove carcinogens from
the market look like a human response to unkind pressure—very unkind
pressure. Worse come to worst [Peter would say] a corporation's leaders
had all they could do to rub together two nickels in a society so depraved
that it was hard to meet their responsibilities to their shareowners at all.

At 2:30 John reached the cafe in Ely. Ely was everyone's idea of a
beautiful northern town. It had three products to endear itself to tourists
at loose ends: stores with imported Scandinavian sweaters, stores with
weapons for killing large game as well as mallards, and restaurants for
both steak eaters and ethnic gourmets.

John and his boss took a front center table, not a cozy booth toward the rear where spies would meet one another if Ely had industrial
or government spies. No one in their right mind would conduct sensitive business at a table like this one, right up front, right out in the open.
People, therefore, would take you for sales reps, John's trainer had told

him decades ago. A second piece of industrial psychology from long ago: while you're eating there, at your central table right up front, in your suit and tie and all, just slouch slightly: you looked like someone more comfortable in knitted clothes than woven, but the firm you do technical support for ordered a three-piece suit on the job. If people *still* seemed in the least interested in you, chew gum. Gum, John's trainer told them at the start, was to clothes what caraway seed is to rye bread. If you make white bread and put in caraway seed they take it for rye. If you wear Armani and chew gum, the Armani changes into Wal-Mart. Anyone who chews gum is delivery-boy-made-good who never got it that gum, and the spit to go with it, made the glue that glued the glass ceiling firmly onto the top of your head.

They ordered. They talked about four or five new out-sourced public relations principals. When they got around to John's work with Peter, the supervisor told him he had just found out last night, actually, from its CEO, that the mid-sized chemical engineering group called Wrack had lost a promising young fellow from St. Fursey, Minnesota. The man had quit. A man whom Tenebray had recommended to them three-plus years ago.

John set down his coffee. "Vern Denham," he said. "Was that employee a fellow named Denham?" He decided the least poisonous menu item today was a patty melt.

The Wrack president had apparently told John's supervisor they wouldn't mind much, since God knew the United States economy was a hirer's market, except for the fact that they had liked this man, Vern Denham. They had been keeping an eye out for nice upper-end niches for him to work into—but he ups and quits.

John said, "They know why?"

His supervisor went on. The Wrack man had told him not only had Denham up and quit, what they didn't like was that he was the third person of four who had quit, all recently, and all for the same reason.

"Wait a sec," John said. "You said the third of four, and he just quit this last Friday. Has someone else quit *since*?"

The supervisor nodded. "I asked him about that. This president of Wrack is not one of your more elegant guys, but I've always liked him. I asked him, were we talking dirty towels in the men's or what? That was supposed to be funny. Well, it wasn't. He felt beat up about it. He said that Denham quit because of 5 Lab—and after he quit, get this, John—*after* he quit, their vice-president for some sort of H.R. drivel, the officer who terminated Denham, apparently walked herself over to 5 Lab, used her override, and had a look in the science rooms. She'd already e-memoed in about Denham, at 4:30. At 5:30, she sent another memo that just said, 'That does it, you guys. Count me out, too.' The president was in Washington that week, but was accessing mail. He felt worked up, and he tried to telephone. By then, everyone was gone for the weekend, so he sent her an e-letter and got a audio back that said she had terminated with Wrack Chemical Company. Now here's what's funny about this, John. That particular woman was hard as nails. I mean hard as nails. In fact, I met her at one of those tomfool Christmas parties and the Wrack pres said, 'Oh, hey, there's a woman I want you to meet,' so we went over and he introduced me and after a while she and I were talking a little, and one thing led to another, you know, hell, a Christmas party. Suddenly she twisted my ear. Twisting your ear, that's very different from you decide to give a pretty woman a treat and she hauls off and slaps you, which everyone can see and hear, but that isn't what this pretty lady did. All skinny, all in black with spangles, that cat—she twisted my ear like a Marine and nobody sees it and there I was with my eyes filling with tears and the pain was out of sight. I actually couldn't speak. Somebody came by spilling their drink and slurred something about 'Lady, your boyfriend's crying' and do you know what she said? I couldn't even see but I could hear. She told him, 'I know, his pet rabbit died and here it is Christmas and he really liked that rabbit.' Then there was a little group of them gathered around, saying 'His pet what? What'd it die of?'

"Well, the Wrack president is just a chemist, he doesn't know how to top-hire anyone. He supposed he had a sure thing in that woman, an attorney of the vicious persuasion. Smart and businesslike. Businesslike, to a simple chemist, means you hire someone for human resources and they do human resources; they don't prowl around other parts of a completely different building where they don't work. At Wrack, that means they stay out of 5 Lab and if they hear rumors about 5 Lab, they don't give a damn.

The CEO would have sworn this one was sound, but no. She had accepted the resignation of one Vern Denham, and what's more, she had paid attention to Denham's reason for resigning, and although he had never been her idea of a promising corporate leader, she had trotted around to 5 Lab herself to have a look. She took time, what's more, to glance here and there at two years' worth of the lab journals, thanked the attendant, and handed the books back. He had laid them down on top of some terminated subject's back on one of those scoop 'em pans of theirs, and she went back to her office to send this e-mail. All about cruelty to animals and so on and so on."

John hadn't been eating. Now he went at his patty melt with fork and knife, giving himself time to think. Three of the four quitters had been promising executive potential recommended by Peter Tenebray. John knew that Peter felt some affiliation with Wrack Chemical. He had done an excellent public enhancement job for them in 1999. Peter would have visited around the company facilities in the usual troubleshooting way, talking to delivery boys on up, getting the human feel of everything. He would have been told as a matter of course that 5 Lab was sensitive, but like a gentleman, he wouldn't have asked seeking questions: 5 Lab would have been a side-problem to work around. The Wrack crowd had been pleased with Peter's visit, John knew from his own telephone conversations at the time. John had come in for some praise, too, since he had found them this fellow to address their image needs.

The supervisor looked grave. He said, "Maybe we can't use whiteners as recommenders for jobs. Maybe whitewashing wrecks their judgment. Or maybe just your Peter Tenebray is someone we need to drop. I'd hate to, though. I like his attitude very much."

"I do, too. Peter's genuinely nice," John said, in as casual a tone as he could manage. "If you've laid a tarp over a dead body, he doesn't lift a corner to give himself a buzz."

"Right!" laughed the supervisor. "I know he's awfully good at the job. And he's your man. I guess I was only wondering. Well, all in all, what do you think, John?"

His supervisor's lunch choice was even unhealthier than John's. He was working his way through a gigantic Reuben slavered over with melted USA rat cheese and underlaid with grease-soaked onion slices.

John wasn't easy in his mind at being asked, all in all what did he think? That particular question, he'd come to realize, most often meant not that a policy opinion was being asked for, but that a policy opinion had just *been acted on*. Not always. He decided to use what time he might still have.

"Two qualities I find especially useful in Peter," he said. "First, he never fails to act like a member of some long family line of someones, who are all living off the increment that someone further back was smart enough to accumulate. The family gets more civic-minded every generation until you get to Peter. It's genuine. He genuinely likes civic duty. Now if there is anyone who hates trouble it is someone like that. Peter will never stir up any trouble for us." John, conscious of a sudden ingenious insight, said, "Peter won't even ever stir up trouble in his own family."

John recalled how Peter had confided to him about his grandson four years ago. The daughter, Imogen, had apparently married an egotistical piece of work. Peter and Natalie stood by him because his wife was their daughter, and daughter was family. The couple had a baby boy. When that child was less than a year old the father and some friend of his went boating on one of the exhausted open pits that had been allowed to fill with water. Somehow the young men had allowed the child to fall overside and drown. They said they had simply frozen—become unable to move with horror. What had struck John was that Peter, in his telling, had clearly urged his daughter to *forgive* her husband for this tragic death. Not once, but several times. He had talked to her and talked to her. He had often mentioned it to John.

John had not been surprised that Peter talked and talked. Peter was a talker. He had failed with his daughter, however. Imogen Tenebray divorced the husband and moved to Duluth, where her job was. When she finally did move back to St. Fursey, she didn't take the home offered her by her parents, but moved into a nearly derelict building full of rentals. At least Peter had been able to talk her into accepting major fixing up. He sprang for a handsome, huge window overlooking the meadow west of town. She sometimes came to gatherings at Peter's house—which was where John met her.

John said, "I am telling you all that to show you how serious he is about keeping the peace, even when there isn't much peace to keep. He just isn't going to stir up trouble."

The supervisor started to interrupt.

John said, "Let me make a second point about him."

"Of course."

John said, "Peter has an addiction. In my experience, addicts never get out of line. He would no more get out of line with me than an alcoholic would bomb a liquor store."

John's supervisor said in a casual tone, "What are we talking about here? Some kind of personal attraction to you, John?"

"Nothing like that," John said. "It's speeches."

"What's *that* mean?"

"Peter loves to give talks. He *loves* to. He doesn't just like to. He *loves* to."

The supervisor said, "Good God, I'd do anything not to give a speech!" He paused. Then he said, "Anyway, how does that work into our picture? I know he does good speeches for just about all our clients. He manages to scoop them out of the deepest gutters. But if we have to, we can use other people for that."

"I didn't mean that," John said. "I meant, if I can keep getting him nice gigs here and there—nice meaning preferably East coast—he will never swerve off course."

John now relaxed. He felt that the whole problem had wobbled back into safety, like a blind person caught by the arm at the edge of a chasm.

The supervisor repeated, "Speeches! Good God! What I wouldn't do not to give a talk!"

"I know," John said. "Me, too. Peter is very different from you and from me, both."

"Keep talking," his supervisor said.

"This may sound nuts but I think it's sound. The man loves virtue and he practices a lot of it."

"Be sure not to describe any of it to me!" the other grinned. "I hate virtue. It causes more just plain outright cruelty than any other Boy Scout thing around."

John Rubrick smiled lightly. "I think you're right, but there's a kink in Peter Tenebray's liking for virtue. He likes virtue so much that he believes everyone has a good deal of basic virtue in them. He literally believes that. One of those people who basically thinks Hitler would have been OK if he had just gone to a Rudolf Steiner school and not got so many beatings from his dad. Tenebray really does think that all the bad folks need is to have a chance to develop a taste for the *res publica* and they will respond and become noble men. That's what he thinks. Example: he thinks he and his wife are working on her alcoholism and making progress. 'Working on her drinking problem!'"

"Jesus," his supervisor said appreciatively.

John went on. "Old Peter also has had good cash flow all his life, so it doesn't really occur to him that a lot of people do what they do because they *have* to get their hands on some money within a given period of time. That never crosses his mind. If you told him that's how people live, scraping along from crisis to crisis, he'd looked pained. He'd say, 'Boy, I so much hope you're wrong about that, John.' Whenever I tell him *any* bad news of why people do what they do, he looks at me as if I were quoting from Wikipedia.

"This genuine belief in virtue now," John's supervisor said. "I'm glad I don't see more of it than I have to. It makes me nervous. It can be very hard to read. Very hard to get a bead on—well, so where's all this going?" the supervisor said. "I feel kind of stuffed into a Sunday School. I want out."

John leaned forward. "When Peter Tenebray takes on a whitewash, he believes that he can present that company's interests in the light of that company's good intentions and potential good behavior. He sees himself as a sort of God-driven defense attorney for a serial killer who, he believes, did not mean to hurt anyone. That's his view!"

The supervisor had looked ready to sneer, but now his expression steadied. "Christ," he said quietly.

"Bring you fellows anything?" their waitress said, hovering.

"More coffee, if you would," John's supervisor said.

John said, "I'd keep Tenebray. Don't worry. If he suddenly listens to a critical mass of what his little circle of young people's try to tell him, so any of it sinks in, that will be time enough to take steps."

The supervisor said, "OK. I will think about it some more. I have begun thinking about this. "

"Oh? Do I know about that?"

Instead of replying his supervisor said, "You had some further point you were going to make? Why we should keep him on?"

John said, "Yes—it's the basic logic behind how Peter works. The reason he is such a good whitewash is that he can't distinguish bad from good. He never *sees* evil, so to speak. Excuse the Sunday School language. Let's say, he seldom has any 'concerns' because he always feels that anything wrong anywhere is a temporary glitch, and if you give it some effort and are personable to everyone involved, everybody will join at some level to make things work out."

The older man, with his lined, cynical face, kept stirring his coffee. "Sounds like a nun." He looked up at the waitress, who had returned, "That's the best coffee I've had in a long time."

"Thank you, sir."

The supervisor said, "OK, John. I am going with your proposal. Tenebray stays on the long leash. I am going to assume that no little silvery snail trail will lead from this Vern Denham quitting thing to Peter Tenebray to you, and from you to me, and from me to the others. To our team. I am going to assume that."

"It'll be fine," John said. "I wonder if you can do me a favor?"

"God, this is horrible coffee. Us and the Chinese. We make terrible coffee somehow. What's the favor you want?"

John said, "I have been trying to get Peter some speaking engagements in New Hampshire, Vermont, and Massachusetts. Those are his favorite places. I've dropped the idea to various people, but I haven't been able to make anything happen so far. Could you get him a couple of speeches? Then I will tell him about them—and he'll be glad."

The supervisor smiled and said. "What do you want me to do that you haven't already wangled?"

"His old school, say. Here's three kinds of things I'd like to get him: I would like to get him a respite-sermon for some already-overworked interim pastor in New Hampshire or some place beautiful like that—you know, the white spire and the nice people who he'd relate to, old New

England types. I'd like to get him the sermon for some Sunday in say January or February when the interim minister would want to take off skiing with friends. Second: maybe this is too much to ask. Could you get him a kind of community-life sermon, you know, from the point of view of a businessman, at Phillips Brooks House? Peter was a Harvard man. He would love it. And finally, do you know anybody at Andover who would put Peter on a Visiting Committee of some sort, so maybe he could piggy-back a Sunday talk in the chapel there? I have been looking at a pile of old Andover *Bulletins* from around the time of Peter's class, trying to figure out if any of those classmates were active in the alumni association and could be called to include Peter for any reason. I haven't got any real handle there at all."

A very familiar look came over John's supervisor's face. It was an expression John knew well. He had even used such a look himself. The look said, You have just asked me a question that calls for senior statesmanship—which I have—and I can and I will help you. I have what it is that you're needing but can't do—and I am about to offer it. I am offering it in the spirit of collegiality. It suggested, be grateful. But it also said, I am a nice person, and I am genuinely happy to do you a favor.

Aloud, the other man said, "I'll poke around. I know I can give you the Andover visit more or less immediately. I think there won't be any trouble about the church. Unitarian be OK? Or does it have to be Episcopal or UCC or something? I'll get back to you on your cell this afternoon so you can tell him tonight at dinner. We did agree, didn't we, you're cadging dinner off him tonight? You can even say you expect to hear from the Phillips Brooks people. We will either get him that or we won't, in the next few days."

John smiled appreciatively. "That's fast," he said.

The supervisor said, "It's good you got yourself invited to dinner because you need to talk to him before young Denham gets there, if he's invited, and loads up with liquor so he can tell Peter he's quit the nice job Peter got him. That man is a rolling stone of an idealist. He is always quitting some job because it's too dirty for him."

John now realized that his supervisor had not only known that the Wrack quitter was Vern Denham, but he had already vetted him.

The supervisor continued, "Denham might decide to show up at Tenebrays' and tell all about Wrack Chemical. Here's the ideal case: the ideal case is, you talk to Peter before he talks to Denham. Second part: the No. 1 outcome is Peter makes it clear to Denham that Denham needs to keep his mouth absolutely shut about Wrack just for now, because Peter, old fatherly type that he is, virtuous community leader, means to handle this appalling, inhumane practice at 5 Lab at a very high level—powerful activists in Washington—and finally, the ideal case is: Peter promises that he will keep Denham in the picture as the gratifying results start coming through. But it means Denham shuts his mouth for now. Tenebray expresses gratitude to Denham both for being observant and for having a wonderful moral maturity. But he says to Denham, 'Absolutely leave it to me.' Once he gets all that through Denham's head, then Denham can load up on scotch with the other dinner party guests—but keep his mouth shut. My experience is that once people have decided they are going to do some serious drinking and keep their mouth shut, they feel all geared up with nowhere to go. So they look around for some girl at the party and try to make out instead. Maybe that is tonight's best option for Denham. This plan strike you OK?"

He felt as if the devil had come up to him and said, "Listen, I dyed my horns a brighter red today. Do you think this shade's OK?"

"What's your cell phone number?"

John scribbled his cell phone number onto a deposit slip and held it above their stained cups and saucers. The supervisor leaned forward and read it aloud, without taking it out of John's hands, and said "OK. You haven't changed it." Then he reared up a little to signal the waitress for the bill.

Outside, the snow fell more harshly. It ticked onto the senior man's MacKenzie plaid golf cap, a favorite choice of businessmen going bald. For just a second, John's supervisor looked like an impressionist painting of a pudgy-faced man swinging along on a Midwestern sidewalk. "American in a Snowfall," thought John, "that's what Pissaro would have called it."

He took the back roads to Eveleth. The moment he got onto 53 in Eveleth, his cell phone went off. He picked up the receiver.

"Good news," the supervisor's voice said, thickly, because he, too, was in a car. "Better than I expected. I got you all three talks—two firm, one tentative." He described the speeches.

"Perfect," John said.

They talked over the contact people and addresses and John felt cheered. He would make a point of getting to Peter's very early, say at five. He visualized asking Peter to set down the mixing bowl or whatever he would be doing for dinner, and give him an even ten minutes in his study. He visualized Peter's delight.

The snow closed in around him. He could barely make out the vague swamp pine forest at either side of his route, but enough other people were driving along the highway, in both directions, so they kept blowing the road clear.

The surface was safe enough for as long as he needed it.

CHAPTER TEN

George and Mercein Herzlich had had a horrible fight over something stupid. George thought, why weren't they fighting about sex or money or how the aging parents of one were selfish whereas the other one's aging parents weren't? That was the kind of thing normal couples fought about, but not he and Mercein. He and Mercein were fighting over her knitting because she was always knitting something for their priest and George took that priest to be the most complacent fool in the world.

Three-day fight or no three-day fight, George got over to the auto lot at his usual time on Wednesday morning.

Today Stan looked gathered and up for the day. He always got down to the dealership very early. He would be eating a deli sandwich in his office and reading over mail until George or Kenny showed up. These days, George sometimes found him lying propped up on Silver's couch, either asleep or awake with the worsening black half-circles under his eyes, and a translucence to his skin.

Today, Stan's expression was merely practical. He was picking off any number of Silver's hairs from his jacket cuffs. George was relieved because he had such bad feelings of his own he didn't want to feel even sadder about Stan. Not here in the man's presence.

Stan asked George to get Mercein and would the two of them drive the Impala up to its new owner in Cook as soon as Kenny'd got it washed.

Stan would come along in an hour and meet them at the Montana and buy lunch. For a couple of years, that restaurant had gone partly yuppie, adding bad-breath art-food and sandwiches from which hummus and bean sprouts leaked onto your Garris Autos jacket. At last, the owners seemed to swing back to solid to regular food. They made hamburgers with one third- instead of one fourth-pound of ground sirloin in them, and they grilled the buns on the same beef-greasy stove. Any lunch there was delicious. The coffee was not so black it reamed out your stomach.

George said, "We could start right now and I'll swing around to that natural-wool sheep outlet up there that Mercein likes so much."

George had two nervous-making subjects on his mind. First, the usual one: he really should look around for a better position than Stan Garris's business offered. He forever turned that problem over in his mind like an old dog with an old tasteless bone.

It seemed to him that each day Stan looked sicker. George decided not to show any of the fear that he felt. He didn't want Stan to die. He also, partly, wanted to quit and get another position in a bigger town, but he couldn't ditch a dying man. He could tell Stan already regarded their friendship as holy. That is, Stan's upcoming death was making things seem holy to Stan. George could tell by how he talked. Then the dog was stolen. Just now Stan didn't need to have his only employee with an IQ over 100 up and leave him.

The other subject was worse. Though he and Mercein had quarreled over three days ago, she was still scarcely speaking to him. The quarrel hung all around them. They went down under its gloom. They moved around each other like rats in a crawl space. It was all George could do to get the smallest household tasks done.

He kept trying to clear up the quarrel—at breakfast, at supper, at breakfast again, and supper—but Mercein wouldn't talk to him. She kept her dining room chair pushed away from the table so that her knitting wouldn't get egg smeared onto it. Whenever George tried to speak, she said, "If you're through eating, you can be excused." He hadn't heard that since they were raising the children.

Now he felt that if he could get into a car with her, he and Mercein would talk it out in the hour and a half to Cook. It would be winter driving. Dull white sky. There was nothing to look at so she couldn't just keep pretending to look out the window. He wondered if she'd bring that damned knitting with her. He couldn't prevent that. But he would make her talk at last.

He had been faithful. He did not regret it, either. Mercein always, always, got to him, some way. She still did, even when she was being a pissant like in these last three days. She did not double-cross the children by talking about them at coffee klatches. She did not double-cross George or do a sidewinder act at New Year's Eve parties, where husbands and wives for some reason would let loose with a lot of mean comments, all feathered back, of course, to sound like hey, just kidding.

Mercein loved their children. That wasn't supposed to be unusual in a mother, but the fact was, George had seen a lot of women go straight gimlet-eyed when their kids came up and asked for something. The kids felt it. George felt it. Thanksgiving wasn't the pathetic sham at their house that other families suffered through. When it was Mercein's turn to have "them"—the relations—for Thanksgiving it was bright-hearted like a TV sit com ad for Thanksgiving.

George was proud of himself, too. He made money without being a sleaze. Once he got a potential used-car buyer out into the back lot, George would sell him the best the fellow could pay for. True, he made good use of The Varmint, but that didn't hurt anybody. The Varmint was a still-good-looking, no-rust Volvo that George and Stan kept parked at the north edge of the slab. Next to The Varmint, when he could, George parked one or another GM vehicle of the same year, or if they happened to have one in, a Volvo that looked older than the Varmint. He and Stan had Kenny move all the cars around every other day or so, so that any regular gawker—and St. Fursey had 10 or 11 of those, even in a hard winter—would get the sense that Garris's dealership kept turning over its used cars. If a genuine customer was looking at anything near The Varmint, George would make sure they saw it. If they paused to eye it, George would say, "Yes, I know. That Volvo is wonderful looking. You don't want that car. The catalytic converter is shot. Someone might repair it, but I doubt it. It's a compacter."

George left it to Stan, as proprietor, to do the major sweetening around the community. He left it to Stan to drop around at big shots' shops and offices—even to drive up to that fancy think-tank resort north of town. Mysterious high-end people—that was for Stan, not George. One of George's particular specialties was knowing which kids in town did good body work and rust removal and painting and which kids in town did good desktop promoting of their body work and their rust-removal and their painting. He tried not to offend any of these kids, because they were the people who didn't leave St. Fursey right after high school. The familiar pattern was a couple of boys would get someone's corrugated shed and believe in themselves for two years. They believed they would make money. Few of them could, but once they had stayed two years in St. Fursey after high school, they tended to stay the rest of their lives. Eventually, they would do business with George, because the poor guys were down to trying to find happiness in driving a nice car. People who failed in automotive, especially in body work, bought more cars in a 20-year period than richer men who didn't know a tire from a doughnut. Actually, these failed young men loved cars. George waited for them.

One of George's side jobs was keeping crooked mechanics, out on their own, from clipping reliable Garris Autos customers. Each year, the number of crooks grew. George stayed on tiptoe. It was easy enough to spot poor auto repair itself. What was a challenge was to figure out which of these sleaze mechanics would subcontract out little jobs George might give them to their incompetent, lazy, or meth-tweaking friends. It was a constant surprise to George how some really good worker, who had actually got signed off on On-Board Diagnostics or Transfer Cases at a real school, would think he had to do a favor for a slob friend. So George steered his used-car customers to the good kids. The bad kids sometimes came to the Garris Autos lot to beg outright.

They would arrive in their matched work clothes, light khaki shirts and pants, and offer George the latest cards they'd had printed up. Before Silver got stolen, they would praise her. They would approach her sofa with soft expressions. Silver, however, loved only three or four people in all, so she would lay her ears flat back, and wait. "Yeah, well, nice girl," the young cons would say, and back off before she went for their fingers.

"Yeah, but George, I mean Mr. Herzlich," one of them said the last time. "How about you give our card to some people you sell inventory to?"

"No, you guys, no, no, no," George said, "Not just because you told Imogen Tenebray she had a faulty windshield when she didn't, and you charged her to replace it with a new one, when all she needed was for you to press around the edges to re-firm the bond on the perfectly good one she had. And how do I know you bought her a new one? You probably just left hers in and charged her for a new one—after you pressed around the bond of the one she had. Not just that. You tried to sell Walt Steinzeiter two resonating pipes in the same year. It's a wonder he didn't flatten you. I'll say this for you guys. You're brave enough. Do you have any idea what would happen to you if a 300-pounder like Walt decided he was irritated with you?"

George sometimes told Mercein his adventures with crooks. She had a very satisfactory hatred of criminality. She would pretend to be shocked: how could those boys have turned out so bad when she had known their mothers back when, in Christian Mothers or CCD? She would press George for all the details. She had a sparkle to her when she was disgusted.

All cute women had a causticness about them, George thought. They were not zombies who talked out of eight sides of their mouths.

But now he and Mercein had quarreled in such a stupid way.

He felt galled that only he, not she, seemed to be oppressed by it. Perhaps he was galled because he was the one who had started it.

They had been sitting at breakfast. He said, "Honey, is that *another* chasuble for Father?"

She laid down the lugubrious dark green knitting. Her eyes got motionless and bright.

He said, "All that knitting for Father makes me feel stupid."

That was all he had said. Was that so bad?

She pointed out in a practical tone that she had knit him, George, so many sweaters and Fair Isle vests and Settesdal koftes and Icelandic windbreakers and Turkish three-end-knitted ethnic socks that there wasn't anything more she could knit for him. She had knit four sweaters each for their boys, who now lived all over the United States. She had knit baby blankets for all sorts of Christian Mothers groups whom she didn't even like very well. She had fitted out all her and George's grandchildren with buntings and blankets and toddler sweaters. Was he saying, she asked, that he was jealous? Jealous of their priest? All because she wanted to see if a chasuble *could* be knitted at all? Perhaps chasubles had to be woven, because they were so heavy.

George repeated, "It's only that it makes me feel stupid."

But then he made a second mistake. He explained that there were two sorry muddles a man didn't want in his wife—first, no one wanted their wife to fall in love with the doctor who attended the birth of her first child, and second, no one wanted their wife to hang around whoever the current pastor was. It made George's skin crawl, just thinking about it.

She looked up when he said that about his skin crawling. He allowed it was probably a mistake to mention that.

Mercein then gave him a perfectly balanced look, straight and cold, like old weight scales in a hardware. She rose with huge dignity. She went outdoors to lay their climbing rose into its trench for the winter.

George watched from the dining room window, while she competently dumped spadeful after spadeful of chill dirt on top of the thorns and leaves.

At their next meal, he tried to apologize, but Mercein said she didn't care to hear whatever it was he thought he was going to say.

She went on with the chasuble. The damned thing was in green, too—meaning she'd been carefully thinking ahead and was allowing herself enough time before Trinity season when the church color would be green. He thought she'd chosen a remarkably dirty green, too. That damned clumsy thing looked like the shelter half his dad had been issued in the army. They weren't even in Advent yet which meant that that dark muck-green pile was going to be around his house, bloused up on one or another chair seat for months.

The worst aspect of it all was that she wasn't knitting miserably. She was happy. He couldn't get through to her. Yesterday, then, when they were beginning their fourth supper in silence, he flung at her, "If you ask me, you're too old to still be working with Christian Mothers!"

He had counted on her bursting into tears at such blaring cruelty.

Mercein gave a disdainful glance at his uneaten supper and remarked, "I'll bring your dessert." She had been knitting with her chair pushed back from the kitchen snack table. She laid aside her current skein and the bulky chasuble. She brought out a single piece of chess pie from the refrigerator.

"I had better put some ice cream on it," she said, as if she were offering to take care of a mistake some puppy had made on the carpet.

That was yesterday, dammit.

Today, George now told himself, we will *have* to talk to each other on this car ride.

The vehicle Stan wanted him to deliver still had the new-car smell of vinyl and metal cleaning agents. For all the thousands of times George had climbed into new cars, he still noted and loved the smell. Garris Autos policy was to leave in the paper foot protection for its delivery so that no workmen's boots would muddy the floor fabric. George wouldn't take those away until they had got the car into their customer's own driveway. He thought about the nice drop cloth he kept so that Mercein could rest her yarn and knitting project on the floor without getting it dirty. He went to transfer it from his car to the Impala. He stopped. She wants it, she can just ask, he said to himself. The shock of their quarrel was gradually wearing off. He felt himself no longer freshly wounded. He thought up vengeful things to say.

He drove from the lot to his home to pick up Mercein. He opened the house door and shouted, "You ready?" There he was, ready to pick her up in the new sale.

Then he clapped his mouth shut. Another woman stood next to his wife, coat in hand. It was Pearl, the ecumenical chorus accompanist and casino gambler. Pearl also managed the VFW lounge. In all three of her occupations, what Pearl was known for was an uncertain temper.

Mercein said in a sparkling, purely hostile tone, "Pearl wanted to go along for the ride." She sailed past George, carrying her bag which he felt, gloomily, was heavy with that chasuble. She was dressed up, he saw, but not for him. Dressed up *against* him, if anything.

Mercein wasn't wearing her usual slacks and home-knits. She wore her deep rose woolen suit and under it, a wide-necked deeper rose blouse of silk. He knew that she had put on that silk—silk with all its chic—the way an officer would decide on full decorations. She went around to the passenger side and sat down with great delicacy.

He couldn't help telling her she looked pretty. Pretty, shit. She was stunning.

He said, "You look pretty."

She gave him a sniff.

They took off. George could see in the rearview mirror that Pearl, in the back seat, was gazing balefully out at the wintry day. Mercein had moxie. What inspired her to pick up that Pearl for this trip? Just meanness is what. He had heard that if you got hold of Pearl at the right moment, she could tell more gossip than anyone else from the Iron Range down to the Twin Cities. She was what church committees called a supply organist. You called her up when your regular organist had failed you. Pearl knew more filth than anyone else about everybody, no matter which church they went to or didn't go to, and her guesses about the real meanings that might lie behind local happenings were very engaging. She was unstinting with her speculations, too. Pearl never said, "Go figure" or "How would I know?" or "You have to kind of wonder, don't you?" She never, ever wondered about anything. For example, Pearl hadn't minded saying that the dead kid the police had found along highway 53 last week had probably been killed by someone from that big-shot think tank in the woods north of town. People at the VFW had immediately snorted. Now why would those smart people do something like that? Pearl had sneered right back, "If I knew why big shots in think tanks do what they do, I would lick every house in every casino at blackjack."

Pearl had been the first person in town to know that the deputy cop was terrified someone might hit him in his face.

Now how would she know that?—the guys laughed as they asked because it was satisfying to think of a cop being chicken, so chicken a woman noticed. That cop had tried out for state trooper, didn't make it, worked security for a while at a casino. While he had that job Pearl had seen him. "Who, him?" she was supposed to have said, getting out cold beers for people at the VF. "Not much there," she then remarked.

She passed bowls of chips and nuts across the counter. "Nope," she'd said thoughtfully. "Not much there." Not much of what was the question—brains, perhaps she meant—or perhaps she meant not much manhood. No vital signs, perhaps she meant. Whatever she meant, it came from her own authoritative repertoire of loathsome humanity. Pearl was like seawater pollution of a given specific gravity: she swayed suspended at that given level under the surface of St. Fursey society. She recognized the other creatures moving around lethargically at her level. She had an eye for creatures of like density. *She* herself wasn't going anywhere. She could spot other people who weren't going anywhere. Between the occasional witticism at someone's expense, and once or twice striking a cop, once assaulting a casino goer, even, Pearl seemed to live partly in a trance. A low-level sour-mindedness clung to her. It began to permeate the mood in the new car.

Well, OK, Pearl, George thought, as he took an occasional glance at her in the rearview mirror, all I ask is don't do anything to mess up the back seat of this new vehicle. I don't own it.

Once George got them established going north on 53, Mercein took out her knitting and appeared engrossed in solving some problem with it. She had the directions and the yarn spread out on top of the safety balloon panel on her side of the dash. She spoke to the knitting pattern in a low, bored voice, like a test pilot repeating specs to a tape. "Kl K2 to-gether, all right," she ground out, "OK, if you say so, if you say so. Ask me, though, that is going to be lumpy. OK. Let's run this past us again. Kl K2 together for the first 12 stitches," she repeated.

George gave up on any possibility of talk. The car ran beautifully under a viscous sky. The sky's faint light was more like the gleam of stone than air.

George grew bored. Maybe he could rouse Pearl to say some unpleasant thing.

"Hey, Pearl," he said into the rearview. "How do you like that sky? Think it means snow?"

She said, "Naw. Just your typical shit weather for this time of year."

Then Pearl leaned forward between their seats. "Your gas tank's awfully low, George."

Idiot of an upset husband that he was, George had not remembered to check it. The dash was flashing amber.

"I'll stop in Etheridge," he said.

He pulled in alongside a three-pump island he thought he recalled the owner of—a young fellow who had bought an old Jetta that Stan had taken in trade. The man wasn't there, however. Through the station window, George saw only a woman covering the register, and a customer investigating the cold-drinks cabinet, probably the one who owned the Buick on the other side of the fuel island. In the office back doorway to the garage, George made out some mechanic's feet jerking on the dolly under their lift.

He replaced the pump handle and went in to pay.

"I'm on four," he told the woman leisurely. Over her head he read the Minnesota lottery figures and the Powerball, one hundred and thirty-one million today.

But the woman's head jerked up from the till and she shouted, "Hey! Hey! Hey!"

George spun around to see what she was shouting about.

Garris Autos brand new Chevy Impala was tearing out fast past the pumps, tires screeching. At least the fuel pump handle wasn't dragging.

George lit out, the station server right after him. When he had got out into the middle of the second lane, where he had fueled up, he caught sight of his car stopped about a hundred feet away, engine running.

He ran over. Pearl was sitting in the driver's seat. She dropped the window. "Just get in, George, and move it!" she snapped.

Mercein was now in the back. George went around front and got into the passenger's side.

Pearl clumped her elbow on the all-door lock and glanced in the rearview mirror.

"Oh oh," she said mildly. A man was closing on them. He lurched right up to the driver's side and pounded both hands on the glass.

"Oh no—not on this new Chevy," George howled and started to get out his side.

"Stay put!" Pearl told him.

She lowered her window and said to the man in a lyrical tone,

"Would it be OK if I explained to you what I am doing? I mean before you wreck my new car and smash my face? Would that be OK? This is my first time ever to drive a good new car. I have saved up for this car for four and a half years and today I bought it. I run out of gas on my first trip because the company is too chintzy to give me a tankful. I get it filled. So the shifting is new to me, so I make a mistake and go forward when I was trying to just check out that it was in park. So I finally get it going. This is the first time in my life I have ever owned any new vehicle. And have I got this right, some totally strange clown—you tell me if I have this right—some totally strange clown like you comes along and—although I like your suit," she interrupted herself. "I like that kind of nubbly rough tie very much. I always think that heavy texture is so much better than the shiny stuff. You come along and go crazy trying to break my window! On a new car! Please, mister. That is so *mean*! What I don't understand is, why would you want to *be* like that, so mean?"

The fellow's features contorted. "Ma'am," he said. "I am so sorry. It's just that someone just stole my new hunting dog and when you took off like that, I guess I just thought it was you."

Pearl narrowed her eyes. She spoke very slowly. "I would put a filthy flea-infested dog in my new car? That is some kind of joke?"

"I'm sorry," he said. Still, his eyes were wandering over to George in the front seat and then to what he must have taken for a chilled old lady bundled up under a dark green afghan in the back.

"I'm sorry," he said and he backed up, but still shaking his head.

Pearl flashed him a blazing smile. "OK to go now, officer?"

"Oh goll," he said. He raised a weak hand.

Infinitely gently, Pearl lowered the lever to Drive4 and the Chevy moved out to the farthest end of the service station lot. They had to wait for traffic to get by.

Pearl told the others, "We'll circle around and then come back, and George, you can pay the bill. You got a cell phone, George? Call that station if you know the number, and tell them we're returning to pay the bill, but we'd really appreciate it if they would get that crazy sex molester off the lot before we stop and open a car door."

Mercein had taken on new life. She swung her head 180° left, then right, looked out all the windows, like someone riding shotgun.

Pearl said, "When you were in there, you see anybody you know, George?"

"The guy I know who owns that place wasn't there."

"Well, then," she said, "this is your twice-lucky day."

She got onto the highway, made two turns onto a back road, made another turn, which took them into the service fueling area again. The woman cashier and the distraught-looking mechanic were now both standing out in front.

Mercein said from the back seat, "You'd better go on and do the bill paying, George. If I were you, I would tell them that was the last time you were going to get into a car with a crazy new car owner, period."

George didn't know what Pearl and Mercein were up to but whatever it was, it was the end of over three days of silent temper from Mercein. For a split second he even wondered, was it possible that women got as bored with ordinary life as men do, so they, too, are glad when just any damned thing happens? He felt springy, all of a sudden—really springy.

George stepped out of the car. "I've come to pay the pump," he said to the attendant and the mechanic.

George decided he would pay cash, all things considered. He brought out his best sheepish tone, with a fool's grin, and said, "Look, guys, do me a favor, will you? Don't even ask me what happened."

What the attendant and the mechanic saw was a handsome grey-headed man who had kept himself as trim as a gentleman. In a very high-end, very new car he had one middle-aged woman and one older-middle-aged woman, both of them smiling pretty strangely, probably mental, the both of them.

"The wife?" the mechanic asked, sympathetically.

Back out in the Impala, no one said anything.

As soon as they got clear and northbound out of Etheridge, Pearl made a left turn onto a county highway, 44.

"No," George said. "We stay right on 53 the whole way."

Pearl said, "We stop here on this road because I am going to catch my breath. And while I am catching my breath, your wife can tell you what happened. Then we will trade places, only I will sit in front and

Mercein can stay back there, and catch fleas and what all else crap from that animal."

George turned around.

Mercein pushed away the chasuble and said, "OK, Silver, you don't have to *stay* any more."

Stan Garris's stolen Labrador immediately leapt forward. She picked her way over the gear panel to kiss George, the second favorite person of her life. She planted her bottom and her powerful back haunches in his lap.

They told him how it had gone. They had caught sight of Silver in the car at that next fueling lane. The owner seemed to be gazing at the Powerball and Minnesota Gopher 5 strips in the station office.

They decided to make things simple. They just opened the back door of his car and the back door of the Impala and told Silver to come.

In the Impala, Pearl told Mercein, "I don't like dogs. You get in back with her and I'll drive us out of here." She ran to the front. Mercein told Silver to stay, and kept petting her. She made Pearl pass her back the knitting. She grabbed the chasuble. One of its dangling in-the-round type needles dropped 140 stitches off the left side. Mercein pulled the needle completely out of the wool, and covered Silver and most of herself with it. Meantime, Pearl had gunned the engine and raced off to the point where George had spotted them.

Now George said, "Honey, you covered up Silver with that, that, that—whatsit for the priest?"

Everyone laughed.

Pearl said, "You let that dog kiss you all over your face like that, George, you're going to have so many diseases come time they won't bury you alongside other people." Pearl got out of the car. George made Silver get into the back with Mercein. As he adjusted the rear view mirror and Pearl did up her seat belt, he heard Mercein say, "Oh no you don't, Silver; you don't drool on that new customer's car seat. Here. You have to drool, you drool on that chasuble."

All the rest of the way to the Montana Cafe the three of them traded opinions on what Stan Garris would do, and what he would say, when he came breezing into that restaurant and saw his friends and his dog waiting for him.

CHAPTER ELEVEN

Eliza, the Rector of St. Fursey Church, was like anyone about to be fired: she felt fired already.

Behind the church's altar, she emptied both the inhumane mouse trap and the humane one with its rope. To empty the inhumane one you grab the little beast by its tail, pry up the strangle bar, and drop the mouse out. Easy enough. Arlene, who cleaned the church—or even the catty Flower Rota women—would have been perfectly willing to empty both traps, just as they usually did, but Eliza now wanted the job herself.

The garroted mouse she took into hands. She noticed its exquisite ears and astounding silky coat. She laid it on the entrance-table tracts while she put her coat on.

As for the live, or so-called humane trap, she raised its tiny portcullis just outside the church door so its victims went free into the crouching, frozen hosta—this instead of carrying both trap and its prisoners to St. Fursey Creek and lowering them to soak for a quarter-hour at the bottom.

It was Saturday morning of what might well be her last week on the job. The Bishop would not show up until eleven. Against church policy, Eliza had agreed to see a young server beforehand. Adults knew enough to leave their rector alone on Saturdays. Katie's wanting to come meant that Eliza was still of some use to someone. What's more, today being Arlene's half-day cleaning at St. Fursey, Eliza meant to have just one more try at getting the poor woman to make a charge against her husband for battering. Brad Stropp was a universal type of a no-good male. He beat his wife. He got fired from nearly every job at the bottom of the town's scattershot places of work. He shot wildlife out of season and without a permit. He had recently killed a Minnesota black bearcub. He battered Arlene every three or four months.

Eliza mooned around outside, between the church and lychgate and rectory, waiting for Katie, waiting for Arlene, dreading the Bishop's visit.

Eliza and her old Seminary pals, especially Bill Plaice, her boyfriend of three years ago, had walked leisurely around grinning over the ironies at this charming little St. Fursey Episcopal Church in its doomed north-woods setting—especially its heart-breaking Poor Box, so old that its wooden top was soft as fur. There were only three such Poor Boxes in the Diocese of Minnesota. Their gapey slots were made for sovereigns, not dollar bills. Bill had said, "Clearly not intended for chewing-gum wrappers."

A little of the snow promised for today now came wavering down.

It was only six days, not years and years, since she had sent the a thousand times ill-advised e-mail letter to the Bishop. In one swoop she ended her career as an Episcopal priest. A loser thing to do.

She was not used to being a loser. Eliza had never been one of the Twin Cities' hang-about loser priests. Younger than most of them—she was only 27 even now—her vanity had never been flattened like the vanity of ordained people whom the Bishop wouldn't give a church to. Diocesan secretaries never treated Eliza the way they treated those casuals who agreed to be part-time chaplains for sheltered shops. She had never been gently, tolerantly, kidded by lay leaders who bounded about the Diocesan meeting rooms and offices on one or another energetic task of the lay ministry. Once through Seabury-Western, Eliza had been immediately installed as rector of St. Fursey's Church, St. Fursey, Minnesota.

She supposed that the Bishop had seen something in her. Well, she had seen something in herself, too. Like any 21st century seminarian, she was partly cynical. Well, this was modern America. Anyone with any grasp of reality had to be cynical. Earnestness was so last year. Perhaps the Bishop no longer cared whether or not his clergy were cynical. Bill Plaice was cynical and he had won the plum—a Twin Cities parish.

Reality check, then: Eliza's college and seminary grades had been high. She herself was beautiful, or at least she was not one of the ever-present, stocky-bodied, good-willed female clerics tramping around the Diocese. She loved nature, especially northern Minnesota forestland, and always had. She didn't crave a Twin Cities parish like most of her classmates. She had said as much in her career statement. The Bishop gave her St. Fursey St. Fursey, as they called it in the trade, identifying each church by its patron and its location.

All that until six days ago.

Now her young server arrived on a bike despite the weather. A half-hour early. Good. Eliza would lightly take care of whatever was bothering Katie and still have a quarter-hour to talk to Arlene the sexton about her options as a battered wife.

Katie locked her bike to the metal sign that read *Rector Only Don't even think of parking here.* Katie was one terrific little kid and whatever she had to say would be as good as it gets from a fourteen-year-old *H.sapiens.*

"Come on, let's go in my study," Eliza said.

She took her office chair and waved to Katie to sit beside the desk rather than opposite. The girl remained standing. Right—classic old bodyspeak for I have a problem which I will lay before you, my rector, but chances are you are too chicken to solve it so I therefore disrespect you. I would take this problem to a psychotherapist or a lawyer but they cost money and you are free. I will therefore remain standing. Eliza read the body language and gave a smile.

Katie said, "Two things, Eliza. First, there is a slob around town you probably don't know because he doesn't go to our church, if they let him in anywhere. His name is Brad Stropp."

Eliza did know about him, though. He was the wife-battering husband of her St. Fursey's Church cleaning woman.

Katie said, "Anyhow, we have had a mother bear and two cubs wandering around the edges of town for the last two weeks. This time of year is when bears feed up so they can sleep out the winter on their own fat. Well, this slob Brad Stropp shot one of the cubs last week and he bragged to someone in the VFW he was going to shoot the other cub if nobody got in his way. You're the priest, Eliza. Will you please do something about this?"

Eliza said, "I am hearing you, Katie. Let's hold that one a minute. What is your second thing?"

Katie said. "Marty Hanks has been rubbing boogers off on the underside of the communion rail. Does he get to do that just because he is one of your servers? Eliza, he is so repulsive."

Katie got that much right.

Eliza said, "About Brad Stropp, Katie. I will talk to the Senior Warden and see what we can come up with."

"I already talked to him," Katie said. "Mr. Tenebray said if he asked the chief of police to trail people like Brad Stropp to keep them from killing wildlife out of season, they would never have time to stop any other crime."

Eliza said, "I'll remind him, again. And about Marty Hanks and the communion rail, I will talk to *him*."

But she felt like the chief of police: if she tried to track young Marty Hanks and keep him from only one or two of the offenses he seemed to commit in a day, she wouldn't have time for any of her other work.

"Look, Katie," she said. "I'm on it. OK? Come on. I'll walk you out."

Katie said, "I was pretty sure there wouldn't be anything you could do about it."

Eliza was cool. "For now, let me just say, I am on it." She stood up and followed Katie out to the bikestand.

Eliza said, "It's Saturday, isn't it, Katie? Are you still building on your tree house?"

Eliza watched while Katie punched a combination lock.

"Do you have to lock the bike, even here in St. Fursey?" she asked.

"Especially here in St. Fursey. Town's full of crooks. Listen, Eliza. You're a priest. You know people suck."

"Still, Katie," Eliza said, as the girl raised a foot to the pedal. "People everywhere are basically good. That's something not to forget. Not ever."

"Sounds good, Eliza. And everyone says it. But what if it just isn't true? What if it's just one more lie?"

But then the girl switched back to being a well-behaved Episcopal-church server with good manners. "Thanks for seeing me, Eliza," she said.

Eliza fled into the rectory to change. She braced herself to talk to Arlene.

Arlene spoke to her as little as possible. Eliza couldn't hide it from herself that the church cleaning woman was a counseling failure of hers.

She heard the nearly-animal scratching at her door.

Eliza said, "Arlene, you have a right to knock a regular out loud-knock like everyone else. Come in! Come in! Come in!"

"I thought you might be busy," she said.

If Eliza were busy, she would have to answer to animal scratchings just as much as answer to an ordinary human knock.

Aloud, Eliza said, "I'm glad you came. Come on in."

Arlene left her bucket with its chemicals and rubber gloves and cloths in the hallway.

"It's about my husband," she said. The bruise that had bloomed roseate on her left cheek last week now showed only a faint yellow, but this morning, there was something covered with Band-Aid on the opposite jaw.

Eliza thought, "What a stroke of luck! Here it's my last chance to get that woman to request a restraining order."

"I don't know what you can do exactly," said Arlene.

Eliza said over again, "You haven't told me, do about what. Exactly what is going on with Brad?"

"It's about that mother bear," Arlene said. "My husband is still sneaking around all over the edges of town trying to kill her and that other cub she still has. He already shot one."

Damn it all. Arlene still wasn't seeking help for the battering.

Eliza said, "I have already gotten a complaint about that and I am going to do something. I will have a word with the police, for starters."

Arlene retied her apron sash. That summer-print apron for cleaning hung in the choir room alongside Eliza's and the servers' vestments. Eliza was proud about it. Her first-class asshole of a parishioner, the father of her first-class asshole of a server, Marty Hanks, had wanted, of all things, that it should be "reflected in the Vestry Minutes" that no sexton's apron should be hooked up there right next to spiritual vestments like Eliza's chasuble and the servers' cassocks and everyone's surplices. People who wanted things "reflected in the minutes!"

"Oh, yes, it should though," Eliza had said. "That's where it's staying, too."

Arlene said now, "I already talked to the chief of police and he probably isn't going to do anything, Eliza. Flat out, he said that."

Eliza said, "He would actually have to catch Brad in the act, gun and all."

"I knew it wouldn't do any good to ask you," Arlene said. She went to the door.

"Arlene, have you got a moment to sit down?"

Arlene turned in a flash. "No, Eliza, I don't have a moment to sit down! I know what you want to talk about! Same as the chief of police! Same as the doctor! You want me to complain against my own husband! Well, if you had a husband yourself, you'd know better!"—and now the woman got out the door and shut it behind her.

Three years of parish work had toughened up Eliza to being a single person in a culture where any single woman of over 21 had less cachet than even a battered wife like Arlene.

She sat on, turning her glance out the gorgeous soldered-paned casement. There was the little glade. There was the salt lick. Snow was falling on it. Beyond the glade stood the evergreen forest, dying off a half-mile on its south edge each year, a gloomy truth you took in only if you were looking for it.

She finally stalked into the nave to change the hymn boards in the usual way. Then she caught sight of Vern, a man who helped his father run the town bakery. She had never actually gone out with him, because they met regularly enough at one of the parish families' nearly weekly buffet suppers. As the fourteen or sixteen, sometimes even twenty, educated Episcopalians went back and forth filling their plates with salmon and cilantro and refilling their glasses they got to know one another. They were the intellectuals scattered around the area. They made up the leadership of St. Fursey Church. Leadership! They were really like small animals warming themselves at the same hearth.

Vern swung up the walk towards her with a huge smile.

He was a man with perfect male beauty. Despite it, he managed not to look vacant. His eyes were prematurely crinkled a little. From the first, he moved her. From the first she watched him while appearing, as she must, not to be looking.

Even though she was clergy, Eliza was gradually eased into the loop of town gossip. She found that Vern Denham was an educated man who now worked in the town's one bakery. The gossip was that he had just left some high-end corporate job in midtown St. Paul for ethical reasons. He strode up the paved stones toward her.

She said to herself, "I knew he would come. I knew he would! Sooner or later."

And so he had. His face blazed, too. With happiness. Unmistakably.

To him, she said, "You hiked down here all the way from your place! You probably feel so fit I bet you don't want to come into any stuffy old rectory! Shall we stand around outside in the snow instead?"

He laughed again. They were at her door. "No! No!" he cried. "What I've got to say is too big! We have to go in!"

She pitched ahead of him, like a harbor tug bringing a huge liner into its slip.

"What a stunner of a view!" Vern said, going fast to the sitting-room window. "This is why we all want to live up here, isn't it? It's the wild forest." He stood there silently.

Her heart was full but also languorous. Let him take his time. This moment in their life would never come for them again. She chose not to go up to the window and stand beside him.

Then he turned around. Since the snow light outdoors was now behind him, she couldn't see his face so well but she felt joy steeping in him.

At last he said, "Well—this isn't really so much church business I came on as a personal thing!"

Inside herself, she felt somber and blessed.

"I'm going to get married, Eliza! Married! And so I've come to find out what needs to happen when an old fallen-away Lutheran like me wants to get married to a dyed-in-the-wool Episcopalian! You will want to instruct us, won't you?"

He gave a tender, furry laugh, with a little thrum to it.

Deep in the engine-room of her mind, Eliza gathered all the discipline and skills she had. She gave Vern what she hoped looked like a beatific smile.

He laughed again, like chiming. "Aren't you even going to ask me who I'm marrying?"

"Of course I am! Of course I am! Who are you marrying?"

"Imogen," he cried. "Imogen Tenebray! I thought you might guess since you see us together so much at the Tenebrays'—those weekend things of her parents."

Eliza got herself across the room perfectly OK. She shook his hand. "Congratulations, Vern," she said. She felt sublime, like someone who has just been shot, but even mortally wounded, can pull off one more good thing. She took his shoulders and gave him a hug.

He had any number of questions to ask, about instructions, baptism papers—his were Lutheran, if he could find them at all, did she mind?—confirmation credentials, what must he do?—she must be wondering, he exclaimed, why he had not brought Imogen, but she had an appointment that day. He wanted to explain every detail.

Eliza did everything she had to do. She shredded a mental picture of herself holding a first child of Vern's and Imogen's for its baptism, and then a second child, perhaps a third even—she stopped herself. She told herself, you need only last another minute. Surely, Vern was ready to get up and go now.

Some more minutes passed. She told herself, perhaps he is just going now. Long before he left, she told herself, maybe he really is done now. Perhaps he will get out. Perhaps he will get out, out, before more minutes go by.

At last he had leapt towards her. His hug struck her the way and-irons grapple and close on a log.

A week earlier she had telephoned down to Minneapolis, to her old seminary pal. Bill said, "Come down! Come down, Eliza! Evening Prayer at 6:30. Then come back to the house and Molly and I will give you supper."

The interstate, 35W, had a slowdown. When Eliza and drivers in other cars were finally waved past, they saw one car lying upside down in a deep section of ditch. Its four wheels pointed haplessly upward like animal paws when the dead belly has begun to swell.

So she was late to Bill's Evening Prayer. As she crept in at the back of the nave, Bill was waiting to process. Ahead of Bill, his crucifer stood stiff with the cross. They were awaiting the organist's signal.

Eliza realized she had never seen Bill in profile before. She didn't recall that his mouth had an elegant, slight downturn at either end. Even standing there, in his garb, solemn, the mouth looked sardonic, because of that downturn. He turned just then, caught sight of her, and rolled his eyes. Then she remembered him. He used to roll his eyes up at all the unbelievable idiocies of their seminary life. Oh, and she had done it, too. She had, she had.

The organist's hand flagged in her mirror. The pedals dropped *lieblich gedeckt* and went full bass—Bill gave her a grin before he took off with his little entourage. All is friendly, his grin said. He was there for her, his grin said. But everything, really, is a little idiotic. And as for people, *people* now—there were only the witty ones, and then the idiots.

Eliza gave him a minute to get up the aisle.

She fled back to her car.

She had then driven home in two and a half hours, no better than the self-centered drunks who regularly endangered I-35.

Once home, she slid her mouse off sleep, and sent off the electronic letter which now was to end her career.

The days fled.

At last it was exactly eleven o'clock. And here was the Bishop right on the hour.

Eliza tried for jauntiness with herself. "Here we go, Tip," she said, aloud, still alone and free, in the rectory vestibule, still a cloaked priest. "Here we go, Tip!"—as if it were just a question of who will paddle bow and who will paddle stern. No one called the Bishop "Tip" except his real friends, or behind his back, witty seminary students, in the cowed, supercilious way that boot camp recruits refer to officers.

The Bishop remained in his car for a moment. He seemed to be looking at something leant up against the steering wheel. Probably his notes or schedule for the rest of the day's travel. It probably said: Fire Eliza at 11 at St. Fursey St. Fursey. See so-and-so at St. Thomas Hibbing. See so-and-so-else at St. Helen's Ely. Eliza wondered how much time was allotted to her, St. Fursey St. Fursey.

She must now gear up. Several of her classmates at Seabury-Western did not believe the most central tenets of Christian doctrine. Eliza knew that. But she didn't think there was safety in numbers. This Bishop, who was two generations older than she, wouldn't be an unbeliever. He was not going to be sympathetic.

He came up the walk. With his ascetic forehead and the decided mouth. Eliza had forgotten how that face gave off competence—intelligence, of course, but especially competence. And especially now, how naturally authoritative the man looked. She tried to jeer to herself in the old way. Competent, *right*! What's so holy about competence? But her sodden heart wouldn't jeer.

Eliza bounded away from the window to open the door. She put out her hand quickly.

"It's awfully good to see you, Bishop," she said.

"Hello, Eliza! Hello! Hello!" he cried.

They grasped hands, then hugged.

The Bishop looked around, as comfortable as an old dog. "I always forget how beautiful this place is!" he said. "Certainly this has got to be one of the prettiest churches and rectories in the Diocese. Each time I come, those huge old oaks look even taller."

"Come in, Bishop!"

"Let's just stand here a minute," he said. "I want to look around for a second."

This Bishop was in his seventies. He had retired from a large parish in New Hampshire, where, word was, everyone loved him. He had come to serve Minnesota as Bishop at about the time Eliza was installed as rector of St. Fursey.

Most Bishops at most installations gave peaceable sermons about how we are all learning this business of being a Christian together, even ordained people—the usual message seeming to say, everyone is equal. The usual slush that had regularly made Bill Plaice and Eliza roll their eyes.

This new Bishop of Minnesota did not give that pitch.

He had told them about St. Cyprian. Cyprian had been Bishop in Carthage at the time of the Diocletian abuses. When the plague came,

Cyprian cleared out of town because, sensibly enough, as his followers told him, they were going to need him, their spiritual leader, *alive*, to fight another day. Cyprian wrote spirit-filled letters to those Christians remaining in Carthage. The Christians who stayed behind cared for the sick first, then sickened themselves, then mostly died.

The second time the plague came around, Cyprian stayed in town. He helped with the stricken, improved the system for removal of the dead, organized transport for survivors.

The Romans renewed their persecutions. This time, they executed Cyprian. Cyprian had learned to be brave, although as usual—the Bishop had said—one must realize that bravery is much less practical than cowardice. In fact, this Bishop had said, Christianity had little to do with practicality, and much to do with courage. Christianity was uniformly impractical.

The Bishop now said, "Let's cross over into the church."

Quickly and naturally, like a habitué tipping a doorman, the Bishop jammed a bill into the Poor Box slot. He gave only a brief glance at the little high table piled with the regular tracts showing animals strapped down to be tortured by surgical students or by chemists working for perfume companies and the like.

Eliza put out a hand by way of steering and welcoming the Bishop into her office just off the hall.

"No, no!" cried the old man. "Let's go sit in the back of the nave."

He swung open one of the double-doors himself and led the way in, as if he, not Eliza, ran the place. Eliza felt two things: she had just lost authority, although it was officially still her church, and she felt comforted. Maybe it wouldn't take very long. He would fire her, and leave.

"Do you want the lights on, Bishop?" she said.

He waved a wrist. He said, "Don't bother."

The Bishop gave a fast glance at the Reserved Host in its pisc. He knelt and crossed himself, spent a moment in silence, then finally took a seat in the back pew, leaving space for Eliza to join him.

The entire nave was lighted only by the snowfall outside.

The Bishop turned sideways to half-face Eliza. "All right. Your letter said you were having a 'crisis of faith.' Tell me about it."

Eliza was trained in the drill of counseling with downhearted parishioners. She supposed the Bishop was about to put these theologian's skills into practice with her. He would ask some questions, let Eliza explain her feelings, and then do whatever he might do in his role as boss. Warn Eliza. Or advise her. Or command her to resign. First, though, right now, he would give Eliza the requisite eye contact and keep his own face interested but neutral.

None of that happened.

The old man said, "First, in your letter you used that phrase 'crisis of faith.' What in hell does that phrase actually mean?"

Eliza muttered that she did not believe in God.

The Bishop comfortably crossed his legs, and laid both hands over his top knee. He simply began to talk.

"I am going to make three points about believing and disbelieving," he said, "and ask you some questions. Then I will tell you what we'll do. First of all, let me say this much. You are one of the best priests I have ever had anything to do with, and I have been around priests for decades, as you must know. I want to say that much straight off, before you allow yourself any foaming-martyr notions about resigning.

"Second, do not tell anyone else about this 'crisis of faith,' as you call it. I will always be where you can find me, at the Diocese or on one of my various visits around the state. You can say whatever you like to me, but keep your mouth shut to others. For one thing, what you are experiencing, which you called 'a crisis of faith,' isn't a crisis at all. It is a simple loss. And it is only your loss, not God's. We can probably fix it.

"First, we have to get clear. For starters, I don't know when this loss came on. Did you ever have faith, Eliza?"

Eliza mustered some dignity. "Well, it depends on what you mean by faith."

The Bishop said, without malice, "It doesn't depend for one minute on anything like 'what someone means by faith.' People with faith know they have it. People without it usually, basically, know they haven't got it. They ease their feelings by pointing out how we need to define what we mean by such-and-such. Whenever people say, 'We need to define what we mean by' something, they are just gassing. Nathan Hale never defined what he meant by patriotism, as far as I know, and the British who hanged him never defined what they meant by rope.

"Besides, Eliza, why should anyone have faith? So much of Christian doctrine is preposterous—the way most doctrine of any religion I have ever read about is preposterous. But how can someone admit such a thing aloud? They'd lose their jobs. Unbelievers know they are unbelievers but they still yearn for belief. So they invent by-pass language like 'depends on what you mean by faith.'"

The old man fell silent.

This was totally not going well and it wasn't going to be quick, either.

Eliza's voice clattered, like a bag of small stones. "I never believed either of the creeds, Bishop."

He laid a hand on her hand, gave it a pat, withdrew his.

"Thank you for not lying, Eliza," he said. "If you have *never* believed, then you have lied your way through seminary. If you can remember back to your confirmation, three years before college, did you lie your way through that?"

"Yes," Eliza said.

"Thank you again for not lying to me now," the Bishop said. "You have lied through confirmation, through college, through seminary, and every Sunday or so at St. Fursey. You've had this parish three years, take out a two-week holiday for each. Three years gives us one hundred and fifty Sundays of the Apostles' or the Nicene Creed. It's good to get it exact."

Eliza seethed.

She should not be getting this excoriation. This Bishop had to have known hundreds and hundreds of disbelieving parishioners out East where, as any fool knew, to be an Episcopalian had little to do with doctrine. Why beat up on one rural Midwest priest like herself?

He couldn't have needled all those well-heeled New Englanders. This Bishop's reputation had preceded him to Minnesota. "A fine priest." "A much loved spiritual leader as well as able administrator." Et cetera, et cetera, et cetera. The Diocesan rag of the time had said that "young people in his care had learned to trust the *Things Unseen*." Other praise not in print but carefully looked into and just as carefully leaked to the Diocese of Minnesota: the man hadn't left behind unpaid parish bills. He had not dumped mission churches into escrow. He had not arranged to steal failed parish buildings from whatever little towns they stood in and then liquefy them to beef up Diocesan coffers.

"Now, then." —the Bishop again, in a bracing change of tone: "A question for you, Eliza."

But Eliza was too upset to be afraid. She had already lost all. All. She was a confounded liar in the eyes of a leader whose mentorship had once touched her.

The Bishop said, "Now, tell me carefully. Have you told any *other* lies to members of this parish?"

Eliza nearly shouted. "No!"

She was fed up with feeling guilty. If the Bishop only knew what kind of creeps made up his stable of priests!—if he knew, he would get off *her* back.

The Bishop said, "Good. I didn't think you had. As I said, Eliza, you are one of the best priests I've known."

Oh yes, she thought, I forgot he said that. Still, counselors always say some favorable thing at the start. It was part of the famous process of building a trust relationship. Eliza knew that old drill.

The man was talking again. "So far as I can tell, you haven't lied for the sake of money, sex, or other self-interest. I think you are a serious rector. One more question: when is the last time you have prayed *alone* at your communion rail? Private prayer, not service prayer done for the congregation?"

A moment of silence.

In a relaxed, casual tone, the Bishop said, "Have you ever come in here alone, Eliza, and gone up to the rail and prayed?"

"I have not."

"All right," the Bishop said. "We'll fix that. The still-accepted theory is that the quality of a parish priest depends entirely on the quality of the priest's *prayer life*. A ridiculous idea. A good parish depends on any number of things. In a minute, we will go up to your rail. I am going to pray for you."

Kindness as clean as snow fell on her from this old man. Still, it was only snow on a hot wound. The feeling of it vanished as fast as it landed.

She did not believe there was a God and so the Bishop's praying for her at the altar was pathetically retro. Retro. Still, totally kind. Shaky kindness was falling on her.

The Bishop said, "Now, the way to handle the problem of having no faith is to decide consciously what you can do inside yourself and what you *cannot* do inside yourself. In your case, though, since you do *not* believe in God," and the old man gave an abrupt wave of the hand, "you will have to stop admiring yourself for being so independent. Forget all the drivel about a higher power. Forget it. At the same time, don't blame people for making up fancy words for God because look, Eliza, they don't pay you a fortune at St. Fursey, but they do pay you. In the United States, other people can lose their jobs, their pensions, their everything, if word gets out that they don't believe in God. Don't forget that. If you have some atheists in your parish, be tolerant with them. Think of how easily a police state, should we become one, could decide to frame anyone who had said aloud, anywhere, that he or she was not just a liberal or a dissenter, but *an atheist.* They'd sting you dead before you heard the rattle of their tails."

Eliza now said, "Bishop—Bishop, I want to hear everything you are saying. But I am having trouble. I am in trouble just now. I'm sorry. I can't follow what you are saying anymore. I can't listen anymore. I can't think anymore."

The old man lifted one of Eliza's hands, covered it with both of his own, as if to warm it. Then he laid it back.

"Stick, Eliza," he said. "Only one more point. If you can, learn the knack of talking to God with parishioners overhearing you, rather than the knack of talking to parishioners with God doing the overhearing. Bear in mind that most people can't get a single idea through their heads except by *celebrating.* Or maybe they never do learn anything, but the celebrating at least puts an eddy into the slow, cruel flow of their practical lives. Have you ever seen lightning on a summer night over a solid waste dump? There was one at my last parish. One evening I was walking at the beginning of a storm. I got through some woods and just as I came out to what had once been a dairyman's meadow, a huge general lightning flash showed me a whole scene of trash—junked cars, refrigerators, skids leaning in a pile—all of it lighted up in blue. I never saw such stunning lightning before. I was sorry that the lightning showed how hideous a human landscape is, compared to natural landscape—but I was excited. That's the way churchgoing is for a good many people. I think it's what people mean when they say they love 'the beauty of the service.'"

The old man gave a gentle laugh.

The chancel and rood screen of St. Fursey were surprisingly dark for the noon hour. They went up to the rail. The Bishop said, "Don't make any of the responses, Eliza. I will do the whole thing. This time, you get to just let yourself be prayed for. Don't double-think anything."

Eliza was bored at first. The Bishop started with two Versicles and Responds that she hadn't heard since a totally crazy English canon had visited Seabury-Western one Good Friday. He had dragged everyone through an arcane *sarum* service.

Then the Bishop eased over to an ordinary collect of the morning service. He skipped to the extra prayers at the back of 1928 and prayed for All Sorts and Conditions of Men. He wound up with what Eliza and other young Episcopalians had called the labor-union prayer "for all those whose toil is difficult or troublesome for them." By the time the Bishop had finished those set prayers and parts of collects, Eliza had lost all desire to make any responses.

But now, somehow, the Bishop left her behind. She could hear the old man's voice but it sounded like the receding voice of someone who has trotted ahead on a path while you are merely standing. Eliza paid attention again. The Bishop was explaining to God that this Eliza was a sinner just as he himself was a sinner. OK, the usual modesty-rhetoric thing. She made herself listen, though. The Bishop told God that Eliza did not practice avarice and that her nature was surprisingly merciful. He reminded God that mercy was rare in people only 27 years old. He told God that Eliza had two bad habits.

At this, Eliza shook herself. Lying, yes. What was this other, second one?

The Bishop told God that Eliza allowed herself to be afraid. She was too scared too much of the time. The Bishop asked God to help Eliza recognize fear when it showed up and to say to herself, "Right—here we go again. I am afraid" and then to tie up the fear in a package, a package of some manageable size, say, a brick-sized package, on her desk. The fear might never move away. She might know that fear all the rest of her life, but it would not wildly banner and writhe like Northern Lights across her mind. It would be contained in the little cage she had made for it.

The Bishop reminded God: "Please help me take care of her. Help me, O Almighty God," he said. Then he said, "O almighty God, who does not require the death of a sinner, please help me."

Now the Bishop raced even further ahead.

In a bizarre, unpleasant tone from deep in his throat, the Bishop said, "O God, help me to keep seeing your holy joy because my country has disgraced itself with cruelty and I can't hide from thinking about it. I am so afraid."

At last he wound up in the conventional way, but still very fast, clearly to keep Eliza out of it. "This I ask in the name of the Father and of the Son and of the Holy Spirit, Amen."

The Bishop got to his feet.

Eliza stood up.

The Bishop turned to her as if just reminded that she was there.

He said in a jocular tone, "Someone has been desecrating your communion rail, Eliza. Rubbing off smut on the under side. I'd have a word with your servers. It's usually the servers, not ordinary parishioners, who do that. If you make the whole group of them wipe it clean with soapy water and rags and then dry it, it will do wonders for whichever of them is the wrong 'un. You can tell the group it is too revolting a job to wish off on to the Fair Linen Guild, if you have one, or even onto the sexton. By the way, Eliza, if you haven't got a Fair Linen Guild, you might ask the women to form one. A good tough Guild can do wonders. Of course, there's some risk. They will be either for you or against you—but either way, they will do some of your dirty work for you. If you tell them that an acolyte is rubbing off snot onto the under side of the communion rail they will look at you as if you were vulgar for mentioning such things. Don't be deceived, Eliza. Within a week, they will have it all over the parish that a certain acolyte had been rubbing snot onto the rail but 'our rector put a fast stop to that.'"

The Bishop himself was meanwhile wiping along the rail with a beautiful, gigantic white monogrammed handkerchief of his own. He showed Eliza the cupped handkerchief full of chewing gum wads, what looked like killed spiders, and worse.

"Your rail really is bad," he remarked in a companionable tone. "Also, if you have a sexton? You might mention someone left a dead mouse on top of the entrance sign-up table."

Eliza opened her mouth to laugh with him, but no sound came out. She opened her mouth again, this time to thank him. Again, no sound came out.

The Bishop waited a moment, then shook hands and said. "I'll tell you something, Eliza. Only people who have some sort of good inside them are ever struck dumb by prayer. Struck dumb. Like you. Get that through your head."

He practically trotted back down the aisle. Eliza hustled after him.

At the door, the Bishop shook hands again, then turned his back and was fleet as a kid escaping, getting out to his natty little Jetta.

Eliza watched from the lychgate, meaning to feel lightly amused and affectionate. But she was not amused or affectionate and the Bishop, for all his doctrine that she didn't believe in, was *not* just "a nice old fellow." He was a lot more complex a person than she was. Most of her acquaintance were *less* complicated than she was. Not this one.

After a while, Eliza went to the vestibule closet and pulled out her down-filled jacket, heavy gloves, and visor cap with ear flaps.

She drove east and then north along the highway. She tried to recite her plan aloud to herself in the car. Her voice had not come back yet. Go see Katie's tree house. If Katie still needed help raising her 2x6s for the ridgepole or rafters, if she was having rafters, then Eliza could help.

She parked on the shoulder above the road with its old sign still legible: *Solid Waste Transfer Station: $700 fine for dumping outside the gates.* The gate had been half-open for years, ever since the station was abandoned. People and creatures made various uses of the place. The poor of St. Fursey saved $33 a month on garbage pick-up. They slipped into the fence opening and dumped. Lovers left contraceptive kits, several kinds, top-drawer and bottom-drawer, all around what had once been the main burning area. Fireweed had seeded itself out everywhere. Bears, skunks, deer, voles, and mice searched skillfully among the busted skids and furnace filters. Katie Anderson and a couple of her tomboy friends had got up the floor part of a tree house onto a lower three-branch spread of an oak.

Eliza saw the girl's bike getting furred with snow. Katie herself sat quietly upon her platform. She had left her ladder hanging. When she saw Eliza, she put a finger to her lips with one hand, and signalled her up the ladder with the other. Eliza went up.

Katie must have been holding still for a long time, her shoulders and cap covered with undisturbed snow as they were. Eliza looked where the girl now pointed. She made out a huge, dark, liquidly moving bear on the other side of the center junk. The mother was eating. A black cub stood beside her with its delicate nose moving about.

Eliza raised a joyful fist to Katie and Katie made a fist back.

In back of them, a car drove up and stopped behind Eliza's car on the highway shoulder. It was hard to hear its quiet engine in all that snow, but the baby bear rose up onto its back legs. Eliza and Katie turned around. A man carrying a 12-gauge descended gingerly from the highway shoulder and let himself pad along into the enclosure. He raised his gun. He was leaning his cheek to the stock where he would brace his point in the time-honored, concentrated way. He looked to be less than forty yards from the bears.

Eliza leapt off the tree house platform, and began shouting, "No! No! No! Absolutely no!"

Then she ran, waving her arms, still shouting, keeping a slant course towards the bears, so the shooter would startle, and be put off his point.

The Episcopal priest died nearly immediately. She did not learn that she had been accidentally killed by the wife-battering husband of her cleaning woman. She did not learn that her body itself was what had spoiled his shot, and that both of the wild animals, mother and cub, had streamed back safe into the whitened forest.

Also, she did not learn that her server, a fourteen-year-old kid, leapt up at the supper given after the Requiem, and in a voice coarsened by tears, had shouted, "I always thought our rector was just some kind of a chicken shit, but turns out I was wrong."

Chapter Twelve

Peter had this Saturday morning to himself. Nat had vanished into the music room to plan the music for rehearsal and to proofread the sheets for each chorister's folder.

Outside the huge study window, the night's snowfall lay about the glade that Peter Tenebray, like his dad and granddad, kept between the forest and the short back lawn. Before the first oaks and one basswood tree stood a deerlick and a birdfeeder whose wobbling saucer-shaped guard had never defeated the most thick-headed squirrel.

Most early evenings, Peter and Natalie brought their drinks to the big study window. Several times they saw the huge mother bear they heard about. At first they thought they saw her with two cubs but, apparently, she had only one. Her large tracks lay here and there among smaller creatures' tracks, this morning showing up in the snow.

Peter sat happily, genuinely happily, at his desk. He kept his thin mug of morning coffee on a pewter pad on a small side table. He came from a line of men who had the luck and sense to retire at 60 or earlier. He was only two-thirds retired, of course. He did any work John Rubrick gave him, and kept it, along with school Old Boys' correspondence, in the exquisite little drawers and cubby holes of his desk. St. Fursey Vestry Meeting minutes, however, he from time to time took over to the church itself. He filed them in the Undercroft. They joined the long record of Tenebray family members' work as Senior Wardens. All the notes to one or another Rector, all the Minutes, all the handouts to the Vestry—hard work, all that. He would put it at the front of a file case whose file drawers, those farthest back, had Minutes and correspondence kept by his grandfather.

Records of jobs, jobs his friend John Rubrick brought him—speaking to civic groups, watchdog groups, the occasional gatherings of one or another corporate directors—he kept at home. He was delighted he had the talent John loudly admired. Thoreau was right: most people's work, and non-working hours as well, were brutish and nasty. Peter's weren't. His life was wonderful.

His desk had been his great-grandfather's, a Wooton, the Rockefeller model. Peter set himself happily to this morning's work. He liked being able to see the guest wing lying to the north. Its beautiful stonework half-framed his view. The four-generation Tenebray house was not made of brick like other Minnesota mansions of the 1890s and 1910s. It was stone, a mixture of roseate and gray stone. Each stone had been custom-cut into one of four different oblong shapes, then fitted so exactly, that the house could nearly have been drywall work. The masons Peter's great-grandfather brought over from Cornwall didn't merely lay level courses of stones, and then fit the ends: they blocked the walls, custom-fitting vertically as well as horizontally. The effect never failed to delight Peter.

He was grateful for the security and leisure in his life, but a close second feeling was his enjoyment of beauty around him. Too bad he was likely the last *pater familias* for the family. He firmly told himself that if he felt wistful about the death of his infant grandson, poor Imogen must feel it a thousand times more.

The Tenebray men had always had the knack of happiness in their home study. Peter, like the others, kept the operations office in Hibbing, and the Tenebray Properties office in Duluth. In the St. Fursey house, therefore, the only papers lying about, the only books in the handsome anteroom off the sitting room, were private work and leisure reading of his own. As he had done several times in the past two weeks, he glanced up at the desk's beautiful gallery. An accident had broken some of the decorative gallery and torn all three hinges away from one cabinet door. Poor Arlene, who cleaned for the Tenebrays as well as for Doc Anderson and the Episcopal Church and St. Fursey Elementary, was the most considerate creature in the world. She sometimes came to work bruised. Peter hated to open the door to her and then covertly see, as she picked up and read Nat's list of instructions on the sideboard, that one eye was sometimes darkened, one cheek black and blue. It pained him. There was nothing you could do, of course, about the quarrelling between husbands and wives. He knew that wretched axiom well enough.

It was now several weeks since Arlene had missed her step while working in his study. He had been waiting for her to finish. He had hoped to speed things up by telling her to by no means try to do anything with his desk. He heard a horrible crash and a woman's outcry. She had tripped and, in falling, had grabbed the open cabinet door of the secretary and yanked it out.

"Your beautiful desk!" she wept.

Natalie came in from the music room. It was only 10:00 or so in the morning so she wasn't tight. "Nonsense, Arlene!" Nat said briskly. "Those old desks—something is always happening to them, and look, all that's happened here is a matter of one hinged door—easily fixed, Arlene!"

"She's right," Peter came in promptly. "This desk spends more time at the repair people's than it spends here! Don't worry about it at all. You know what central heating does, Arlene: it dries out houses so everything breaks like matchsticks."

She was consoled. Peter had called down to his dad's favorite restoration place in St. Paul. He described what damage he could see. No, he didn't want to arrange to ship it. Would they come up and fetch it with their van? He would have a boy here to help lift. Good enough. They talked it over. The restorer said she was pleased she had a beautiful stick of walnut already on hand—that was one good thing. It might run him something between $2000 and $2500, including travel. Might be more if she found dried and loosened veneer, say, on the raised panels or anywhere. She had a record of that desk in their shop. Mr. James Tenebray had once had a part of the gallery replaced and carved "It'll be your call," Peter said. "Whatever it takes. I've loved that desk since it was my grandpapa's and I wasn't tall enough to see over the top of it."

It was back now and he was grateful. All the three weeks it was gone,

Arlene had over and over told both Natalie and Peter that she couldn't think what was matter with her that she didn't think to tell them her Brad could have repaired the desk for them. That was so dumb of her, she said. And Brad would have done it reasonable, too, because he'd mentioned, different times, maybe getting into the furniture repair business. He couldn't decide between furniture repair and automotive. A job like Mr. and Mrs. Tenebray's would have helped make up his mind for him. It was so dumb of her not to.

This morning's work was especially pleasant. It fell right down the center of Peter's best capability. He therefore made himself take care of a small dutiful note to an Andover classmate first.

He sometimes felt chafed that his schoolmates didn't originate many letters to him. Why not? Why didn't they? He was a good correspondent. Perhaps it was that their lives were busier than his. Even when his class had long since left school and graduated from their colleges, Peter had not had to work the extraordinary hours that his friends reported in the Class Notes and in their Christmas letters. A family business was not a law firm. No heartless eagle eyes had ever watched Peter for billable hours. Peter hadn't much to report about family affairs. Imogen was born, grew up, married, had one child, not three or four. Peter lived in the old family home, not an Ohio cornfield converted to a suburb. For sadnesses to report, he had only a grandchild's death. Natalie and he were battling her drinking problem, but a drinking problem is not fighting cancer, and in any case was unreportable.

He gradually grew hesitant about starting up any correspondence with men who had shown no interest in hearing from him. It would not be pushing, however, to come up with an annual Christmas letter. Besides, he knew exactly what a Christmas letter should be. Three to five paragraphs: warm greetings, personal news of the last year, but reporting only surgeries or internists' diagnoses that led to happy endings, with a final paragraph expressing worry about "the times" or "the world" but with no specific mention of the United States. In fact, never put that phrase, "the United States," into a Christmas letter.

This morning he meant to give a moment to a man who had sent what was frankly a form letter to all of his classmates. Peter couldn't recall his name. He consulted all eight of his huge, but tidy mailing lists and couldn't find him. He had even looked up Bennett Solutions, the man's employer, on the web but its restrained home page in deep red and a lighter orange didn't link you to a list of its officers.

Peter felt he must reply, if only out of plain human sympathy.

The man had written, without a complimentary heading of any sort: "I will be stepping down from Bennett Solutions." From there, he went into his appreciation for having worked with remarkable colleagues who provided him with intellectual stimulation and so forth. At the end, he said he intended to spend some time to "find the right context in which to develop my range of options."

Peter shook his head. The phrase was a soundless scream. Language gave away a person's pain: "transition," an expression used in The Classes part of the *Harvard Magazine*, meaning someone's husband had done a bunk. Now the ex-wife was *in transition. The right context in which to develop one's range of options* meant any lead, please, a job—any job, please, God. Dear classmates, please. A job. If you hear of anything.

Peter thought it all over and decided on Brief and Respectful. He found half-size letterhead in the second drawer, decided against using Tenebray Properties letterhead, fumbled for personal letterhead and wrote Dear—he had to look again to remind himself of the fellow's first name—*Dear Jay, Very, very best luck with all of it,* and signed the letter Peter. Then he underlined all twice because he meant it. Then he added a P.S.: *This is the damnedest economy.*

At last Peter was free to attend to his morning's task. John Rubrick had asked him to talk informally with the executives of a smart little wholesaler who had been watchdogged for renaming and continuing to sell a carcinogenic ingredient in soft drinks. The company very much hoped to keep on using this ingredient because it apparently was just addictive enough to make young people ask for that soft drink by brand name without attracting notice—so far as their marketing people knew—from anyone connected to the FDA. So far they had only citizens' activists' groups to deal with. The Company wouldn't have to worry about these groups so long as they did not appear to be planning to join forces with one another.

John and Peter agreed on a two-stage solution: first, they must heal the PR lesion caused by the watchdoggers. Next, they should gauge how intense and how durable would be the memory of the issue. That is, if the company recovered its prestige or even took steps to improve it, might they again rename the chemicals in question, and use them again. Peter began drafting out a rough syllabus for himself.

First, the Company must address the legal necessities.

Second—but close to the same time, of course, because it should start immediately—the Company should develop a handsome reputation of a kind to kill adult idealists' interest. They needn't look more attractive to the teenagers drinking the stuff. They might be well advised to work up a little new advertising about how this beverage caused weight loss. If you shouldn't lose weight, consult your physician before imbibing. Peter scorned that particular strategy. He had been shown stats for how well it worked, however, so he didn't quarrel with the pros. One of the noticeable markings of his work was how much conciliation or tolerant turning of a deaf ear one must do. He complained once, just once, about it, years ago, to John. "Well, but you are good at that!" John had laughed. John made it sound as though Peter did nothing but soothe criminals or the like.

"Nonsense," John had said, "Peter, ask yourself: why does this Company want to hire you to preserve their public esteem for them? Because you get along with idealists. Idealists like you. You also get along with the Fed, and then, very talented of you, you get along with the kind of CEOs who know that, in the end, they will have to do whatever it takes, so why not start with bottom-down strategy right now and save a lot of time?"

Peter shook his head, but he gave his friend a smile.

John said, "Well, people like your moral taste."

Peter began to divide the papers about this morning's job into two piles: the Company's central and peripheral memos, and public response to Company policies. He read over their January Annual Meeting booklet. John Rubrick had put a Post-It on each of the Stockholder Proposals and on the Company's responses to each. There were only four for the most recent annual meeting, all of them from Roman Catholic nuns with their order initials after their names. The Meeting editors would have weeded out all other complaints on the same subject, so that an average reader saw only that a bunch of nuns—wouldn't you know, what did they know of the necessities of business—were howling about something again, so what else was new? Peter had been around stockholders too long not to know that a good many sensible businessmen complained in their own minds about evils that only the Catholic sisters criticized aloud, so he did not sneer at the letters. He read each one through.

He was already seeing how his timing might go—first, some modest publicity—friendly projects, high-school lyceums, town library talks— then giving some words to the wise—identifying who was likely to promote a serious campaign against the Company and seeing what might palliate them. All that would give him time to design a change of general attitude. For example, if you were selling beverages with aspartame in it that looked bad in 1994, but by 2006 or 2007 had gotten screened back out of memory to just one more carcinogen among millions. The best thing to do with protesters who were young is offer to meet with them and tell them the Company had had to go back to the drawing board. It was costing them money, they would say, showing some slides, but "we don't want that kind of thing." The young people would feel they had won. Last time Peter had conducted a program like that, a number of 20-year-old men and women had later got into a queue-up to shake hands with him afterwards.

Now, Natalie interrupted him.

She put her head around his door and said, "Bernie Stokowski's here and he didn't ask if it was convenient. He's out of uniform."

By leaning forward, Peter could see about half of the driveway turnaround. The parked car was a Ford, not the town patrol car.

He stood up and went out into the living room. Bernie Stokowski was removing his snowy boots and letting snowmelt pool onto the gray and olive vestibule tiles. He wore reversible woods clothes, orange side out, and lifted a large packsack that Peter hadn't noticed right away.

"Hi, Bernie," Peter said.

"Hi, Peter." The man glanced around the living room with a speculative look. Natalie had disappeared into the music room.

"Have a seat," Peter said. "How about coffee? I've got it all set up and just have to turn on the maker."

"That'd be good," the cop said, brightening a little.

"Well, sit down, Bernie."

"Say, Peter. This is private. Do you want to—" again his eyes roved around the living room.

Peter told him Nat was working on the violinists' bowing in the music room. Would Peter's study do? He pointed. "In there," he said. "I'll just turn on the coffee."

As he went into the kitchen, he thought, what's this going to be? The man wants advice about something. Wife? Gladys? He didn't think so. Peter knew that people sometimes regarded him as a community sage of some sort. They asked his advice on the damnedest things, but not about wives. Job? No. Bernie's kids were too young for him to be looking around for job contacts. Wanted to turn Episcopalian? Wondering how to do it without "tearing the family wide open?" People thought one thing or another would tear the town wide open or it'd tear the family wide open or it would tear the United States wide open but it never did. Anyway, only eager churchgoers switched passionate loyalties from one church to another. Casuals, as Peter understood Gladys and Bernie Stokowski to be, stayed casual. Maybe Pearl the accompanist was in trouble again. Perhaps Bernie wanted to know if Peter by any chance knew where she went after she closed down the VFW. He shuddered at the thought of where all she might have gone.

He returned to the study, and saw the strong cop sitting on his grandmother's needlepointed chair seat with its glorious *grospoint* of pink and lighter pink azaleas. He fervently hoped that Bernie had come to him on his way to go hunting and not on his way back, with blood and mud and snowmelt on his trousers.

"How can I help?" he said simply, hands half opened out over the papers that covered the whole desk top.

The policeman gave a nervous laugh. "This time it's me helping you. Let me tell you this way. I am going to tell you from the beginning because you'll get the point. But Peter, please believe me. This absolutely has to stay between us two. I wouldn't tell you at all except that I think you have a right to know. Not a legal right. Some kind of other right. I mean, I just think you have a right to know."

Peter waited.

"So you don't pass any of this on?" Bernie said.

"I don't pass any of this on," Peter said. "Wait a minute," Peter added. "This will take some time. Let's see if the coffee's done. How about I defrost and microwave some very good left-over deli sandwiches that Nat and I brought home a few days ago?"

Bernie smiled. "Yeah," he said. "Sounds good. But Peter—would this be a thing where your wife will see that we're eating and want to come join us?"

"No," Peter said. "It's a promise."

He went fast into the kitchen, heated the sandwiches, filled his own cup and a clean one for Bernie, put paper napkins on a tray, and brought it all in. He set it on top of his work on the desk.

"That's really good," Bernie said with his mouth full.

Peter saw it was going to take forever for Bernie to get going with his story. He settled himself and glanced out the window. Peter himself ate enough of the sliced-ham-sliced-Swiss-sliced-red-onion-and-mayo-and-Dijon to make the policeman feel at ease. He slowly drank coffee that he also didn't want, and waited.

Bernie began to talk. He started way back.

His father had been the chief of police in St. Fursey and Cullough both, a long time ago, when he was just a little boy. Like any child, he hadn't known the ins and outs of his father's work. He had admired the man. From earliest childhood, he had loved it when his father lifted him up, when first coming into the house out of the cold. His uniform tunic was cold, and the buttons were icy. His father's face shined red and smiling.

Years passed. One early fall day, Fort Leavenworth sent a Calling All Cars that was picked up by every cop in northeastern Minnesota: one of their most violent repeat murderers had escaped and was believed to be heading north on US 61. Bernie's dad gathered his wife and children, tucked them into his car, and drove into the Superior National Forest— Toohy Lake, a beautiful place that Bernie never forgot. There they camped for a few days. Bernie's dad told him how to tell the straddle of a mouse's track in snow, how to tell if the mouse was trotting or galloping. He showed them a woodpecker's hole in a tree, lifting the smallest child up close. He explained how the woodpecker dug the hole on the under-slant of a tree trunk, on the south side, so that it would get sunlight and warmth, and when it rained, very little runoff went into the bird's cozy home.

Their dad and mother cooked them fried meals. Bernie was charmed that his dad insisted on doing the dishes, a job his mother normally did. His dad trotted around in the fire-red light and near dark of their camp site. He talked to himself, locating what he needed in the dark, telling the dishes, Stay there. Don't fall off. Don't go away—all in very good humor. The little boys could see the shadow of their mother, with her flashlight, inside the family's heavy canvas tent. They were longing for her to be ready, so they could get out of the heavy, languid, dark cold that had come down on them. At last, she called them in and made them take off their clothes and put on their clean underwear which she had warmed for them under her jacket. They smelled of wood fire and of her. She put them into one of the serious, goosedown sleeping bags where she had put hot water bags filled with boiling water from the fire.

Bernie had thought he would never be so happy in his life as he was that first night, just before sleep, watching his mother as she moved things around in the flashlight light, listening for his father, who was still clomping about outside when the boys fell asleep.

He did not find out for years that the reason his father had taken them winter camping all of a sudden like that was that he was afraid to try to pull in a repeat murderer. Bernie got into a fifth-grade fight with a boy who said his father was a coward cop. From then on, he knew that the town knew. Everyone in the county knew. A state patrolman from way west of Bagley had finally apprehended the murderer, so the countryside was safe again. It was safe, but never again right-feeling to Bernie.

He grew up and became a policeman himself. Like a lot of people in their late teens and early twenties, he just wandered into a kind of work, got some training, and took the job they taught him. Police work, in his case.

One day, he was upending a couple of beers with old high school classmates and someone said, "Going to be a cop, huh? Way to go, Bern! State patrol?"

He did not *want* to try for the much coveted state patrol—he wanted to work up to be chief of police of St. Fursey. Once he actually *noticed* that, he set down his beer can and thought, of course. What I want to do is do well what my dad did badly—not to show him up or compete with him—but to recover his good name, *our* good name.

Still, Bernie told Peter between mouthfuls of sandwich, he wasn't a very good cop at first. He arrested everything in sight. He all but brought in turtles for crossing the white line. He wanted to find crooks here and felons there.

Finally, he settled down.

Now Bernie Stokowski paused and said, "You must be wondering when I am ever going to get to what I want to say. I'm getting there, Peter."

"I'm listening," Peter said. He added, "I am not in a hurry." He had been longing to concentrate on his job notes. He had been sorry that this earnest policeman showed up. However, he shut it out of his mind because any fool could feel the urgency in this man's unburdening himself so strangely. Peter felt a spark of pride, too, that an upstanding member of the local police, the chief himself, needed his help.

Bernie picked up his story with the finding of last Friday's dead body alongside Highway 53. Right away, Bernie told Peter, he had scented large-scale crime, or part of some *large-scale* crime, not just some crack-trashed serial killer. He wanted more luck than he'd needed before. This was trouble from far away, which meant someone knew exactly what they were doing. What's more, this someone had enough money, another way of saying enough personnel, to carry off any crime so simple as a single-corpse murder. People came from Duluth to identify and study the crime scene, but left again. Bernie remarked to Peter with a wry smile that they hadn't even stayed long enough to have doughnuts with the locals—the locals being him and Darrel.

Darrel, Peter thought. Oh yes, that unpromising looking deputy policeman.

Bernie said, "So I told Darrel that homicide in Duluth would be doing the investigation. I needed to have Darrel think that, because although those officers, two cars of them, whoever they were, handed the P.M. over to us and asked us to ask our M.E. to send in the results, they left us the body. They said they would fill us in on whatever they found. I said, OK. I saw that Doc Anderson did the body in Cullough Hospital where they are set up for examinations. Dr. Anderson wrote out his P.M. and we sent it to the Duluth address they gave us. We never heard anything after that.

"I wasn't surprised. There are a lot of police in Duluth. The men I saw milling around that morning weren't anyone I'd ever seen before, but I haven't seen a tenth of their people."

Bernie said at this point, "I am not a particularly brave man, Peter. I pulled my deputy away from those people. There were two cars full of them—unmarked Caprices. I don't suppose they would have objected to a local cop who was willing to have a look around. Still, I thought of Gladys and the kids.

"While Darrel and I fooled around in the station, waiting to see if any of that crew—in their ties and shirt and jackets under their overcoats—would show up for coffee, poor Darrel wanted to dig up the whole area between the highway and Small Bass Lake because he's young. He wants to bring in a killer.

"I got rid of Darrel by telling him he had to go out and throw the book at Walt Steinzeiter about an infringement."

Peter said, "That the heavy-set gravel man?"

Bernie nodded. "Weighs 300 plus. He's had a flag dangling across County 10 ever since 9/11, a nice big flag, too, but it's against the law. That got Darrel out of the station and I spent some of Friday afternoon following my own hunches. I also spent most of Saturday morning. I was going to do a little searching on Sunday morning, too, but I didn't want to tell Gladys anything, so I went to church with her as usual. On Sunday afternoon, I went out again, by now pretty sure of what I was looking for. Gladys asked if I wasn't going to watch the Vikes cream the Patriots. I told her no, it wouldn't be much of a game; I was going to see if I could find a partridge or anything. I got into my cammos.

"By the way, you guys in that Thanksgiving choir were rehearsing. I was driving home when you were still rehearsing. It was very pretty. You all were pretty good on Sunday afternoon.

"The next morning, I left Darrel to call up and wait for the school principal to come and sign for a kid. I brought the stuff I had into Forensics. It took them three days. So they called and I drove over to talk to them. They told me what I was afraid they might tell me."

Now the policeman leaned over and undid the straps on the Duluth Pack by his feet. A trowel dropped out onto Peter and Nat's Viss rug but it missed his grandmother's needlepointed chair seat.

"This I don't guess is yours," Bernie said, handing Peter a plastic bag with what looked like bright blue socks in it. "No!" Bernie said sharply. "Don't open it. Just tell me if you recognize it at all."

Peter said, "Natalie's been missing a blue knitted scarf just like that. But I'd have to look to be sure."

Bernie reached across to retrieve the bag. He went into another pocket, took out plastic gloves, put them on, and then opened the bag. He dangled a torn, bright blue scarf so Peter could see the whole length of it. Bernie turned it backside to, moved it closer, so Peter could read the label. Peter squinted and moved a hand up, but Bernie said rudely, "Get your hand down!"

"Norsk Turistforeningen," Peter read. His voice changed. "Where'd you get this, Bernie? It's been missing for weeks and weeks. We've looked everywhere. And where's it *been* anyhow? It looks like hell."

"I'll show you the other stuff and then explain everything. You tell me, though, if some of this stuff is *not* yours."

One by one, he took out small plastic bags with single-zip closures, and Peter, feeling nearly faint, identified twelve of them. There were fourteen items in all, two of which were only threads, presumably of clothing, and Peter couldn't be sure. Should he go get out a pair of slacks they might have come from? A snag had drawn up in one cuff of his Harris sport jacket. He could check.

"That's OK," Bernie said. "I don't need to take this stuff to those people again. You've identified enough. The scarf, a handkerchief, a piece of rosin. I take it that's something that you might have in your pocket? Other little stuff. The chapstick had one good and a couple of not-good finger prints of yours on it. The handkerchief, which had been used, would have your DNA."

Bernie replaced each little bag into his packsack.

Peter spoke nearly in a whisper, "What are you saying, Bernie?"

Then he straightened himself up and cleared his throat. "Are you saying you are looking for proof that I was involved in that girl's death?"

"That's exactly what I am *not* saying," said Bernie without a pause. "Long ago, I noticed a category of people who just never would kill for any reason except to save kids or save their country. Like you, Peter. You are in that category. Dieter Stolz is in that category—speaking of which, in fact, at first I thought someone might have it in mind to frame Stolz for the murder of that girl. Then I realized that was a mistake."

Bernie was systematically strapping his pack shut. "No." he said. "What we have here is either one person, which I don't think it is, or a very tight-thinking organization, and they have laid a sleeper trail leading to you.

"A sleeper trail is a trail you can leave after a crime which doesn't get found unless someone goes looking for it. It just sleeps until needed. There are probably more sleeper trails left around in the United States than there are unexploded claymores in Vietnam. Generally, the organization that leaves one doesn't necessarily intend to use it, but they leave it because it is cheap and low-tech, very low-tech, and it *might* come in handy later. Since the trail has to be left near the time of the victim's death, they think ahead: they ask themselves, might we want a sleeper trail here? Look at all this stuff of yours and your wife's. They probably collected the stuff ahead, anywhere, weeks ahead, and then when they decided on the murder, they got some one-time person to lay the trail. They tell the one-time hire that it is undercover police work or some darn thing that sounds manly or romantic. If they can get an idealistic teenager to do it, they do. It is cheap. Some trails even get laid before they have fine-tuned the crime itself. In those cases, they have the trail layer put several objects along some trajectory they have decided on, some snagged on bushes, some lightly buried. Later, when they are ready to pull off the crime, they choose one of their sleeper trails and move the crime *to* it. For example, the body of that teenage girl we found on Highway 53 had been kept *frozen* for at least a week before they dumped."

Peter began to open his mouth.

"Wait a minute," Bernie said. "Let me tell you what *might* be their thinking. Then you can ask questions. Whoever these people are, they may perfectly well never intend to compromise you or your wife. They likely don't know you from Adam and Eve. Only if they ever need to finger you.

Say, if it looked as if one of their friends might get fingered for it, then they might wake up the trail to you instead. I don't know that any one of us can be sure just how those people think. All I know is, Peter, when they want something to happen, we need to figure they are big enough to make it happen. If they decide to blame someone for it, they probably pull that off, too."

Peter had to clear his throat. Even so, his voice came out scruffy and weak. "But why would they want to blame me or Nat?"

Bernie said, "Nothing personal, most likely. And as I say, they may not ever use it."

"But what kind of people *are* such people?" Peter cried. "If they knew me—if they only knew me—they wouldn't want to frame me..."

Bernie twiddled his thumbs a little. "Here's a different way to look at it. They don't know you but they don't care what happens to you, either. For all I know, they are like bomber pilots. If you are in some city being bombed, you don't ask what the pilot has against you. They may perfectly well not have known the young woman of the case, either. And she is *dead*. At least, Peter, you're still alive.

"Who would *do* such a thing?" Peter asked again.

Bernie gave an ugly gust of a laugh. "That's an easy one," he said. "Bad people. Sometimes large crime groups, sometimes large business groups, sometimes government groups of one government or another. Whoever these bad people are, they have substantial resources. Your happenstance sex killer or even serial killer doesn't have equipment to freeze a body and then to keep it frozen at a steady temperature for a week."

"I suppose I thought that kind of thing wouldn't happen to me," Peter said.

Bernie gave him the look that grownups give children who pity themselves.

Peter saw it and stiffened. "All right, Bernie—I think I know people I can get on to about this. Whoever these criminals are, they don't get to get away with this. I know some people, so I will start—I have contacts."

"Wait, Peter," Bernie said. "That is why I am here. This is why I am telling you all this instead of taking the evidence to serious police. You can't solve this, and you can't make the right thing happen. Not with these people, you can't. Just to show you how serious this is, I took back the bags of stuff you just looked at, and I am going to replace each item exactly where I found it. If they send someone around to check on the trail for any reason you and I both need for them to find it undisturbed. I have been very careful. I will continue to be careful."

Peter looked at the stalwart, open face in front of him. A nice man. A good policeman, he bet. But a man of a simple background. Without connections, poor fellow.

"Bernie," he said, "I don't want to intrude on your turf, but this sounds like a question of who you know. I know people who know other people who can handle serious, large, bad things like this. I even know a reliable place to start. I have a colleague in some of my public relations work, a good friend, John Rubrick. I will consult with John."

Bernie's face went pale.

"Now that's what you *can't* do," the policeman said. "Don't talk to your John Rubrick, Peter, Actually, don't talk to anybody, but especially don't talk to John Rubrick."

"He's an old, and trusted friend—from way back—" Peter added deliberately, "He's a gentleman. He's just not anyone who would kill people."

The policeman said, "Pay attention, Peter. You're not listening. Please. You don't understand. These people who would do anything so cruel are big and very bad. Please somehow get that through your head."

"John will—"

The policeman was now quite livid around the eyes.

He cut in. "Don't talk about this to John Rubrick ... of all people." He hesitated and added, "Look, if not for yourself, then please think of me and my wife and my children."

Peter's heart hardened. "What can you possibly have against John Rubrick?"

Bernie hung tough. "I don't like his friends—the ones I have looked up," he said. "Worse, he has other friends whom I don't even want to check into because I would be afraid to have them know that I had checked them out. Peter, I don't want to be rude but the fact is you don't know much about him, either. You probably *think* you do, because he is so familiar to you, but in fact, you don't know what all he does. Please, Peter.

Don't talk to that man. I am plainly begging you."

Peter was impressed that although a simple man, Bernie had not let Peter override his will. Peter felt some force in him.

"All right," he said. "I won't. And Bernie, frankly, I am grateful you have done this crime search and have told me. I think you are probably one policeman in a million."

Bernie picked up the Duluth Pack and carefully Velcroed shut his own pocket flaps. The two men ambled to the front door talking about the weather.

It calmed them. At least, it calmed Peter. He felt his heart slowing to normal beat. He felt the blood retiring from his face. He held the outer door while Bernie lifted each boot from its little pool of snowmelt in the vestibule.

Peter waited until the Stokowski family car left the driveway. He supposed that Bernie would go back out to the Solid Waste Transfer Site, and then hike along that path that led eastward to the little lake, then southward along the shore until it turned west again to go to Peter's dad's old horse barn with the outbuildings. He imagined Bernie would carry a shotgun in the crook of his arm so if someone saw him scuffing along, they'd think he was tracking and hunting. He remembered the trowel that Bernie had jammed into an outer pocket of his pack. He felt bemused by the policeman's fear. He had never felt such fear himself, but then he had never been a policeman or a soldier.

Some of Bernie's terror had got into Peter but, thank God, it was wearing off. What he felt, as he finally shut the heavy door, was loneliness. His body was a little stiff, too. He returned to the kitchen to turn off the coffee maker. How nice—there was Nat taking a break, coffee cup in hand.

Her eyes were still a remarkable blue and even in her fifties, her figure was slender. OK, so she drank. She was his beautiful wife and he wanted to talk to her.

She turned her back to him to gouge at a spill on the stove. She said, "Your friend called. He's coming by. I didn't want to interrupt you in your study…"

Clearly, she was curious but the least a husband could do was spare his wife scary stories from the local police.

"What friend?" he said, smiling, and lightly sliding up to her. He went to take her lightly into his arms. He said, "Theoretically, I have more than one in this town. In theory," he said, approaching Natalie's back, "I am not only respected but loved by a cast of thousands!"

"The friend who's coming is John. I am off to do some shopping. He sounded as if you two have business to talk about."

"Why don't you stay! We could all scarf down some coffee! That pig of a Bernie drank up the whole pot!" he cried, feeling a kind of growing gaiety because not two minutes ago, he had felt desolate but now, here was his wife, and not only that, his good friend was coming.

The door bell sounded.

Nat vanished into the music room and Peter opened to John Rubrick. John looked buoyant and boyish with a dusting of clean white on his hair and shoulders.

"I thought you just drove up!" cried Peter. "How'd you get all that snow on you?"

John said, "You have a beautiful place, Peter. Really, really beautiful. I've just been standing outside here a few minutes. You've done all the right things. The clearing so a person can see the snow through the first tree trunks."

"That was my grandfather's idea," Peter said. "My father and I just kept it going."

John came in and slapped snow off his coat.

Peter took him into the study, and they sat down, as usual, half facing each other, half turned to the window.

Peter looked at the smiling, sober, familiar face. "I've just had the damnedest morning," he said. "I'm glad you've come."

Peter realized he could tell the outline, just the outline, of what had happened without breaking his word to Bernie. John listened to him politely, with no visible interest.

"Cardinal," John interrupted him once to say, half rising from his chair. The stunning bird dropped from an evergreen to the top of the deer lick, paused, and then returned to the tree. John said, "Sorry—you're used to beautiful birds around here. I shouldn't have interrupted. Oh, and when you're done, I've got nice news for you."

Peter gave an outline of Bernie's remarks. "Well, it shows that po- licemen can have a paranoid imagination as well as the next person!" he added, with a smile.

"Still, you have to hand it to him," John said, "bothering to work out a theory at least. A lot of loudmouth paranoids don't *do* anything about awful things they insist are going on. You have to hand it to him, he was unusually conscientious for a state trooper."

"Oh, but he's not a state trooper," Peter explained. "Just our local town chief of police."

Peter heard himself, and felt his soul shrink. I can't have done this, he thought. How can I have done this?

John merely said, "Then you have to hand it to him even more, don't you?"

His tone lightly changed: "Well, Peter—on another subject—New Hampshire and Vermont must be jack sprat filled with lazy interim pas- tors trying to duck their work. I've got you a second sermon and service, if you would do it, for the week after you supply for that other minister. Would you be up for, say, eight days out East, in one shot? I might be able to suggest they get some other Sunday, but they seem to have planned a ski weekend."

John looked up from one of those digital hand memos that didn't ap- peal to Peter. He seemed to have picked up on Peter's wretched feelings.

"Oh hey," John said, "you don't have to take on this extra talk! No need at all! I get the feeling it's worrying you."

"No! No! It isn't that," said Peter. He made himself smile but his whole mind was shaken and cold. "No, I'm delighted! Absolutely delight- ed! And Nat won't mind, right in the middle of winter. She'll be glad to get rid of me. I am always trying to drag her to see people, to have them for dinner, and all."

John smiled back at him. "I've got to be off," he said, rising. "I had no business stopping here but I was passing through, so I wanted to tell you about that extra sermon talk in New England, in case you could work it in."

The day that had started happily hours and hours ago had gone on and on. How unused to self-castigation Peter was! Maybe, he thought, he had never done any self-castigation. Like any Episcopal lay-reader, he knew the words, but this horror, this self-condemnation, for the first time lay like a glacier over his heart.

He was not only afraid that Bernie Stokowski really might be on to some criminals too close, whoever they were, and too powerful, to halt, but he was appalled at himself.

How could he have done exactly what Bernie Stokowski asked him *not* to do? The poor fellow had actually begged. Naturally, Stokowski had to be mistaken about John Rubrick. There was no way a man like Stokowski would understand a man like John. Still, Peter had given his word. And now he again heard his voice chirping like a baby bird, "Oh, it was just our local town chief of police!"

I know what I'm going to do, he said to himself: I will go see Imogen! I absolutely, oh, absolutely, will not burden her with any of this—dear Imogen, his little girl who somehow had grown up to be a kind-hearted person. He would not burden her with his new fears, but she would console him. He knew she would! A person who spent hours and days as she did, working kindly with such a mixed bag of people. It must take such patience, he thought. People are stupid, stupid. For the first time, he felt that stupidity, like some disease the whole species had, inside himself. Perhaps he wasn't so lost as he supposed Imogen's clients or patients to be, but he had been stupid. Not just this morning, which he would not talk to her about, but he would confess to her that four years ago, when her husband somehow failed to save his grandson from drowning, Peter—stupid, stupid Peter!—had had the complacence to suggest to the dead boy's mother that she *forgive* the husband. He would tell Imogen how wrong he had been... how facile, how unfeeling. What a sanctimonious, what a positively magisterial, ass he was! What did he know about losing a child?

Peter decided to walk across town to her apartment, although it was a good half mile and the snow was still falling. The temperature was fast dropping. As the first brittle chill scraped across his eyes, he stopped to rewind his scarf. The miserable cold felt chastening to him.

Imogen's building was a ratty place that he had gone round and round about with his Tenebray Properties manager. It ought to come down, he had said. The manager had said there was lots of life in it yet, by which he meant that if one put $11,000 in some beam replacements and basement footings, then it would be a good income property for fifteen more years. They had left it like that. They didn't replace the double-but-spacer-filled 8 x 12s at all. For the moment, they shimmed three of the 4 x 6 supporting posts in the basement, but made a note of planning to tear up the floor and put in footings within four years.

To cheer himself as he trudged along, he imagined how the mid-day light must be filling Imogen's living room. She would be there. Surely, she would be there. He hadn't called ahead for a coward's reason: she might say he shouldn't come.

He was chilled straight through. Adults of his acquaintance were seldom chilled through—at war, maybe, but even men and women who skied the ferocious mountains of New England had elaborate insulation for their faces and bodies. He hadn't been this cold since a November Saturday afternoon, in 1966, when he had suited up to kick Exeter.

He let himself into the building without ringing and waiting for an answer. His old knees, good old knees, took him up the unlighted staircase. Good heavens, he felt like a slum landlord who wouldn't replace a 60-watt bulb on a landing. On the other hand, why ever did Imogen want to live in a place like this, when she could live in her wonderful childhood home with Natalie and him? That was one of the exasperating aspects of any younger generation. They always try to show you how tough and frugal they are. Peter himself once came all the way from Boston on a Greyhound when his father had already bought him a Capital Airlines ticket from Logan to Minneapolis. And as James Tenebray was bawling out Peter, he had suddenly got an absent-minded look on his face. James confessed that he had once sat up all night in a coach on The New England States to Chicago, although his own father had bought him Pullman reservations for both nights of the trip. And here was Imogen, living in this dump, when Tenebray Properties could have found her something simple, but rat-free.

Imogen's doorbell seemed to be out of order. He would let himself in with the key she'd given him.

The warm, dry apartment-house air made him sigh with relief. He went in gingerly. He sat in one of three chairs pulled up to the fireplace and held out his hands to a few blooming coals and ends of sticks still aflame. So she'd been in the house recently. Probably out shopping now. She'd return.

The bedroom door opened behind him. If she had a burglar, Peter was glad he was there. He was just in the mood to do something heroic. He reached for tongs, didn't see any. All right, bare hands it would have to be.

Peter's daughter, tying the braided cord of a dressing gown, came towards him with a pleasant exclamation. "Yay, Dad!" she cried, like a kid.

After her came Vern Denham. Clearly they had been in Imogen's bed. Neither Imogen's nor Vern's hair was combed.

Peter thought: they will be furious that I let myself into the house, and I—he came to a stop. A man doesn't really like to think of his daughter being in bed with anybody, not really, not even with a husband. Not even with a man you know to be principled. Whatever that ancient, primitive aversion is, Peter thought, I am having it.

Peter had automatically risen from his chair, to strangle a burglar. He stayed on his feet.

Imogen was smiling at him. Her face was roseate and calm.

"Yay, Dad," she said again. "You look frozen. You didn't walk! Did you walk all the way here?"

"Hello, Peter," Vern said. The young man came over naturally, even though he was wearing what looked like pajama bottoms of Imogen's along with his own shirt and sports jacket. They shook hands.

"What'll we have, Im?" Vern called.

"Hot tea. Here, I'll get it, Vern. Oh, the hell with it," she said in a reasonable tone. "I'll bring us drinks. Dad, what do you want to drink?"

Peter heard it all. He felt everything, mainly a mix of solemnity and hilarity. Here was a new couple acting domestic. It partly reminded him of finding a litter of puppies that you hadn't known were in the old horse barn. Imogen and Vern were acting like a man and a woman who had already made love many times, and would again, many more times, thousands of times before their deaths, and their deaths would be decades and decades away.

They were inviting him to their hearth. Vern was brisking up the fire. He added a birch log and two chunks of oak.

"Sir?" said Vern's voice, because Peter had fallen into daydream. Vern bent over him with a flat bowl in which lay some desperately stale-looking Cheez-its.

"Damn right," Peter said. "Thank you, Vern."

He sees that I feel shy and definitely *de trop*, Peter thought. Vern sat opposite him, crossing his legs in the flowered women's pajamas. Vern began to patter along about Imogen's skills in decorating this apartment. The young man's steady, cheerful voice, as meaningless as wallpaper, gave Peter time to recover from embarrassment or shyness or anything else he might be suffering from.

"Oh, good! Here she is!" Vern said. He leapt up and took the tray from Imogen. Three tall whiskeys, it looked like.

Imogen sat down.

At last, Peter laughed. "I want to give a toast in the worst way," he said.

"Give it, sir," said Vern—using the outmoded language with deliberate irony.

Peter looked back and forth between their faces. "The toast is to you two," he said. "I have seen a lot of people in 58 years but I have never seen any two of them look so happy as you. And nice. I bet there isn't anyone else in Minnesota or anywhere today who has walked in on two people in bed and they've treated him so kindly!"

They drank.

Then a shy pause overtook them all. Then Vern said, "Tell you what, Peter, it's time to tell you what my intentions are."

Everybody laughed.

Vern began to explain their engagement, and his interest in modernizing his dad's bakery.

A huge switch of power took place quietly, ghosting in without either of the young people's noticing it. It was not like a mutiny in which at one moment a captain is captain and in the next is walking a plank. This changeover of power was like a mist moving across a landscape that only a moment before had looked ordinary. You don't ever exactly see the edges of a mist and nothing is wounded by its movement. The most fragile grassheads do not stir.

No, that was not what it felt like. This power was like a serious, civil animal that had ambled over to take the scent of the guest, but now was moving heavily back over to its true owners.

Peter, warmed by his daughter's fire, and flattered by her lover's courtesy, was just now losing all of his power.

Peter went on listening to this sandy-haired fellow—of course, he could do that much and he did, and of course, he put in a question now and then, about whole wheat bread marketing, getting married, anything, the kitchen sink would have done—it made no difference. Underneath the young people's voices, Peter realized he was turning over much of his remaining happiness to them. He was like someone who has gift-wrapped something and is handing it to others who are talking: they scarcely notice that they've taken this package into their hands, or if it is addressed to anybody.

CHAPTER THIRTEEN

The choir director was thin in the way of big-shot women. Her chic, very narrow, mannish tweed jacket made her all the more feminine. Natalie Tenebray began, as always, by leading the group in a hymn that both synods of Lutherans, the Episcopalians, and the sprinkle of Catholics would know. Some latecomers—the slower of the aged, or the irresolute poor—could get settled in the rear.

The regular ecumenical choir singers pretended to take direction from Natalie. Now they were belting out *Dona Nobis Pacem* in the canon, rather than the round, form. They belted out what they knew, and yawed lightly over what they didn't know. Tenors who couldn't read music at all leaned heads toward anyone in their section who could, such as Dieter Stolz. They took his note from him, a split second late. Pearl slammed the piano keys to punish people back onto the beat when they lagged.

At this last rehearsal, as last year and years before, the two heavy-set violinists with their shirt cuffs hanging loose and their imitation Norwegian-knit vests bulging around their bodies, played their instruments perfectly. They made no mistakes in the fingering. They studiously kept to the slash-and-*U* bowing that Natalie had penciled in for them. One of them played with a respectable vibrato, the other with a palsied left-hand jiggling. Their bows did not sail over the strings: this was hard labor so they labored. Natalie smiled at them, cued them in and off from time to time, scolded a couple of sopranos for being flat when they could perfectly well have trusted the violins for their note—this with a smile at the strings players.

Natalie Tenebray wore two hats until the post-Thanksgiving chorale was over. She was always the wife of the town's biggest big shot, but on Sundays in the autumn, she was a glorious, authoritative martinet of a music director. These annual minions of hers never received serious discipline in anything else. They smiled nervous smiles and even low laughs when Natalie Tenebray swatted her two palms together until the male singers heard her over their own voices.

"Stop, oh, for the love of God, *would* you stop!" she shouted.

She made them listen while she sang whatever parts had disgraced basses or tenors, whichever section had got it wrong.

The old people and the poor people who sat along the back wall, were grateful for a new electric strip just under their seats this afternoon. "Oh, if that didn't make a difference!" they exclaimed to each other. None of them really sang, but they dutifully lowered their eyes to their sheet music as Natalie berated people. They noticed everything they possibly could. If Natalie Tenebray was scolding the others, they took the scolding, too. This was Sunday afternoon, free of the Patriots, free of the Pack, both of whom were what their grandchildren came to visit if they came at all. Here, these rehearsals now, were a social occasion among the other people in their own town. They remarked on everything they could. They noticed the curious presence of Arlene Stropp, who cleaned houses. Her husband was in jail, arraigned and charged for shooting the Episcopal priest. They studied what they could make out of the back of her head, as if the truth about manslaughter was hidden in her, somehow. She'd never been there before, not even sitting at the back with them, but here she was, big as life in that alto section.

This week the "lunch," as it was called, although it was a mid-afternoon snack, was from Marty Hanks's Super Valu. Everyone knew the differences and similarities between food from Denham's Bakery and food from the Super Valu. They liked all of it. Just thinking about it reminded them that the first half must be about over soon. The moment Natalie said, "Time to eat!" Stan Garris got up and came back, and told everyone back there to come right up and take a plate with the others.

Ward Hines, the oldest man in the room, felt very good about that. He remembered back to when people voluntarily brought the lunch to rehearsals. One Sunday, nothing came in but jello and boughten chocolate chip cookies from the Super Valu. Ward remembered clearly what happened. Mr. Peter Tenebray went to the telephone and ordered in deli. People thought the poor and the old liked trans-crap—as Ward's wife called it—for food, but it wasn't true. They were grateful for some protein when it was offered.

In the second half of rehearsal, the director got angry.

Mrs. Tenebray swore at them. "For the love of God!" she cried. "*Would* you please stop singing when I need your attention!"

At last, the couple of basses closed their mouths. They had rushed to rehearsal from watching two and three-quarters of the Vikes' game. They'd acted humble about coming into the church drunk as they were, but then they loved the sound of their voices swinging through the Tallis Canon. They looked sullen when Natalie told them to shut up.

Natalie said, "You've got to learn to listen to someone besides yourself! Look—Pearl, go back to C and play the bass line."

She made the men repeat the bad passage.

"All right then!" she called. "*Tutti!* Everybody! Try it again!"

The sturdy women raised their violins and bows.

Natalie stopped them after a second.

Natalie said. "Would you put down your music, please, and just sing with me? Just sing with me! 'Love divine all loves excelling'—Strings on parts 1 and 2, please—Pearl, no piano. Note, please."

Pearl tapped on E flat. They all watched Natalie, all of them sullen, but as they sang on, they cheered up. The beauty of it reached into them, and their voices began to peel upward, instead of just slamming the air. Their director let them do it again.

They regarded her with solemn happiness.

"O my dears," Natalie cried, "You're lovely when you put your minds to it! Lovely! OK. Housekeeping now?"

Peter came forward from his place among the basses. His wife had already turned to one side to put her music into its briefcase. She kept at it as he began to speak.

Peter told them that, as they knew, they would be using the St. Fursey Church cassocks this year. He reminded them where their choir booklets would be and when to meet in the side room of the school auditorium.

He turned to the violinists. "You two all clear to go?" he smiled. "Music stands? Anything else?"

They reminded him that they always brought their own stands.

Peter cried, "Don't forget Wednesday night! Annual Veterans' Evening! And it will be very special this year. Starting promptly at 7:30."

A bass called out, "What time on Wednesday then?"

"He just said!" snarled a couple of the sopranos in unison.

"Seven thirty, everybody! All right then!" shouted Peter. "One more announcement only. As you know, at St. Fursey Episcopal Church, we have lost our Rector this past week. This is a tragedy for us, not only because Eliza was so young to die—but because we loved her. Some of you who are not Episcopalians had come to love Eliza, too, in her three years among us all. Eliza especially loved serious music. So here is my thought for us: let's dedicate our concert coming up to her memory and to the memory of everyone we have loved in our lives who enjoyed music. Let's make it a celebration for each of them."

A quiet clapping from someone in the tenor section. It caught on. Then everyone clapped quietly, steadily.

Peter came down the aisle to Arlene. "Stay for a minute, will you?" he said. "We have a cassock for you, but let's make sure of the size."

Ward Hines was painfully stiff, but he helped the other men clank together the backs and seats of metal chairs. Katie Anderson collected all the music and brought it forward into a neat stack. Stan Garris went out into the kitchen and stopped them packing up leftover sandwiches. He grabbed eight of them and folded them into those sheets that threatened choir directors with prosecution if they made photocopies of copyrighted anthems. He had no trouble finding Ward Hines still at the back. Stan's mother was holding out the jacket sleeve for the stiff old fellow.

"Ride with us," Stan told him. "And Mom, take these, will you, and divide them up when you get home, you and Ward and Michelle and the gang up at the Apartments."

At last, Peter and Natalie sat in their living room, martinis in hand. Peter's ears still heard how one person had started that light clapping and kept it up until the others, in twos and threes, and finally everybody, had joined in. His heart bloomed. It was mysterious to him that when he had stood in front of the singers and urged them to do their best for poor Eliza, he had felt sure of his message. Now that he was back home, he could not remember whether or not Eliza had ever shown any feeling for music.

Now he was telling Natalie that he had been asked to fill for an interim pastor service in New Hampshire, late in January. He had been appointed to a Visiting Committee to Andover, too, to plan new film material for the school. He had hoped, he told Natalie, that he could combine those two trips, but it wouldn't work. They wanted him to take Morning chapel on the Friday for the School. But the New Hampshire church had put him off another week. He had meant to keep news of his third gig to himself until it was a sure thing, but Natalie was looking so graceful and agreeable, even affable, as she sat down across from him, that he blurted it out. "And I may have to do a third trip," he told her. "Phillips Brooks House."

"Sounds wonderful," Natalie said. "Did they give you a subject or have you chosen your own?"

She almost never asked him about talks he got scheduled. She had not changed her clothes since the rehearsal. Even in that no-doubt smart, but to him, harsh, style of pinstriped suit, she was fine. He didn't detect a drop of sarcasm or irony about her at the moment. She was so often truculent about tiny issues, or so it felt to him, that this present, warm moment made him want to tell her everything in his heart. Even if old Nat drank too much, and mostly alone, he knew she still preferred to drink with him at the conventional cocktail hour.

The combination of her beauty and her elegant relaxation touched him. She so often grew angry when he praised her that he now hesitated. He looked at her speculatively. How could he make her know how much he admired her kindness in sharing her music like this? What a beautiful rehearsal it had been! He wanted to exclaim that her leading that humdrum choir was a major, major kindness to ordinary people. He felt as if the world—well, all right, weren't such things bound to sound stupid!— but still, if there were only more of such kindnesses, helping ordinary people make beautiful sounds—if there were more of that, then wouldn't the world—well, he didn't have to be specific about it.

"Oh, Nat," he said, now rising to take the pitcher over to replenish her glass. "I so often feel guilty about your musical career!"

Her face went expressionless.

He hung onto his idea anyway. He said, "I mean, if you and I had not lived here in the middle of the continent and raised our daughter here, you might have had a very different kind of career... in Boston, say. In New York. We have no way of guessing, European tours maybe."

Her face grew so irate that he hurried on. "But, of course, it is wonderful for this whole community—and for me—especially for me—that you exercise your talent here and brighten the lives of all of us."

"Drinks, Peter," she said. She had emptied her glass.

"Yes, of course," he said hastily, but he called back over his shoulder from the ice bucket, "it's true, though, Nat: all that top-drawer career you've given up has been a huge boon to our community."

Back in the living room, he refilled her glass. Her face had settled back into the obdurate expression that was habitual with her. Like all people who don't drink addictively, he had no real clue as to what made Natalie take four martinis instead of two each evening—and if he offered her only two, she would retire to the guest wing where she artfully hid her liquor. He himself never wanted to load up with booze, especially in the middle of the day as she sometimes did. He had no instinct to lie down on a guest bed in order to sleep off a half-bottle of something. He supposed she didn't understand some of his pleasures, either. Maybe she hadn't the slightest desire to fly East for a weekend in order to give a talk. And old friendships. She didn't seem to keep in touch with her school or college classmates, either. Still, what if she felt stuck back home, here in this uncultivated little town, while he got to address groups of variously educated people?

"Nat, when I get jobs to give talks in different places—and now these three sermons—"

"Not three whole sermons, is it, Peter?" she said. "One church sermon in New Hampshire. One ten-minute morning chapel address for prep school kids. One lay talk at Phillips Brooks House?"

"Of course you're right," he said. "But Nat—when I get jobs like this—and take off for the Duluth or Minneapolis airport to fly to them—does it remind you of a life you haven't—well, does it remind you that you have a huge talent in music and aren't getting much chance to fulfill it?"

She now upended her glass. She drank off the third entire straight-up martini that he had poured her a minute ago. "No, Peter, it doesn't remind me of anything like that."

"I only wondered," he said.

"It doesn't remind me of anything like that," she repeated. "For one thing, I haven't got any huge musical talent, and I never did have. What you see me and hear me doing is all I can do. I am a singing teacher. I am a director of an ecumenical choir who at their best sing at one-third volume. Most of them can't sight-read at all. None of them except Dieter have the least idea of dynamics. What interest they do have is so low-key and childish, that if we tried to run that choir an additional six weeks instead of just the October and November six we do have laid on, they'd quit. I am able to help the accompanist and the two strings players do what they can, but at bottom, I look on them as damage control: their mission is to be ready at all times to drown out the singers if worse comes to worst."

Peter flung at her: "But Nat, you shouted to them! You shouted 'O my dears! Sometimes you do a lovely job!'" cried Peter. "You've praised them before, too! And you did it again this afternoon!"

Natalie said calmly, "I'm a music teacher. I love good sound when I hear it. Sometimes some of them, this afternoon even a critical mass of them, make good sound. I tell them when it happens."

"But Nat! That's so—"

Now she stood up. "I know you mean to be encouraging, Peter. But the truth is, I am just like you. I am a mid-sized fish of no particular color in a pond of no particular size. You and I—we're promoters. I am not an artist. I am about one step better than a publicist about music. Yes!" she called back over her shoulder, on her way to the guest room. Her tone sounded malignant. "A publicist! Like you," she added. "We're both publicists for the nice life!"

He didn't mean to run after her and beg. His feet took him, nonetheless, and when he caught up with her in front of the bookcase wall he grasped her shoulders.

"You're coming back, Nat. Come on, we'll have another drink and we'll talk over what needs to be talked over."

He looked at her infuriated face. He said, "I don't think of my work as being publicist work. And I don't think of my community interests—like church and ecumenical choir—as publicist work. And I don't think of what *you* do as publicist's work either. Damned if I must take such insult! And—damned if I can imagine why you would even want to make such demeaning remarks!"

He would give her a moment. Peter went around to three of the table lamps and lighted them.

Now she spoke. She said, "You always try to brighten and shine up everything. It drives me nearly crazy."

He said, "That's a lie. I wasn't trying to brighten up what you did for the singers over at church this afternoon. It was wonderful, so I said it was wonderful."

She said, "All right. So it was good community ambiance. And I like singing, too. I think it is the more serious things that drive me crazy. When you try to gloss over very bad cruel things, it drives me crazy, Peter. I thought it was my fault for years. It was only four years ago that I got it through my head that it was your fault."

He waited. Four years ago. Four years ago?

Nat said, "You were always trying to get Imogen not to worry about Strog."

"She married him," Peter said in a brutal tone. "Marriage is marriage."

Nat went on. "He had a propensity for recklessness, and you've got to have seen that just as well as I did. When they invited us up to that Thief River Falls place they'd rented."

He couldn't help smiling at the recollection. He said, "I'll never forget that! They were so happy in that wild place! All that nature and how they loved it! Do you remember how that one afternoon, Strog supplied us all with guns, and we walked through a cornfield looking to rouse up some pheasants?"

It had been a late Saturday afternoon in the fall. The farmer had picked, but not yet disked down, a half acre for plowing. Their little group took rows four feet apart. Only two pheasants got up at the end. Strog winged one, and Peter didn't get his gun up in time for the other.

They started across another field. Suddenly, a rabbit leapt up, alternately jumping and galloping, down rows, then cutting across, then coming back up towards them in another row.

"Get him! Get him!" shouted Strog.

Peter had no desire to kill that rabbit. Rabbits were Easter bunnies.

A sharp seeding of shell spread very near him. Strog had taken the animal cross-row, right in front of Peter. For an excellent shot like Strog, it probably wasn't even dangerous. Peter came up to the dying animal. Its huge, amazing back legs still plunged and plunged in the corn leaves that the picker had left.

Peter's daughter cried, "Goddammit! You didn't have to do that, Strog!"

Her young husband ignored the remark. He came bounding across rows, breaking down more stubble.

"Sorry, Pete," he said. "I didn't want to miss that one. He's a big fellow!" He picked it up in front of Peter and broke its neck over backwards.

Now Peter said to his wife, "You had to hand it to Strog, how he had survival skills. He cleaned and skinned that rabbit for us. He told me the trick of the skinning, too, but darned if I can remember it. I think he soaked the pieces in vinegar, not exactly a marinade. Then he rolled everything in whole wheat flour and tarragon. Don't you remember, Nat? He not only fried it for us but he made a pan gravy, too."

Nat said, "What I remember is how, when the baby came, he loved it and would toss it up into air and then catch it again."

Peter smiled. "True enough. Men do that. It irritates women, I know."

Nat said, "Imogen used to leave the room."

Peter was feeling nearly joyful, he was so relieved that they were just discussing the past in a civilized way. This was the first time he had been able to get Nat back on track, so to speak, once she lost her temper. It felt like a good omen to him.

CHAPTER FOURTEEN

The countryside between the Iron Range and Minneapolis looked wonderfully interesting to Imogen as she drove south. The November morning was so early that the sky hadn't yet drunk up any light from the sun. She was nearly weightless, happy, with what little she could make out in the green-black hood of clouds. She had a delicate stomach, but otherwise was as strong as most people at age 34. She threw up a lot, but not in the car.

Like any rural Northerner in any helping profession, she knew her usual routes by heart. She knew where the rest stops were, where the less poisonous of the fast-food sites were, where the most poisonous—and most delicious—were. She knew where you must watch for wild animals although there were no crossings signs. Deer stood lightly on the highway shoulders. It was scary guesswork for them. They angled their heads this way and that, half-drugged with headlights, deciding to cross, deciding no, no, don't cross after all, trying to make judgments with their tiny non-neocortical thinking sites, their pathetic amygdalae. It had been hundreds of thousands of years since Imogen's species, *homo sapiens*, had had to guide its decisions by terror alone.

She anticipated having a happy break from work. She liked her work and she liked her life. She was a school social worker who was in love for the second time, and happily so. On the other hand, she worked in what the field of social work called "a secondary setting." A primary setting was some place like an agency where there were other professional social workers, so you weren't the only person on the premises whose mission was different from everyone else's missions. A small school, like St. Fursey Elementary and Middle, was always a secondary setting. The social worker was the only person with social-work aims and social-work ethical constraints. Everyone else had other professional goals. The superintendent was driven to maintain the entire structure. The principal wanted to keep the peace between administration and the parents. Over half of the teachers were saints. Imogen noticed that they invited little kids into getting a kick out of their own imaginations. Other teachers were so terrified of chaos or loss of power they would trample flat any idea they hadn't heard of over and over. It scarcely mattered if the idea came from adults or children. If it was original—original! *Original!* Original was all very well and good but you couldn't tell where it might go. Some teachers even rolled their eyes to the rest in the class—inviting them to sneer—Oh, quietly! Not really sneering, of course not, only trying to show the fact that, look, you had to have a sense of humor about some things.

Imogen was like an old fox with its own bag of tricks. She watched her back. She had even stood off the bullhead principal, Donald Menzies.

Still, how wonderful it was to be driving by herself in the lightening day to the MSSWA conference. She planned to park outside the Earl Browne Center just as the keynote speaker was being introduced. That way she could slide into a back seat and hear him without much prefacing. Later, she would find some colleagues and eat lunch with them. The whole day she would not have to protect her psychological or physical space from a principal or anyone else. Everyone would trade real truths instead of small talk. How had they liked the plenary guy? What was the beastliest thing that had happened in *their* school recently? What great moments of truth had *they* rejoiced in recently?

In the crush of the lunch line, she found her friends all right, but one of them had brought along a guest. As non-professionals sometimes did when visiting helping professionals, this guest brought out some psychological theories to make an impression. She said she hadn't liked the keynote speaker because he talked about *evil*, verbatim, and any ethical practitioner knows that one person's evil is someone else's everyday custom. They all ate steadily from their sandwich boxes which were full of food that was bad for you but tasted wonderful. The conversation moved on. It turned to men, and Imogen perked up a little. The guest said that the real attraction between men and women was mutual high-mindedness. She went on about it some and the others dumped out the chips and commercial cookies and offered them around to one another with raised eyebrows. It seemed too bad that no one picked up on such a cheerful idea as men and women are initially attracted to one another by intuiting like-minded idealism. Nothing about the idea was unpleasant. Imogen couldn't help with the conversation, however, because her attraction to Vern—her current squeeze—was his sandy-colored hair. You can't just join some conference conversation with the remark that you preferred sandy-colored body hair as well as sandy-colored head hair and that you had been delighted to find Vern had it, now that you two had got to know each other in the past two weeks. And that she had noticed the sandy-colored hair before she knew he had quit a high-paying position because his company tortured rabbits as part of product development. No matter how comfy the little table of acquaintances who had managed to get their lunch trays and take them over to a table, you couldn't add that into a conversation just to put a guest at her ease. And it wouldn't improve anything if you further added that not only did you like the sandy-colored hair of your present man, but it had been a factor in how you had chosen your husband, too, from whom you were divorced.

Imogen merely listened for a while. The others consulted their packets to make choices for the afternoon.

Imogen looked about until she caught sight of the morning's speaker. She went gingerly between the hilarious or raucous or shy-sounding table conversations along the way. He stopped eating to smile at her. His face said, you may tell me you loved my talk this morning; others have been doing that. Or his face said, whatever reason you have come to speak to me is OK with me.

"Just a question," Imogen said. "I was just wondering if you ever take a last-minute emergency client for a session."

He said without any pause at all: "That's the main kind. Hang on a second." He laid down his fork and got a card out of his jacket pocket.

This encouraged her enough so she could lie cheerfully to the table group about why she'd had a word with the speaker.

Now the guest at their table was announcing that you lose power only if you give it away. *No one can take power from you,* she said. Imogen felt too buoyed up inside herself to ask for some examples. Or why it was that those with money and educational privilege seemed to manage all sorts of stunts that single moms in poorish rural towns couldn't pull off?

She had paid for the conference. They had her money; they had given her one totally good speech, she needn't give them her time as well. She now longed for her own life, which she had left at 4:30 that morning. She decided to leave for home.

Her family had always had power. And a taste for rhetoric. A gassy bunch, she said to herself. She was even named for the daughter of the composer Gustaf Holst, of all things. This made her a very funny kind of social worker. Money and privilege did not always combine to make stupidity, however. For example, there was one reason and *only* one reason that the St. Fursey, Minnesota, Elementary School didn't have windowless walls like other schools built in the late 1960s and early 1970s.

Her great-grandfather and her grandfather together had used force and money in 1970. Pure force. Pure money. Old Cornelius Tenebray, even so old as he had been then, and his son James had had money all their lives. Generations of money equals rhetoric, Imogen thought as she drove back north. Cornelius and James had bullied a venal school principal and his passive, startled (and chicken) local Board of Education into taking the architectural design those two men wanted instead of the more conventional design types being presented by a Duluth architectural firm.

That St. Fursey Elementary principal in 1970 had been a sleaze, but not so bad a sleaze as the present man, Imogen's boss, Donald Menzies. In 1970, the school principal just wanted to do a favor for friends in Duluth. LaserSpace was an architectural company that did a lot of schools. There was nothing particularly criminal in the principal's machinations.

His meeting to publicize LaserSpace's proposals was announced, as it had to be, twice in the St. Fursey newspaper. Light refreshments, the announcement read, would be served. In that town, refreshments, without the world "light," meant coffee brewed on the spot by the principal's secretary and fresh cookies from the St. Fursey Bakery. "Light refreshments," on the other hand, meant cardboard-boxed cookies from the Super Valu.

LaserSpace sent their president and an engineer with drawings for the St. Fursey School Board to look at. The meeting was poorly attended. Schools are schools and someone has to build them. The promised "light refreshments" protected the meeting from a roomful of indifferent citizenry whose votes could not be augured ahead. As it was, one school board member in a Vikings sweatshirt, whose obvious drunkenness said "loose cannon" to the principal, had to feel along the back of his intended chair to make sure he got his bottom into it safely. The principal decided not to worry about that one vote, but he was very sorry to see not one, but two, members of St. Fursey's leading family at the meeting.

Both Cornelius and James Tenebray did attend. Cornelius was 81 at the time, and couldn't hear much. It didn't matter. He was there to talk, not hear. James Tenebray did not guide his old dad by the arm, but they entered the library meeting room with James very close behind his father, looking like an equerry who whispers cues to a powerful, aged king.

The principal was a jerk but he wasn't stupid. He knew a lost cause when he saw one. Still, once a meeting is set, you had to run it. He stood in front of the large newsprint stand. He thanked everybody for coming. He bowed to the two Tenebrays and smiled, though he had spent a restless night, fully hoping that neither one of those two rich bastards would show up on one of their goddamned power trips.

He introduced an architect named Reg Lazer to the group. He also said they were lucky that Reg—everyone was first names because that was the climate—had brought his chief engineer with him. It meant the group could ask any questions they had and one or both of these two smart guys would have answers. Everyone smiled. The principal introduced Reg Lazer's engineer. Then he said that, without further ado, he would turn everything over to them.

The Lazer company men took turns speaking.

They carefully said that they were a three-generation family company. Lazers had been born in Minnesota for three generations, actually. While one spoke, the other laid fresh drawings and charts on the newsprint stand. They made a handsome presentation. They didn't recognize the Tenebrays, so they didn't jiggle their feet the way the school principal did. Like any human beings who have successfully made a business proposal exactly as planned, they were completely, sincerely happy to take questions. They nodded to the first person to raise a hand.

"Yes, sir!" Reg cried energetically, because the man looked very old and his suit was unmistakable Savile Row. Reg felt an element of relief as well, because he had noted that one of the locals present was informally dressed and looked drunk. He had been hoping that man wouldn't squeeze in the first question.

His joy vanished in the next half-second.

Cornelius and James Tenebray rose together. James brought forward a three-foot wide color photo of a very top-drawer building and asked Reg if it would be all right to set it on top of their stand.

Cornelius started the talking. He asked everybody to notice the windows. He argued for expensive fenestration for the entire building. He asked everybody to notice the long low building of one wing after another, with a short cul de sac of a wing for Administration. The old man said to the Board that they did not want a high-security prison to educate their children in. Please, he repeated, let's have windows. True, he said, lots of brick and no windows was much cheaper than first-rate glazing and good interior space. The old man sat down.

James Tenebray had been passing packets of papers around, offering them between shoulders like a waiter with a hot platter. He did not forget the school secretary.

Then he moved to the front. Using no notes, he told the Board that cheapness was being wished off on them by the Lazer firm. Let's not let them wish that off on *our* town, James said. He said, "Many of us will be dead, but our children's children will still be going to St. Fursey Elementary School. Let's stick up for our kids, and their kids, and St. Fursey, Minnesota, kids to come."

In general, the group let their mouths sag open. The Vikings fan made a thumbs-up sign. The younger Tenebray reseated himself.

The principal knew all was lost but he wasn't yellow. What's more, he was very, very sick of being pushed around by Tenebrays. That family even ran the church he went to. Just because they were anglophiles or whatever you called a UK freak, that church ran services that hadn't been used since they hanged you for stealing a sheep. The principal had been waiting his chance.

He drew himself up and said "That *does* look very expensive, Mr. Tenebray—and James."

"It will be," old Mr. Tenebray said. "It will take two and three-quarters millions and here are—" whereupon his son James came forward again, to the principal and then to the chairman of the Board of Education, and handed each a large blueprint roll: "—here are preliminary drawings."

The principal had a moment of hope. "Thank you," he said crisply. "You will remember that our Board here is a fiduciary instrument of the State of Minnesota. We can't duck the question of the expense."

James Tenebray returned to his seat. He whispered to his father. He had rested one index finger on the table. Now he swiveled it 30 degrees so it pointed to the board chair. His father nodded.

Old Mr. Cornelius rose again. They all could see that it took him a minute to get the blood running through his legs so he could walk. "You're right," the old man said. He carried what people took for two small pieces of paper in his hand. He came forward behind the seated people again and handed one paper to the chairman. He brought the other around to the school secretary.

The chairman glanced at the paper and then stood up at his place with a shining, obsequious look. He cleared his throat. He said, "Mr. Tenebray has just given me an affidavit which I will read aloud to you. 'It will be the pleasure of the Tenebray Family Foundation, jointly with Tenebray Properties, Ltd. to pay nine-tenths of the cost of the St. Fursey Elementary School's new building, namely $2,475,000, half when the work is taken in hand and the other half upon completion, excluding landscaping.'"

It hadn't made news that much interested the VFW crowd, but it went along a route natural to its kind. First stop was the 19th hole of the Northland Country Club in Duluth. Reg Lazer had never been the Club president but he had taken one or another office from time to time. His detractors found it interesting that someone in some foxy little town called St. Fursey had finessed him.

From there, the story mysteriously returned to St. Fursey. Next year, as the building went up, the School Board members came to believe that they had pulled off something wonderful. They began to recall and repeat bits of the speeches of Cornelius and James. Sometimes these speeches were attributed to them, sometimes to others.

Private money and family privilege had given St. Fursey Elementary a building with windows all down one side of every hallway and huge picture windows in every single office. Each schoolroom had a swath of window glass from two and a half feet above the floor to within two feet of the ceiling. The only places you couldn't look outdoors from were the janitors' four supply closets and the lavatories. The smallest children could rush to the windowsills to see a bear family, if it passed within sight. Teachers could and did interrupt their work with the kids to say, "Hey, everyone, look at that" because a stag was bringing his does just within the forest edge on the other side of Tenebray Creek.

Now, this autumn, a week passed after the conference Imogen Tenebray had attended. Three wolves trotted along the near side of the Creek. Imogen got some cachet in telling a troubled little girl in her office, "Wait. A fourth wolf might follow after a hundred yards or so." They both waited. A full minute. Then another. Then a handsome beast came slouching along at a slow trot, gray, low to the ground.

November grew darker and colder. Imogen welcomed it because it discouraged the extroverted cheer that sunshine tended to build up in human beings. Other social workers had said there was no more futile exercise than agreeing to do psychological work with clients in California: they came to their first sessions full of cheer like expectant shoppers for in-season organic fruit. It took them two full sessions to get inside their own minds enough to concentrate on anything more serious than complaints about their mothers having given no help with menstruation. But the sunshine, the beach, the outdoor stalls of organic fruits and vegetables called to them to be happy the way they had been happy before. They often quit therapy at three weeks.

A drawback to hallways so exposed to the out-of-doors as St. Fursey School's was that if you threw up in the hall outside your office, you could be seen by anyone in the front parking lot. Imogen's nausea attack on this

Thursday morning came after Donald Menzies had spent a half hour doing business in her office. Imogen's policy, in the four years since she took
an MSW, was to make it out to the hall for all vomiting. She was usually
able to spare other people by clearing out of whatever room they were
in—her office, or the nave of St. Fursey Episcopal Church, for example.

After Menzies left, his laughter, along with the sound of her own
retching, was thick in her ears. He had fortunately turned the corner into
the short Administrative wing and didn't hear her.

"OK," she said aloud to herself as she went off to the familiar broom
closet for pail and rag. "OK. Now you don't put it off any more. I will
remind you," she continued to herself, but aloud, "You don't get to ar-
gue any more that you are only one-tenth crazed instead of nine-tenths
crazed. Your own four years of professional advice to clients has been to
treat all lesions early on."

Oh, but people can and do work these things out, a few thousand
dendritic synapses in her brain said. No they can't either, a few thousand
receptors said back to them. People—adult clients—had told Imogen
they could work through their drinking habits if they had them, but they
didn't do it. Other clients were going to work out getting the husband to
stop being a wife-batterer, but they didn't do it. She was going to work
through uncontrollably throwing up every time the death of any small
child was mentioned, but would she do it?

"But of course, unlike others, you are not crazy," her mind remarked
glossily. "Look, you even heal other people." She reminded her mind that
she had thrown up at the DECC in Duluth just because two tenors sang a
song about Abraham and Isaac. In St. Fursey Episcopal Church, she had
thrown up during the reading of the Second Lesson on December 28th
just this past last year. And now, especially neurotically, she had thrown
up because a principal, whose general coarseness she should have been
300% immune to by now, had laughed about a dead bear cub that the cop
had picked up. Her mind said, "So what's wrong with throwing up now
and then? People do it." She firmly shut the closet door after rinsing the
pail. "There's more," her mind said. "You can't even remember the *name*
of your ex-husband's child! You really are crazy."

Back in her office, shaken, she said to herself. "I will give myself ten minutes to calm down. I might remember the name of Strog's infant son if I concentrate. I might. If I do, then I will work through the throwing-up part later." She said it several times.

Donald Menzies was such an appalling school principal he was uniformly disliked by everyone. It wasn't even refreshing to gossip about him in the Denham Bakery because everyone knew he was no good. Even Imogen's father, who felt some liking for everybody, had asked Imogen once if she had any idea why the Bishop, a frequent visitor to the house, had exclaimed, "So *you're* the ones got that fellow for elementary school principal now?"

Imogen had lightly said, "He was probably just referring to the fact that Donald takes the bad boys down to the basement near the lockers and beats their heads against the wall."

"Surely, that can't be true," her father said.

Surely, it was true, however.

She thought, there is no end to the way psychological street wisdom can be wrong. In her family, for example, her mother, being the alcoholic in the family, should by rights be in all sensible psychological theory considered the villain—the one who yanks around the rest of the family so they are somehow to blame for her addiction. But it wasn't true. Her *father* was the one who wouldn't allow an unaffectionate thing to be said about anybody. Anybody! Donald Menzies!

Donald Menzies and Imogen were so clearly enemies they never argued anymore. He kept his eyes open for any chance to fire her. If the grown-up clients of school social workers were less likely than others to cost the people of the United States $34,000 a year for room and board at Sandstone or Dannemora or Leavenworth, that made no odds to Donald Menzies. What he needed was what he had built up carefully—a school board tending toward neutrality on all issues. He wanted them to be cross about tax paying. Their opinion of him depended on what they called his "down-to-earth" humor. When the question of the school social worker came up, he always repeated to them her salary—for which, he would hint, she did goodness only knew what with the kids that she shanghaied into her office. But then, he would confess, what would he know?

On her part, she watched eagerly for any 8th grade boy who could get outside the culture enough to make himself accuse the principal of physical abuse—as in head-bashing near the lockers.

This past Tuesday morning at 7:30 Imogen had come around the hallway corner in time to see the two janitors locking up her office. She found they had stood three five-foot-tall Title I files in the center of her space. No problem, really. In order to get them out, she first removed each of the 12 file drawers because they were heavy with paperwork. Then she was able to toe-and-heel all three tall cases out into the hallway. She replaced the drawers. Then she sat down at her desk to look out the window at some pretty snow that lay as light as lace on the broken brome outside. She estimated Vern and she would be together again in nine hours provided she didn't have to arrange respite care for anyone, or drive any kids back to Residential who'd run. She thought about bed with Vern for a few minutes.

At 8:30 the principal found those gray metal cases standing right in the middle of his hall where kids would soon be coursing past on both sides. He pushed open Imogen's door with a red face.

She called to him pleasantly from her desk by the window, "Oh yes! Those darn things. Sorry, Donald, didn't know what else to do with them. Somebody goofed and put them in my office. I am up to my ears in work so I just took time enough to get them out of my way."

"Nobody goofed!" he shrieked. "I *ordered* those files moved in here. It's the perfect place for them!"

Imogen noted that he was actually trembling. That wasn't much, but it was something.

"Am I ever glad you told me," she said. "Because I was going to complain around until I found out who did it."

He flung himself back out into the hall, striking and tipping one of the file cases against the second case. It made a ten-inch, bright metal, fuzzy-edged scratch right through the khaki paint.

The next day, he burst in without knocking.

"Sorry, Donald," she said. "I'm with someone right now. Can you come back in half an hour?"

The child in her office looked astonished.

Donald reappeared on Thursday, apparently not to sit down. He ambled easily here and there, picking up things, setting them down. He spoke very casually. "I'm afraid we are going to have to ask you to share the work that has to be done in our school." He studied one of her little animal statues in his hand, "Namely—

1. playground supervision when needed.

2. lunchroom supervision, but it wouldn't be every day.

3. bus checking mornings or afternoons when needed."

Imogen got her mouth open to speak and then shut it.

He said, "These little animals you got are cute. Speaking of cute animals, last Friday afternoon, I had to go to the station to sign for one of our kids as per usual and there was the cop getting out of the patrol car. I went over and there was such a cute thing. For some reason, the cop had a dead bear cub sitting in the cage, sitting up looking as sweet as you please in the back seat. Its head had fallen over to one side, onto its shoulder, so it looked just like a kid who's fallen asleep in his car seat. I said as much to the cop. I told him, 'Hey Bernie, you driving bear cubs around so they'll fall asleep and take their nap? Never mind,' I told him, 'Just kidding. This one you got here's not waking up from any nap.' Yup, that baby bear was having the nap no one wakes up from. Probably a cub of that mother bear that people have sighted around town."

He had rounded the corner before Imogen retched in the hall. She cleaned it up.

She dialed that keynote speaker's number that she had been carrying with her since the MSSWA conference. A receptionist came on the line and told her he was with a client.

Imogen said, "Will you please tell him this is urgent? Will you have him call me fast? I am in St. Fursey. Tell him I want to drive down to Minneapolis tomorrow. Please will you get back to me on my cell? Here's the number. Please tell him we talked at the Minnesota school social worker conference."

The next day Imogen managed what should have been a three-and-a-half hour drive in two and a half. She drove the whole way far too fast because she was driving with ingenuity, lighted up with the technical agility sometimes given to people when half of their common sense has cut out on them. The only part of the brain working noticeably at all is the triggering motor skills linkage between thalamus and cerebellum and from there to hands and legs. Emotionally, Imogen was nearly out of it. She estimated her present IQ wavering around 79 or 80, perfect for risk-taking behavior in a car.

She passed some I-35 drivers obviously nearly asleep at their wheels, wrists hanging over the steering, eyelids lowered. She might be a half-crazed lady who finally got her head on straight enough to seek help because she needed help and now had found help and was going to the help and soon would be there, but at least she wasn't asleep and if she killed anyone she wouldn't have done it asleep, without noticing.

Suddenly she was there. Faster than GoogleEarth. Better.

Out of the car. Inside the building. Hovering near what had to be the receptionist's desk, in a room empty of people. Warm air moved about. The building's air-exchange system gently hummed its tuneless voice. She listened to it carefully.

Really, she told herself, this therapist's office was a pleasant, modern place. One really should try to live a pleasant, modern life, and stay in touch with real things. Look, life was blessed. She had been too freaked. Why freak over something so small as vomiting? Of all the things people had wrong with their lives! And all she had was vomiting now and then? And why should she, Imogen, who thought she was so smart, keep gnawing at the old bone of whatever Strog had done with that little boy of his? That was his affair, wasn't it, and shouldn't Imogen move on?

Moving on—she had been wrong—Oh, wrong!—to object when clients made that gender-specific remark: "I know I should let it go. I know I should get on with my life! I know I should 'move on!'" She should have *helped* them "let it go!" True, only very badly licked women went for that phrase—but still! Now that Imogen had taken a seat in a warm, soothing room she wondered, who in the world had she thought she was?

The building kept giving its faultless hum. So what if it was contrived white noise? She was stupid to sneer at white noise! If we human beings didn't know how to give ourselves white noise, we would be grieving all the time over dead children in Afghanistan and Iraq and places like those, places that were far away or long past or both. Half of what one hears was white noise—fair enough. When that receptionist returned, she would apologize and explain that she had been mistaken in making this appointment. She would explain that she was going to do what any sane person does. She was going to get on with her death—her life. She stood up, her jacket over one arm, all set to give her casual, courteous explanation for when the receptionist returned.

But it was a different receptionist who entered the room, and from a side door that Imogen hadn't noticed. This woman asked her if she were Imogen.

"I'll take you right in," she said.

As they moved, either quickly or slowly, whichever it was, Imogen found it impossible to start the perfectly sensible speech she had planned, with its apology for having caused these awfully nice people so much inconvenience. She could not remember how it went.

Now she was seated somewhere again. An intelligent face regarded her.

She was being lowered into herself. It was too late to apologize and take leave. Another human being was inviting herself into a half-eclipsed place inside herself. How could she ever have spent even a moment willing to be influenced by mechanical sound?

All she wanted now was to hear the sound of her own voice. It came to her ears as two sounds. One was a lyrical storytelling fountain of a voice, the other throttled growling. Both sounds were hers. A person ought to be ashamed to make noises like that, she thought, but only for a second. The lyrical storytelling voice was the voice of a girl scout explaining her failure to earn merit badges. That voice told the therapist how her parents were very civilized people who had asked her to forgive Strog, a man she had been married to. They still thought well of him. They were wistful about him.

The shame passed. Imogen leaned forward from her chair. She talked with hardly pause for breath to this utterly strange, professional person. Far beneath any conscious decision-making inside her, she knew that this man was going help her reconnect some damaged part of her mind. She hoped it wouldn't kill her.

He sat opposite. He, like her, leaned forward.

Imogen could barely speak but she was doing it.

When she choked, she stopped. She said, "Sorry, I am going to choke for a second."

Each time, this man's voice was quieter when he replied. Soon he was nearly whispering his replies and questions. They bent toward each other. They were like two people bailing, in perfect tandem, while inside one of them a hurricane flung itself again and again against the shelter of their vessel. At least there were two of them.

She told him that her ex-husband's name was Strog.

You would think, she told the therapist, that he would love his infant son enough not to endanger its health. She could not remember his son's name. She promised to tell the therapist that child's name as soon as it came to mind.

The therapist listened. She told him how the father of that child loved him and loved to show him off when he was out with friends.

The therapist said, "Did Strog have other children?"

"Just that one," she said.

She told him that on that day, Strog and his friend—he had several friends—were fishing in one of those lakes that lie here and there on the Iron Range when a depleted iron mine was allowed to fill with groundwater.

The therapist asked if Strog's child could stand up or walk by itself.

"Not yet," Imogen said. "He could not pull himself up yet."

By this time, both client and therapist were speaking so quietly that they heard each other's breathing.

The therapist then said, "So that infant son of his....he couldn't have pulled himself up and over the boat's edge?"

"He couldn't physically have done it," she said. "Excuse me. I am going to choke. I won't throw up, though. I am fairly sure I will not throw up. I throw up a good deal but I will not do it here."

He said, "You can throw up if you need to." He had risen already. He brought her a wastepaper basket.

The choking passed.

"I don't think that child could have got out. I don't think his child could have fallen out of that boat by himself."

The therapist waited.

Then she said in an even fainter whisper than before, "I am not saying that he lifted his child out and deliberately threw or dropped him overside. I don't know that. I think he had to have lifted the child up, and then, for the fun of it, likely, swung him around a little, because he liked swinging him around. Especially when he had friends around. They would look anxious, but he would grin. Then he must have lost him. Or he dropped him in to see if he could swim, New-Age style. You see, I don't think he intended murder. I think he wanted so much to show the other man... he did it for the fun. He was a genuinely joyful, adventurous dad. I bet he was doing that and then he froze up and didn't save the child. And the friend...well, maybe they were both smoking. You would think Strog would be more careful around his son."

She stopped talking. Then she said, "I have never been so afraid as I am just this minute."

A minute passed.

The therapist said, "Where did you go just now?"

She said, "Wait a second. I might be going to choke for a second. Just wait a second."

"I can wait," the therapist said.

She did a little choking.

Then she said, "If I could come back some time..."

"Yes, you can," he said promptly. "You can come back soon."

"I want to talk about the other things—if that would be all right."

In some dim recess of her ears, she heard herself doing what her clients sometimes did—an odd thing—ask if it would be all right to talk about something very, very bad. For a pretty murderous species, we are certainly courteous, she thought, splitting herself for a second back into her old self, the therapist and ordinary person who was going to marry a very nice person named Vern. She was an ordinary school social worker with some private practice—splitting herself back and forward from that person to this deeper self which lifted itself slowly up and down in her head like a very long swell at sea.

"I want to come back," she said. "I want to be more OK than I am now."

The therapist said, "You have said that Strog must have lifted up his son... in that boat."

"Yes, he must have. But, I want to repeat," she cried, "I didn't say he meant to murder his son. I think he was having fun with him. He was impressing his friend. He loved to have fun."

The therapist glanced down, regarding his knuckles.

"You're not even listening."

"I'm listening," he said. He waited a minute. Then he said, "I want to ask you. You call that little boy Strog's son. I am going to ask you, can you say who was the mother of that little boy?"

She told herself, "Listen, Imogen, you know this world of therapy. You know nobody can do it if they're chicken. You know that! So do it."

So she sat up very straight in order not to choke. She said, "I am the mother of that little boy."

The therapist started to speak, but he had trouble.

Oh yes, he is having trouble, too, Imogen thought. It is nice he is having trouble, too.

Then he said, "You are the parent of a little boy who died possibly because the other parent was showing off to a friend then."

Neither of them spoke for a moment.

Then he said, "I'm not sure I could have borne that."

She said, "That's right. I can hardly bear it. I have been able to hardly bear it. And now I am through for today. I can't do any more."

"But you have done so much," the therapist said. "You've done such a lot. You have so much courage. It's enough for one day."

She looked at him wonderingly. "But I still can't think of that little boy's name."

He spoke firmly. "You will think of it. You don't have to think of his name today."

Still, the day wasn't over. Imogen was not throwing up but she realized that she might howl. She might howl. She gave the therapist a covert glance. She knew it would sound horrible if she howled.

He now said very fast in a low voice, "There is still time."

It came out. The howling was a thousand times louder and more torn-sounding than she had been afraid it would be. A thousand times.

At last it stopped. She found she was kneeling on the floor. She found that the therapist was kneeling, too, and had held her shoulders all the while. He did not hug her. He just held her shoulders.

They both got to their feet.

"What are you going to do right now?" he asked. "Are you driving back north? Is someone driving you?"

"I'm driving," she said. "I will be safe." Then she said, "I can't believe it's been four whole years!"

"Four years is almost nothing," he said. "Not in anything to do with love it isn't. It will always be sad. Always. You will always have lost this child. You may have other children, but you will have always have lost this little boy. You will never, ever forget him."

She could hardly bear it, but she remained standing.

He said, "We will work very hard."

They talked schedule. They both were spoken for all of the next eight or nine days—he because he was a famous therapist in Minneapolis and she because she was putting together a package income with no perks.

"No, eight or nine days is too long from now," the therapist said. "Do you have to cook on Thanksgiving morning or anything? Cheer for a football team or anything?"

They both laughed. He said if she could show up early on Thanksgiving morning, they could do one hour and he would have another hour free, too, if they wanted it.

They were walking toward the door.

"Now, here's advice. Please take it," he said. "Drive very slowly home. Very slowly. And when you feel any difficult feeling coming on, pull over to the side. About those rest stops at least as far as Duluth. Pull off at each of them. You may likely get very sleepy. Go to sleep in every one of the them if you feel like it."

He gave her a respectful smile and said, "Can you stand one more piece of advice?"

She said, "I know a good therapist when I see one. What's the one more piece of advice?"

"This may sound dumb," he said, "It isn't. Sometimes a person's eyes fill with tears while they think over a profound conversation. We don't know for certain what those tears are about. Sometimes those tears seem to come only because so much truth has been got at that a person's heart is surprised by it—by so much truth just for its own sake. Anyway, if your eyes fill with tears for any reason, pull off the road."

Back outside, Imogen's remote made her car give its baby animal bleats. She climbed in. She drove so slowly north it was as if the earth were trying to grasp her tires. It was clutching at her car. All right then, she thought, not complaining. A lot of people have never been married to someone who for years fancied the edge, taking chances, frightening people—for years—before actually killing. Yet such people must be around us all the time, nearby or not. She added, yes, and inside the rest of us somewhere, too.

She knew that much. She wasn't a therapist for nothing.

CHAPTER FIFTEEN

Whenever you put on a public celebration, somebody gets their feelings hurt. Men and women in departments of state and in armies get inured to it by the time they're 30 or they'd be crying on their desktops every day. That is the way it's always been. Those in the loop that counts march after the Colors, or get handsomely seated in the first row.

Still, ordinary civilians and especially small-town people keep hoping that somehow the honors will be dealt out fairly—really fairly, this once—just this once. They never are, and somebody always gets their vanity kicked.

At St. Fursey's most carefully planned annual occasion, Veterans' Evening, there were this year three different sets of hurt feelings. First, George Herzlich happened to be serving as mayor. He would be the one to walk up the aisle to the platform, immediately followed by the big-shot speaker who had been brought in from out of town. That part was OK and he had figured out exactly what had to happen and what he himself would say. But Peter Tenebray, who wasn't mayor or a St. Fursey Public Library official, got deferred to like God because there had to be a dinner party before the doings. There had to be a private home for the speaker to stay at, and it had to be a sumptuous private home.

The Herzlichs' house was a nice place but its one guest room and both of the boys' old rooms were filled with Mercein's knitting projects and skeins and two old Brother machines that George kept straightening the needles on. What's more, Mercein froze at the very idea of cooking for someone who would be used to fancy food. You couldn't fry up pork chops and make frozen beans-and-mushroom-soup hot dish for a general—and as for overnight! Even if she got all the stuff off one of the beds, she and George hadn't bought new sheets for decades. You couldn't tell some big-shot general that the reason his top sheet had a neatly sewn patch on it was that his hosts had saved up and then sent two children to college and then even made both of them huge loans at 3% to eke out down payments on houses. George felt embarrassed.

Stan Garris, without whose aged mother this big shot wouldn't be coming to St. Fursey at all, hadn't health or house or wife to do a crispy little dinner plus overnight stay for the speaker. Stan had cancer and looked like hell and probably felt like hell, too, because Doc Anderson had bawled him out for missing the chemo appointments set up for him in Duluth. He had given in at last, and started the therapy. He had decided he was dying and the doctor told him he wasn't, but Stan couldn't get convinced that the doctor was telling him the truth. Even without the sickness, however, Stan was definitely not one of those St. Fursey area out-of-the-knothole-top-drawer intellectuals. He and his visibly, audibly, famously horrible wife had never even been invited to the Tenebrays' dinner parties.

Peter and Natalie Tenebray found out at the last minute that the speaker was a retired American brigadier general. The Tenebrays would have liked to be in the loop with the town leaders pulling off this event but they hadn't been. Peter hid his personal hurt. He asked the mayor if he and his Nat could do a very simple supper before the presentation, a Chicken Marengo, say, because advance prep left you free to join the guests? And, of course, George and his Committee might have already arranged something else, but if not, might Peter and Nat put the general up for the night? George was most relieved and said so. When you had a retired brigadier general coming on a three-and-half-hour drive to do a freebie, the Tenebrays' was the right thing. Peter took a small notebook from his vest pocket. If George would give him the list, he would see they all got invited to dinner. And, if George thought it suitable, the World War II vets—at least those who'd fought on our side? Peter laughed. Of course, it was all a good idea. This was Tenebray-type stuff, not Herzlich-type stuff. Chicken Marengo, whatever the heck that might be! Of course, everyone would want to eat it, and drink whatever was offered before it and during it. About the World War II vets, those on our side, George opened his mouth as though to say something and closed it again.

Even Natalie Tenebray's feelings were harrowed up, because Peter told her hands down she had to clear the guest wing of all dead soldiers (empties) and do it immediately, and he would inspect. Arlene Stropp was proud that Mr. Tenebray trusted her to make sure of the sheets, pillow cases, blanket, a new unused bar of soap in the second, larger guest-wing bath. Would it be all right to break open that package of new towels and matching facecloths she'd seen?

"Way to go, Arlene!" Peter shouted.

One no-account person got his feelings hurt. This was Darrel, the deputy cop. Darrel was a member of the VFW at its second lowest level. At the local Post, he had somehow been made sergeant-at-arms. This meant he should have been the one to carry the colors up the aisle of the Library meeting room, up the two steps to the platform, do a smart heel swivel about, and place the United States flag at right, as the audience would see it, leaving the Minnesota flag in its stand at left.

The mayor, however, explained to Darrel that it was to be the sergeant-at-arms of the Auxiliary who would carry colors on Veterans' Evening.

Darrel grew red and showed a hand palm up. "The Auxiliary!"

George said "Pearl has offered to go down to the Cities and pick up the general and drive him both ways."

Darrel raised his voice. "I could do that!" he said.

Herzlich said, "Garris Autos is providing a 2007 Buick Terraza."

Darrel said, "I can sure drive as safe as Pearl, any day of the week!" He added, "I should think you'd want a man doing a man's job!"

A little of Darrel's spit struck George Herzlich.

"The answer is no," George said.

On the night itself, the St. Fursey Public Library was beautiful. Bridget Garris had been authorized by the Committee to spend some money on flowers. She decided to decorate not only the Meeting Room itself but the small back lounge which served as her office. The city had put in a handsome sofa for her. Years ago two ladies had crocheted some throw pillows and a matching afghan for the Senior Citizens' Center. When the Center was given over to the chief of police, these ladies brought their knitted materials over to the Library because a) Bridget Garris, who was still the librarian for all these years, wasn't getting any younger, and she might appreciate them, and b) there was no point in leaving hand-made craftwork for that dirty-looking young deputy to ruin.

Bridget imagined ahead how it would be: Pearl would be in her uniform white blouse and royal blue VFW suit. She would bring that Buick around from Tenebrays' when they were through with supper. They would use the back door with the glass window so Pearl could park, and because she would be in uniform, she would show good snap when she opened the passenger door for the general. Things were democratic these days. He would probably sit up front with Pearl. The other supper guests would have gone ahead to get themselves seats in the Meeting Room. Pearl would lead the general to Bridget's office. Bridget jotted down: pitcher, water, glass.

Bridget said to herself, it was actually all going to happen! If only Stan weren't so sick—she still could hardly get it through her head that a child of hers might die before she herself did—otherwise, she felt happy.

The meeting room filled fast. In his Boy Scout uniform, Marty Hanks, Jr. did not look like someone who picked his nose in a church chancel. He guided the World War II veterans to their armchairs in the front row. Ward Hines. Walt Steinzeiter. Everyone else just had ordinary auditorium chairs. Walt Steinzeiter weighed almost 300 pounds so he walked without any spring to his step, but his son had ordered for him a custom-fitted VFW dress blue uniform. Walt knew he looked good, even if he was a heavy fellow. His huge face was bright with Peter Tenebray's single-malt. As he made his way up to the reserved seat, he noted here and there in the audience the local clowns he knew he could still beat the pants off. He saw that six-foot-one piece of shit, the deputy cop, too. He meant to straighten him out later tonight after the doings. Darrel was seated on the aisle in his police uniform.

Others crowded in who had not been invited to the Tenebrays' and were not full of Peter Tenebray's booze. Most of them were up for some hilarity anyhow. They shouted greetings and chaff—making too much noise to hear much other than themselves.

The Boy Scouts urged the guests of honor to keep moving forward.

Marty Hanks said, "Sir, you want to come along now? They got your seat reserved for you!"

A third armchair was marked *Reserved* on the righthand side.

Marty said, "You're on this side, sir. Next to Mr. Hines."

Walt belched and pointed: "Who's that one for then?"

Marty said firmly, "You're on *this* side, sir."

At last, it was 7:30. People instinctively lowered their voices, knowing that the m.c. for the evening would shush them any second now.

Two high school seniors came forward, one with a trumpet damped and the other with a flute. They went up onto the platform, behind the lectern, to their skinny metal music stands.

At last, a stir at the back.

Ordinary people didn't set much store by whoever happened to be the mayor of St. Fursey. None of the town's affairs went through his hands at all. St. Fursey was a town run by its clergy and a car dealer who was a nice guy of long standing and the Tenebray family. Still, here is the mayor —George Herzlich this year. OK. Nothing wrong with George Herzlich.

The high school kids did a fanfare and then a march that was more lyrical than military. People didn't stand.

The VFW Auxiliary's Sergeant-at-Arms came by with the flag. Next came the Mayor. Then the Commander of the Veterans of Foreign Wars. The two Boy Scouts who had returned from ushering so they could be in this procession.

The little procession got slower since those at the head paused before taking the step to get up onto the dais.

The music stopped. Silence.

George Herzlich returned down the aisle. Some voice in the audience said too loudly, "Now what's wrong?" A woman's voice said, "Why don't you wait and see? Can't you ever just wait without making a fuss once?"

George was not in his navy-green Garris Autos suit. He wore what the mayors always wore on Veterans' Evening—dark suit, white shirt, and a black tie in mourning for the American dead of all wars.

It was so quiet you could hear here a cough, there a mild creak of a chair.

Then George Herzlich's voice very clear in the back: "Sir? If you'll come up now?"

To the delight of everyone in the room, a straight-backed, elegant old soldier in the rarely seen dress-blue of the Army was now accompanying George forward. He was of medium height, with a strong neck and wavy, completely silver hair shaved rather high in back, in the military way. He carried his cap under his arm. He brought no notes to speak from. He walked firmly.

People took in the uniform and those who knew insignia whispered to those who didn't. The word got passed along. The words, "It's a brigadier general!" lifted lightly and went around the room.

"A brigadier general! A real one!" Other whispers followed. "That's the European Theatre of Operations medal." "That's a Bronze Star." "No, it isn't either. That's a Silver Star." "I can't see, would you move your head." "Oh, don't fuss. Once he gets up there he'll turn around and you'll see all you want."

When everyone stood on the platform, George Herzlich came forward to the lectern. He tinkered with the mic a minute, looked over to the piano at the far right. Pearl, having set the flag into its standing bracket, raised a thumb.

"Welcome, everybody," George said. "Our national anthem."

Everyone stood up as fast as they could. Pearl played the last bars.

Everyone sang as loud as they could.

George Herzlich then waited until everyone had sat down.

He said, "We have a very special speaker tonight. And he is bringing a wonderful message especially for us, here in St. Fursey."

George turned to smile at the general, who smiled back. "*Because* we have this special speaker and program, we are shortening our usual Veterans' Day agenda a little. We won't have Taps. But we will have the reading of the names of all St. Fursey men and women who have served in the wars. Then we will introduce our speaker and he will take over from there. Well—" and here George turned on his car-sales charm, "I ask you, if a brigadier general in the United States Army can't take over, then we'd be in bad shape!"

Everyone was pleased to laugh. They'd been delighted to be awed. They'd been pleased to sing "The Star Spangled Banner" solemnly instead of in the half-assed way that overpaid entertainers hyped it up at Super Bowls. And they would be pleased to give some thought, a short invisible inward salute to people who never got to live past their youth. When the names were read aloud, they planned to be pleased to imagine—as well as they could—the dead Civil War privates of the Minnesota First Infantry. But for *this* moment, they wanted to laugh at George's gag. The visiting general laughed, too. Everyone on the podium sat down.

Old Walt Steinzeiter got up from his chair. He opened the sheet he would read from. No one brought him the battery-run mic. When his voice came out, however, it was loud. The sixteen-year-olds in the room could hear names of dead men and feel the force of what it means to live and then inevitably to die, even if you got decorated by President Lincoln.

Walt sat down.

George nodded to Marty Hanks, Jr. The Boy Scout went down the two steps and down the aisle. There was a silence, during which George also came down and stood before them in silence. Now the Scout was escorting a man forward, and George smiled. When they got near, George reached out his hand and shook hands with Dieter Stolz. With the other hand he showed him to the right-side armchair that had been kept for him. If the German-American farmer was amazed, he didn't show it.

Not everyone knew Dieter Stolz, but everybody had heard of him. Well, people thought, and their hearts warmed because everyone on the podium was smiling. Besides, it was over a half-century since this fellow had served in Wehrmacht.

The mayor said it was his great pleasure to introduce to them Brigadier General Frank Gorretter, United States Army, Retired.

The officer rose and stood in front of them. He said, "I am very happy to be here among you. Where is Bridget Garris?" He made Bridget stand. "I would never have known to come to St. Fursey if it weren't for her! Then I really never would have had the right people to tell my story to. That's because you citizens of St. Fursey are the right people.

"I'm going to tell you one particular part of my life as a soldier during World War II. There are others here tonight who served in that war. I want to greet them as one old soldier to another"—and here he looked down at the front row of three old men in their armchairs and smiled at them, face by face. Then he looked up at the whole audience again. "I want to tell you my story because it has something to say not just to soldiers but to all of us."

He had been born a second-generation German-American in a family that still spoke German. His draft board of late 1943, learning that this latest 1-A recruit spoke fluent German, immediately recommended him for military intelligence.

"Good thing!" he said with a laugh, looking all over the room, gathering everyone into his story as if it were a joke. They grinned back at him. "A *very* good thing! I was a terrible shot! I expect every one of you men in this room is a better shot than I was!"

He trained for Intelligence. He was sent to Europe where his first experience in combat was to be taken prisoner. No heroism there.

He explained the difficulties of the Ardennes forest in early spring of 1945. Snowfall, cold, loss of air support, encirclement by German units. One night, he got lost. Here and there, dead American soldiers lay in the snow. Snow had drifted against some of them. He himself was not wounded, but he had turned his ankle on a smashed-up jumble of snow-covered tank tread. He was nineteen.

"Perhaps some of you," the old man said with a genial look, "were brave at nineteen. I happened not to be. In addition to the fact that I wasn't even a good shot."

He had thought, I can walk if I put my mind to it. He couldn't. He sat down, his wool coat long since sopped through with snow. He tried to plan. He had his sector map but was so disoriented that he might have been crawling about in an area off the map.

A wrecked Sherman stood nearby. A wrecked half-track lay on its side with a hole through its driver's door. Night was coming.

Then he heard someone moving cautiously. His heart leapt. If only it were an American, even an American from some other outfit! It might not be, however, so he had better play dead in case the person creeping around was a German. So he lowered his upper body and half hid his face with one hand. He had taken his glove off, but didn't dare reach for it lest it make a sound. Please be a G.I., he breathed. His fingers began to ache with cold.

Between his fingers, he opened his upper eye a crack. A German sergeant was creeping about from one dead American soldier to another, getting closer. He was collecting something—probably food, or both food and ammunition. Some German troops had been regularly short of ammunition. They counted on picking up Garand rifles, and the bullets to go with them. This fellow was now clearly approaching.

Don't get out your knife, he prayed silently. Don't get out your knife. Look. I'm dead. Anyone can see I'm dead. He told himself to leave his eyes open because it is the living who have shut eyes. The dead's eyes are open.

The German approached, now crawling to get under the bent long-rifle of the nearest tank. He was coming. Don't move your pupils at all, Frank said to himself.

The German seemed to be collecting K-rations. Frank didn't have any. The German glanced right into Frank's eye between the fingers. He paused. Then he came still closer and now brushed Frank's hand away from his face. Frank's fingers felt cold even to himself, but he was afraid they were not cold like dead men's hands. The German bolted upright and leveled into Frank's face an American pistol, a .38 of the kind officers sometimes wore. No, don't kill me, Frank thought.

He decided to beg. After all, he spoke German so he *could* beg.

Now the old man paused to smile at his St. Fursey audience. He said, "The better side of valor is begging. Don't let 'em tell you different!"

Everyone laughed gratefully. They still felt the dread of his story, but now he had included them so they felt comradely. Some of them wondered if they themselves would have begged.

The German was Frank's age or perhaps a year older, not more.

Frank said, in German, "Please."

He asked Frank what was *los* with him. Frank felt lucky it was only an ankle. If he had been hopelessly wounded, nearly dying, the German sergeant likely would have killed him. As it was, he held that revolver on him, and asked him to show him his ankle.

It was badly swollen. He said, "Ach," the way Germans do.

The brigadier general looked at one of the program committee sitting just below the podium, a gigantic fat fellow he had met at his hosts' house. He shouted down to him, "You guys still say 'Ach!' I bet!"

Walt Steinzeitter went rosy in his huge face. "Ja, we say Ach!—and worse!" he cried.

The brigadier general let the laughter rove around the room and then picked up his story.

The German sergeant told him to stay there.

Frank said, "I am not going anywhere."

The German actually gave him the ghost of a smile. "No, I don't suppose you are."

He went off and came back with three or four little boys. They had a blanket which he made them turn into a rough seat. They got Frank onto it. They carried him off—making hard work of it. They were just kids, but suited up as Wehrmacht privates. One of them even had the Waffen-SS insignia.

The brigadier general explained to his St. Fursey audience that various units in the West had Waffen-SS personnel attached to them to keep up morale. To keep up morale, one learned, was to prevent squads and platoons or whole Patrol Gruppen from finding Amis and surrendering to them.

They were taking him off to woods he hadn't explored. They came across fewer dumps of equipment and fewer bodies scattered about. They seemed familiar with the terrain because although it was getting very dark, they didn't barge into things, like tank treads, the way he'd done. At last they came to a small clearance. There were a few tents set up. They were like our shelter halfs, but in quarters. Now he saw a few other soldiers. Kids had a low fire going.

The sergeant told them to heat up what he'd brought them. He was like an old fox bringing back dinner for the kits. It looked like the mix of stuff that Frank had gotten his hands on before, when lost. Now that enemy patrol, if that's what they were, would be eating together for days— five-in-ones, which were like K-rations but intended for five men to heat and eat together. Some K-rations. Some C-rations.

The old soldier now told the audience he would make a three weeks' story short. Those Germans kept him alive. They splinted his ankle for him and fed him as well as themselves. He and their leader, the sergeant, talked. The men sat around in cheerful circles at night, drinking from a healthy supply of brandy they had unearthed. They shot small deer, and fried chunks of the meat in rendered K-ration bacon. The bacon itself they ate for a kind of rough canapé while they waited for dinner.

There were only eight of them, and except for their sergeant, were all 14 years old. What was left of their uniforms seemed to fit, but the helmets were outsized, made for men. The boys wound woolen sock strips inside the head supports. Now and again, they shared what they had left of German rations with him—a fairly tasty mix of cooked rice and sausage meat.

Their mission, he began to realize as they kept him with them, was to be taken prisoner. They regarded him, the sergeant explained, as the American who could best lead them back to American forces. That was the sergeant's tactful way of saying that when they found U.S. troops in great enough numbers to surrender to, they would keep him, in his uniform, out in front of them as they came in. Their principal danger was that Americans were much less likely to take prisoners in fewer numbers than 40 or 50.

The German sergeant kept them going partly on humor, partly on their depending on him to think for them. The sergeant had a kind of mental alacrity which is always interesting just in itself. Frank would have liked to talk more with that German. The fellow clearly was a civilized kind of person, and clearly meant to get all of his men *and* Frank as well alive into Allied hands. Frank found that he trusted him absolutely.

There was a problem, however. Whenever he and the German sat smoking wet *cigarettes de troupe* that they found in some dead soldier's cache of souvenirs, the SS boy would inch himself up near them. That boy had an unpleasant look of intent in his eye. Frank's intelligence training had taught him that most of these very young Waffen-SS boys had been indoctrinated later and more severely than the other boys: it was possible that this boy would not want to surrender.

There was an unspoken skirmishing of wills between the boy and the sergeant. Clearly, the SS boy wanted to kill Americans. He kept offering to serve guard duty over Frank, so that the sergeant could sleep longer. Frank's heart would pound at the very thought. They all urinated more or less right anywhere they were, merely facing outward by way of civility. They moved off several yards, however, in order to defecate in a place already assigned. Frank knew that if that boy were his guard when he went to the Scheissengrund, he would kill him for attempting to escape. Fortunately, the sergeant always gave prisoner guard duty to one of the others.

At night, they heard a good deal of firing—of carbines, which suggested that Americans were popping away at those same forest small-deer that they hunted. On nights when they couldn't hear any firing of either carbines or ordinary M-1s, they would make a nearly decent-sized fire, as opposed to the tiny fires they could shade with a shelter *Viertel*.

On those nights, the sergeant would let the boys feed up, drink up, and then he'd give them lectures. He kept their spirits up. Once he tried to make Frank give them English lessons, but the SS boy lost his mind. He shouted that they would have no use for English when the war was over.

The sergeant covered his back. "Of course," the sergeant said mildly. So they had no English lessons.

The brigadier general said, "I remember one of these evenings I especially admired him for. He had gone off by himself all afternoon, prowling about, leaving me guarded by three of the others. The remaining boys were told to make as good a dinner as they could. 'We will be celebrating,' he said.

"'What were we celebrating?' I asked, since no one else asked.

"'Today is the birthday of Paul Josef Goebbels,' he said, looking me squarely in the eye.

"When he returned we all ate a reheated leg of deer from the day before, the last of their rice-and-sausage casserole, and some fried scrambled-egg sandwiches from some very good C-ration that had been better protected than the rest of our scavenged food because it had lain under a tipped over field kitchen.

"We had a *Real Politik* lesson. 'Why were the Amis able to make landings on Fortress Europe at all?' the sergeant would ask. 'Why are they able to push us back into Germany?'

"The SS boy answered first and no one interrupted him. 'They will not push us back into Germany,' he said in his stout tone. Everything he said he said as announcement to prisoners in a Stalag. They were all patient with him.

"'Of course not,' the sergeant would say, 'Ganz richtig, Jurgen. Anyone else?'

"'They have industry and money,' someone said. 'If we had those aircraft and weapons that they have they wouldn't be here.'

"'Right,' said the German sergeant amiably. 'But another point, which is nearly a military secret of the United States.'

"'The United States,' he explained, 'had its northern boundary exactly on the 49th parallel of North Latitude. Now this boundary was not guarded. Anybody could visit the Dominion of Canada whenever they wanted. Canadians could visit the United States. Now why was this useful to the Americans?'

"No one had the least idea. All I myself remembered was that the Rush-Baggot treaty of 1818 or 1828, one or the other, stressed an unpoliced border except that each nation was allowed two police boats on the Great Lakes.

"'It is this,' the sergeant told his little troupe. 'That open border let Americans go to the north of Ontario and Manitoba,' which he explained were provinces north of Minnesota, especially to find polar bears each season when they migrated.

"'Polar bear flesh was all right, but it was not strategic food for soldiers. What was strategic food,' he said, speaking with serious emphasis, 'for the reason that it gave so much energy, was polar bear stool.'

"The boys tentatively smiled—but when the sergeant's severe glance went round their fire-lighted faces, their smiles disappeared. They weren't a hundred percent sure of what it all meant.

"At last he said, 'I have been lucky. I have found some for you. I looked all over this afternoon and I found some.'

"He unstrapped his bread bag. In it were not two or three but about nine or ten, of what I recognized as USA D-rations—chocolate candy bars, the delight of soldiers throughout the ages. The trouble with these, the D-ration version, was that they were frankly—the printing on the packaging said as much—manufactured in Kansas City, Missouri, in 1933. They were plenty stale before some canny Army supplier got the contract to sell them. Each candy bar was nearly completely coated white with age.

"'Now,' the sergeant said, 'Everybody gets one, after which we will cut up the others for seconds. But I want everybody to eat one, because it will give you the energy to repel these invaders who want to take the Fatherland. A wunderbare *Energie*—Polar bear scat—you must eat.'

"He had his knife out. He looked at their half-doubting, half-horrified faces. 'Have courage,' he said. 'You're in luck. Someone in Kansas City, Missouri, it says so on the packaging, put chocolate flavor into them. It makes them much, much more palatable. If the Amis who had these were alive and knew you were eating them, they would be yellow with envy. I, for one, am glad,' he said as though confiding something, in the way that complacent upper-grade noncommissioned officers sometimes decide to be pals with privates. 'I am partial to a sweet after dinner.'

"He passed them around and saw that each man bit into his candy bar. Each face, in turn, filled with delight. It was chocolate. There is nothing like chocolate. They knew that much.

"That was our last meal together, as it happened, the birthday of Goebbels.

"The next day, we heard firing closer. The sergeant took his little patrol along a faint animal path in the woods, going on a diagonal toward the sound. He kept me beside him. He kept the SS boy in the rear. I believe he had told that boy to be sure no one made a dash to escape to the American lines through the woods.

"Then he and I, twelve meters ahead of the others, saw a declivity in front of us. And there we found what surpassed our best hopes: parked on a kind of logging trail below us stood a Jeep. In it sat one enlisted driver and three officers.

"I looked at the sergeant and he looked at me. I will never forget that moment. We were nearly friends by then. Still, war is war, and each of us had to keep reassuring the other one that we intended no treachery. I grinned at him and told him that we were in luck. Those were officers off having a private little drinking party. The three of them seemed to be sharing a bottle with their driver. The only weapons we could see were light carbines jammed into those vertical holders. I couldn't be sure about pistols because I couldn't see their right hips.

"My sergeant looked at me as if to say, Now that we have come this far, I am not going to shove you in front of me with my weapon. He said, 'You stay behind. I will go talk to them.'

"That was the first I knew he spoke English. I should have guessed he might. Some day he would matriculate as a student.

"I told him, I'd better go with him. What if those fellows were drunk? If they saw one Feldwebel alone, even approaching very slowly with his hands up, they might decide to be heroes and shoot him.

"In the weeks before I was captured I had seen Germans sneaking along hedgerows to join one another, the idea being to make up a large enough group so that when they surrendered, the Americans they approached would feel obliged to take prisoners.

"I told him we'd slide down onto that road together but I would talk loud to them in English all the time we approached the Jeep.

"He turned around and told his men to lie down, and not show themselves.

"Then, laying down his own MP-40, he pulled out a white cloth—which he had kept hidden from all of us so far. He held it above his head. We skidded down the little incline together.

"The Americans were startled.

"I kept shouting at them. He did, too.

"'No! No!' he kept saying in an English accent he'd been taught. 'Do not stretch for your weapons. My men have you covered on both sides.'

"He told them in quaint, rather elegant English, that he had eight and forty men on the other side aimed at the Jeep right now. And on our side, he had thirty.

"He told them to sit still. He would explain his plan. He said, 'I do not want war. Here is what we want, all first,' he said.

"I said, 'First of all.' Prompting.

"'First of all,' he said. 'That smell is tobacco. We want cigarettes. We want to take just a few back to our men.'

"I had been staying half in front of him, just to make sure. I let him do the talking. My war was now over, I thought. He was managing fine.

"The corporal in the driver's seat handed over a package with most of the 20 cigarettes in it. Field matches, too.

"The German read the yellow and gold. 'Looky Streek-a,' he said, then corrected himself. 'Lucky Strike. Thank you.'

"Then he explained he would return to his men and instruct them to come out at three-meter intervals, hands upward, and without their weapons. 'I am going to bring out my men on either side of the road, starting against over your Jeep. Then they will move forward. You already face to the American lines, so when all my men are here, you will escort us and we are surrendered to you. Is all understood?'

"One of the officers nodded and said to me, 'Tell him OK.'

"I climbed back up off the road and into the woods with him.

"He made the boys crawl up close. They looked very worried. He calmed them. He said, 'This is a type called a Lucky Strike cigarette.'

"He explained what he wanted them to do when he signaled.

"I ambled along back the path we had come on. The German boys were too excited to light their cigarettes. They each took one from the pack and put it in his pocket.

"Now he spoke very quietly so they wouldn't get twitchy. I realized the moment he started talking that he had rehearsed this speech over and over. Possibly for weeks. He said, 'Now you lay down your weapons. Your duties to the Fuehrer are now over. And my duty to your mothers has just begun. I am going to deliver all of you alive to your mothers. You are going to grow up and go to University, and marry, and be fathers of children.'

"'Everybody ready? Obey me then, this last time!'

"I watched, fascinated, as one by one they laid down their pathetic weapons. Three M-40s with no bullets. Two picked-up M-1s. The poor kids had been told they'd be shot if they laid down their weapons. It was hard for them now, but they trusted their sergeant. They obeyed him.

"'Vorwaerts!' he shouted, and they stood up. 'Every three meters,' he told them.

"They went slowly out of the woods, slid down the embankment, and lined up alongside the road, with curious glances at the Americans in the Jeep. I watched for a half-second or so and then I dropped back behind a tree. It might be hours before we could relieve ourselves in a prison camp.

"They were moving so slowly I would catch up without trouble.

"After a few minutes the Americans were shouting at me, so I shouted back and got out of those woods for the last time. The German sergeant and his men were standing, hands up, along the road as he had promised.

"The first-lieutenant in the back seat said, 'OK. Where are all the others?'

"The German sergeant said, 'This is all I have. They are fourteen years old. No—one is fifteen. The others are fourteen.' Then he added, 'Please.'

"'OK,' the lieutenant said. He turned to the driver. 'Home, James.'

"The little cavalcade started off. The American driver said to me, 'You want to ride?'

"'Naw,' I told him. 'But they all want to put their hands down and smoke their cigarettes.'

"It all went very well. As soon as we got to the nearest Americans, the sergeant and I were questioned. He and his men were put into a huge field with a lot of other German troops. It was a very smelly place because it was three-fourths surrounded by a 10-foot-wide latrine ditch. I was told how to reach my unit, after they had heard my story of being a prisoner. I shook hands with my German sergeant."

The brigadier general broke off his story.

"Well, that was over half a century ago," he said. The entire audience hung silent.

The brigadier general said, "You know, that German sergeant did something unusual for a human being. He made up his mind, on his own, that the Fuehrer was wrong in consigning those young boys to be killed in hopeless battle. So he saved them. He simply made the decision. To save children. How many people can think for themselves—and do a merciful risky act which their own government might label treason? Few."

The room was dead still. Then the retired brigadier general gave everyone a smile. "That man who made up his own mind is here tonight. I feel honored. Most of you know him but some of you may not, so let me introduce him to you. I will ask him to join me up here. He is Carl Dieter Stolz, sergeant in the 19th German infantry, IV Corps, from 1944 to 1945."

Slowly, the old strawberry farmer went up the steps to shake hands with the general.

People cried, as people do.

At last, everyone had left but Bridget Garris who had the keys, and Peter Tenebray. The two old soldiers still stood talking in the glass doorway of the library office.

Peter half wanted to remind them that Dieter Stolz could join them for a nightcap at his house, yet he didn't like to interrupt. They had moved over into speaking German. Peter supposed they were getting down to fine points. He hung back and pretended to confer with Bridget about closing up.

Only later did he find out what they were talking about. Dieter bowed out of Peter's offer of a nightcap. Back at Peter's house, the general repeated for him the conversation he and Dieter Stolz had carried on in the library doorway.

"Why did you take so long coming down out of the woods?" Dieter had said. "I had almost given up on you. I couldn't imagine what you were up to."

"I was hiding behind a tree," laughed the general. "I didn't want my drunk countrymen to change their minds and decide to shoot you down as you came out of the woods. So I was no hero. I hid."

Dieter laughed. He paused. Then he said, "But you know, one of my men never did come out. When I asked the others they didn't know. Some thought he must have gone ahead. Others thought he was lagging. I myself wondered if he was such a patriotic little SS fellow that he would refuse to surrender."

"O that," the general said. "From behind my tree, I watched those kids wait their distance, and then go out, hands over their heads. Jurgen was last. He waited his three meters, too. He stood up, but then stooped down. I thought he had dropped his cigarette you'd passed out. But no. Then I thought he was doing something we all did. Picking up souvenirs. What he had his hands on was the last kid's little machine pistol.

Then he raised it. I was a little slow on the pickup. I think a whole second passed, before I realized that he was going to mow all of us down from behind. And then, who knows, if he still had enough ammo, perhaps get the Americans in their Jeep. Maybe he dreamed of a Ritter First Class, if they were still being awarded."

A silence fell on the two men.

"So?" Dieter finally asked, a little coldly.

"So I crept up on him from behind. I wasn't sorry I had no weapon. I probably would have missed, and in any case, those Americans would have heard the shot and reacted. Besides, what they taught me in intelligence was bare-hands work. Jurgen was a determined little patriot. He would have killed as many of us as he could."

Natalie and Peter had lighted the library fire, and Natalie had given them each a brandy. It should have been extraordinarily pleasant. Extraordinarily, Peter thought. Not just a cordial ending to an evening carried off so well. An extraordinarily successful occasion.

What was wrong with him, Peter thought. He slightly tipped and turned his globe with its sea of drink. In these last few days, he had had to fake his usual high spirits. That is, usually, when he found himself in a room with people he loved or even just expected to love, when he knew them better, his mind would fly forward towards them, full of gaiety. He would let his own gaiety bear everyone along. Just looking into their faces, Peter could recall people's interests and hobbies, the recent events of their lives, whatever they had once mentioned to him and might like to talk about some more. His own happiness would gather them up and shoo people breezily into their stories.

Now, however, he got the idea that his own life as a simple man was over.

The American general's story was not just some anecdote. It would always lie underneath whatever other conversations Peter heard from now on. Of course, Peter would go on rejoicing that his daughter was starting a happy life. Of course, of course. From now on, though, he would always know that when you learned any bad news, you had to make yourself believe that bad news fast—very fast—and act as if it were true, if you really meant to give shelter or safety to anyone, even to yourself.

CAROL BLY died in December of 2007. She was an ardent champion of the joys of an intellectual life. Her short stories, essays and this novel speak to her belief that writing is an ethical person's best weapon against the cruelty of governments and the indifference of the immoral. Born in Duluth, and a great lover of Minnesota's northern woods, Carol often placed her work in confident little Minnesota towns where she lived a great deal of her life.

In addition to her fiction and essays, Carol wrote books about how to write and how to teach creative writing. She taught widely, at the University of Minnesota, at Hamline University, at the University of Iowa, and Carlton College, among others. Carol was the recipient of the 2001 Minnesota Humanities Award for Literature, as well as being chosen the University of Minnesota's Edelstein-Keller Distinguished Author in 1998-99, and the *Minnesota Women's Press* Favorite Woman Author of 2000.

In her story "Gunnar's Sword," an elderly woman realizes that she "was very surprised to find that she hadn't spent eighty-two years in love with all there is, with tiny things like pebbles..." Carol Bly kept faith with pebbles, and all the rest of life's fierce, strange complexities. *Shelter Half,* published posthumously, contains all that Carol Bly believed made life worthwhile: challenging the cruelty we see around us, having and defending strong beliefs, serious study of art and literature, love of nature, and learning to give the best of ourselves to each other.

ALBERTA MARANA graduated from Hamline University with a degree in Art and Sociology in 1973. She graduated with a Master's in Studio art from the University of Wisconsin, Superior, in 1995. She has been working with pastels since the mid-1980s. She started using that medium when she was a full-time parent of small children. Pastels were handy to use in that she could pack them in her car and drive to a spot where she could work on location.

Much of her work is of scenes from northeastern Minnesota and northwestern Wisconsin. She especially loves working in the fall, when the colors of the trees are at their peak. Since her move to Duluth in 2002, she has become inspired by the evocative mood that the lights of the city create at night.

She has exhibited nationally and internationally and has won several awards, including a Milwaukee Arts Commission Purchase Award, First Place at the Florida Pastel Society Show in 1995, and Best of Show at the Duluth Art Institute, 1990. In 2003 she was a recipient of a Career Development Grant from the Arrowhead Regional Arts Council and, in 2007, a McKnight/ARAC Individual Artist Fellowship.

Her work can be seen in Duluth, Minnesota at Lizzard's and the Sivertson Gallery; in Madison, Wisconsin at the Grace Chosy Gallery; at the Katie Gingrass Gallery in Milwaukee, Wisconsin; and at Opening Night in Minneapolis, Minnesota.